FOXED BY THE ALPHA

THE ALPHA KING'S BREEDER
BOOK SEVENTEEN

BELLA MOONDRAGON

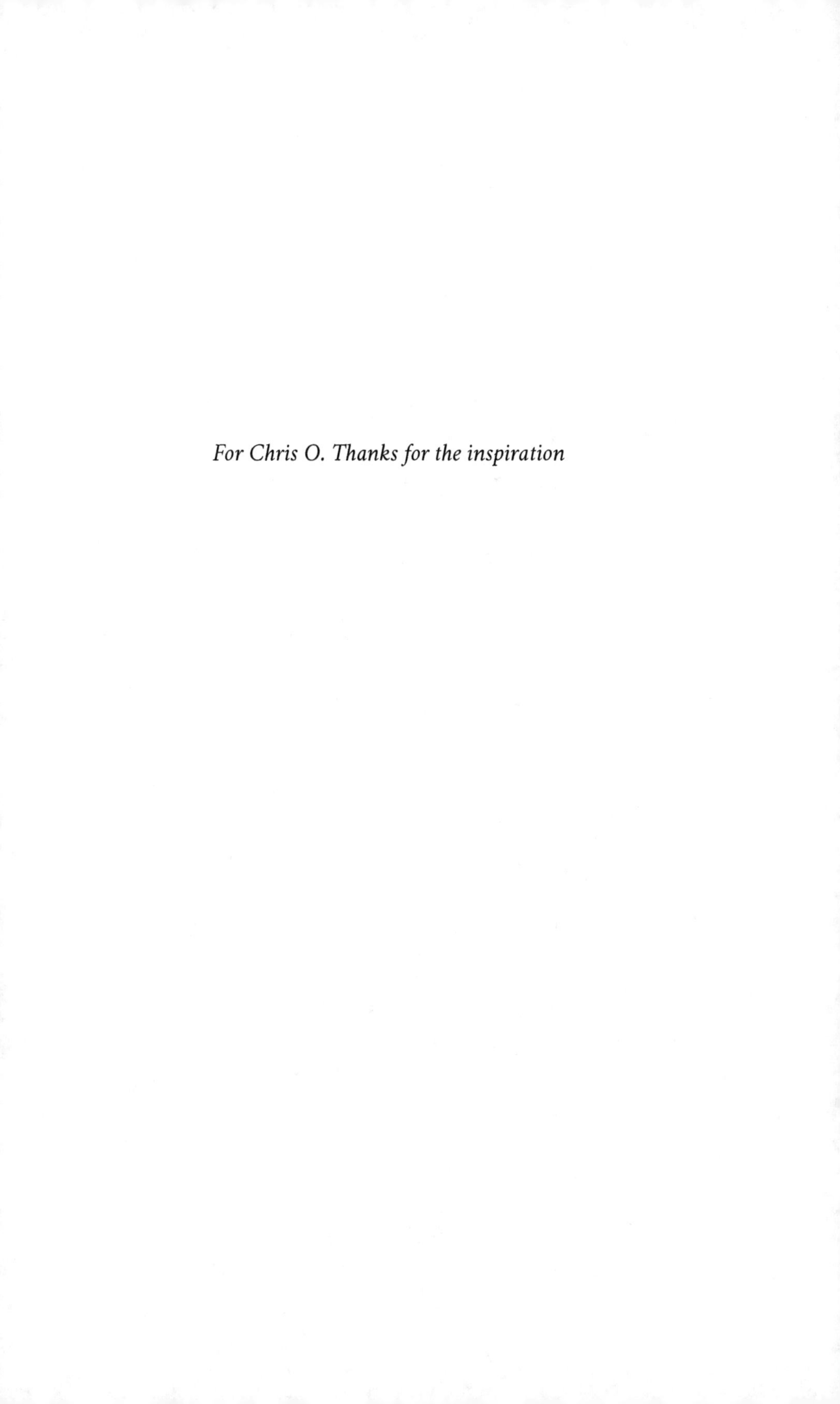

For Chris O. Thanks for the inspiration

CONTENTS

SUMMER HOME

POSEY

"*OH, MY GODDESS.*" WILLOW'S SLEEK DARK BROWN HAIR FANS AROUND her face as she pulls her baby blue convertible to a screeching halt, the smell of burning rubber scorching my nostrils. She pushes her sunglasses down the bridge of her nose and gasps as the shadow of a massive, three-story stone house from a begotten era swallows us whole, stained glass windows glaring down at us, four spires twisting to the clouds and nearly blocking the sun. "*This* is where we're staying? How old is this place?"

"That's a very good question. Probably ancient. Everything this size in Veiled Valley is–"

Her door slams shut. She's already out of the car and falling into the shadow of the–well, I suppose it's a castle. A miniature castle, probably the home of some long-dead aristocrat or Alpha that built it during the time of the original Firestone Witches. Two wings branch off the center of the structure with perfectly trimmed hedges juxtaposed against a remarkably modern and meticulously landscaped front lawn. It's a strange combination, but estates like this are all over Veiled Valley, and especially here, in the Gem Lake district.

"Holy shit, Posey!" Willow squeals, spinning in a circle, her crop top and jean shorts making her look like a time traveler as she hops up the dark stone steps. "You have to take my picture. This place is insane! It's haunted, isn't it? Puh-lease tell me it is!"

"Unlikely." I reach for the keys still dangling in the ignition, switching off the car.

Willow peeks through a front window then darts across the porch, vibrating like a rabbit in a trap while I fish my suitcase out of her backseat and drop it on the white gravel.

"No fucking way! This is incredible! We don't have many places like this in Crescent Falls!"

The front door swings open, and Willow jumps back, her hand flying over her chest. Roman steps out onto the front porch wearing an expression of mock annoyance and glances at me, then his watch. If he had a teasing remark about how late we've arrived, it's lost in a gust of breath when Willow launches into the air and collides with him, wrapping her arms around his neck.

"Roman! It's been ages! Wow, you're like, really muscular now!"

My brother artfully lowers Willow back to the ground and takes a calculated step away, giving her a polite, but disgustingly rehearsed, smile. The kind of smile every son and heir of an Alpha has down to a science. "Willow. It's never quite long enough."

The dig goes right over the top of her head. She bounds past him, gasping and shrieking as she's swallowed by the house, but I can still hear the excited clack of her sandals when Roman arches a brow in my direction and says, "Sister."

"Brother."

"So nice of you to join me… three hours late. I was about to call in the Ghosts."

"Willow would have had a fit. She loves a man in uniform."

"Keep her away from Aris then, unless you want her ruined for life." He snorts a laugh, jogging down the stairs to gather my suitcase. "He has a bad habit of playing tricks with his Ghost issued gloves."

"I didn't think he was really coming." I narrow my eyes at Roman. Aris is notoriously flaky. Not that I've kept track or anything. I gave up on his attendance to any significant life events years ago. He's a prince, which gives him an eternal pass to be an asshole, so no one has ever called him out on it.

He did text me earlier this morning, but I'd mostly ignored it. I generally do.

I don't dislike him by any means but he–he's just... *Aris*. It's always been so hard to explain. He's hard to explain.

"He is. He'll get here any minute, actually. I thought you'd beat him by a few hours." He tucks my suitcase under his arm and turns back to the house. "Should I get her things, too?"

"Yeah, I'm sure she'll be expecting that." I toss her keys in the front seat of the car with a sigh.

Roman sizes me up, giving me an arch of his thick, dark brow. He looks like our dad. He's a mirror image, everyone says. I can see it, the striking family resemblance, the DNA that missed me by a mile. Roman and our dad, Farrow, the Alpha of Sapphire Ridge, are both tall and broad shouldered, with all the physical blessings of an Alpha family line. They share the same deep, chocolate brown hair and skin that tans to a cool bronze the second they step into the sun. Roman even got the eyes our pack was named after. They are a bright, glossy, and flawless sapphire blue.

There are similarities between us but not many. I have the same soft waves and bouncy texture in my hair. The straight, narrow nose and rounded cheeks are, apparently, a Sapphire Ridge family trait, but that's as far as the similarities stretch. I look like our mother, Oulette. I have her strawberry-blonde hair and pale green eyes–forest green, Dad likes to say, because of the flakes of yellow and brown around my pupils and the deep green that edges my irises. Still, it's nothing compared to that perfect blue. I've been reminded of these differences my entire life.

I'm also shorter than I probably should be, given my genetics. Both of my parents are tall, whereas the top of my head barely reaches Roman's shoulder. We walk side by side into the massive summer rental house Aris probably put on his family's coffers. Where my family tends to be on the lean side, I was told recently by a decrypted old crone at the apothecary that I have child bearing hips and a chest to match. She'd meant it in a nice way, I think. Told me I was "blessed" and crinkled her nose when I'd purchase several contraceptive drafts. In my defense, they're for Willow. She needs them a whole hell of a lot more than I ever have.

"I am glad you're here, you know. One last summer before we have to grow up and be something," Roman says with a smirk. I follow him up a set of stairs to the eastern wing. We've lost Willow already, but she's rather loud, so it won't be long until we can easily pinpoint her location. He glances around for a moment, turning to face the western wing, which rests across a sweeping balcony overlooking the foyer. The inside of the house is modern, totally redone, and smells sharply of floor polish. I can see my reflection in the cherry wood floorboards when Roman murmurs, "I was going to put you on the second floor next to Willow, but based on how heavy your suitcase is, I'm guessing you packed every book you own?"

"Not *every* book."

"You're going to be studying, aren't you?"

"I have my entrance exams at the end of summer, so… yeah. A bit."

He adjusts his hold on the suitcase, doing another scan of the area. "Well, in that case, you'll want quiet from the rest of us. Come on, then. We have another flight of stairs."

He guides me through the eastern wing, past at least six doors, until another, smaller, less grand staircase comes into view. I hesitate before following him up.

"Aris is staying right across the hallway. Technically, this suite adjoins his, but I doubt he'll mind. He doesn't bring women back to his bed, so you won't be bothered up here."

I crinkle my nose, chuckling, "He hasn't changed a bit, has he?"

"When was the last time you saw him, anyway?" Roman opens a door to the left, and the room opens before me. Large windows let in southern facing sunlight, now faded with the setting sun, but it's bright and airy, nonetheless. I smooth my hands over the pale blue duvet cover on the bed.

"Um, years ago. I have no idea."

"He asked about you. He was surprised you were coming."

"I'm surprised I'm here," I admit with a small laugh, but Roman's expression darkens.

He sinks onto the foot of the bed, crossing his ankle over his knee and taps his foot, his arms crossed over his chest in a very familiar way. He tends to… hug himself when he's stressed or unhappy about something, like the future I've decided for myself.

"You're really doing this, aren't you?"

I turn to the window, pretending to be invested in the wooded backyard. There's also a view of the pristine lake. "Why is everyone so upset about it? It solves every issue our family has about–about *me*."

"It's your whole life, Posey. Dedicating your entire life to someone–"

"I'm making the right decision for everyone," I cut in, throwing him a look over my shoulder. "You get it. I know you do."

"Not having a wolf isn't that big of a deal."

"In our family it is."

Roman chews his lower lip, shaking his head. He won't press. He never does. No one has really fought for me to change my mind, so I haven't.

Voices drift from downstairs, and Roman rises, tucking his hands in the pockets of his jeans. "That's probably the guys. Come downstairs and say hello."

"I will. Just give me a minute. I've been in the car all day with Willow."

"Social battery running a little low?" He smirks then glances at the door. "How are you friends with someone like her anyway?"

"You know she's great. She's just excitable."

"You need more friends like you, Posey."

I don't know anyone else like me. There's no one else like me.

"Where the fuck is he?"

I freeze as a trio of male voices barrel toward the open door. Aris is the first to come into view, and for a moment, my heart stops. I haven't seen him in five or six years. He's not a scrawny teenager anymore.

That's for damn sure.

His dark blond hair curls around his ears, ruffled, like he doesn't have a care in the world, especially about his appearance. The boyish, utterly charming curve of his mouth is the same, however, as well as the chiseled angles of his face, like he was carved by a master in the style of the effigies of the old gods. Everyone in his family is like that—beautiful. Handsome. The works.

Tate and a man I might know but just don't remember come to a stop behind him, totally blocking the doorway.

Aris looks from Roman to me, his silver eyes glimmering with mirth as he leans against the doorframe, his biceps flexed and rippling under his thin cotton shirt. He looks straight at me, a boyish smirk touching the corners of his mouth. "Posey."

"A-Aris," I stammer, then blush. I can't hide it. The heat spreads down my neck and flares across my chest where the strappy tank top I wore to try to cut through the dead heat of summer doesn't hide a Goddess damned thing.

I barely register the conversation about room assignments taking place around me. Roman leaves, taking Miles, *right, that's his name,* and Tate with him. I assume Aris will follow, but when I finally look up from my toes, he's still standing there, darkening my doorway.

"What?" I cross my arms, wetting my lips before fixing him with a look. A glare. At least, I try.

"I thought I told you this was *my* part of the house. I sent a text. I know you saw it." He smiles down at me, the same look he used to give me as a kid whenever he broke one of my toys or wanted me to play war games with him and Roman, with me being the dragon they meant to slay, or worse, a bridge troll. It's meant to disarm me and always has. That's his gift—not shadow play or storms of darkness. No, he's fully weaponized his good looks and charm.

But I'm immune at this point.

"Take it up with Roman," I tell him with a curt smile. "Don't worry.

He already said you don't bring girls back to your bed, so it's not like I'll be in your way."

His silver gaze turns suddenly cold. "He knows too much about me and my habits."

"Bad habits."

He hums a laugh, glancing around my room. "I guess this is fine. Just keep that door–" he points across the room. "Keep that door locked. It joins our suites. I wouldn't want you getting any crazy ideas."

"Me?" I laugh, and he playfully glares. "You were the one who sleepwalked until you were in warrior training."

He winks and turns for the door, saying over his shoulder, "Yeah, well, I know for a fact you still sleep with a night light, Posey. Come downstairs soon. We're going out. There's a bar nearby–"

"I'm staying in tonight. I need to unpack."

He slowly turns back in my direction. "You're staying in on a full moon?"

"I have the whole summer to go out. It's fine." My chest tightens. It's not a good enough excuse. If anyone can see right through me this summer, it's going to be Aris.

Aris scans me from head to toe before heading through the doorway. "I see you haven't changed a bit."

A LAPSE

Aris

WILLOW IS EXACTLY THE TYPE OF GIRL MILES, OUR FRIEND FROM OUR early warrior training days, would fall for.

It's a damn shame she's all over Roman at the moment.

Miles tilts his pint of beer back and sighs, shaking his head while Roman and Willow stand at the bar across the room. Tate raises a brow, his close cropped black hair catching the dim, flickering neon lights plastered across the wall to our backs.

"What?" Miles gripes, running his fingers through his dark, equally short, hair. Both men are in the Ghost forces, low ranking, low enough that taking several weeks of leave wasn't that big of a deal.

"Roman's not interested in her, man. He'd love someone to save him right now." Tate shrugs, hazel eyes glistening. "Just go talk to her."

Miles grumbles something incoherent and twists his empty glass in a circle. I roll my eyes to Tate, who shrugs again before sipping his beer.

"She's staying for a while, according to Roman," Tate offers. Miles glares.

"She doesn't seem like the kind of girl Posey would be friends with," Miles argues.

"Posey met her at Wellington," I tell them. I'm not sure why I even spoke. Posey going to Wellington had been a huge deal for her family. Farrow hadn't been happy she was leaving Veiled Valley, which has perfectly fine universities, but Posey was adamant, and Posey, despite her pixie-like size and overall doll-like qualities, is a manipulative little thing. She gets away with everything she wants–always has.

"Speaking of Posey," Tate grins, blowing out his breath as he leans back. "Damn. She grew up."

I narrow my eyes. "What do you mean?"

Miles glances at Roman before leaning forward with his hands extended away from his chest like he's holding two melons. "I mean… she *grew up.*"

"That's Roman's little sister." My warning tone settles in the center of the table, blooming like a death knell. "Don't let him hear you talking like that."

Miles and Tate glance at each other and then straighten as Roman approaches the table, carrying our third round with Willow's help.

She sits between me and Roman, giggling and excusing herself while she squeezes in. Her long, almost black hair nearly reaches her waist, pin straight. She's hot, I'll give her that. But she was also just fine leaving her friend behind at the house.

I lose myself in my beer for several minutes and come to just as she says, "I studied communications. I'm starting a job at a local news place in Crescent Falls this fall." She flips her hair over her shoulder, beaming. A million-dollar smile. "I'll be a nightly news anchor."

"You met Posey in school, right?" It's Tate asking. I throw him a look, and he throws one back before turning his eyes to Willow, his brow raised.

"Oh, yeah, we were roommates our final year at Wellington. She's the absolute best! I love her so much. I really do. There's no one as smart or as kind as Posey." She takes a deep drink from some fruity cocktail before continuing. "She's so studious. I could never get her to go out with me, but when I told her I was taking a road trip around Eastonia this summer, she offered to let me stay with her in Veiled Valley for a while and then Roman–" She nudges him, batting her eyelashes, "Invited her to the lake, and I couldn't let her turn down the offer."

"So this is your first time in Eastonia?" Miles finally gets the nerve to speak. He seems about ready to throw up when she looks at him with a smile bright enough to light the night sky.

"Yeah! It's been amazing! So old. Like, seriously, the oldest place I've ever seen in my life." Her giggle turns heads from across the room. "Aris, you're like, the queen's cousin, aren't you?"

Roman purses his lips.

"Maeve is my little sister."

"Oh, my Goddess! I would totally love to meet her."

I blink, then shake my head, giving her a polite but slightly dismissive smile. "That's practically impossible. Maeve is rather busy at the moment."

"Oh," Willow says, nodding viciously. "I bet. The fae thing, right?"

The fae thing. I can't totally fault her for her ignorance. The people of Crescent Falls were generally unaffected by the acts of Hannibal, the Viper, and everything that happened and is still happening between Eastonia and Pantharas. Maeve has been hosting summits for months now, and Emberfyll has become an allied base where the new fae leaders and leaders from our kingdom can meet peacefully without the need to step onto each other's soil. It hasn't even been a year since everything happened. Nothing feels certain. Peace doesn't feel certain... yet.

But I'm not here to talk or even think about politics.

When I don't answer immediately, the conversation moves on without me. I finish my drink and rise to fetch another, wanting a buzz before shifting with the group tonight ,but my body angles toward the door with something else in mind.

"Do you need anything from the house?" I ask Roman when he follows me to the bar. He orders another drink, but I pay the tab for the group, wincing at the price.

"Uh, no, I don't think so. Why? Are you going back?"

"Just for a minute. I want to lay out some clothes in the event anyone goes out to shift and ruins what they're currently wearing." I take my card back and tuck it into my wallet. I'm sure Grandpa Ryatt is fully aware of my spending habits, but I think he understands I get a pass this summer... I hope. He seemed pleased, at least, when I told him my plans, but I assume he expects me to come home and take more interest in my Shadowsynger duties, which are bound to double, or triple, in the coming years.

"Check on Posey for me?" Roman brings his drink to his lips.

I shrug, nodding, and quickly leave the slightly rundown bar right on the edge of the lake. It's only a half mile from the house, which used to belong to an Alpha. This whole area–the house, the village–is ancient, but a new community has risen from its ashes. Now, the entirety of Gem Lake–a system of lakes that feed into each other, creating islands and causeways–is home to at least six different packs and a variety of villages like this one, most catering to tourists. Neon lights reflect off the water where boats and small yachts bob at both private and public docks. Lake houses rise through the trees, most modern new-builds. The house I rented is one of the last standing from an era before the veil fell.

I bought it. I used nearly my entire inheritance to do so. I'm not sure why, but the moment I saw it, I just knew it was mine.

So I took it.

The Gem Lake district is still part of the Kingdom of Veiled Valley but a hundred miles away from Veiled Valley, the capital, where my family lives. Where I live. The river separates the two areas, and it's a long, winding journey to get here that includes a ferry and at least an hour or more, depending on the weather, of driving. The magic of Veiled Valley is still thick in the air when I round a corner, and the gravel begins to fade from a deep rust brown to glimmers of white, and the house comes into view.

Only a few interior lights are on.

I take a step past the gate and catch an unfamiliar scent that immediately riles my senses. It's not totally foreign, which makes me nervous. I pause between the columns, the gate open, just like we left it, the driveway stretching out before me under the glow of the full moon, white gravel sparkling like fallen stars.

There're small critters all over Gem Lake, but this scent isn't something natural. Shifters carry an underlying human scent, and that's exactly what I'm picking up as I take a tentative step forward, then stop.

It's a fox. Undoubtedly.

A fox shifter.

"Fuck me," I snarl, scanning the area.

Fox shifters are more than rare. They're nearly impossible. Well, there are a few exceptions, and one of them is my grandmother, Amanda, the only known fox shifter in our entire world, as far as we've been able to gather. It's a rare recessive gene that sometimes makes its presence known in Alpha bloodlines. Fox shifters, in our lore and history, are notoriously violent, cunning, and mischievous and shouldn't be fucked with.

I'd know because I am one.

I have the ability to shift into a fox, at least. I have both forms, just like my dad, Evander. The public is still wary of any shifters who aren't wolves, and even with three foxes in my own family, the royals have kept it a secret—with good reason.

Wolves *love* to hunt foxes. Foxes are considered evil, an act against the Goddess. Even my royal status wouldn't be enough to sway public opinion the other way.

Now, there's one here somewhere. Or there was. The scent is so faint I quickly lose it.

Unnerved, I enter the house, resisting the urge to sweep through every room and closet, but the scent doesn't carry inside.

I find Posey on her bed, sitting crisscross with a half-moon circle of textbooks around her and several notebooks, papers scattered across the bedspread. She looks up as I throw open the door. "What?"

"Are you good?" I step into the room, glancing around. "No one came into the house, right?"

She's wearing massive tortoiseshell glasses with impossibly thick lenses that make her eyes look three sizes bigger than they normally are. The smell of cherries and amber shampoo hangs heavy between us, and I notice her hair is damp, loose waves piled on the top of her head and pinned back with a clip. She blinks, tilting her head. "No. I'm the only one here. Why?"

I step deeper into the room, crossing my arms over my chest with a sigh. "Nothing. Just being paranoid."

"I think you get a pass in that department after everything that happened last year." She exhales deeply and takes off her glasses, massaging the bridge of her nose. "How are you doing?"

"Me?" No one asks me that. I barely fought in the small skirmishes that littered the Roguelands when the Viper had power. I wasn't in Teshka when an entire regiment of royal warriors was slaughtered, and Lexa was taken. I didn't go to Pantharas with Dad's Ghost forces and Tarsian's navy. I stayed here, in Veiled Valley. Doing what Shadowsyngers do... a whole lot of nothing. Talking to apparitions and shit. Playing with my shadows when I desperately needed entertainment.

"I'm doing fine." I think it's the truth. I ignore the unsettling feeling gripping my chest and scan her bedspread, noting the heavy textbooks and notebook pages covered in religious symbolism. "What are you doing?"

"Studying," she replies pointedly.

"You came all this way to do this all summer?"

"I'm not–this is just–" she waves a hand at the mess before gingerly gathering the loose pages and closing the textbooks. "I have an exam coming up in a few weeks. All I needed to do tonight was make some kind of studying schedule for the summer, but I got a little carried away."

A bright pink blush creeps over her cheeks and down her neck, flaring over the curve of her... yeah, very large breasts. Miles wasn't that far off with his crude description. I look away. This is Posey.

She's beautiful, sure, but I've known her since we were kids, and we're… friends. At least, I've always considered her a friend.

I'm sure to her, I'm more of a bully. Maybe. Hopefully, a bit of both.

"What are you studying?"

"It'll bore you to death. Shouldn't you be out tonight? I thought you all were going shifting and exploring the islands?"

"We are, but everyone is at the bar as it stands, trying to catch up with me." I brace my hands against the mattress, leaning over the bed to scan the titles of the textbooks before she stacks them. "Theology?"

She ignores me, saying under her breath, "You don't seem drunk to me at all."

"I'm a master of my craft," I tease, and her bright green eyes meet mine. "I'm going to join them again, but I wanted to check in and make sure you weren't getting into trouble on your own."

"What trouble would I get into, Aris?"

"Nothing without me, I hope."

She gives me the smallest curve of her lips in lieu of a smile. I don't think I've ever seen her smile with teeth. One day, I will. I'll make it my mission this summer to make her laugh. What a challenge that'll be.

"Go back to your wolfish games, Aris. I'm going to bed." She slides off the mattress in nothing but shorts and a light, fluffy cardigan covering her gray tank top. She sets the massive stack of textbooks on the dresser with a thud before padding back in my direction, her hands resting on her hips.

"Why not come out with us? It's a full moon, Posey. It's the best time to shift. You'll feel–"

"I'll feel nothing, Aris. it doesn't affect me."

"The full moon affects everyone."

"I'm a lapse." She looks up at me, curling her arms around her middle like she's shielding herself from view. "I thought you knew."

I haven't heard that term used in years. It's considered derogatory. "What–what do you mean?"

"I don't have a wolf. I never developed the gifts." She shrugs. "I can't shift into a wolf, Aris. That's all it is. The full moon means nothing to me." She turns toward the bed, squeezing her eyes shut. "Please, just… don't make a big deal out of it, okay? I'm the daughter of an Alpha. Something like me–it looks bad for our family."

PRINCESS POSEY

Aris

"WHY DIDN'T YOU TELL ME POSEY CAN'T SHIFT?"

Roman squints into the midmorning sunlight, his tan skin going rosy along his cheekbones. The dock off the back of the house is empty save for the two of us taking up residence in wicker chairs, watching the fog roll off the lake. A loon floats by, diving under the water.

Everyone else is still in the house sleeping off their hangovers.

I couldn't sleep. Haven't slept. Probably won't until I get this cleared up.

Roman exhales deeply, scrubbing his forehead like he can swipe his hangover away. "It's not something she likes people to know."

"Obviously."

"She never came into it, never showed any signs of developing gifts in that realm. My parents said she just needed more time, but Posey produced a report from the healers in Sapphire Ridge that confirmed she didn't possess any lupine powers, and that was that. Mom's in pieces about it, worried about Posey's marriage prospects."

17

I shake my head, bringing my steaming mug of coffee to my lips. In any other circumstance, the idea of an arranged marriage would be ludicrous, but the Sapphire family has been in power for as long as my line of the royal family, the Westfalls of Veiled Valley, have. Their line goes back centuries, if not thousands of years, and their wealth could easily put mine to shame, and I'm a prince. Posey is a princess in her own right, even if she's not related to an Alpha King. The Sapphires have been allies with the Shadowsyngers since the dawn of time. They also have other gifts that determine things like mating—and marriage—to keep their line strong and powerful.

"What about her alchemy?"

Roman hisses out a breath. "She hasn't said a word."

"And yours?"

"I'm training, but it doesn't seem necessary. It's more of a tradition, if anything. Our family hasn't made magical weapons or riches for yours in hundreds of years?" He gives me a look, arching a brow. "Prove me wrong?"

"I can't." I shrug, sipping from my mug and then resting it on my knee. The Sapphires have a gift, and that gift is the manipulation of metal, turning a cord of iron into anything they desire just by touching it. Those gifts take years to develop and even longer to perfect. Roman can make iron into gold and copper into jewels, but it's not perfect yet.

Long ago, the Sapphire family helped create the Sword of Shadow, several diadems, and the mask and bracelets I found in the cave during my ascension into the Shadowsynger guild. Their alchemized jewels hold our power like no other gems, not even a precious, sacred moonstone, can. His father was the one who crafted the necklace that gave Maeve a shot of having a real childhood without the risk of setting everything she touched on fire.

"If Posey is an alchemist, she hasn't said so."

"Why don't you push the subject? She called herself a *lapse*."

"I know. I've heard her say it, too. She's rather manipulative if you haven't noticed over the twenty years you've known her, Aris. She's an artist, a master, when it comes to deflection." He leans back in the chair, tilting his head to the sun. "She left for college, made it clear she was going to be a teacher, and my parents allowed it with the stipulation that she come back to Sapphire Ridge to teach, and she has. Now, she has it in mind to join some graduate program. It's tearing the family apart, but she's adamant." He winces, shaking his head.

"What program?"

"I was looking for you guys." Tate's tread is heavy and uneven as he moves down the dock. He plops onto the boards, hanging his legs over the edge, his bare feet barely touching the surface of the lake.

"Anyone else awake yet?"

"Just us and Posey." Tate leans his face into the sunlight with a wince.

I stiffen at the mention of her name, and Roman notices. He discreetly shakes his head, silently willing me to keep our conversation between us.

"What's my darling sister up to this morning?" Roman drawls in his practiced Alpha's voice.

"Making breakfast," Tate says with a grateful smile. "It smells great, but she nearly bit my hand off when I tried to steal a few pieces of bacon."

I methodically rise. "I need a refill." I tilt my head toward my mug. "Anyone else?"

Both of them shake their heads.

"I say we take the boat out after breakfast. There's so much lake to explore. We can grab lunch in Ruby Row," Roman offers, and I nod my agreement before turning on my heel and stalking toward the house, the back windows reflecting morning sunlight over the freshly cut lawn.

Posey's in the kitchen, her hair pulled back in a ponytail while she perfectly flips a pancake. Miles is leaning groggily against the kitchen island, looking worse for wear as he gingerly takes a sip of his coffee. The pot is now empty.

"The guys are outside discussing plans for the day," I tell him in a form of dismissal. He takes the bait and saunters through the kitchen and adjoining open dining area, where large glass doors open to the backyard. I watch him until he disappears into the glare of the sun.

I can feel Posey watching me when I move toward the coffeemaker.

"If you're going to ask how I'm feeling, don't bother. I'm not hungover in the slightest." I set to work making another pot of coffee, the sizzle of her skillet as she pours more batter filling the silence between us.

"Do you eat carbs?" she asks, sliding a plate piled high with every kind of breakfast food imaginable in my direction while I lean against the kitchen island. Pancakes drenched in syrup with whipped cream and berries, bacon, eggs with cheese and flaked with green onions, and sausage links that will pop the second I bite into one.

"Of course I eat carbs. Who do you think I am?"

"Tate and Miles told me they wouldn't touch the pancakes because it will undo their progress at the gym."

"Well, they're stupid beasts, so that doesn't surprise me." I grab a fork out of the drawer at my side and make a show of sinking it through four layers of carbs, fat, and sugar, my eyes on hers when I finally take a bite.

Posey takes a breath and smiles at me but then gives me her back, resuming the arduous task of pouring batter.

For whatever reason, her inability to take the bait I just wiggled in front of her settles so deep in my chest it makes my ribs sing with pain. I've always teased her, tried to get a rise out of her. It was second nature. I have two sisters, for the Goddess's sake. Our family's love language has always been acts of bullying. I treated Posey the same because I didn't know how to do it differently.

But even a searing, slightly flirtatious look into her eyes does... nothing for her. She's totally immune.

"Roman said you're trying to get into a graduate program."

Her shoulders tighten. "Yeah, I am."

"Where?"

She sighs heavily, looking at me over her shoulder. "I'd rather not talk about school. You're the one who gave me a hard time last night about not going out and staying home with my books, anyway. I am here to enjoy myself. I know that probably surprises you–"

"I didn't know you couldn't shift," I cut in under my breath.

"Does that bother you?"

"Kind of."

"Well," she huffs, chuckling. "Good thing it's none of your business and shouldn't affect you in the slightest."

I abandon the delicious breakfast and come to her side, leaning my hip against the counter and effectively stepping into her personal space. She doesn't step away. "I hate the idea you're out there in the world without a way to defend yourself."

She rolls her eyes to mine. "It's none of your business, Aris. Give me a break."

"I could train you."

"In what?" She flips a pancake with so much force it splatters all over the skillet.

"A little hand to hand." I shrug, watching her expression twist.

"It's not necessary."

"Listen, I caught a scent last night just outside of the house. There was something here while you were alone."

She stills, looking away from me.

"And while you are perfectly free to have visitors…"

"Aris!" she hisses, slapping my arm with her spatula.

"I'm just saying. If you're going to be alone more often than not, it would make me feel better knowing you can at least defend yourself."

"I will be totally fine!" She scoffs, rolling her eyes back to the now burned pancake. She grumbles a rather colorful curse under her breath before snatching the skillet and carrying it to the trash can, scraping the blackened remains into the bin. I hover beside her, waiting for her to just give in. "Will you go finish your breakfast and leave me alone? I have things to do today."

"Yeah, you do. You're going to Ruby Row with us. There's shopping and a market, and we're taking the boat. It'll be fun." I snatch the skillet from her hands and toss it in the sink, arching my brow and silently daring her to challenge me.

"That wasn't my plan."

"You're in my house for the summer. You're my guest, and it's my duty to ensure you have a good time."

"You rented this house."

"I bought it a few weeks ago."

She eyes me skeptically. "Congratulations on your newfound homeownership."

"What's wrong with you, Posey? Do you have a problem with everyone or just me?"

"I don't have a problem with you, Aris. But you're bugging me. You never took any interest in me and my goals before, so why start now? Why be bothered by the fact that I need to spend some time studying this summer? Why care that I can't shift?"

"I am worried about–"

"About someone coming here to assault me?" She laughs, but it's bitter. "Aris, be serious."

"I'm serious as death." I step into her, looking down into those bright eyes. "If I have to drag you to every activity, I will."

"Am I on vacation or at summer camp?"

"You're at *Camp Aris.*"

"You're so annoying," she chuckles, stepping around me. She lays out several plates for whenever the rest of the guests rouse themselves enough to eat. "You're not my brother, you know. You have no authority over me."

"What am I to you, then?"

"You're my friend. You always have been."

"If I were really your friend, you would have told me about the fact that you couldn't shift ages ago!"

"Will you keep your voice down!" she hisses, glancing around. "It's not a big deal to me at all, Aris, okay? I couldn't care less. I'm fine. Everything is fine. You don't need to hover over me all summer and treat me like a charity case because I don't have a wolf. Leave me be and chill out, please."

She tears herself from the room with a huff. I roll my eyes back to my plate, which I've been eyeing over the course of the argument, and scarf down the delicious breakfast. Eventually, the guys come back to eat, and Willow makes her presence known in a grand way by tripping and falling down the stairs. Thankfully, she doesn't maim herself too badly, and she's numbed to the bone by the alcohol still swimming through her system, so she doesn't feel a thing.

Posey doesn't return to the group until an hour later, when Roman and I are loading up the boat that came with the purchase of the house. It's a slick sailboat perfect for the amount of people going out on the water today.

Posey looks bored as she walks down the dock carrying a wicker bag, sporting huge sunglasses and wearing nothing but a soft blue bikini and crocheted swim cover, the tip of her nose already turning pink from the sun.

I can tell she's scowling at me under the gleam of her sunglasses, but I give her a gracious smile, bowing deeply at the waist. "Princess Posey. How kind of you to grace us with your presence."

She frowns deeply.

"Do you guys have to start this now? Already?" Roman asks, exasperated.

I extend my hand, clutching her fingers, and help her onto my boat.

TAKE THE PLUNGE

Aris

"WE SHOULD HAVE SPENT MORE TIME HERE GROWING UP," ROMAN quips, sprawled on the smooth wooden deck of the sailboat, the sun relentlessly beating down on him, but he smiles under the shade of his hand.

"Neither of us had access to our wealth until recently. Even just visiting Gem Lake is expensive." I gently bank the boat to the left, gliding just close enough to shore to see the houses peeking out over the tree line. We're one of a few boats on the water this morning navigating the wider areas of the interconnected lake systems and narrow passageways. Small towns and villages rest along the shore every couple of miles, but private homes and pack communities are abundant.

Veiled Valley has thrived when other kingdoms have not. That's clear as I scan the shore, watching ancient architecture blur against a wash of modern homes and businesses. Magnolia trees hang heavy with blooms over the water, their white petals dappling the shore.

The air is heavy, humid, and stifling hot, and I know for a fact the water is the perfect temperature for swimming.

"Are we still going to Ruby?" I ask over the gentle snapping of the sails. There's barely a breeze, and the engine hums beneath me as I squint through my sunglasses at the curve of the shoreline where the forest grows heavy and the lake narrows significantly. "There's a cove I want to check out before we get lunch."

No one answers. Roman sits up and takes off his shirt, tossing it onto the growing pile of discarded clothing as the heat rises. Willow's head whips in our direction from the far end of the boat. She slides her sunglasses down the bridge of her nose and stares appraisingly at Roman, but I'm staring past her, just for a moment, just to peek at the woman behind her.

Posey has her legs dangling over the side of the boat, her toes barely skimming the water while she hugs the railing, her cheek pressed to her arm while she smiles and chats with Tate. I can't hear their conversation, but he's gesturing enthusiastically about something, and her smile keeps growing. She's never smiled at me like that, that's for damn sure.

I turn from the scene, rolling the tension from my shoulders just in time to guide the boat through the narrow channel connecting this inlet to the next one. Trees tall enough to cast shade over the boat stretch their branches overhead, vines dangling from the limbs. The mingled conversations die behind me as the boat is swallowed by cool shadows, and the busy center of the lake fades to forested solitude and the sound of cicadas singing.

I feel Posey's presence before I turn to see her. She kneels beside me, her fingers curling over the railing as she looks up at the vines brushing the sails.

"Scared?" I ask with a cool smirk.

"Of what? You steering this ungodly expensive boat into the bank? The water's only a few feet deep here. I doubt I'll drown."

That smirk angles into a frown. I turn from her to look out over the water again, quickly guiding the boat right, then left again, following the increasingly narrow water channel through the woods.

"Do you even know where you're taking us?"

"I sure hope so because I can't turn around here, so if we get stuck, we'll have to shift, and… seeing as you can't…" I arch a brow, stealing a glance in her direction, but her expression is stoically blank, "you'll have to ride on my back."

"How do you think Roman would feel about me riding you? Having to grip you with my thighs?" She cocks her head to the side. "I doubt he'd like it very much."

Goddess above. I didn't think she had it in her.

"I think he'd be the only one feeling that way." I resist the urge to bite down on my lower lip when that blush paints her skin a deep, rosy pink. What the fuck is my problem?

A chorus of gasps ring out behind us, and the moment dissolves as quickly as it came. Posey rises to see the new startling view of the lake. Rocky cliffs overlook the water, the forest continuing above us rather than on all sides, and I angle the boat to continue riding the shore until the cliff edge splits, revealing a cove of pure, glassy water.

Willow's sharp inhale cuts through the air as she gasps, shouting, "A waterfall!"

Ours is not the only boat taking up residence in the cove this morning. Two other sailboats bob in the shallows, and blurred shadows dot the cliff face, where a trail to the lowest of the falls has been etched out of the dark stone. The same note of astonishment from Willow punctuates each splash when people leap off the cliff behind the falls and into the water. Then, she begs and pleads for one of us to go with her.

"Oh, come on, Posey! Please? I have to do it. If I don't, I'll be thinking about it forever, regretting it for the rest of my life!"

"I'm not a big fan of heights." Posey laughs, but I can tell she's doing her best to let Willow down easy without having to give her an outright no.

Roman ignores the conversation and takes over the rudders while I strip down to nothing but my swim trunks and jump over the railing, the water only chest deep, and guide the boat as close as I can to the shore to tie it off. Tate jumps in next but with much more drama.

His splash rocks the entire boat, and Roman snarls while Willow titters, but Posey remains clutching the railing like her life depends on it.

"Does she know how to swim?" I ask Roman, squinting up at him, then wincing when Miles follows Tate's lead with a backflip.

"Who? Posey? Of course she does."

Willow leaps gracefully, giggling the whole four feet down, and lands without a sound, but Posey remains glued to the railing, watching everyone else with marked skepticism.

Roman looks at his sister, shrugging a shoulder. "What's your deal?"

"I don't have a deal. What do you expect? A flip?"

I take a few steps away from the boat and float on my back for a moment, observing the bickering above. "*Come on*, Posey. The water feels great. You're missing out!"

She disappears from view, walking to the far side of the boat. Roman sighs before climbing over the railing and jumping in but swims past me to where Tate, Miles, and Willow are nearing the shore—a soft, gently sloping beach with shiny taupe sand. Music drifts from the dunes, flowing against the constant hum of the waterfalls, but I wait forever for Posey to reappear.

"Posey!"

"What!?" She swims around the boat, obviously having scaled the ladder on the far side, her hair piled on top of her hair and eyes narrowed into cat-like slits. I can just make out the blue swimsuit she's wearing beneath the gentle waves. Her skin is a rosy alabaster against a wash of deep blue.

I suck my teeth, remembering again the conversation at the bar when Roman was, thankfully, outside of earshot. Cool pearls of fresh water slide between her breasts, which are… exactly as Mile's described. Fuck me.

She stares at me for a moment, her rosy-blonde eyebrows arched in a look of pure annoyance.

"I was just making sure you weren't eaten by a shark." That's all I can manage.

She stills, huffing, obviously struggling to touch the bottom. "There're no sharks here. It's freshwater."

"I've seen a shark here before."

"You haven't. You're not a very good liar, Aris. You never have been."

She gracefully glides past me while the others call out to us. Willow is already on the beach, tugging Miles to go to the waterfall with her.

"I don't want her jumping off that," Posey says, finally reaching a spot where she can stand with ease. The water laps against her shoulders. She tucks rogue strands of hair behind her ears and pushes her sunglasses up on top of her head. "She'll break her neck, and I'll be responsible for it."

"Oh, please, what makes you responsible for anything she does?"

"I'm her tour guide while she's in Veiled Valley."

"Does that mean you're her bodyguard?"

"I've just always kept her out of trouble. That's been my job, I guess. Dragging her out of frat houses and driving her home when–"

"Do you even like her?"

Posey startles, looking up at me like I just slapped her across the face. There's only a foot of space between us as it stands, and I can see the water droplets on her skin, shining like liquid sliver in the sunlight. The same color as my eyes. "Of course I like her. I love her. This is the last time we'll be able to see–" She abruptly shuts her mouth, her lips pinched.

"Your last, what?" I walk closer to shore until I can sit down in the water without it rolling over the top of my head. Waist deep, the cool, fresh water is a welcome relief from the heat. The sun has crested directly above us. Posey remains in the shallows, watching Willow scale the cliff–alone–while everyone below cheers her on.

"The program I'm starting is going to be grueling, and I–I likely won't see her for years."

"Why not? She could visit. Hell, you can just go to Crescent Falls–"

"I don't think… I'm… what… I'm trying to do–" Posey goes silent, her eyes following a body flinging off the cliff as the woman seems to fall in slow motion.

"Shit!" I jolt upright, sprinting through the tide line. Roman is leagues ahead, his body careening off the beach and into the water in a smooth dive toward Willow, who just landed head first and hasn't reemerged. The shore beneath my feet drops off abruptly. Posey is right behind me and unprepared for the depth. She resurfaces, choking, and I snatch her arm, pulling her against my chest in an attempt to keep her chin above the water just as Roman dives beneath the surface and is under for several aching seconds before breaking the glassy glow of the water with Willow in his arms.

Posey clutches my shoulder and takes several deep breaths, but I can feel her heart pounding rapidly through the single slice of fabric between us.

"She's fine. See?" My voice shakes despite my best effort. "She's exactly where she wants to be."

Willow's arms are wrapped around Roman's neck as he bobs in the water, trying to juggle her and swim back to shore. The crazy woman is smiling, her eyes shining with triumph. She waves to the shocked onlookers on the beach.

"She wasn't hurt in the slightest, Posey. Everything's fine," I continue with a sigh, but Posey's still clutching my shoulder like her life depends on it. I tread water, turning with her in my arms. "Are you in shock or something?"

"No, I just–" Her grip tightens. "I just need a moment. Stay still, please."

She fumbles between her chest and mine, her cheeks burning with a blush edging on blood red.

"What's going on?"

"My bikini top," she growls. "It's falling off, I can't–" She shoves off me, barely able to keep her face above water as she grips her bikini to try to keep in place while treading water in the deepest point of the cove. The straps that should be tied along her back are floating on either side of her.

I roll my eyes, taking her by the elbow and pulling her through the water until her feet touch the bottom again.

"Turn around."

"I can do it!"

"Chill, for fuck's sake. It's not that big of a deal."

"That's easy for you to say," she murmurs, huffing with frustration when I grow tired of her pouting and whirl her to face away from me. "You only have to worry about your swim trucks falling off. I only have strings keeping me clothed as it stands."

I skillfully redo the straps, securing the top tighter than necessary, but she... needs the support.

I clear my throat; my fingers brush over her soft skin. "Do you like anything, Posey?"

"What kind of question is that?"

"Do you enjoy anything in life other than complaining about it?"

"I like being inside," she says without skipping a beat. "Alone, preferably. I like quiet, and dim lighting, and... everything you'd find boring."

"Why'd you come?" I turn her around. "I don't get it. Why come if you were going to hate it this much?"

"I don't hate it. I just don't have–Look, I–"

Roman calls out Posey's name. My hands drop from her upper arms. and I find myself taking a step away from her without meaning to, like just the sound of her brother's voice is enough to drive a wedge into what should have been an innocent moment.

"Are you okay?" I ask her, and for a brief moment, I see a flicker of raw emotion behind her normally trained green eyes.

"I'm totally fine, Aris. Why does everyone always ask me that?"

A PAINFUL TOUCH

POSEY

WILLOW SNEAKS THROUGH THE DOOR INTO MY ROOM DRESSED IN A THIN nightgown that barely brushes her knees. She grins at me like she has a secret stuck to the tip of her tongue, her eyes wide and bright with mischief.

I smile through the mirror, catching her reflection, and shake my head. "What are you doing up here? I thought you were going out again tonight."

"I had about all the fun I needed for the day." She jumps onto the bed, ignoring the books, and rests on her belly with a sigh. Her eyes meet mine in the mirror. "A little sunburned?"

"A bit." I continue slathering a cooling gel on my chest and shoulders. Willow, who tans like a dream, cocks her head. I move the straps of my tank top out of the way, revealing the color my skin turns in the sun. Pink.

She clicks her tongue, saying, "*Ouch.*"

"Speaking of *ouch,* how's your head?"

"Are you asking about my plummet off the falls? I knew exactly what I was doing and who'd run to save me." She twirls her hair around her finger, looking smug.

"You forget your savior is my brother, and he would have blamed himself for eternity if you'd broken your neck."

"You Sapphires are all the same, aren't you? Loyal to a fault."

I turn to face her, crossing my legs on the little vanity chair.

She rests her chin on her fist and arches her brow. It's an odd standoff–something we've done since our Wellington days. Willow talks and talks while I like to remain silent and observe. She says I can read her mind. It's true in a way. She just wears every emotion, inner plot, and her schemes plainly on her face and always has.

I adore Willow. I haven't had many friends, and it's my preference to keep it that way. I like my time alone. I like quiet. I was being honest when I told Aris that today at the cove.

Willow didn't give me a choice about being her friend, however. She's always liked me the way I am. That's why I've kept her in my life, and for some reason, despite my faults, she's kept me.

I hold her gaze until she breaks with a deep exhale.

"How would you feel about me sleeping with Roman?"

"Wouldn't that be breaking a cardinal rule in our friendship?" I ask, fighting a teasing smile. She rolls her eyes.

"We've never set those kinds of rules, first of all. Our friendship has always been unorthodox because you are a strange person, Posey."

I frown. She's not wrong–not entirely. "Well, second of all, you're grossly underestimating Roman's sense of control. If you're hoping he'll get sloppy and let you into his bed, you're delusional."

"So… you wouldn't be opposed to me fucking your brother?"

"I honestly don't care." It's the truth. "I'd be more shocked that you accomplished it, actually. I'd be more likely to give you a trophy for your efforts than be mad."

She sits up, intrigued. "What do you mean by that? How hard can it be? He's a man, after all."

"He's a Sapphire, just like you said. If we weren't wolves, we'd be akin to dragons, hoarding things we thought were ours and never letting go. You sleep with him, and you'll belong to him. I'm warning you. There's a reason he keeps women at arm's length."

"You're a strange family."

"Veiled Valley is a strange place, just like the old families who still live here. I tried to explain this to you, but I doubt you listened."

"Roman is *hot!*" she whines, flopping onto her back. "It shouldn't be this complicated to check sleeping with someone from Veiled Valley off my list. Tate and Miles don't count because they're just stationed here. *Boring.*"

I'm halfway turned back to the vanity to continue getting ready for bed when her words hit me. I curl inward and pause, glancing at her over my shoulder. "What list?"

"I have a bucket list I've been trying to work through for the past couple of months while traveling. You know, just things I wanted to do, wanted to experience, before I fuse myself with monotony and work a real job, settle down, and maybe find my mate." She blows out her breath and then looks at me, grinning like a cat with cream. "Conquering Roman wasn't necessarily on that list, but Veiled Valley men are so foreign. I'd like to try one, at least. And he's here, somewhat willing. I'm still working on that front, but I may give up soon and find someone else. It won't be that hard."

"Oh, my Goodness," I breathe, then laugh out loud, the sound reverberating around the room. "Willow, you slut!"

"Oh, please, you don't get to judge me!" Now she's laughing. "In fact, I'm judging you for how you're going about this… this *life change* of yours. You should write a list. You only have a few weeks until you do something I know you're going to come to regret anyway. What have you always wanted to do? Wanted to see? Wanted to *taste?*"

I stare at her as the words settle. "I haven't thought about it. I'm happy where I am. I've traveled before, seen Crescent Falls and other parts of Eastonia. I've seen enough–"

"You've never been with anyone, Posey. Never even kissed a boy. And you're about to throw all of that away!"

"I'm not throwing anything away."

"Uh, just your entire life?" She fixes me with a hard look. I flinch. "Ah, there it is, that piece of you that knows you're making a mistake."

"I've made up my mind. You know that."

Willow bites her lip, shaking her head. "Fine. I don't like it."

"You don't have to like it. It's my decision. My life."

"Don't you want to experience life before… doing this?"

"Like what?" I turn to the mirror and avoid making eye contact with my reflection.

"I don't know…. I mean, you'll be trapping yourself in a world of solitude until you grow old and die. Don't you want to know what it's like to be… drunk? Drunk and dancing on a beach, dancing with a guy who… who you find handsome… and he makes you feel all… hot?"

I glare at her, but she's grinning again, enjoying my discomfort, seeing right through the armor I've tried to don over the course of the conversation.

"Don't you want to kiss someone before you take the oath?"

"Who would kiss me, Willow? Be serious."

She scoffs. "Have you looked in the mirror? Better yet, have you seen the way Tate and Miles gawk at you? It's your boobs. They're wonderful. Perfect, actually. You're the Goddess's favorite, for sure."

"Willow," I grind out, shaking my head. "What?"

"And Aris!" She blows out her breath in a whoosh. "Did you know about his crush on you? Gods, he practically drools when he sees you, and then he just stares at you like he's confused about how he's supposed to feel about his best friend's little sister."

"Don't," I say, cutting her off. "Don't even start with that. I might be unfazed by the idea of you sleeping with my brother, but he'd freak out on Aris about that, okay?"

"Would he really? I don't believe you in the slightest. I think Roman would be relieved you were letting loose for once in your life."

"Well, it wouldn't be with Aris. He can be with anyone he wants. It doesn't matter. It would never be me." I'm not sure why the words catch in my throat. Willow drags her fingertips over the collection of books scattered on my bedspread with a sigh.

"I'm just saying… how do you know this is really what you want when you haven't experienced the other options yet?"

"I don't have options, Willow." I wish there were something I could say to make her understand. I've told her about my family and our role in Veiled Valley society, but it's terribly difficult and almost downright impossible to explain the significance of the lines of power and the promise of magical genetics to someone from somewhere as modern as Crescent Falls.

I can't marry because I cannot have children.

I just… can't risk it.

And… Goddess forbid I find my mate, as impossible as that would be, and then what? Curse another generation with *what I'm not?*

I close my eyes, reaching blindly for my hairbrush.

"Well, I'm tucking in for the night. I'm still kind of hungover." The bed shifts as she rolls off the mattress. "Think about it, okay? Just because you don't have a wolf doesn't mean you're not allowed to get a taste of life before you throw it all away."

To appease her and end the conversation for what I hope is for good, I reply, "I'll think about it."

Her footsteps are soft on the carpet until they fade, and the door closes with a soft click.

I stay up. Not because I'm not tired after a long day in the sun, on a boat, sailing around the Ruby district of Gem Lake.. It's gorgeous here, and even the small town of Ruby, where the Alpha lives and most of his pack resides, was like something out of a fairytale, and that's coming from someone who grew up in a village older than most of the Firestone era ruins dotted across Eastonia.

I can't sleep. I don't even bother to try, knowing I'll just toss and turn, pouring through my conversation with Willow over and over again, so I slink out of my room and wander the mostly empty house. I peek into Willow's room and find her fast asleep. She's always slept like the dead, even when we were back in college. She never cared about my lamp being on or the sound of pages turning in the middle of the night.

The guys aren't home. They left to go to some bar nearby once we'd arrived back at Aris's lake house. So, I'm safe to wander, to explore, to look into every room and judge the decor Aris likely hasn't touched since he bought the place.

I find a small, but decently stocked, library on the first floor and start thumbing through the shelves, my fingertips slipping over old, leathery spines. None of this is Aris's doing. I don't think he's much of a reader. All of these books must have come with the house.

My fingers stop on a copper bookend, and a rush of warmth tingles down my arm into my fingertips. I pull them back with a hiss, clutching them against my chest as they throb. Three fingerprint-sized indents glisten on the bookend, now slightly warped from my touch.

Copper and I are not friends. I much prefer iron. Silver is great to work with, seeing as I don't have to worry about the side effects since I don't have a wolf. But copper is–

"Still up?"

"Oh!" I whirl, clamping my lips shut and stepping discreetly to the side to block the shelf I'd just been examining and the damage I did to the bookend. I'll fix it once he leaves, even if it makes my bones sing with pain.

Aris steps into the room, shirtless, the missing article of clothing in question scrunched in his fist. He's damp with sweat, wearing nothing but a pair of shorts. Barefoot, muscles rippling...

"Did you shift?"

"Yeah," he says, nodding, inspecting my face like he's suspicious about something. About me. "What are you doing up? It's almost three in the morning."

I shrug, my spine biting into the shelves behind me. "I couldn't sleep. I had too much fun today."

He cocks a brow. "Oh, yeah? I'll make note of the fact that you're having fun the next time you look absolutely miserable." His gaze drops to my bare shoulders and upper chest. "Have you ever been in the sun before, Posey, or was today the first time?"

"Did you come here to tease me, or are you picking out a book to read before you fall asleep?" I shoot back, motioning to the stacks.

"I'm just doing my rounds. Roman and the guys are staying in town tonight. I wanted to make sure whoever was here last night hasn't returned."

The scent. Of course. "Well, it was a full moon when that happened. Everyone shifts on a full moon. It could have been anyone."

"Sure," he says skeptically, looking at me like he's trying to pick through my thoughts. "Not a boyfriend of yours or anything?"

"Who do you think I am? Do you think I'd lie to you, Aris?"

"You've grown into a very mysterious woman. That's all. I feel like I'm meeting you for the first time all over again."

"Do you have anything nice to say to me?"

"I could try." He looks suddenly bored, giving me a smug little shrug.

"You actually think I snuck someone into the house, don't you?" I can't move, not without him seeing the bookend, but if I could, I'd be going toe to toe with the prince, that's for sure. "I'm not a little girl anymore, Aris. I hope you can see that."

His gaze drops to my chest, and he sighs, closing his eyes. "Oh, trust me, *I can.*"

"What?" I barely heard him. I risk stepping forward. "I didn't sneak anyone in here."

"I know. I just like seeing you all riled up. Goodnight, Posey." He turns like it's painful, fighting every step, and disappears into the darkness. I wait for his footsteps to recede before hastily turning to the shelf and running my fingers over the bookend, smoothing the copper with a pained wince.

WHAT A WASTE

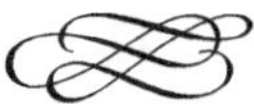

Aris

"YOU DIDN'T HAVE TO COME," ROMAN SAYS. WE WALK SIDE BY SIDE through the market that's held in Ruby every weekend. It's crowded with locals and summer tourists alike, but through the noise and bobbing crowd, I catch a glimpse of Posey's reddish-blonde hair as she weaves toward a stall selling an incredible array of freshly cut flowers.

"I was either going to sleep half the day away or this." I motion toward the market. "I had no other plans."

"Well, we've been going a hundred miles an hour since we arrived," he says with a sigh. "I'm kind of looking forward to a break this weekend; I'm not going to lie."

"Are we getting old, Roman?"

He smirks, shrugging. "I suppose the fun has to come to an end at some point."

"Hold this," Posey says quickly before darting away, leaving Roman with the giant basket she brought, which is now full to the brim with vegetables, two loaves of bread, three bottles of wine from a local vineyard, and several small bags of herbs.

Roman adjusts the weight and smiles softly to himself. Posey returns to the flower stall. I watch her with interest as she drops into conversation with the young man helping what looks like his mother sell the flowers. She seems happy–smiling and laughing in a way she won't do around me. I've noticed how quickly she shuts her mouth and curls inward when I'm around, especially over the past week of our vacation. It's been a full seven days since everyone arrived, and it's only gotten worse.

I'm not sure where or how I offended her, but the way she's acting around me now makes me wonder if I owe her an apology for something.

"Posey has a garden back home," Roman says while we walk aimlessly through the market, keeping Posey within our sights while she hops from stall to stall, filling her second basket. "She's got a knack for it, honestly. No one had touched the old garden beds since my great-grandparents were alive, but she turned them around. Dad even made her a greenhouse. She grows mostly flowers and herbs for our alchemy, but you should see the cucumbers she has growing right now. It's impressive."

"I thought you said she wasn't an alchemist?"

"I mean for me and Dad. We need some stuff. Tinctures, mostly. Posey started making them herself. I think she just needed something to do to pass the time, you know, since coming back to Sapphire Ridge."

I pause, looking over at him. "She's a teacher, right? That's what she studied in school?"

"Yeah, she taught for about a year and then decided to join a different program, got swept into it." He tapers off, looking suddenly pale. "Our parents are to blame. I keep telling myself that if they weren't so shocked, so beyond upset about Posey not developing wolf gifts and her lack of alchemy skills, we wouldn't be in this situation with her right now. They pushed her into this, whether they believe it or not."

"Dude, what are you talking about? Isn't she just going to grad school?"

Roman turns to me looking equally confused. "Grad school?"

"All the books she brought." I shake my head, wondering where the disconnect is. Roman looks utterly lost as I continue, "She's been studying most nights. She won't go out with us, for one, and every time I come back to the house to check on her, she's reading from those massive theology texts."

"She's joining the seminary in Sapphire Ridge," Roman says. "She's decided she's going to be a priestess."

"*What?*" I gasp, but Posey returns with the other basket and thrusts it into my arms. I nearly drop it. She's gone again before I can even catch a glimpse of her this time, lost in a sea of shoppers. I turn back to Roman, and the look on my face must give away everything I'm feeling. Shock? Mostly. Disbelief? Incredibly so. Confusion? Regret? Grief? "What the fuck are you talking about?"

Roman heaves a breath before tilting his head toward a break between two stalls, silently commanding me to follow him to a grassy hill overlooking the market. I do, looking over my shoulder just once in search of Posey, but she's nowhere to be seen.

"Look," he says the second we're alone and the noise of the crowd is nothing more than a gentle hum. "This is a new thing she's cooked up."

"Then you can put a stop to it."

"It's not my decision to make, Aris. Posey made up her mind. A few months ago, when it became clear she wasn't getting a wolf, she had it confirmed, just like I said. She brought proof, records, blood testing back from the apothecary stating she was... not gifted with wolf powers or alchemy and then announced she was joining the Temple of the Moon Goddess as a priestess."

"And your parents are allowing this?"

He licks his lips, struggling with how to word what happened. "Aris, it's complicated. You know how these things go–"

"I don't. Enlighten me." The edge in my tone isn't something I didn't anticipate. Real anger burbles through my system, twisting like a knife in my chest. Posey? A priestess? No. No, this feels like an incredible waste. She always wanted to be a teacher. She loves kids. I thought she'd grow up and have a family of her own one day, and I'd be the weird pseudo-uncle who bullied them just like I bullied her when we were younger.

Right? That's why I feel so fucking… furious right now?

"Alchemists only come from Sapphire Ridge, our family, especially. I–I have the family gift. She does not. I will go on to have kids who also carry the gift, and she will not, so–"

"Are you saying they–they pretty much agreed with the fact she thinks she's useless?"

"It's not about that," Roman rushes out, but his eyes betray the truth.

"She's joining the temple because she thinks that because she doesn't have a wolf or alchemy gifts there's no other option for her? Are you fucking joking?"

"What is your problem, Aris? This isn't about you. It's about Posey and what she wants, and she wants this, apparently. She's been driving us all fucking mad since spring when she decided. I don't like it, trust me. Mom had a match for her, another alchemist from a weak line, yeah. Possibly related to us in some distant way, but an alchemist all the same."

"So it was this or marry her cousin?" I snap, and Roman glowers.

"You know how things are. You're a Shadowsynger, for fuck's sake. Your ancestors wouldn't have been able to keep Veiled Valley hidden and safe had it not been for mine!"

I take several steps away from him and turn, dragging a hand down my face. "You've got to be fucking kidding me, Roman."

"I wish I were. We've all tried to get her to change her mind, but she knows what's coming. Dad's old. He'll step down from his position as Alpha soon, and I will rise to power. I'll have to find a wife and start my line. She'll have no place in Sapphire Ridge. Everyone will become aware of the fact she's–she's–"

"A lapse?" The word is like acid on my tongue.

"She's the first one in our family who doesn't have a single drop of power, and yeah, it would make us look horrible. There would be questions about my own validity." Roman's expression shatters as he stares past me, just over my shoulder. "Fuck, Posey–" Roman takes a step in my direction as I turn, catching a single glimpse of Posey before she darts away. He tries to run after her, but I stop him, pressing the basket I've been holding against his chest.

"You've said enough. I'll talk to her."

I walk off before Roman can protest, reeling, barely thinking past my elevated heartbeat drumming in my ears.

I walk the length of the market three times before deciding Posey is no longer here. I try to pick up her amber and dark cherry scent, but it's lost in the crowd leaving the market, spreading out into the small town beyond. She wouldn't go where people gather. I'm not going to find her hiding in a cafe or bookstore along the lakeshore.

I turn toward the woods, following a wolf trail until I reach the lake again, and keep going until the trail melds with a rocky beach overlooking a wide swatch of water and several small islands.

She's sitting on a fallen log, her back to me, her long hair falling loose from a scrunchy and lifting off her shoulders in a breeze as she stares out over the water, still holding a bouquet of flowers.

"Posey?"

Her spine straightens, but she doesn't turn around. I kick a few pebbles, unsure if I should even approach her or not. "Hey, listen, Roman and I–we shouldn't have even been discussing that."

"You're right. It's none of your business."

I roll my lower lip between my teeth and let it go. "Can I sit with you?"

"No."

"Can I talk to you, at least?"

"There's nothing else to say. Roman covered it."

"He was being a fucking dick, I agree, but I was trying to defend you. Pose, come on. Is this really what you want?"

She turns her head ever so slightly to the side at the sound of her nickname, and I notice her tear-stained cheek, her tears leaving a trail of silver.

I approach her like she's a wild, skittish animal, and one wrong move will have her fleeing. "I understand why you feel like you have to do this–join the temple, sign your entire life away to the priestesses, but you don't have to do it."

"I am not interested in explaining this to you because it doesn't matter, and you'd never understand." She turns back the water and then further when I sit beside her, angling her body away from mine so I can't see her face.

She's been picking petals off the flowers until several are nothing more than stems.

"You're not useless to your family because you don't have a wolf, Posey. When Roman said–"

"When he said other people would know my little secret, he was right. What he didn't say, what he was going to say, is that it would harm the family forever and ruin his prospects when it came to marrying."

"Roman will find his mate–"

"He doesn't care about that. None of them have. Our parents aren't mates, Aris. You know that, don't you? My father is an alchemist. He chose my mother because she came from a good, strong, local family who had alchemists in their bloodline–long dormant. It should have still meant strong, dominant power in my generation. That's all. That was the reason. I don't have a wolf. That directly affects my ability to use alchemy. If it gets out that I have neither, it'll be a stain on Roman when he rises to power."

"I will be Alpha King one day. I have Roman's reputation in my hands."

"No, you don't." She rises, but I catch her wrist.

"Why are you doing this? Really? I want a real answer, Posey. Joining the temple is for life. It means forsaking everything else. *Is that really what you want?*"

She pulls her arm out of my grasp and walks away, leaving the flowers behind. I know better than to chase after her, but I rise, saying, "This is why you came, isn't it? Roman wanted you to come, to spend some time with him before you locked yourself away forever, right?"

She stops walking and turns to face me, her expression grim.

I take a few steps toward her and stop, holding out a hand in surrender. "He thinks he can convince you to change your mind, doesn't he? You know that, though. You came anyway just to appease him."

"I'll be taking my entrance exam to join the seminary in a few weeks. If I get in, I'll train in Moonrise for three months before being placed at a temple–anywhere. It could be a few years before I see him again, so... I agreed to come. Then Willow came to visit, and I thought it would be good for both of them to see me and come to terms with it."

"So you're really doing this?"

"Why do you care so much, Aris?"

"Because I think it's a waste."

"For who?" She laughs bitterly and cuts into the woods.

WHAT NORMAL PEOPLE DO

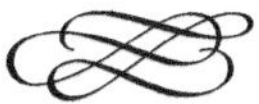

Posey

"WELL, THAT TAKES CARE OF THAT, I GUESS." WILLOW CUTS ME A LOOK as she stuffs her clothes in her suitcase, leaning her weight against it. "I did tell you he was interested in you."

I slouch on the edge of her bed on the second floor of the lake house, the room full of tangerine-hued light from the sunset. "He's not interested in me. He's interested in my business. There's a difference. Aris has always had to know everything about everyone."

She rolls her eyes and yanks on the zipper several times before it gives and allows her to close the suitcase, which she promptly dumps on the floor with a reverberating thud. "I'm here for one more night, and the one thing I want more than anything is to see you let loose and have fun with me. Can you do that? Your secret is out, so it doesn't matter."

My chest tightens. "My-my secret?"

She tosses her hair over her shoulder. "Uh, yeah? The fact you'll forever be a virgin?"

My chest relaxes as relief sweeps through me like a tidal wave.

"Oh, I, um. I don't have to be a virgin to be a priestess. I just have to abstain after taking my vows–"

"So you weren't keeping the fact you're going to live at a dusty, haunted temple a secret? Or was it just a secret from Aris?"

"I was under the impression he knew. It's not a secret. I don't know why he cares. He shouldn't have an opinion at all."

"He has the hots for you, girl."

"He doesn't."

"I say... add him to your list."

"I don't have a list." I rise and walk to the window. This room has a view of the backyard. Aris is nowhere to be seen, but Miles, Tate, and Roman, who hasn't spoken to me since the market fiasco this morning, are lounging in the grass drinking cans of beer–pregaming for the bonfire tonight.

Willow is heading out tomorrow to continue her grand tour of Eastonia, her next stop being Twin Rivers before she hops over to Tarsian... all in her little blue convertible.

I'm not nearly as brave as her. I never have been. She's spent her whole summer having new adventures, checking things off a list, before settling into her new life.

I've been ignoring the freedoms I'm leaving behind. Ignoring my curiosities. Ignoring the desires I had for a life I've been robbed of.

"What's on your list, exactly?"

Willow, now doing her makeup in the ensuite, pokes her head through the door with a grin. "You really want to know?"

I nod, and she squeals, then disappears from her room entirely, coming back five minutes later with a bottle of wine and two glasses, which she fills to the brim recites the list, which is apparently completely mental, in detail.

Willow, who is convinced her mate is out there, and she'll meet him when she gets back to Crescent Falls, has decided she's going to not only visit every major city in Eastonia, but sleep with someone from each one. Her sexual prowess has already made her successful on that front, except for here, because just like I thought, Roman has ignored the bait entirely.

"It doesn't make me a… well, you know," she says, halfway through her second glass of wine. "I just know what I like, and I always find it. I'm just… testing all the flavors until I find my favorite."

"Until you find your mate?" I smirk over the rim of my glass—still nursing my first, but I'm nearly finished. I already feel lightheaded as she grins and rolls her eyes to the ceiling.

"He's not going to care, I know that much about him because he's probably just like me… sleeping through every pack until he finds me."

I laugh, and she follows, both of us pink in the face and so distracted by the faint buzz in our veins to notice Roman in the doorway.

"Am I interrupting?" he asks, and his deep voice slices through me, the buzz turning sour. "We're leaving for the other side of the island in a few minutes. For the bonfire. If you're going." He's looking at Willow, refusing to make eye contact with me.

Willow picks up the bottle of wine and tops off her glass before looking at me with an arch of her brow.

I think about it for a moment, about how I could, like every night for the past week, go upstairs and study. I could be alone, enjoying the quiet solitude and the shadows that seem to dance around my room, keeping me company.

I tilt my empty glass toward the bottle, and she presses her lips together in an excited, but subdued, grin.

Roman stiffens as the wine pours, but Willow turns her practiced, seductive smile on him. "We'll be ready in, like, twenty minutes. Posey still needs to get ready."

"You're coming?"

I look away from my brother. "Yeah, is that a problem for you?"

Roman just sighs, rolling unsaid words over his tongue, and leaves. Willow jumps into action, exclaiming, "All right, we have work to do!" and rips open her already packed suitcase.

MY ENTIRE BODY FEELS LOOSE AND UNSTEADY AS I WALK BESIDE Willow down a wood-lined road. It's fully dark now, not a single light shining to illuminate our path, but Roman, Miles, and Tate have it covered as they hoot and holler several yards ahead, the backyard beers, apparently, having given way to a bottle of whiskey that Roman finished off.

I've never seen him this drunk. I've never seen him laugh this freely, but anytime his glazed eyes slide in my direction, they darken, and I eventually refuse to even look at him.

"He'll forget the fight by morning," Willow says breezily, soaking in the warm night air. "Trust me. He's obliterated already, and we're not even at the party yet."

"It wasn't even a fight. He's just—he's mad because he knows I'm upset with him. It's his way."

"He's ruining your vibe." She playfully pinches my arm. "You know what? I still have a night left. I'll… distract him for you. Maybe I'll get my way after all!"

"You don't have to—" Her arm slips from mine, and then she's flouncing toward him through the darkness, giggling as she comes to a stop, purring like a cat hooking her claws into his forearm. He doesn't fight it this time.

"She's a cunning little witch, isn't she?"

I close my eyes and take a deep, restorative breath as Aris's voice sounds out behind me.

"How long have you been lurking in the shadows?"

"Long enough to hear the entirety of your conversation with our resident lady of the night." Aris sidles up beside me, his hands tucked in the pockets of his jeans. His muscled frame is on display in a simple thin white T-shirt. He looks normal, a far cry from the prince he is. I doubt many people will recognize him like this.

"Willow isn't a witch, and even if she is a lady of the night, she's proud of it, and I'm proud of her for being so brave."

"You think sleeping with anyone with a pulse is brave?"

"She's rather calculating about it, actually. You could learn a thing or two from her seeing as you do exactly what you accused her of."

"Tell that to the tabloids, Pose. I fear I've ruined my reputation past the point of no return, so it doesn't matter."

"It is rather bad. Everyone knows you *will* sleep with anyone with a pulse."

"I'm rather picky, actually."

"How so?"

Music wafts toward us when we reach the outskirts of a quiet, lakeside town. Beyond the trees now growing sparse, the moon glimmers over the lake, which is teeming with boats, all of them anchored just off the shoreline where a huge party is taking place. It's a warm night. A calm one. It's not enough to thaw the chill between me and Aris after the fight this morning, but he's obviously trying.

"I tend to lean toward people who want the same thing I do." His voice drops to a low whisper, the words meant for me and me alone.

"And what's that?"

He shrugs. "Feeling like... I have someone, even if it's just for a moment."

I startle but stifle it. "That's kind of deep."

He quickly corrects himself. "It never means anything. It's casual. Always. No strings attached."

"You make it sound easy."

A heavy, speculative silence settles between us for several heartbeats. "Aren't you going into a convent?"

"I am, I just... Willow mentioned I should make a list of things I want to do and experience before I take my vows, and I think she's right. There're things I should know."

"Are you saying you're... hunting tonight?" There's a gleam in his eyes I'm not sure I understand. He's either impressed or seriously concerned.

"Hunting for what?"

"Posey! Come on!" Willow jumps up and down, waving her arms.

I pick up the pace, walking steadily in her direction. The ground turns to thick sand, but Aris's touch on my wrist burns through me like a fire heating a forge.

"Don't do anything stupid," he says, his thumb resting over my pulse. I try to pull out of his grasp, but I meet his gaze, and I feel suddenly, inexplicably trapped in place. His eyes are a stunning clear silver. A flawless silver. The kind I can so easily bend to my will.

"I wouldn't do anything you'd do. Don't worry."

He lets me go, but I feel his stare following me through the crowd.

Willow and I move across the beach. I've never seen anything like this—this many people our age gathered in such a small space. I never went to the college parties Willow was always trying to drag me to. Going to college in the first place had been a miracle because my parents were so incredibly opposed to me leaving Sapphire Ridge, and the idea of messing it up had me in tatters.

I spent the majority of my years at Wellington alone in the library or my dorm room, praying I'd remain under the radar, that no one would catch my eye and vice versa. It was before I knew that I don't have a wolf. It was also before my secret alchemy gifts had shown up. I'd been raised knowing I'd marry someone someday who'd strengthen my alchemy gifts, and anyone else would soil our carefully crafted bloodline.

Someone in that bloodline lied, however.

And now I'm never going to know what it feels like to dance against the backdrop of an open flame, my mate's mouth on mine, his hands...

"Damn." A deep, rolling male voice sounds directly above my head. I look up just as a dark-haired fortress of a man catches my arm, stopping me from tripping over a cooler parked in the sand. His hazel eyes scan mine before mapping the planes of my face, and when they meet mine again, they're a shade darker than they were before. "I haven't seen you around. Just visiting?"

"Yeah." He lets me go, and my arm drops limp at my side. Willow, realizing I'm no longer beside her, whirls to the group of men with me standing precariously at the edge of their semicircle.

"I'm Mason."

"I'm—I'm Posey."

"Northern girl. Haven't heard an accent like that around these parts in a while." He smiles, and it's charming, something that exudes heat that makes my stomach pinch. He's flirting, isn't he? This is my shot, isn't it? At affection? At a taste of something Aris and Willow find so easily? "Where are you from, Miss Posey?"

I open my mouth, but Willow latches herself to my side, her smile blinding and immediately entrancing the group. "We're from Crescent Falls. And... who are you, exactly?"

Mason smirks, giving Willow an appraising once over. "My father's the Alpha of Ruby. You're on my property as it stands." His eyes slide to mine once more. "I have a few rules, especially for tourists as pretty as you two."

Part of me wants to tell him the truth–I'm also from Veiled Valley–the northern part, yes. He'd been right about my lifted accent, so different from the slow roll of his vowels, but... he doesn't know me. He doesn't know anything about me. *He doesn't need to.*

"Oh, yeah? What rules?" Willow's smile is coy like a cat, her eyes gleaming in the firelight.

Mason reaches down and plucks two beers from the cooler. "If you're going to stand by my fire, you have to drink to it"

"To what?" I manage, my throat suddenly thick with something akin to excitement–or dread. I'm not sure. I fight the urge to turn to look for... Aris, of all people. But this is what normal people my age do, don't they?

"To new friends," he says smoothly, cracking open a beer and handing it to me. His touch lingers on my fingers when they meet. "And a long night ahead."

JUST A KISS

Aris

I SHOULD BE LOVING THIS. THIS IS ACTUALLY WHAT I WANTED OUT OF my last summer of freedom before I submit to my grandfather and let him turn me into the new king of shadows he's been pestering me to be since I was little more than fourteen.

I should be shitfaced right now with my tongue down some stranger woman's throat, but instead, I'm watching the beach and the hundred or so people I don't know mingle and rally like this is their last night in the Goddess's kingdom.

Half an hour ago, I'd been finishing my second beer while watching Posey talk to a tall, dark-haired idiot I immediately recognized as the Alpha of Ruby's son, Mason. I've only met the guy once, when I came to view the lake house for the first time, and didn't hate him then, but I sure as hell do now because I can't find the knuckle-dragging bastard anywhere, and I'm guessing wherever he went, he took Posey with him.

I can't relax, even after downing a third, then fourth drink... Well, perhaps this is my sixth, judging by the scattered beer cans. My body is on fire from within. I scan the crowd below, shadows snaking from my fingertips in a blurry dance, also feeling the effects of the cheap booze weakening my system. No one notices them. It's dark, and my shadows merge with the natural shadows being cast by the fire. They pick through the crowd, searching, clawing for any sign of Posey.

Just to make sure she's fine. That she's not being taken advantage of. Not because I actually, deeply care. Just because… if I don't find her, I'll scream. I swear on the Goddess–

"Where'd Roman go? I just saw him and Willow like ten minutes ago." Tate is suddenly at my side, stumbling, a woman I don't recognize swaying under the weight of his arm resting over her shoulders. She giggles but can't form a single syllable. I frown at them. Tate is barely lucid. He takes a single step and sits directly on the sand at my feet.

"I don't know where Roman is, and I don't care. Where's Posey?"

"Oh, she went home like an hour ago," he says with a wave of his hand. "She was all bent out of shape about something and–"

I turn, leaving him behind mid-sentence, and break into a near sprint until I reach the tree line where the beach ends and the forest hugging the small town begins. My clothing shreds into ribbons when I involuntarily shift and promptly disappear into a wolf of pure, nearly invisible shadow. It's unnecessary, but it's not up to me. My senses propel me forward. I'm driven by my thundering heartbeat with every rapid step. I barely breathe until my paws touch the smooth white gravel driveway, and I skid to a stop, spraying pebbles all over the porch and tumbling into my human form without being able to even remotely stop the shift from happening.

I storm into the house prepared to fight, shoulders squared, haphazardly snatching a pair of shorts off the staircase railing that likely belong to Tate or Miles and pulling them on while the house blurs and adrenaline rushes, blinding me to the world. Posey's door is open when I climb the final staircase to the top floor of the house. A shadow moves through the stream of light pouring through the crack then pauses, halting mid-step.

I charge, fist drawn back, prepared to flatten the Alpha's son who followed Posey home to torment her further and…

"ARIS!" Posey's scream bounces from wall to wall, booming through my ears. The noise rattles me to the bone, snapping me out of my delirium in a heartbeat, and then the booze, nerves, and overwhelm crush me, sweeping me into a furious current I can't find the footing to fight.

"What–are–you–doing–here?" I choke out, panting, gripping either side of the doorframe as I look down at her.

She's white as a ghost and dressed in nothing but an old Wellington T-shirt that brushes the top of her thighs, her face free of the makeup I know Willow piled on. Her hair falls loosely over her shoulders, and her eyes–as wide and round as tea-saucers–wildly scan my face. I can almost feel her racing heartbeat through the floorboards between us. Her left hand is fused to her chest like she's trying to steady it.

"You scared me to death! What's wrong with you?" she shouts. "I thought…. Were you going to hit me?"

"Of course not." I heave a sharp breath and enter her room, kicking the door closed with a crunch. My face is glazed with sweat, and my skin prickles as I move across the soft carpet to the edge of her bed, where I sit, ignoring the scattered books and trinkets, nearly crushing her glasses. She snatches them out of my hand and inspects the thick lenses before gripping them like a weapon, her cheeks finally turning from a pale cream to a rosy, furious pink again.

"What the hell is wrong with you?"

"Why do you need those anyway? Your eyesight can't be that bad." I motion to the glasses, and she glowers, tucking them behind her back. I take several more deep breaths, trying to fill and calm my lungs.

"I don't have a wolf, remember? You can thank your wolf for your better-than-perfect eyesight. I wasn't as blessed." She sets the glasses carefully on her side table before forming a fist. "I almost had a stroke, Aris. I heard you sprinting up the stairs and thought someone was, in fact, here to kill me–or worse."

"I heard you left the bonfire and wanted to make sure you were okay." I can't be this out of control. Now, I'm the one with a hand clasped against my chest, my body screaming from excretion, my skin slick with sweat.

"Did you sprint the entire way back?" she hisses, moving across the room. She turns, giving me her back, and begins to twist her hair into a bun on the top of her head, the shirt lifting ever so slightly to reveal the tight boy shorts beneath. Panties. *Fuck.*

I look away, coughing, struggling to clear my throat. "I–I shifted. It was faster that way."

"You're actually insane. What is your deal? Why are you so concerned about me and what I do?" She tosses out the questions like they're insults.

"Why'd you come back?"

"I wasn't having fun anymore. Everyone else was drunk, so I figured it didn't matter. I just wanted to be home."

"You should have told me."

"I told Willow I was leaving."

"You should have told *me.*"

"You are not my brother. You're not responsible for me in the slightest. I'm a grown woman, Aris. I'm capable of making my own decisions." She walks into the bathroom and shuts off the light like I'd interrupted her just as she was getting ready for bed, which explains the books and the glasses I nearly snapped in half sitting on the bedspread.

I don't take the hint and move when she approaches the bed, so she gestures to me, to my unkempt state. "Are those even your shorts? They barely fit."

"I think they're Tate's. He's a lot smaller than me."

"Are you okay?"

I blink, spiraling back to reality as my wolf senses fade. "Yeah. I just wanted to check on you."

"Well, I'm in one piece–"

"Did something happen?" I meet her eyes. She's standing only a few feet away, and I can tell the question is hanging in the air between us as she ponders her answer, then surrenders, her shoulders slumping. She sits down beside me. Her leg brushes mine when she reaches behind her for a small tube of cherry lotion, that scent I keep catching when she's around.

She smooths it onto her hands, slowly massaging it along each digit. "I came home before anything could happen." She purses her lips and shakes her head. "If you really want to know."

"What do you mean?"

"What do you think I mean? Gods, you were just asking if I was hunting tonight. Maybe I was, Aris, and then realized how grossly unprepared I am for the real world and something as simple and innocent as flirting with someone who showed even the smallest fraction of interest in me." Her cheeks flare, turning from rosy to a deep red. "I felt awful, so I left. I didn't like it. That feeling."

"What feeling?" My voice is low enough to be barely audible, but she chuckles darkly, her eyes suddenly glossy like she's on the verge of tears.

"You know, I have done everything right. I'm pretty." She meets my eyes briefly. "I apparently have childbearing hips and breasts to match. My mom had the highest hopes that I'd make a good, strong match." That dark chuckle turns self-deprecating. "I grew up thinking I'd be like Dad and Roman–an alchemist. Gods, that's all I wanted. I wanted a room in the spires in Sapphire Ridge where I bent metal all day. I didn't care if it meant making uniforms for the Ghost army or little trinkets for your extended family. I wanted that. And then I realized what was happening to me, and I went off to college to give myself some space to figure it out. I was terrified the whole time. I didn't know how to talk to people. I didn't know how to want anything other than the future I'd carved for myself that was getting ripped away second by second, and I couldn't do anything to stop it."

She looks at me again with tired eyes that scream for me to understand, to see her.

"You're not worthless because you don't have a wolf."

She searches my gaze. Unsaid words sit on the tip of her tongue, which she bites. "Mom wanted me to come home after school, so I did. That was the deal–I could leave and go to college in Crescent Falls, but I'd have to return and… be who I promised I'd be. Marry who I promised I'd marry. But I made those promises when I thought I could still be an alchemist. I can't now. And I can't remain… I'm a stain on the family's name."

"You're not."

"You don't understand–"

"You know my family. You know what we're capable of. One word of this to my parents–"

"No," she breathes, shaking her head. "You don't understand, and I can't make you understand my reasoning for signing my life away to the temple."

"Why there? Why do it, Posey? You're right, I don't understand. You can do anything you want. You're not tied to your parents and their expectations." I turn toward her, the space between us shrinking.

"You heard Roman."

"I don't give a shit about how Roman feels about this."

"He's your best friend."

"You're my friend, too."

Posey stares at me for several seconds before looking away, taking a deep, slow breath. "Aris–"

"Why'd you leave the bonfire?"

"I already told you."

"Why did you leave and not tell *me*? Have I done something to offend you, Posey? You know…how I act around you… what I say to you sometimes… it's just who I am, and it doesn't mean anything."

"I know."

"Then what's going on?"

Her nostrils flare, but she looks down at her lap, her blush creeping down her neck. "Willow has a list, you know. To sleep with someone from every place she visits. She's doing it because she likes it but also because she thinks she'll meet her mate when she gets back to Crescent Falls, and then it's over. Her life begins."

She wrings her hands, scrubbing the lotion in deeper, like her fingers hurt, especially the tips.

"It's like everything is changing at the end of the summer for everyone, and everyone has these plans to experience stuff, to check things off a list, and I've been so–" She sucks in a breath, letting it out slowly. She doesn't finish the sentence, but the look on her face crushes me.

"What's on your list?"

Posey blinks, shaking her head. "I don't have one. I thought... maybe tonight I'd try to be more like Willow and allow myself to... just talk to someone, but it's not what I think I wanted."

"Posey, come on." I nudge her, but her answering smile is half-hearted and faint.

"Don't laugh."

"I'll try."

"I wanted to kiss someone. I just... wanted to know what it felt like." She rolls her lower lip between her teeth before looking up at me, those doe-eyes unraveling any traces of common sense I have to my name. "It's so stupid."

"Kiss me."

"What?" She starts to laugh, but I lean in, and she doesn't lean away.

"It's just a kiss, Posey. If you want to know what it feels like, kiss me. It doesn't have to mean anything every time."

She looks at my lips and back up again, that blush creeping back into existence.

"Aris..."

I wait for the *"we can't"* to follow.

It doesn't.

"Tell me no," I tell her.

She looks into my eyes. I give her the space of a breath, of a single heartbeat, to say the word.

She... doesn't.

It's just a kiss. Something I've done a million times before. If my best-friend's little sister is serious about joining a fucking convent... kissing her is the least I can do. The *least*.

I lean in, my fingers stroking her cheek. I angle my mouth over hers, and she closes her eyes.

"It feels like this," I whisper against her mouth.

And kiss her.

HE DIDN'T HURT ME

POSEY

ARIS'S LIPS ARE SUPPLE AND WARM—SOFTER THAN I EXPECTED. I'M NOT sure what I anticipated, but it wasn't… this.

His mouth presses to mine—tender, soft, innocent. His hand remains on my cheek, holding me in place as he slowly eases the pressure and angles away ever so slightly. The distance is unbearable, like he's taken the very breath from my lungs.

I realize I've pinned my eyes closed, holding my breath, so I open them, looking up at him in disbelief. His fingers curl around the back of my neck, and he takes a shallow breath, his eyes searching mine before he presses our foreheads together, our mouths only centimeters apart.

My stomach tumbles, my body floods with warmth like a sudden fever, and my heart feels like it's about to race out of my chest.

"That's what it feels like," he whispers, his thumb smoothing over my cheekbone.

"Every time?"

His eyes meet mine and hold, darkening several shades until they resemble raw iron. He leans forward, our lips nearly touching again. My lips part, chasing his by instinct. He inhales deeply and groans, dropping his hand and making a tight fist as he rises.

Reality hits me like a bucket of ice being dumped over my head.

"I–"

"No," he says with effort, cutting me off with a quick but firm gesture of his hand.

"I'm sorry–"

"No," he repeats, running his fingers through his hair. He smiles, but it's tight. "No, don't apologize. Posey, I'm drunk. Shit faced. I shouldn't have–I probably shouldn't have kissed you."

"I–I won't tell Roman if that's what you're–"

Aris raises his brows and looks at me like I've just slapped him upside the head. "Roman? You're thinking about *Roman* right now?"

"Your friend and my brother?"

"I know who he is." His voice is suddenly caustic. It catches me off guard. I've never heard him use such ice in his tone.

A strange sense of unease cloaks the room. I suffocate, turning from Aris so he can't see the look on my face as rejection sweeps through me, numbing me to the bone.

"I–" He pauses then hisses out a breath before abruptly walking out of the room, leaving the door wide open. I hear his bedroom door close down the hallway, and the house falls silent while I sit on the edge of the bed, pressing my fingers to my lower lip.

Reeling.

MORNING SUNLIGHT DRIFTS THROUGH THE OPEN WINDOWS IN THE kitchen. The house is as quiet as the night before while I sip my coffee and stare at the glassy reflection of the lake, at the family of ducks bobbing on the mirrored surface. I smile at one of the baby ducks beneath the water, and the mother squawks in annoyance when it falls behind.

My spine straightens, however, when I hear footsteps behind me—a familiar tread that echoed in my dreams last night.

I can feel Aris's gaze sweeping over my body from head to toe before he enters the room. I'm leaning against the kitchen island when he moves to my side, reaching over my head to where the coffee mugs are neatly stacked on a shelf.

"Good morning."

"Morning." My throat feels impossibly tight when his arm brushes mine.

"I'm going on a walk. I'd like you to come with me," he says in a near whisper. His tone, however, edges on commanding as his silver eyes meet mine in the bright glare of the morning sun. "We need to talk."

"Okay."

A rough, choking sob shudders from the hallway. We both freeze, and Aris slowly turns toward the archway leading off the kitchen. When another rattling sigh and the sound of suitcase wheels bumping over his waxed wood floors scurries toward us, he moves, but I grab his arm. Willow passes the archway hauling her suitcase and moves out of sight again.

The kitchen is a blur of coffee scented air and sunlight. I sprint in Willow's directly, catching a single glimpse of her undone state as she slips through the front door.

"Willow!" I chase her down, the white gravel biting into my bare feet, but she's already at her car, roughly tossing her suitcase into the back-seat. I glance behind us, seeing Aris standing in the shadow of the front porch, his eyes shining a bright silver in the dim light, and when I pivot to face my friend, I see her tears. "What's wrong? What are you doing?"

She wipes her tears and steps toward the driver's side door, but I step in her way. "I'm fine," she grinds out, but her voice cracks. I've never seen her cry before. She's... eternally happy and optimistic, always has been. Even in the worst situations, she's sunshine and rainbows.

Now, she looks sullen and gray in a matching terrycloth lounge set in a soft butter yellow. Her normally perfect hair is pulled tight away from her face in a lopsided bun on the top of her head, straight strands falling loose behind her ears, and she's not wearing a lick of makeup.

Her eyes are bloodshot from crying.

"Willow?" I breathe, reaching to take her by the arms, but she steps out of my touch.

A cold, creeping presence fills the driveway, and I turn back to the porch. Roman stands in the shadows looking just as undone, shirtless. Then I see his eyes as he looks at Willow…

I grab her arm and move her to the back of her car. "What happened?"

"I'm fine. Everything is just fine," she replies hoarsely, trying to smile, but she looks more like she's in serious pain.

I look her over for injuries. She snaps her hands back, shaking her head.

"I'm catching the midday ferry back to the capital and then traveling to the port."

"The port? Of Avalon? What are you talking about? You're going to Tarsian next." The main port of Veiled Valley expands in my mind. From Veiled Valley in the west, it's only a few days' journey by boat to the Kingdom of Maatua and a few days more to Crescent Falls. It's the opposite direction of where she's supposed to be going. "Willow?"

She's looking up at the porch.

At Roman.

"I'm ready to go home. I've seen and done enough."

Willow leaps into action, skirting around me before I can catch her, and yanks open her car door. I have to leap out of her way when she revs the engine and peels out of the driveway in a tight circle, spraying gravel, and disappears in a flash of baby blue.

My heart rate soars. I slowly turn to the porch, to my brother. "What have you done?"

"Go inside," Roman sneers. "This doesn't involve you."

Aris whips in his direction, but I'm already stalking across the driveway toward my brother, hackles raised, my vision blurred red with rage. "What did you do to her? Roman?"

He licks his lip, glancing between me and Aris. "Nothing. Nothing that concerns you!"

Aris grabs Roman's arm and pulls him inside so aggressively my brother nearly trips over the doormat. I chase after them through the foyer and down the hallway, but when I reach the kitchen, Aris is shoving Roman through the patio door and into the backyard.

"Aris." His name leaves my lips in a pitched exhale. He pauses with his hand on the door. Behind him, Roman walks out onto the grass, repeatedly running his fingers through his hair, pacing.

"Call her and make sure she's okay. I'll call the port authority and ensure she has a suite on whatever ferries are departing from Avalon tonight. She'll have a ticket waiting for her when she gets there." He steps into the sunlight and shuts the door firmly behind him. He approaches Roman, and my brother turns, yelling something muffled by the glass windows next to the kitchen table.

My heart aches. I turn from the scene and hurry upstairs to my room, out of breath by the time I reach the side table where my phone is resting on its charger.

Willow doesn't answer. Not the first, second, or third time I call. But on the fourth, half an hour after she tore off the property like her life depended on it, her voice radiates through the phone, broken but steadier than before.

"Posey." She takes a shaky breath. "I'm sorry. I'm sorry I took off like that. I'm okay. I want you to know that." The call fizzles. I hiss a curse when I pull the phone away from my ear and see the single damning bar of service.

"What the hell is going on? Did Roman do something to you?"

She sighs deeply. In the background, I hear faint music and the hum of her engine. She's driving. Driving to the small ferry port that will take her across the river back to the capital of Veiled Valley.

"He... hurt me. It's a long story."

I sit on the edge of my bed. A shadow darkens the doorway, and I know it's Aris before looking up. I ignore him, asking, "Can you tell me?"

"It's really nothing. I slept with him." She laughs, but it's bittersweet. "Finally checked a guy from Veiled Valley off my list. I need to go, okay? I'll come visit when you're in Moonrise, okay? You're gonna get into the seminary, I know it. You don't even have to study, Posey. They'd be lucky to have you." Her words fade as the connection shudders.

"Willow?"

The call drops. I stare blankly at my phone for several seconds before looking up at Aris. "What happened? Where's Roman?"

"I sent him out to shift, to burn off his hangover and come back to his senses. He won't be back until nightfall, and even then, I think after our conversation he might take me up on his offer to stay at one of the hotels a few towns over. For a few days, at least."

"Why?" I rise, nervous, not liking the conflicting look behind Aris's eyes.

"I want him to keep his distance from you for a little while, honestly. He's not thinking straight." Aris moves deeper into the room, running his fingertips over my dresser, picking up a hairbrush and putting it down again. "Is Willow okay?"

"I don't know. What happened? Did he–did hurt her? I don't believe her."

Aris meets my gaze. "No."

"Then what–"

"About that walk," he says, cutting me off. "Get dressed. We'll be gone for a while."

He starts to turn to leave, but I step in his way. His chest rises and falls deeply, like he hasn't taken a full breath since all of this began. "Willow is my friend, and I've never seen her so upset. If you know something… please, Aris. You have to tell me."

"I need a moment to process what he told me." His expression is apologetic but firm. "We'll talk once we've both had more coffee and are out of this house. Tate and Miles will be waking up soon, and I'd rather not be forced to rope them into this, too. It's none of their business."

He looks down at me, searching my gaze, likely waiting for me to argue. I have a feeling he'd tell me right now if I really pushed the subject, but he looks… tired. Worn thin.

When his eyes drop to my lips and hold for a few seconds longer than they should, I blink and turn from him to hide the heat painting my cheeks pink in the glare of morning sunlight warming the room… or maybe that's just my body reacting like it did last night. *I'm so stupid. There's no way he's thinking the same way about me.*

"Okay. I'll get dressed."

"I'll make coffee to go. Do you still take yours without sugar?"

I nod, and he wordlessly leaves, closing the door behind him. The silence that follows is too much.

Twenty minutes later, I'm standing in the kitchen accepting a to-go mug from him, both of us dressed for the day. My sundress is thin but not thin enough to stop the raw burn of the unrelenting sun. It doesn't matter. It's going to be another hot day, I can already tell. Aris tilts his head toward the backyard, and I follow, sliding my feet into my shoes.

"Where are we going?"

"Somewhere private. There're a few things I want to discuss with you."

"Roman and Willow?"

He pauses where the grass merges with the tree line and a faint, barely used wolf trail. "Yes. And something else."

OOPS, HE DID IT AGAIN

Posey

ARIS MOVES LIKE A WOLF EVEN IN HIS HUMAN FORM. EVERY STEP IS calculated and sure-footed. I follow him down a wolf trail just above the rocky beach. He keeps his eyes trained on the forest, turning his head ever so slightly to every sound, but he hasn't said a word to me in over two miles.

I can't say I mind the silence, the walk itself. *The hike.* This is exactly the kind of activity I enjoy. It's a beautiful day, and after this morning, my mind was in a tangle. Now, it's quiet. The overstimulation I felt back at the house is nothing more than a gentle hum of noise in the back of my mind while I focus on everything and nothing at all.

Gem Lake as a whole is a melting pot of environments, and here, in the Ruby district, the beaches tend to be rocky and steep, and the trees, mostly magnolia, silverbell, and dogwood, grow thick, giving much needed shade. Further south along the Gem Lake system, like the cove we visited, the beaches thin, the sand growing soft and pale, and the water is nearly translucent to the very bottom.

But here, wherever we are, as the trees give way to marshes, and as the wolf trail begins to blend with our surroundings, the path lost to nature entirely, I feel like I'm somewhere untouched and unseen, like my eyes are the first to discover it.

Aris, however, holds claim to this place. It's obvious. He knows where he's going and has likely been here several times before. I follow him like a loyal dog, watching herons lift from the marsh while he picks our path forward. The sun is relentless, drumming down on the top of my head, but the heat washes away any lingering nerves that had been plaguing me, and now it's just... perfect. Perfectly still. Perfectly quiet. Like I'm utterly, blissfully alone—with him.

We eventually duck back into the forest again, and the landscape shifts from sun to shade and shadow. Magnolia blossoms are scattered across the forest floor. Aris leads me further and further away from his property. I'm sure we've walked close to three miles, spent an hour in silence, when he finally comes to a stop and steps aside to allow me to move forward and see the view.

"Woah," I whisper, praying my voice isn't loud enough to break the spell. Six feet below, the path drops off, revealing an entirely private and protected area of the lake—another cove but much smaller than the one we visited. A rocky beach dappled with fallen, washed up logs is surrounded by the forest, covered in deliciously cool shade, and the water here is so calm I can see to the bottom of the deepest point of the water, where the rocks and logs below shine the richest blue against the cerulean water lapping the shore.

"Careful." Aris takes my hand and leads me down to the beach, steadying us both. I slip and slide down the embankment. My lips part in awe when I look up at the massive trees and their interconnected canopy keeping the cove shaded from the sun. It's likely ten degrees cooler here, and it's a welcome relief. "You like it?"

I look up at him, seeing his face in full for the first time in an hour. His eyes gleam with boyish excitement, but his mouth remains neutral, a hopeful smile tugging at the corners of his lips. "How long have you known about this place?"

"A few weeks. I don't know who owns this section of Ruby, but no one has stopped me from coming here yet." He shrugs a shoulder. "I haven't shown anyone this cove. Just you."

"I like it." I glance around, his fingers falling from mine as I step closer to the water.

"Why are you whispering?"

"It feels rather mystical here. I don't want to disturb it."

I sink onto a fallen log, resting my tired legs. I've barely touched the to-go cup of coffee Aris made, but I pop the lid and drink deeply, and all the while, he watches me. I meet his eyes, arching a brow, fighting the urge to curl into myself when the memory of our kiss sprints through the forefront of my mind, but I quickly banish it.

We're definitely not here to talk about that. I guarantee it.

"So, about that kiss."

I cringe, gritting my teeth as he paces a few yards away before sitting down on another log. The distance between us feels safe enough, at least. "What about it?"

"Is it what you expected?"

"Well, I didn't expect you to stick your tongue down my throat and ravish me, if that's what you're asking, so yes, I suppose it went exactly like I thought it would."

He arches one blond brow and chuckles low. "What kind of movies have you been watching?"

"What are you actually trying to ask, Aris?"

"Did it check anything off your list?"

I look into my coffee cup to refrain from meeting his gaze. "Yes. I've kissed someone. I can now go into a life of celibacy without any regrets."

"You're a stronger person than I am. I can't imagine." He sips his coffee, and I look up, peeking at him through my lashes. He's no longer looking at me, but I have a full view of him, his handsome, chiseled features, the way his chest rises and falls with a steady breath. "Is that all you wanted to experience?"

I should say no. I should ignore his bait and the obvious offer on the metaphorical table between us. He doesn't look at me when he says it, and maybe I'm reading too deeply between the lines, because this is Aris, someone I've known my entire life. He's in my earliest memories. A friend.

"No, but… I can't really think about it now. I can't stop thinking about Willow and everything that happened this morning."

He rises like he's being called into action. "Roman and Willow are mates."

"What?" I gasp, the word falling from my tongue before I can stop it.

He doesn't look at me but shrugs, shaking his head. "That's really all there is to it. They slept together." Now, he's looking right at me, pained, like this knowledge is going to undo my friendship with Willow.

"I was aware she'd set her sights on him, if you're wondering. I don't care in the slightest." But if the roles were reversed, and it was Roman standing here and Aris admitting to kissing me? The conversation wouldn't be nearly as calm, and there would be a whole lot of blood involved for certain. "But they can't actually be mates. That's insane."

"Is it really that hard to believe? The mate bond can happen at any time."

"But she was so certain her mate would be back in Crescent Falls waiting for her. She had everything planned out. She was going to finish her grand tour of Eastonia and go home, start her job, and…" It clicks. I hang my head. "Oh, Willow. This changes everything for her."

"Not necessarily." Aris is suddenly seated beside me, resting his to-go cup between his knees.

"Of course it does. They're mates! That's the endgame for them. She'll have to move to Sapphire Ridge. Roman will be Alpha one day and–"

"She made it perfectly clear to him that she has no intention of doing that."

I look up, startled. "What?"

"And Roman made it clear to her that… he will require someone else for the job," he continues, caustically, rolling the words over his tongue before gritting his teeth. "They may have rejected each other."

I'm blindsided. Thoroughly shaken to speechlessness. "No, they didn't."

"It explains Willow's state and Roman's violent behavior. I'm not sure if it actually happened. I couldn't get it out of Roman, but I will."

"Doesn't it hurt?"

"Being rejected? Yes. My sister–Brie and Logan rejected each other when they first found out. Obviously, it didn't last long, and now they're mates again and married with two kids. Brie told me what it felt like, even though it was a mutual rejection. It's like… falling into pieces and not being able to put yourself back together again. It can drive people to madness, which we saw this morning."

"Willow wouldn't have rejected him. She's obsessed with the idea of finding her mate. It's a huge deal to her!"

"Then, maybe Roman did the rejecting, but again, he was beyond being able to talk about it. I was able to get enough out of him to know for a fact they slept together and felt the bond. But I couldn't beat the idea that he's allowed to have a mate, even someone not magically aligned, into him."

His words are a crushing blow to my psyche. I press my knees to my chest, hugging my legs tightly. "He's a Sapphire, Aris. Of course, something like that matters to him."

"And yet, here you are, throwing your life away to join a convent while being a Sapphire as well."

"This has nothing to do with me!"

"In my humble opinion, it does. I look at Roman, my best friend, a man I've known my entire life, and I barely recognize him anymore. He didn't use to be like this, especially toward you. So high and fucking mighty about his bloodline and the idea of passing his alchemy down to the next generation."

"Aris, please."

"And you, ostracized by your own family for not having a wolf." He sucks his teeth, his calmness melting into sudden, utter fury. "I plan on giving your father a piece of my mind about it. I outrank him as prince, you know. It wouldn't be out of line."

"Aris."

"And your lack of alchemy skills? This is all because of marriage and bloodlines to you, Roman, and your family. It shouldn't matter that you don't have alchemy, and Willow shouldn't have to suffer either–"

"I do have alchemy gifts."

The forest around us stills like it can feel the sudden burst of tension in the air as the words hang between us.

I press my legs to my chest, refusing to look at him.

"You do?"

"Yeah." It's a quick, nearly silent reply while internally I'm berating myself for even opening my mouth. How could I be so stupid?

"You told me yourself that lacking a wolf meant your alchemy skills never surfaced. Can you shift, Posey?"

I exhale deeply, finally finding the nerve to meet his eyes. "I'm not a wolf, Aris. That hasn't changed."

"Does Roman know?"

"No, and don't tell him."

"Why not? If it stops you from having to join the temple–"

"I am joining by my own free will. It's what I want!" I rise, my temper, which is normally easily controlled, flaring. I ignore the shadows weaving between his fingers as I slowly face him, the space between us only inches while I point a finger into the center of his chest. "You have no authority over me. How often do I need to remind you of that? I cannot practice alchemy in the open without drawing questions about why I can't shift. That's the meat of it, Aris. Me joining a convent... it's an easier thing for my parents to explain. They can say I'm just *so virtuous, so humble,* and that I was called to a life of worship, and they'll be able to get away with that. Roman can carry on our bloodline. There are no other options for me. I don't have a choice!"

"You do have a choice!"

"And I'll ruin my family forever! I know you don't get it. I know your family can just breed with anyone without having to worry about your powers, but mine can't. Alchemy is already so rare. You know that! Your family keeps us a secret because of it! I doubt most of them know what we can do!"

He swallows hard, his Adam's apple bobbing.

"Look at me and tell me I'm wrong," I grind out, teeth bared. "Tell me I'm wrong. Tell me my other options are… marrying a distant relative, perhaps, with enough alchemy skills to pass on to the next generation and hope and pray that's enough to make up for what I lack–"

He grabs me. It's not a tender touch and the kiss that follows… is aggressive. Overwhelming. *Life altering.*

I gasp, my lips parting with a sound I've never heard leaving my tongue, and then his arms are around me, pulling me so close my chest is flush with his. He parts my lips further with his tongue, and I… fold. Melt into a puddle. My eyelids flutter closed, my body relaxing into a heap of heat and delusion. For several seconds, it's nothing but bliss. A much needed distraction.

He pulls away breathless, panting as he grips the back of my neck to keep me fixed in place. "You're wrong."

"I'm not wrong."

Another kiss, just as bruising as the first, steals my words away. Heat blooms through my body. I'm acutely aware of his hands, one pressed to my lower back and the other tangling in my hair. My body feels both featherlight and overwhelmingly sensitive–like one new touch to an aching part of my body I often ignore will send me over the edge, and I… *want that.*

I want to know what it feels like to be touched that way–by him.

But I'm the one who shoves him away this time.

He just looks down at me, shaking his head, his expression dripping in disappointment, and not about the kiss or my heated reaction–the fact that I gave in. He's disappointed in me in general, and I can practically taste it.

"Your secret is safe with me," he says, biting back the edge to his voice as he wipes his mouth on the back of his hand. "But you're not a waste of space. I'm sick of hearing you talk like that. I'll kiss you again if you do. In front of Roman, if I must."

"Is that a threat?"

"It's a fucking promise."

"Why did you kiss me again in the first place?" I'm chilled to the bone without his body pressed to mine despite the thick, humid heat of midday. I can't let this ridiculous sensation of want get into my head. I have a plan. A goal. *An out.* I can't let him get in the way of what I must do, even if Willow's carnal explorations have awakened mine, and now Aris is lighting the match that's going to undo everything.

I want to know how far this feeling can stretch before it bursts.

I need to know before I take the vows and put this life, this identity, behind me.

Aris scans my face, looking so deeply into my eyes I wonder if he can see the thoughts, the desires, I'm trying to banish.

"I wanted to kiss you again," he says without an ounce of reservation, his voice like gravel. Then, he turns, snatching both of our cups off the ground. "Tate and Miles aren't far off. I can smell them. We need to go."

TIME TO GO

Aris

What I should have done is sent Roman back to Sapphire Ridge to chill the fuck out.

What I did instead was nothing. It's been three days since Willow stormed out, Roman shut down, and I kissed Posey not once, but twice against my better judgment. Three days of pretending like everything is okay, that I didn't do something that will forever ruin my friendship with Posey and her brother if he finds out, which he *won't*.

I'm not even thinking about Roman, however. He's a grown-ass man. An Alpha's son. He'll be fine, but his presence is currently grating on my nerves, and him leaving would be the best option. He'd go back to his responsibilities, and he'd have the opportunity to bury whatever he's going through and refuses to talk to me about it. But if he leaves, so will Posey. I can't allow that quite yet.

I tell myself it's not because he'll take Posey with him, and I feel like I'm on the cusp of changing her mind, but because I need this summer as well. Like Roman and Posey, I will leave Gem Lake and immediately step into responsibilities that have, so far, not manifested. I made promises I have to keep. I have a duty to my family, to my parents, to take being an Alpha one day seriously.

Being the Shadowsynger heir is a whole other monster.

Brie's voice is a welcome relief when I answer her call. Kieran sings loudly and unintelligibly in the background while I walk around the backyard looking for better reception. All of this power, and not to mention the handful of engineers in our family, but we haven't solved the cell tower issue in Eastonia yet, apparently. Our family does have its weaknesses.

"I came bearing news," she says, her grin audible through the screen. "Good news. It feels like so long since I've had good news to share."

I can hear her moving through her little house in the Deadlands. Honestly, if someone had told me four years ago that Brie would end up living in a little stone cottage with blue shutters and just enough rooms to keep her family stacked on top of each other all times of the day... I would have believed them wholeheartedly. Brie is the heart of our family. She finally has that–a cozy home with an ever burning hearth and the sound of children laughing and singing to the rafters.

I feel at peace about her. I hated when she was living so far away in Emberfyll.

Now, Logan is spending his summer setting up his pack in a valley near Silverhide, building New Emberfyll piece by piece, with Brie living in domesticated bliss by his side.

"What news?" I reach the very edge of the dock, and the connection snaps into place.

"It's a two-parter. Do you have a minute? I don't want to interrupt your summer of debauchery. I hope you've been using those contraceptive drafts Mom made for you."

My cheeks burn at the memory of Mom's lengthy, totally unnecessary monologue about the uses of the tonics. "What's up, Brie?" I manage to choke out.

"Well, Nora found her mate! I wasn't sure anyone told you, seeing as you've been in Veiled Valley and haven't been back since Blake and Marianna's wedding."

I sink onto the edge of the dock, letting my legs dangle over the water.

She continues, "He lives in Crescent Falls, which came as a shock to everyone. It's one of Liam and Charlotte's friends. She went there to train with a master of realism. You know, for her painting..." Brie tapers off with a soft sigh. "Anyway, it wasn't love at first sight, but Nora is going to spend some time in Crescent Falls with Sarah and Sydney this summer to get to know the man better. His name is Kent. He's, uh, a Beta, I think. Ryan has been silent on the details. I don't think he's happy about the idea of her moving to Crescent Falls, but he's been rather busy the last few days."

I think I know where this is going. My stomach tumbles as I lean forward, resting my elbows on my knees. "Did the baby come?"

Brie is quiet for a moment, but I can hear her smile through the phone. "Yeah, he did. Lexa is doing *so well*. I wanted to be the one to pass the news to everyone who's not in the Deadlands currently. Mom and Misty were both here for the birth. Cole as well. Everything went about as well as it could have. He's a big, healthy boy!"

A knot that's been lodged in my chest since Lexa returned from her adventure, to say the least, eases. I stay silent, waiting for my sister to continue.

"He doesn't have wings, which was their main concern. He does have pointed ears like Kaleb and my boys, but Mom did a power group test, and he's fully shifter."

I close my eyes as the breeze skitters over the lake, lifting my hair from my ears. "That's good news. You're right. Ryan and Aviva must be insanely busy as it stands."

"I think having Logan and Kaleb here is helping Ryan, at least. Both men are now technically just Alphas, but they've been stepping in to help in Silverhide while Ryan handles his daughters."

"Does the baby have a name?"

"Not yet," she breathes. "They can't decide. I think Kaleb is a little stunned. He told Logan he wasn't sure he'd ever be a father, and Lexa was the one who changed his mind about it, but after everything they went through, I'm not surprised they're having trouble believing things can be this easy for them. They have time. Everyone's been calling the boy *the baby*." She laughs lightly. "Kieran has dubbed him Bub, but I doubt that'll stick. He still refuses to acknowledge Griffon as it stands. The novelty is bound to wear off within days."

Now, I'm smiling softly. "I'll come visit you guys in a few weeks. I miss that little monster."

"How's it going there?"

Gods, where do I begin? I roll my lower lip between my teeth. Brie is trustworthy. She's the keeper of secrets in our family and knows everything about everyone without making it other people's business. She's the only one like that.

If I need a sounding board, which I do, it has to be her.

"Do you remember Roman?"

"Roman? Of course I do."

"And his sister?"

"Posey? Goddess, I haven't seen her in years!"

"Well, she's… here." I'm not even sure what I'm trying to say. "I need some advice."

Brie pauses, then murmurs something to who I believe might be Logan, and then the background noise fades, replaced by an echoing kind of silence like she just stepped into an empty room.

"What's up?"

"Roman is… you know he'll be Alpha of Sapphire Ridge one day. Maybe soon, if his father steps down in his stead. He's on the marriage path, stepping into more responsibility." I explain the situation as best as I can without giving away Posey's secrets. But when I mention that Posey is joining the priestesses because she doesn't have a wolf and because she thinks her inability to shift is going to cause issues for Roman's future, Brie sighs heavily. And my voice fades.

"Do you remember how I was four or five years ago? So obsessed with what I thought was the right thing for Maeve?"

"Clearly."

"I thought I needed to marry an Alpha and tormented the family about it. No one could convince me otherwise, that it didn't matter. It took Logan to change my mind."

"So someone needs to change Posey's mind?"

"If she's only doing this because she feels like she has to… yeah. I mean, I would have been trapped in an unhappy marriage had I continued on that path. She'd be giving her life to the Goddess and… the Goddess might not intend that for her. Maybe She'll intervene."

I don't think Posey would even listen if the Goddess sent a bolt of lightning through her skull the second she stepped foot on the steps of the temple.

"If she's going through seminary in Moonrise, it's likely she'll be training at the smaller temple in Old Moonrise, seeing as Blake made such a mess of things last year. The new temple will be under construction for years as it stands."

I'm barely listening as Brie continues, changing the subject to Blake and Marianna, who are apparently living in blissful solitude in their recently finished mansion on the outskirts of Moonrise.

Posey is now in the backyard, slipping her feet into sandals, carrying her market bags. I watch her, losing track of Brie's voice.

"Can you hear me?" Brie asks.

"I think I'm losing you," I lie. "I'll call you later. Tell Lexa congratulations for me."

I hang up before she can reply. I rise, but Posey walks off, not even looking in the direction of the dock, and by the time I reach the lawn, she's gone, having disappeared around the house.

I walk inside with every intention of following her to the market. We haven't had a moment alone since three days ago at the cove, and I feel like I need to explain why I kissed her like that… twice. Aggressively. *Consuming her.*

Fuck.

"Hey."

I whirl to Roman's voice. He's standing in the kitchen, leaning against the island with his hands wrapped around a water bottle. He's shirtless, too, like he just returned from shifting.

"Hey."

"I just wanted to let you know I spoke to Miles. He's in town making a call to the barracks in Veiled Valley. It sounds like he and Tate are being called back to duty, their leave cut short."

"How come?" I glance in the direction of the foyer, trying to catch a glimpse of Posey in the driveway through the ceiling height windows.

"I have no idea, but they need to be back by tomorrow morning at dawn, and both would rather have a night to sleep off their perpetual hangovers, so they're leaving this afternoon, and I'm going with them."

My stomach twists. I brace my hands on the counter preparing to argue my point, which I'm unaware of at the moment, as to why Posey should stay behind, but he continues, "I think it would be wise for Posey to remain *here* for another week or two."

Shock. Uncertainty. The works. They roll through my body, overwhelming a single flicker of relief. I look up, meeting his sharp, sapphire gaze. "Why?"

He shrugs, looking more put together than I've seen him in days. "I have some shit to take care of back home, and she has her entrance exams for the seminary next month. When she returns to Sapphire Ridge, our parents will be all over her about it, and I don't want the distraction of family drama getting in my way. I need her to stay, to study here, take what time she needs to prepare, while I handle my business with our family."

I bite back my rising anger. "So you're going to allow this to happen to her?"

"She doesn't have alchemy or a wolf. She's right. This is her only option. *My* only option."

I straighten at his thick, serious tone.

"I'm packing, but once Miles returns from his errand, we'll take off. I'll make sure Posey is aware of the plan when she gets back from the market."

"Does she know you're leaving her here?"

"I plan on telling her."

Commanding her, more like it.

He starts to turn away, but I ask, "Did you reject Willow?"

He stiffens, clutching his water bottle like his life depends on it. "It's complicated."

"It's a yes or no answer."

"No. Not yet. That's part of why I need to return home–to get my affairs in order and nip that in the bud so I can move on like planned."

"She's Posey's friend."

"Exactly."

"You slept with her, you both felt the bond, and you pushed her away, didn't you?"

"I'm doing what needs to be done for the family, Aris. You should understand, given your position." He looks me up and down, and I feel the rift between us open wide, a cavern I'm not sure we'll ever be able to cross. "I'll come back to get Posey when I'm settled."

He trusts me with her wholeheartedly, which is why he simply walks away without another word, leaving me in the kitchen wondering if two weeks is enough time to change her mind, or if I just have to accept that it's none of my business, and this strange, foreign gnawing in my chest means absolutely nothing in the grand scheme of things.

If Posey really wants to be a priestess… so be it.

But she wanted a kiss.

What else does she want to know before she signs away her life forever?

LIKE GRIM DEATH

POSEY

ROMAN'S DEPARTURE WASN'T THE LEAST BIT SHOCKING. HE HOVERED IN the doorframe of my bedroom in the glare of morning light, posturing, refusing to make eye contact as he rattled off what was happening and his expectations of *me* in the meantime.

"It'll be better for you to stay here. It'll give you a chance to actually put forth an effort in your upcoming entrance exam, and I will finalize the details of your move to Moonrise while at home. You won't have to worry about Mom and Dad's feelings on the matter. You'll be alone here. You'll have all the time you need to prepare for this. To succeed." His voice was monotone but firm—a silent warning, and honestly, a confirmation that he gets it now. *Why I'm doing this. Why I have to go.* Even if his reasons for being okay with it are entirely selfish and only about him and his precious future.

He said nothing about Aris and left after saying, "I'll pick you up in ten days, give or take."

The first thing I did was check my calendar, counting the days until the next full moon, breathing a sigh of relief that I'll be home by then, and cracked open the textbooks I've already studied cover to cover.

I didn't see Aris for an entire day after that. A storm swept through the Gem Lake districts, swamping the lakes and channels in so much rain Miles, Tate, and Roman couldn't catch the ferry until close to midnight. No one bothered me. No one lingered in the kitchen while I cooked a meal for everyone, which went cold because everyone was on edge.

The next day, when the clouds cleared, I woke with a pounding headache that tapered off by midmorning, just as I was easing into my sandals to go to the farmer's market, which has become a ritual during my time here. When I returned to the manor, Aris was standing in the driveway talking to an older man who couldn't be anyone other than the Alpha of Ruby. The way he slightly cowered in Aris's utterly casual, non-offensive presence haunted my brain for the rest of the day. It was a quiet, somewhat lonely, and honestly, perfect day. Just the way I like it.

Aris is an Alpha even without the title. Some people are just born to be one, whether by birth or force. One day soon, I suspect, Aris will inherit all of this. Gem Lake. The various towns of Veiled Valley. The capital city high in the mountains. He doesn't realize the effect he already has on those around him, even the hardened Alphas that will one day live under his rule and command.

The headache returns with a vengeance when night falls, followed by full body chills that wake me in the middle of the night–sweaty and aching. I've felt like this before. My irregular cycles are likely because of my inability to shift into a wolf, and these afflictions normally come when I'm nearing the end of the moon cycle. However, they were never this intense before.

I wake up the morning of the second day after the guys left all alone in the house, drenched in sweat, but feeling well–well enough to spend the morning in the sun at the edge of the dock studying. Aris doesn't say a word to me. He's busy, it seems, or avoiding me, which would make two of us.

I suppose, in another life, before I kissed the lifelong friend of my older brother, being left to my own devices with Aris would have been nothing to fuss over. I wouldn't have thought anything of it. I would have, probably, seen Roman's insistence on leaving me behind to be babysat by Eastonia's most prolific fuckboy as nothing more than a grave annoyance. I would have stayed in my bedroom the entire time, studying, ignoring Aris's many attempts to rile me in whatever way he could because that's who Aris is and what he always does.

But now, the house feels shockingly open. For me.

It's hard to explain, but I feel a weight has been lifted from my shoulders. Anyone else would have made a real list of things they wanted to do, like Willow advised. I would have taken it seriously, spent the next few weeks of freedom checking things off. The food I wanted to try. The people I wanted to meet. The places I wanted to go.

But I'm... boring, to put it simply. I long for the solitude and quiet I've now been awarded. My list would have been short–after those damning kisses...

Or it would have been completely sexual in nature.

I shake those thoughts from my mind and go back inside, leaving the dock behind.

The next day, I brace my hands on the smooth quartz countertop in my ensuite bathroom, staring at my undone reflection in the mirror, and those thoughts come back. It's early morning, three days after Roman left. The sun hasn't risen and won't for another hour or two, but I'm awake and shaken to my bones like I've been through a blender, and I look like it.

Strands of sweat-damp hair stick to my reddened cheeks. My glossy, fevered eyes stare back, my pupils wider than I've ever seen them. I have an overwhelming desire to peel my skin from my body and split my ribcage apart to scoop out whatever's stuck there, hurting me. A virus. A parasite. I don't know, but last night, I woke up repeatedly in a kind of pain I've never experienced, and the only thing that helped the fever that followed was repeatedly dunking myself in a cold bath.

The old T-shirt I wore to bed sticks to my skin. The syrupy feel of it as I peel it off makes me shiver with disgust. I'm still trembling with remnants of the fever as I shower, scrubbing sweat from my hair, letting the cool water ease the blush threatening to stain my cheeks for the rest of the day. My breasts ache. My stomach feels raw and knotted. I thought these cramps must be my moon cycle coming early, but I'm not due for another two weeks, just before the next full moon. I think. I've never been totally sure when it'll come.

I change into another T-shirt, leaving my hair wet enough to cool the back of my neck while I rip the sweat-soaked sheets from my bed. I sweated through to the mattress.

Aris doesn't wake up for another four hours. When he finds me, I'm dozing on the couch in the little library on the first floor, sprawled out without a care in the world with every single window open to a cool morning breeze. Of course, he would choose this morning to finally talk to me.

"Um… what's up?" he asks, scratching his head. He rounds the couch to look down at where I've withered away. "I've been looking for you for like an hour. I figured you went into town, but your sandals are still on the back porch." He scans my body from head to toe, moving slowly up my bare legs before he meets my gaze again with a deep furrow of his brow. "Are you okay?"

"I didn't sleep well."

"Yeah, looks like it." He eases onto the coffee table, using it as a chair even though it creaks under his weight.

He smells… amazing. Like magnolia blossoms and salt. Like the forest after a drenching kind of rain, when everything is alive and fresh. Perspiration glimmers on his shoulders, just visible in the cut-off T-shirt that shows off most of his muscles. I want to rub my face against his shirt. The fabric looks so worn and soft and I…

"I think I might be coming down with something," I admit, meeting his gaze, and he's utterly confused. Just like me.

"Doubtful. Shifters don't get sick–oh." He grits his teeth and leans forward, resting his elbows on his knees. "Right. You can't shift. Well, what can I do? Medicine? Soup? What do people need when they're sick?"

"I think I'm going to just sleep it off. It's just stress, I'm sure."

"Sure." He doesn't sound certain. He eyes me with a deep sense of suspicion before rising and extending his hand. "Let's get you back to bed."

The second we step foot in my room, however, I realize with a crushing sense of embarrassment that my bed is stripped to the mattress, and the evidence of my tossing and turning is... everywhere.

Aris rolls his tongue across the inside of his cheek, looking around at the scattered pillows and books and then down at me. He wordlessly tilts his head to the hallway, and I follow, expecting him to take me to one of the many guest rooms, but he opens his bedroom door.

I haven't been in here yet during my two-week stay. It's dark, a shaded part of the house, and the air is cool and crisp and smells like him. I shiver unintentionally and shake my head. "There're rooms downstairs."

"I have someone coming to clean the house and strip the bedrooms today. I'd rather you not sleep in a bed previously occupied by Tate or Miles and whomever they brought home for their regular evening entertainment." He sucks his teeth, arching a brow. "So, get in bed. Get better because we have plans tonight."

He begins to walk away. "What plans?"

"We're going to a concert on the mainland. I have tickets. Unless you're on your deathbed, you're coming. It'll be good for both of us to get out of the house."

He looks over his shoulder at me, one hand gripping the doorknob.

"I don't like this," he says with effort, and shuts the door behind him when he leaves.

Gentle waves lap the dock. I wait for Aris to help me onto his sailboat. The sun set hours ago, and all across the water, boats bob, their lights casting streaks against a backdrop of the darkest black. The moon is at its weakest now, reflecting the sun's light. Aris reaches for me, clutches my fingers, and helps me step onto the deck. He's wearing jeans and a flannel–totally casual.

I tug my cardigan tighter over my waist. A soft breeze sweeps over the deck, ruffling my sundress, making my skin prickle with a chill. I slept most of the day in Aris's bed, waking in a nest of his blankets, pillows, and shockingly, two of his shirts with no idea how they got there, but my embarrassment is enough to choke me silent.

In his defense, he hasn't said a word about it and stayed away from me like he knew I needed the space.

Now, however, sitting on the deck of his sailboat as he slowly maneuvers out of the shallows and into the deeper, choppier section of the lake, he asks, "Feeling better yet?"

"Just a headache." The pounding in my temples eased the second he touched my hand to help me into the boat, but I don't say it.

"And the fever?"

"Gone." It's the truth. I fold my arms around my knees. The sails catch the wind and send us barreling across the deep. He says nothing, his eyes on the distant shoreline, the mainland, where the river leading back to the capital of Veiled Valley feeds into Gem Lake.

He seems on edge, though. I can see it painting his muscles in shadow, the tension clear in every rippling cord as he steers the boat into a spot at a sprawling fresh-water port. This section of the lake is the most populated, the busiest, with several Alphas claiming territory. I would have liked to avoid it during my time here, but Aris didn't really give me a chance to argue.

We pull into a slip, and he ties us up. "Stay close," he says under his breath, the words fanning against my temple. He helps me off the boat and into a crowd. Music thrums in every direction, melding with my uneven heartbeat. His scent is lost in the mix, and my head begins to hurt again, just a little pinprick behind my eyes, until he intertwines his fingers with mine and tugs me toward a building nestled against the shore with a huge, crowded deck overlooking the glimmering lake.

"I've never been to a concert before," I tell him.

"I know," he breathes, tugging me alone. "Just something to check off your list."

IS SHE A WITCH OR SOMETHING WORSE?

POSEY

"HERE." ARIS SLIDES A GLASS OF PURPLE-HUED LIQUID IN MY DIRECTION. Fizz lifts off the round balls of ice within, and it smells like juniper and lavender.

I immediately wrinkle my nose. I enjoy the occasional glass of wine, but I've never been one for hard alcohol, even during my college days.

"Don't worry. I know you don't like liquor" Aris leans against the railing overlooking the lower level of the bar, where a live band sends a screeching rock melody through the venue. "It's a mocktail. There's nothing in it but soda water and flavor."

I arch a brow. "You're not drinking either?"

He shakes his head once, lifting an identical drink to his mouth. "Nope. I think I've drank enough for an entire lifetime while the boys were here. I want to be clearheaded going forward." His gaze holds mine against the strobing lights. I feel a little off-center despite the crisp, buzz-free flavor of the drink.

He finishes his in a single swallow and sighs, looking over the top of my head at the crowded bar. "Do you like the music?"

"I don't know." I laugh, leaning my arm against the railing. "It kind of sounds like a car accident."

"I think that's what it's supposed to sound like. I didn't do a lot of research into the band."

"Oh. I thought… why are we here, then?"

He shrugs a shoulder, so casual, so aloof. "I haven't seen you in three days. I've been busy, and I wanted to get out, to see… anything." The words unsaid drift between us for several aching seconds, hammering through my ears like he actually had the nerve to say them out loud. *I wanted to come, and I wanted you with me.*

It's written all over his face as he stares down at me.

"Fucking witches." A voice directly behind me grates down my spine. "Always in the fucking way."

I look around to try to find the speaker and spot a trio of young men standing only feet away. All three are staring at me, which is odd. The one in the center lifts a brow, leaning into his companion to loudly say, "I didn't think their kind was allowed in Veiled Valley. Fucking disgusting. They smell awful, too."

I turn back to Aris, trying to look over his shoulders at whoever these jerks are talking about but… I'm the only woman against the railing overlooking the thick of the concert below. My body tingles. Every fine, downy hair lifts on instinct.

I feel that gnawing, sick kind of feeling again, like a wave is heading toward me, threatening to pull me into a fevered, aching embrace–the kind that left me sweating so profusely I could barely crawl out of bed and into the shower this morning.

But then Aris drapes his arm over my shoulder and pulls me close until I'm flush with his chest, his fingers drawing lazy circles over my upper arm. His chin brushes over the top of my head. He looks at the men behind us and chuckles, the sound a low, vibrating reverberation that settles in the base of my spine. "Can I fucking help you guys? You're staring. I'm not keen on other men looking at what's mine. *Back off.*"

A note of unease skitters between our groups. Aris's voice still clings to the edge of charming, play-boyishness, but the undertone is as serious as death. His scent changes, too. Darkening. Deepening. Spiced with sudden violence, and I melt into his touch against my will, my fingers curling over the center of his chest, wrinkling his shirt. I turn to steal a glance at the men over his arm.

The middle idiot looks stunned for a split second before his eyes narrow, but his companions back off, their tails between their legs, so to speak.

"Prince Aris," Middle Idiot bitterly remarks, dropping his head into a brief, shallow, halfhearted bow. "I didn't know you–"

"Back the fuck off before I throw you over the railing," Aris commands so dryly I almost laugh. He's not joking, that's for sure, even if his body remains totally relaxed. I know without a shadow of a doubt he can flip a switch and go from this to deadly in an instant, and I think the guy knows that, too, because he turns on his heel and cowers, disappearing into the crowded balcony.

"What was that about?" I whisper, hoping he can hear me over the pounding screech of the music below.

"Just your typical jackass bar behavior," he replies without skipping a beat, but even when I drop my hand and pull away, his arm remains around my shoulders, his touch damningly present, like he is, in fact, laying a very public claim to me.

"You didn't have to do that for me. They probably weren't even talking about me."

"Oh, they were." He looks down at the band, his silver eyes absorbing every flash of color and light.

"But... I'm not a witch?"

"You're not. You're not a wolf either."

"But they... said I smelled–"

"You smell *unreal*," he says so low I almost mistake the words for a growl. His eyes are on mine again, holding fast, so dark the silver streaks resemble stars. I forget to breathe because I'm *stupid*. Stupidly, irrationally, staring back at Aris like he's the glue that holds my world together, and those kisses meant something. Even the thought of them has me pooling with a feverish kind of heat, and I can't snap myself out of it.

Neither can he.

I'm better than this. Smarter. Quicker. I've always been able to separate carnal needs from what actually must be done. It's how I was raised. I am not my own person. Everything I do and think is for the Alpha. For the pack. For the good of all or none.

I was going to give myself away in an advantageous marriage to whoever my parents saw fit based on my alchemy powers. I was ready to zip my mouth closed and keep my head down after four blissful years of freedom in college because I'd been granted them like they were a divine gift, and I owed something in return.

Then my wolf never came. What replaced it is a monster.

I am worthless. I will beg for forgiveness at the altar of the Goddess for the rest of my life in repentance.

The way Aris is looking at me right now makes me question everything I know to be true.

It's crowded. We're being jostled from both sides as the concert thunders to a remarkable close, and the crowd moves upstairs for air and more drinks. "Let's get out of here," he says against my skin, his lips a gentle brush over my forehead.

I gulp fresh air the second our bodies breach the entrance of the bar. The crowd is young and excited, buzzing around us in every direction, but Aris is a large man and easily shoves a path for us, his steps steady on the uneven cobblestone. It's a humid night. The air is heavy and damp, clinging to my skin. We walk side by side to the port.

An outdoor night market glows, its lights casting streaks of gold and crimson on the wet stones, but all I can feel is him–his hand on my arm. His strength. His scent masks everyone like my body is clinging to it, offended by everyone and everything else.

I feel off kilter. Uneasy. Feral. Things I've never felt before. But then the boat comes into view, and he's helping me onboard, and then...

"Prince Aris!"

Aris nearly kicks off the dock but stops, holding the tethers keeping the boat bound in place. A cool breeze rustles my cardigan. Aris straightens, a shadowed figure jogging into view. It's a tall, good-looking young man. A warrior, based on his build and plain clothes. He smiles widely at Aris and Aris does the same, loosing a disbelieving chuckle, and he hops down onto the dock and embraces the fellow.

"Gods, I haven't seen you in years," the stranger says, blue eyes shining wolflike in the darkness. He smiles up at me with a little salute–charming, but curious. "I didn't mean to interrupt."

"Posey," Aris says, his face alight with what I can only describe as joy, "this is Eric. We went through wolf training together as kids."

"And warrior training in Moonrise after that," Eric continues with a smirk. "But he went back to his fancy castle while I stayed on and got the shit beat out of me for a decade further, by his brother-in-law.."

Aris runs his fingers through his hair. "It's been that long, huh? Yeah, Brie and Logan… They've got two kids now…"

I suddenly feel like I'm the one interrupting, but their conversation is brief, their greetings warm with a few common memories shared. Eric asks about Aris's family and Aris his, then they laugh about a time when they had an instructor who mixed up their names so often they took each other's identities for an entire training season and would have gotten away with it if Logan, a trainer at the time, hadn't been such a "bootlicking smartass."

There's nothing I can add to the conversation, so I just stare, noticing the ease and the smile painting Aris's expression.

Why did I never look this closely at him before?

Because it doesn't matter. If he knew the truth, he'd hate me. *He'd scorn me.* His hatred would have deadly consequences.

And that might be what I'm most afraid of.

"I was just in Ruby visiting my brother," Eric explains, and I'm instantly drawn back into the conversation. "Were you aware of the hunting party they're gathering? The Beta called it into action."

"A hunt for what? I just spoke to their Alpha a day ago, and he didn't mention anything." Aris shifts his weight.

"You're never going to believe it. They think there's a fox on the island."

Aris's entire body changes. His posture becomes so rigid I can see every fine angle of muscle beneath his shirt. "You're kidding."

"No. I wish I were. My brother thinks it's far-fetched, but his mate is nervous now, and won't let the kids play outside. I'm not sure I believe it, either."

Aris toys with the ropes, stretching them over his fingers while my stomach sinks to my toes. "What reason would they have to believe there's a fox in Ruby?"

"Not just a fox." Eric leans in like he doesn't want to be overheard, but we're the only people in this section of the port, and the dock is empty save for us. "A fox shifter. The Alpha's son is sure. He's a fucking meathead, that guy, but several others reported catching a scent two weeks ago, during the last full moon."

Aris nearly snaps the ropes. He just nods. "Thank you for telling me. I'm in Ruby for another week or two. I'll see how I can be of assistance."

"Can you imagine?" Eric says with a rough, disbelieving laugh. "A fox shifter? An abomination, right? I can't even picture it."

The boat could be capsizing right now, and I wouldn't notice until I tried to breathe and filled my lungs with water. Aris says something under his breath. Eric leaves. I barely register the fact we're moving, the shoreline drifting further and further away, until the rush of undiluted fear loosens, and my heart thumps back into rhythm.

Aris quietly mans the sails, his eyes locked on the distant shoreline, to the archipelago of small islands coming into view—their city lights glimmering like embers.

"Are we safe?" I ask him, and he looks down at me like he forgot I was there.

"Yeah. There's no such thing as fox shifters, Posey. You have nothing to worry about."

WILD WITH FEVER

Aris

THE CLOCK OVER THE STOVE READS 12:57 A.M. POSEY MOVES INTO view wearing a tank top and shorts, her skin shiny with perspiration. She piles her hair in a bun on the top of her head. In the dim light of the kitchen, she's all curves and skin, something soft enough to sink my teeth into.

I bite my lower lip instead, rolling the glass base of my half-empty bottle of beer against the kitchen island. She opens the fridge, scans the contents, and takes two steaks from the bottom self, already rubbed and salted, like cooking a meal in the late hours of the night was always her plan.

"You know you've cooked breakfast, lunch, and dinner like clock-work for the past two weeks. You were under no obligation to do that." I fold my arms over my chest. Her eyes met mine in the hazy glow of the stove light. Thunder booms in the distance as a storm funnels over the lake, but inside it's still warm from the heat of the day and cozy, like we hadn't just spent several hours out on the town and at a concert.

She shrugs, giving me the smallest, tightest smile. "I don't really have an opportunity to do so otherwise. We have cooks at home."

"How'd you learn?"

When she reaches for one of the cast iron skillets hanging over the island, I beat her to it, stepping into her space to rest it on the stovetop. The flames click, spreading, casting a blueish shimmer through the shadows.

She grabs some herbs and chops them. "I used to go down to the kitchen as a kid. I was often hungry. Starving.. My mom was so strict with my diet—our shared diet. She's as thin as a reed, you know. When it became clear I was… softer, was going to be shorter than her by a mile and not nearly as waif-like, she made it her mission to ensure my diet consisted of nothing but vegetables and lean meat. No butter. No sugar. Nothing a growing child wanted. The cooks used to pour me glasses of milk and make secret cookies for me. I'd sit on the stool and watch them work, fascinated." She pauses with a sigh. "I understand where my mom was coming from. I don't want it to sound like she was purposefully starving me."

"Well, that's exactly what it sounds like." I press the steaks onto the skillet, the sizzle radiating through the kitchen.

"She just wanted me to be beautiful, graceful, and fit for marriage one day, but I never managed to rise to her expectations." Another self-deprecating smile touches her lips. "She backed off after a while, especially when I started my garden. I was skilled enough with growing herbs that she allowed a witch to come and teach me how to make some basic tonics and tinctures, and with that, I had full access to the kitchen and needed to learn some basics there, as well, since those two skills go hand in hand. She figured my apothecary skills would be a selling point when it came to marriage, especially if my future husband had notable alchemy skills. Tinctures are so good to ease the burden of our powers in our fingers…"

"That lotion you use?"

She stills, her fingers curling on the handle of her knife. "Wild cherries are great for inflammation. I grind and soak the pits. It's also good for coughs."

"How often are you secretly practicing alchemy, Posey?"

I flip the steaks. She moves to my side with herbs and butter, wordlessly sprinkling them into the pan. The entire kitchen erupts in notes of butter and rosemary, and my stomach pinches, like I've been starving for my entire life, and it's because of those skilled hands, those long, delicate fingers. Not the steaks. Not the promise of a good meal.

"Often enough to be better at it than Roman."

"Why are you hiding it?"

"You know why."

"Because of your lack of–"

"The powers go hand in hand."

"Then there's a chance you have a wolf after all, and she's just taking her sweet time to show up."

"No," she replies simply, shaking her head. "I had it confirmed."

"So then it's wrong."

"No," she repeats more firmly, leaving no room for an argument, and I let it go.

Maybe it's the hunger and the cozy feeling of the kitchen, but we eat in silence. She's ravenous, like something about the night sweeping through Gem Lake has flipped a switch in her brain, bringing her back to her rawest form, even without a wolf inside her. I have the sudden, overwhelming urge to ask if she wants to come outside with me. If she wants to run her fingers through my coat, to ride on my back while I'm in wolf form. But she excuses herself and goes to bed, and the house falls silent once again.

I'm riding a fine edge between sleep and full awareness when a crash echoes from across the hall from my bedroom. I blink into the pitch black of the night, wondering if I'd dreamt the noise, but then I hear Posey crying out in a stifled whimper, and my brain isn't fully awake when I charge into her room within seconds.

"Hey," I rush out as she thrashes and then curls into herself. She's in the center of her bed, which is damp with sweat, and she's sticky and hot with fever. "Hey, Pose, what's going on? What hurts?"

I clutch her face with both hands, smoothing her tears from her cheeks with my thumbs. They're hot. Like she's boiling from the inside out. "Posey, come on. You weren't like this earlier. What happened?"

"My head!" she cries out, choking back a silent sob.

"I have some healing drafts. I'll get them."

She reaches out, clawing my bare shoulders with her fingernails.

"Posey? Listen, I'll be right back, and then you can rest, okay? But you're sick."

"Why do—why do you smell like that?" Her voice is just above a whisper when she finally opens her eyes to fevered slits. Her pupils are blown wide, like she's on the verge of shifting if she had the ability, but her scent is... undoing me. Pulling me apart at the seams. It hits me directly in the chest, blowing past my ribcage, splitting it into pieces. I feel like I'm on the verge of shifting now, either to run away or hunt down whoever and whatever did this to her. It's confusing. The answer is... right there... but just out of my grasp, like I know what's wrong but can't put a name to it.

Her fever spikes. She groans, gasping. I lift her off the soaking wet sheets and carry her across the hall to my bedroom. I kick open the bathroom door so hard the hinges bend. It'll never shut properly again, but it doesn't matter.

Her heat seeps into my skin. I turn on the shower, stepping in fully clothed, pressing her body, draped in nothing but underwear and an old shirt... my shirt, for some reason, to my chest. The water is like ice as it flows over us, but after a few aching minutes, she grows quiet, relaxed, and then the fever breaks, and she shivers. I only leave the shower when her teeth begin to chatter.

I shouldn't do it, but I have no other choice. I pull the soaking wet shirt off her as she slowly comes back to reality, her eyes still wolf-like but hazy. Without looking directly at her, I dress her in an old flannel and toss her in my bed, tucking her in, then collect several more blankets out of a linen closet in the hallway. I build her a pile of blankets and pillows. It's instinctual. I don't know why or how I'm managing it, but it works, and eventually, her eyes flutter closed, and she takes a deep breath before slipping into an even deeper sleep.

I change my clothes and then sink to the ground at the foot of the bed, my head lulling back against the mattress, and I fall asleep like that, waking to the first hint of morning light.

Posey isn't in bed anymore.

I find her in the kitchen making breakfast, and for obvious reasons, it enrages me.

"No," I bellow, and she whirls, clutching a spatula like a weapon. "Put it down and go back to bed. You're sick, Posey. I'm calling for a healer."

"Don't." She sets the spatula down. Her scent is so heavy today. It's everywhere. It embraces me, makes me want to claw out of my skin and shift, but not into the form I would expect. I normally ignore my fox form until I can't. It's happy being dormant most of the time, but now? When it senses a serious threat?

I edge around the kitchen island, brows raised. "You were on the cusp of having a febrile seizure in my arms last night," I growl. "What is happening to you?"

"I don't know. I didn't feel well all day yesterday, and we still–I shouldn't have gone out. I overdid it." She looks up at me with those doe-eyes looking so incredibly pathetic that I have no choice but to brace my hands on the counter so I don't touch her. "Aris, I'm sorry. I didn't mean to wake you up."

"Are you in pain?"

"Not anymore."

"But you were?"

"A little."

"Don't lie to me, Posey." I fix her with a glare. "For fuck's sake. What hurts?"

She turns back to the stove. I'm behind her in an instant, cutting the flames and snatching the skillet and spatula out of her hands.

She goes perfectly still, her back flush with my chest. We stand like that for what feels like eternity–touching ever so slightly, and it's enough contact for my mind to travel somewhere so dark even I'm on the verge of blushing, which I never do.

"I had to take off your clothes last night," I say into her hair, my heart thundering. I needed to tell you. You need a healer. If you're ill, I'm unequipped to take care of you–"

"I'm going to go lie down," she says shakily, and flees. "Don't call for a healer. I'm just going to rest."

I let her go. I don't see her for the rest of the day. She does not leave her room, but she's awake up there, because all I hear for the remainder of the day is scraping, like she's moving furniture around.

But that night, when the moon rises, it happens again. This time, I don't have to invade her space and carry her into my bed.

My wolf wakes me up, sensing something amiss.

I find her downstairs in a daze, trying to open the doors. Trying to get out of the house. Sobbing and telling me to go away when she sees me lurking in the shadows of the foyer, pleading with me not to hate her, and not to call a healer. *"They'll kill me if they find out!"* she screams, completely out of her mind with fever, and there's nothing I can do but hold her close.

I pull her into a cold bath, where I sit with her on my lap until she calms down and the fever breaks, but not fully like last time. I doze with her clutched to my chest.

When I wake, I put her in my bed again, curl my body around hers, and pray.

I don't sleep. I watch her all night, sending silent prayers into the aether that she's not going to die, but she recovers by the time morning light begins to trickle through the curtains.

When she wakes up, I pretend I'm asleep, and she slinks out of the room.

I roll over, inhaling her scent, which is everywhere, and it's everything, and I'm… losing my mind, aren't I?

I avoid her. I shift into my wolf form and spend the earliest hours of the morning running through the woods to try to clear my mind, and it works, at least until I return home.

She doesn't want a healer, but something is wrong. Maybe with both of us.

There's one person I can call, but if I do, I'll never hear the end of it.

THE NEST

Aris

POSEY'S SKIN GLEAMS IN THE MIDMORNING LIGHT. I'VE BEEN STARING AT
her for the past hour while keeping watch on the back porch swing,
giving her the space I can tell she wants. Classical music drifts from
the kitchen where the sound of her knife against the cutting board is
a rhythmic reminder of her presence, but even over the smell of
whatever she's cooking, something rich and deep with hints of maple,
her scent is everywhere.

The last two nights were insane. I can't come up with a better
word for it. Gods, I thought she was dying. I think *she* thought she
was dying. Waking up in the dark hours of early morning with her
sweat-soaked body clutched against mine and her scent enveloping
me had me thinking thoughts I can't say out loud, like whatever's
happening to her has me by the balls, and I'd crawl through fire to
make her feel better.

I twirl my phone over my fingers, stealing a glance through the
open patio doors leading into the kitchen, and slowly rise. Posey

dumps a bowl of bread dough on the counter and kneads it, her body still pink, still gleaming, like the fever remains.

It does. I can smell it. Smell her worry and confusion. She won't meet my eyes.

"Aris! I wasn't expecting a call from you." Mom's voice is lifted and girlish like usual but edged with alarm. I plop onto the end of the dock, the only place I get clear, uninterrupted phone service. "Normally, you only text me back if I ask a yes or no question. Are you all right?"

"I need some advice." I suck in a breath of fresh air that doesn't smell like Posey, and it feels wrong. "I'm still in Gem Lake."

"I'm aware. Your grandpa is holding down the fort. I don't return to Veiled Valley until tomorrow, just so you know. What's going on?" She doesn't like my tone. I can practically see her brows furrowing through the sound of her voice, that pinch of concern.

"I'm here with Posey Sapphire. Roman left a few days ago, and she stayed. I think she's sick."

"Sick how?"

"Either sick or cursed."

"Aris, be serious. What's going on? Her symptoms?"

I run my fingers through my hair, absently taking note of how long it's getting. "She's had a prolonged fever for the last three days, I think. It gets worse, then better, but it never goes away entirely. She's been short with me or..." Desperate. Clawing for my touch, like last night, when I'd held her so close, and she'd clutched me like letting go was a death sentence. And I've been... fuck. "Well, the last two nights she's had these spells of fever and nausea, and it's been extreme."

"What about cramping?"

I wince, nodding even though Mom can't see it. "She's in pain. Cold water helps, but last night I tried to help her. I found her wandering around. She was delirious, trying to get outside, but I stopped her."

"How old is Posey again? Twenty-two?"

"Yes." I brace myself for her diagnosis, for the string of words that will send my mind into a tailspin like when she had to hurry to Moonrise to help Marianna, but they don't come.

"Aris," she says slowly, laughing a bit. "I need you to go to her room for me."

"Why?"

"I just want to confirm one thing. Is she around? I could talk to her directly."

"No," I lie. I'm not sure why, but I have a feeling Posey would rather I not say a word to anyone about what happened, including a midwife and healer, *my own mother.*

"Well then, go to her room."

"Are you going to tell me why?"

"I just need you to confirm something for me. It's not that hard."

I grit my teeth and obey, slinking into the kitchen with my phone pressed to my ear. I hold my breath as I step past Posey. She turns her back, but I notice the way she trembles when I pass her, letting her breath out slow. It's like a taut, vibrating string is being pulled between us, and I want to tug on it just to see what she'd do.

I'm out of my mind when I reach the shared hallway. Her door is closed, but her scent is already everywhere.

I turn the knob, and it hits me like a punch to the gut. Heady. Warm. Beautiful. It makes me hungry for things I've never...

"What do you see? I remember Posey being a rather organized and particular person. Is her room normally clean?"

"Yes," I manage to say, unable to swallow. I'm looking at the beginnings of a mess. On her bed. Which is shielded by the canopy of the four-poster that's now drawn and hiding nearly every single pillow in the house and several comforters, like she spent her entire day yesterday pilfering anything comfortable, cozy, and soft from the house. I pull back the lace canopy. "What is this?"

"If you're seeing what I think you're seeing, she's trying to make herself as comfortable as possible. Her bed–"

"Mom, *what is this?*"

"Oh, Aris, I thought I was far more progressive with your education than I needed to be at the time, but apparently I'm wrong."

Mom's laugh is lost to the way my heartbeat is hammering in my ears like a drum. "Describe what you're seeing."

"Pillows. Blankets. In a–a nest. It looks like a nest." I did this for her in my bed last night without even realizing what I was doing. My heart skips several beats before restarting.

"I thought it might. She's not sick, Aris. Poor thing, though. She should call her mom"

"She's not very close to her mom."

"Oh." Mom's voice lifts in surprise. "I didn't realize. Um, well, is there another woman around–"

"No, it's just us."

"I see."

"What is this?" My voice drops. I can't even hide the edge to it at this point. I need to get out of here. I need to crawl into the blankets and inhale. I need to...

"We do, in fact, call it a nest, but there's a perfectly reasonable biological explanation to what's happening to her, Aris. She's not sick. She's just in heat."

I close my eyes.

"It's awfully startling and confusing. I'm guessing if she doesn't know what's happening to her, this is her first time. She's around the right age for it, especially if she just came into her wolf and hasn't found her mate yet. I don't know if you remember how bad it was for Brie, but shortly after she met her wolf, she went through her first heat, and the first one is always the worst. Oh, she was so sick. She begged me to kill her one night, and your father nearly lost his mind, so I locked him out of the castle and told him to go to Maatua for the next week. You were probably at warrior training then, I think."

I'm barely listening. I have tunnel vision, staring at three of my shirts that are tucked in her... nest. Worn. Likely pilfered from the laundry. Shirts that smell like me... in her bed.

"Brie ended up shifting and ran off into the woods. She was gone for three days, in her wolf form, riding out her first heat. She had such a hard time shifting, but it didn't matter; she was out of her mind, which is normal. After that, her cycles evened out, and it didn't bother her at all."

I'm beyond being squeamish about the bodily functions of my sisters. Par for the course, being a brother sandwiched between two sisters.

My thoughts are on Posey. Focused. Unsteady. Trying not to fall to my knees.

"Posey cannot shift. She doesn't have a wolf. This can't be a heat."

Mom's silent for a moment, but then she sighs heavily. "Oh, that changes things."

"How so? What is this, and what do I need to do?"

"Well, honey, she can still go into heat. Both of her parents are wolves."

"You've seen this before?"

"I'm a midwife, Aris. Of course I have. But for the rare few who never develop the ability to shift, first heats can be… especially difficult to manage. You said this has been going on for how long?"

"Two or three days."

Mom sighs, humming something under her breath. "She really needs another woman there."

"Well, I grew up with two sisters, and none of you were quiet when it came to these things around me, so what does it matter? She's refusing to see a healer."

"Your typical, run-of-the-mill healer wouldn't be able to offer much help."

"Then what do I do?" She has to hear the bite in my voice. I back out of Posey's room and shut the door, bracing my hand against the wall.

"She needs fresh air and distraction. Good food and comfort. It'll pass in another two days or so. Most people will want to be in their wolf form for it because it's much easier that way, but if she doesn't have that ability… get her out in nature. It's the closest thing."

"So you're saying take a fevered, delirious woman on a fucking camping trip?"

"Language, Aris."

I bite my lip, shaking my head.

"In fact, now that I'm thinking about it, a heavy dose of contraceptive tonics may help ease some of the symptoms. The fevered delirium, especially. It should clear it up completely, actually, given that she doesn't have a wolf, but I would still air on the side of caution."

"Why would a contraceptive draft help this situation at all?"

"Honey, she's going into her first heat. What do you think is the reason for that?"

Instead of the blood rushing to my face, I feel it gathering somewhere else against my will. "Is there a reason this is happening now?"

"For her, I don't know. Normally, it's only this intense the first time or when a woman finds her mate, but... that's what mates are for, you know. Some people don't even notice what's happening if their mate is around, but their mate sure will. In Brie's case, she didn't find her mate for a while after that, so her first heat came on very strong, and yes, she was just as sick. Posey doesn't have the ability to shift, so give her the drafts I made you. I know you haven't used them."

I squeeze my eyes shut and force myself to swallow a groan of pure frustration. "Fine. I'll figure this out."

"Just keep her comfortable. It'll pass. Don't let her wander off on her own, either. It's likely other people—especially men—will notice."

Fuck. I see red. "She will not leave the house without me."

"Good. Well, I think you have everything you need. You've always been such good friends with Posey, but I can see why this would be uncomfortable for you both. You—"

The call abruptly drops. I grit my teeth and scrub my fingers through my hair several times before turning on my heel and stalking toward the kitchen.

Posey is setting out a plate for me, just me, when I walk in and shut the door with a thud.

Her fevered eyes meet mine and hold. Looking at her makes me want to scream. Or crawl to her. I'm not sure which.

"Pack a bag."

"Why?"

"We're going on a little adventure."

"No, I don't feel well, Aris. I should stay in. In bed."

"The nest you made? Do you understand what's happening, or did your parents leave you in the dark completely?"

"The *what?*"

I lean over the counter, the two of us nearly nose to nose. "You and I are taking a little trip on my boat for the next two days, and when we come back, we need to have a serious conversation about… everything." I'm not even sure what I'm trying to say. My mind is malfunctioning. Just being in her presence makes me feel unsteady. Surely, this is just the effect of being in a woman's presence during this… time. Right? "Go pack a bag. We're leaving in ten minutes."

She nods, turns, and walks away without an argument.

I pull the plate toward me but find I'm not hungry in the slightest.

THE CABIN IN THE WOODS

POSEY

IT'S AN OVERCAST, DRIZZLING DAY. I WATCH RAINDROPS TRICKLE DOWN
the circular windows of the one-room cabin in Aris's sailboat, tracing
their trails with my index finger. My stomach is tied in multiple tight
knots as the boat rocks on the choppy water. Fog hugs the horizon as
far as I can see. I have no idea where we're going. I packed for two
days but nothing for this kind of weather.

I met Aris at the edge of the dock, and he put me down here,
alone, while sending us into the storm.

The door to the cabin opens, and Aris steps down into the warm,
dry air. Rain drips from his hair onto his shoulders, soaking into the
soft fabric of his worn-out flannel. His silver eyes meet mine briefly,
hooded, lined with dark circles, before he shrugs out of the shirt and
drapes it over the couch. "How are you?"

"Don't," I croak, sniffling as I tear my gaze away from his shoulders, bare in his cut-off T-shirt. "I'm fine."

"You're not fine. You're far from fine."

"Which is why you're taking us into the eye of a storm in the center of the lake?" My voice is thick, my mouth syrupy with the fever that just won't break.

He sighs and bends to dig through the duffle bag he packed. "I need to set something straight."

"What?"

"Us." He meets my eyes and straightens with a little plastic box in his hands. He sits beside me but keeps his distance as he opens it, thumbing through the little vials of… potions.

My spine feels like lead. I lean against the couch, unable to swallow past the knot in my throat.

"Do you trust me, Posey, even after I kissed you?"

"Of course." I'm slightly taken aback by the question.

"It didn't… It didn't mean anything, you know. It shouldn't mean anything." He rolls a vial between his fingers. "I shouldn't have done it. The first kiss was innocent. It was something we both agreed on, but the second and third…"

"I don't–I'm not upset with you about that."

"I'm upset with myself about it." He hands me the vial. "I need you to take this."

"What is it?"

"A contraceptive draft. It's potent, meant to be taken when needed for… immediate effect." His words are thick. "You'll take one now and one tonight. It might make you feel a little lightheaded, but otherwise–"

"Why do I need this?" A rush of unbridled heat burrows deep in my belly, expanding into something so damning and irrational I find it hard not to squirm.

Aris looks at me, his eyes scanning my expression, the blush fanning across my cheeks, and his eyes darken. "Because you're going into your first heat. That's why… why you have a fever. Why you've been building a nest in your room. Why you're so sick unless you're with *me*."

I blink at him, trying to form some kind of rational reaction to the news. "But I can't–"

"It doesn't matter if you can't shift. Your parents are wolves. You're still… a wolf."

I'm not. I wish I could make him understand. I wish I could just tell him, but he'd… hurt me. It's in his nature. All of their natures.

I look down at the little vial in my hands. "Why do I need to take this?"

"Because every symptom you're having aligns with a first heat, which… according to who I spoke to, is very intense and going to get worse unless we do something about it."

"Who did you speak to?"

"It doesn't matter." He shifts his weight beside me, obviously uncomfortable.

"Do I have other options?"

"Riding it out. Which is why we're going to a hunting cabin my family owns. It's secluded, on its own island. You'll have… two miles of shoreline to yourself if you want to go through this without help. It's up to you."

"I don't know anything about heats. I was never taught."

"I figured as much." He runs his fingers through his air. "I did some research while you were packing."

"Oh?" I let out a rough, wet laugh. "Thank the Goddess you're more competent in the matters of women than I am."

"I wanted to make sure I knew what to do for you." His voice is so soft I almost miss it.

I don't know what to say, so I say nothing, curling into myself until my knees are pressed to my chest and the vial of contraceptives is warm in my clenched fist.

I try to focus on his voice as he explains what a heat is. How I'll be fevered and out of my mind for days, doing things I normally wouldn't do—like building a nest, staying up all night in a fever induced delirium, and I'll lose my appetite completely… hungry for only *one thing*. Because… Mm wolf, if I had one, wants only one thing.

A mate. Or, at the very least, someone who can appease the gnawing, feral desire bound to bloom that has one reason. A baby.

Aris explaining all of this to me should be driving me out of my mind with embarrassment, but he's speaking so softly. Calm. Collected. He doesn't patronize or tease me. It's like he's giving a lecture, and I'm a willing student.

For whatever reason, I'm thankful it's him enlightening me.

"You've been stealing my shirts out of the laundry," he says after a moment of sucking silence. I wince, but he continues lightly, "It makes sense now. You think I smell nice. I should bottle up my essence and sell it to the masses."

My mouth quirks into a small, tight smile.

He shrugs, trying to lighten the mood and make me feel better. "You can build as many nests as you want at the cabin. I'll dirty up a few shirts for you."

"It's weird, isn't it?"

"I mean, I kind of built you one in my bed without realizing it. It's a wolf thing."

"It sounds more like a bird thing."

"Maybe we're closer to our winged cousins than we realize."

"It's a totally different clade–" I bite my tongue. "We are not related to birds."

"Crazier things have happened… like me helping my best friend's little sister through her first heat."

Guilt rumbles through me, settling in my heated, fevered bones. I unfurl my fingers and look at the vial, at the milky liquid dappled with flakes of herbs. "I have my own, you know. I brought some for Willow."

"This is much stronger. Again, it's up to you."

"You said I had options. Is it just this or riding it out? There has to be something better."

I've never seen Aris blush before. It suits him. His sun-tanned skin goes ruddy, and he looks down at his lap, letting out an exasperated laugh. "Uh, actually. There's one more thing, but it's not–it's not even worth talking about."

"What is it?"

A rhythmic beeping noise cuts through the cabin, and he rises, relief washing over his features and cutting through the blush. "We're close to the cabin. I have to go back up to the deck. It might be rough for the next twenty minutes or so, but I'd... take the draft. Just my opinion. If it were me... I wouldn't want to go through it." He squeezes my shoulder. The touch ignites like a striking match against my skin. It burns through me, twisting into something hot and unavoidable. I shift away from him. He doesn't notice; he's too busy pulling his arms through his damp flannel. I bet it smells *amazing*. Like rain and *him*.

What's wrong with me? Oh, right, I'm in heat.

I smooth my hand over my face before popping the cork of the vial and downing the bitter contents. I nearly throw it up, my body recoiling and trying to reject the draft the second it touches my esophagus.

IT'S POURING RAIN WHEN ARIS OPENS THE DOOR TO THE HUNTING cabin. I step into the shadows, and the smell of dust hits me, washing over me like the sheets of rain pounding the metal roof.

"The last time I came here I was a kid," he admits, looking around with a skeptical expression. "In fact, I don't think anyone has been here in at least ten years."

I step deeper into the space. Aris drags in our luggage and closes the door, shrouding us in near-total darkness for a few seconds, but then several sconces flicker, swirling at first with silver mist before turning a deep gold. I turn to him and notice he's wearing a bracelet on his left wrist. The band is thick, made of iron, I believe, inlaid with gems that have no name because they're not natural. They glow with his powers.

"Did my father make that for you?" I ask as the house hums to life, Aris's powers igniting every sconce and even the wood stove, which rumbles into a blaze, warming the lower level of the A-frame structure with nothing but embers and ash.

"I doubt it. It's over three thousand years old. Unless your dad is one of those vampires Arthur keeps rambling about, it probably wasn't him."

I cock my head, unsure who he's talking about, Arthur-wise, but he moves past me into the kitchen. There's not even a refrigerator. Everything is as bare-bones as possible.

"I'll hunt for us. That's kind of the whole point of this place, but I did bring some snacks. Water. A bottle of wine." He sighs as he looks up at the ceiling. It drips, and rain pings off the wood floor, warped in a few spots. "I didn't think this through."

"I kind of like it. It's rustic."

"It's likely the ceiling will cave in if the rain gets worse."

I look up again, following the trails of water and rusted metal. There's a loft above us, which I believe is where we're meant to sleep. A single bathroom on the first floor. A small kitchen, a work table, a few wooden chairs… that's it. "I can fix the holes in the roof. I wouldn't need any new material. Maybe just a… ladder?"

"You're not getting on the roof to do alchemy while going through heat, no less."

"Then we'll be wet and cold," I reply with a shrug, and he narrows his eyes.

"I'll think about it." He looks around and then settles his gaze on me again. "I'm going to hunt for dinner."

"I'm not hungry. You don't have to do that."

"Well, I still need to eat, and you should, as well, especially if you're going to ride this out."

"I took the draft." My head, however, still aches, and my body feels like it's held together by craft glue. "I don't know how I'm supposed to feel now."

He seems… disappointed, which I wasn't expecting. "All right. We'll know if it worked tonight."

"Why does night have any effect?"

"Because of the moon, of course. I think." He shrugs, running his fingers through his damp hair like the conversation is uncomfortable, which it is.

I am, however, grateful it's him. I can't explain why. I feel safe. I've always had to rely on myself, but now?

"I'm sorry this is happening. I didn't mean to–to ruin your summer vacation."

Silver eyes gleam in the sconce light. "You haven't ruined anything. I wanted an adventure. I got one. You… wanted to check things off your list, and now you can put a strike through your first heat and spending it at a dilapidated hunting cabin during the worst storm of the summer. What else could you possibly want to experience after this?"

I bite my lip before I say something I'll regret for the rest of my life, and instead reach for him, stepping closer until I close the distance between us. "Can I see it?"

He extends his wrist. I smooth my fingers over the bracelet. It's thick, masculine, obviously made to fit a man–a large one. Someone with strength and a whole lot of power, based on the validity of the gems–moonstone derived, I believe, based on how my powers flare to existence. "You're right. This is very old."

"Do you know about the caves beneath Veiled Valley?"

I shake my head.

"Well, seeing as we have shit else to do, how about a story?"

MAKING AMENDS

After telling me everything he knows about his Shadowsynger ancestors, which is very little, and the strange caves beneath Veiled Valley, which are immense and guarded by some kind of creepy spirit, Aris tears himself from the cabin like being in my presence is painful.

It sucks. I don't know how else to describe it. The knowledge that my scent is suddenly overwhelming to him, like I'm some beckon of fertility and everyone in the nearby vicinity knows it, has me cringing. I assume that's why he brought me here–to the middle of nowhere, miles and miles away from anyone else and trapped on a small island.

Aris left his clothes on the warped front porch in an untidy pile. I missed seeing him in his wolf form, but I gather his damp clothes and hang them to dry in front of the wood stove, using a length of twine I found in the kitchen strung between two sturdy, obviously handmade wooden chairs. I explore, running my fingers over every surface, every touch like an electric shock–all wrong. Too hard. Too cold. Too rough.

Upstairs in the loft, I find a bed. A single, full-sized bed on another handmade frame that took time and skill to produce, I bet. Whoever built this place and furnished it… they did it completely by hand over the course of many years, and it shows.

I pull the dust cover off the bed and find the mattress clean and protected from the roof leaks, but I can't find sheets or blankets anywhere. I can't make a nest without them, can I? That's what I'm supposed to be doing, right? Stealing anything cozy, soft, and warm? To build a nest like a little mother bird?

Annoyed and frustrated with myself, I jog out to the boat, which is rocking in the uneven surf coming off the lake. The storm is funneling in the distance, turning the landscape gray and black, the midday sun completely lost to the thick clouds. I find sheets and a few blankets in the cabin of the boat, but they smell sterile, like a harsh detergent. I wrinkle my nose while I search through the cabinets and snatch the few thin pillows off the couch that I believe unfurls into a bed if needed, and then walk back to the cabin with my horde just as the rain starts again in earnest, thundering against the leaky roof like a pounding, relentless fist.

I make the bed. I walk around, examining every inch of the cabin again. I mend some of the metal strips in the window seams, turning the rusted lengths to shiny… steel, I believe. I find out the cabin does, in fact, have running water while exploring the plumbing under the sink and burn my fingers on the copper pipes, my magic recoiling with silent curses of displeasure.

But I keep looking up at the roof, my skin itching to try it. Meld the metal back together. Flex the powers I've kept secret from everyone but the man currently romping around in his wolf form somewhere on the island. I need a ladder, however.

On my way back to the cabin after fetching the sheets, I noticed an outbuilding tucked in the trees. I race into the rain, squealing as fat drops hammer the top of my head, and find the wide door unlocked by the grace of the Goddess. It swings open with a groan, and I step into dusty shadows, coughing at sawdust lifting from the ground, disturbed by an inrush of outside air.

A single dusty sconce lights the space, swirling with Aris's powers. I was right when I came to the conclusion that someone with wood-working skills built this cabin and its furniture by hand. Saws and other tools are neatly arranged around the room. Several finished projects line shelves, coated in dust. On a wide wood table at the center of the room, a smaller project lays unfinished.

It's a rocking horse meant for a small child. Whoever lived here was still chiseling the details when they abruptly left it behind. Small tools rest in piles of gray, aged sawdust, untouched for... decades.

I turn the rocking horse on its side and find a name etched on the very bottom. *Granger.* Beside it, another name, etched sloppily, like the woman who carved it wasn't practiced in the art. *Amanda.*

"My grandparents on my father's side."

I whirl toward the door. Aris darkens the doorway, shirtless, wearing nothing but a pair of damp jeans. He steps into the light, his body wet with rain. He smells delicious–like the storm, the wet forest, and sweat. It cuts through the smell of sawdust and makes me so dizzy I have to grip the worktable for support, but he's not looking at me and doesn't notice the way I'm struggling to find my breath again.

His silver eyes scan the room before settling on the rocking horse with a small, knowing smile. "Granger and my grandpa Ryatt were best friends back in the days of King Kane. Granger was Ryatt's second in command, his Beta by all means, and Amanda... took care of Grandma Ella when Ella arrived from Crescent Falls. They've been in each other's lives for... fifty or sixty years now."

He steps forward to run his fingertips over their names.

"This was their house?"

He nods. "When the war was won, and Ella and Ryatt came to live in Veiled Valley while Moonrise was being built, the old palace repaired, Granger would spend weeks here with Amanda. She needed–she wanted privacy." He bites back what I can only describe as some deeply guarded secret. It flares behind his eyes regardless, and his unease is palpable. "They didn't come back very often after my dad was born. I have five aunts and uncles on that side of the family. They had kids one right after the other after that." He smiles again, shaking his head. "But this... I believe my grandma went into labor while he was working on this, and they returned to Veiled Valley and didn't come back for a while. Everyone moved to Moonrise after that." He finally looks at me. "What are you doing here? Better not be looking for a ladder."

I purse my lips.

He hums with delight at having read my mind. "Honestly, I'm kind of curious. Fine. Mend the fucking roof. Be my guest. But if you fall off the ladder and break your neck, I'll never forgive you."

"If I broke my neck, there'd be nothing to forgive. I'd be dead!"

He brushes past me, lifting an old, gray ladder off the wall, and carries it like it weighs absolutely nothing. "Do you need anything else to complete the task?"

"Just my fingers."

He looks at my hands, which are still curled around the edge of the worktable. His gaze lingers there for a moment before he slowly meets my eyes, and it's almost like he's in between forms–on the cusp of shifting again, maybe involuntarily.

He blinks, shakes his head like he's trying to dislodge a thought, and moves into the rain. I follow, glancing at the little rocking horse just once before shutting the door tight behind us. Sheets of rain sweep over the grassy, sloping, and severely overgrown garden between the workshop and the cabin. Grass and perennials brush against my waist. I follow Aris back into the house. He pauses with the ladder slung over his shoulder, staring down at the makeshift clothesline I made for his discarded clothing, and sighs, but wordlessly carries the ladder up the narrow, slightly uneven staircase and sets it up in the loft.

The ladder itself nearly touches the ceiling, which is perfect. Aris grumbles but holds the ladder steady while I climb up, examining the larger holes in the rusted slabs and realize with a frown that it's not steel like it hoped. I murmur out loud, "Tin. *Great.*"

"You sound disappointed."

I look down at him, and he looks slightly amused by my frown. "Not that you'll be able to understand, but tin isn't the best for alchemy. It's feeble, unruly, and prone to damage even if it's easy to bend to my will.... I can fix it. I just need it to stay like that." I reach up, pressing my fingers to an undamaged section.

"What are you doing?"

"Feeling for its resonance. Magic, technically."

"Metal is magic?"

"No, not on its own, but it holds magic in different volumes depending on the chemical makeup. It's like… teeny-tiny, damn near microscopic traces of our world's magic trapped within, and people like me can draw it out and manipulate it."

"But you don't like tin, huh?"

"It's pretty worthless. I can manipulate it, sure. There's just hardly a reason to bother normally. If we want to be dry in the morning, I at least have to try." I grit my teeth as the metal warms under my touch. I slowly move my fingers, the tin stretching with the movement and regenerating, and the holes in the metal close like my fingers are a paintbrush, and the roof is my canvas, but just like I thought, the alchemized metal is thin. Too thin to be considered a long-term repair.

"What metal is your favorite to work with?"

"Iron, for sure. It holds the most resonance. It's thick with it, and there's a lot I can do with iron. I can turn it into gold and gems, for one. Copper is great for alchemy, but it hurts me for some reason. It burns when I touch it. Silver–" I pinch my mouth closed, but the damage is done.

Silver can tear a wolf to shreds.

"Silver?" When I don't answer right away, Aris jiggles the ladder.

I hiss with annoyance and peer down at him before moving on with my task, my fingers reaching for the largest, most complicated rusted out holes. "I find silver the easiest for me to work with."

"Oh, yeah? It doesn't burn the fuck out of you?"

"I'm not a wolf, remember? That was part of the reason I started to wonder about it when my wolf abilities failed to show up. Not that silver is useful by any means."

"I could use a few knives."

"Silver knives? Are you planning on killing someone?"

"What else would a silver blade be for, Pose?"

I glare down at him. He shakes the ladder again, loving the way I squirm, and I realize with a start that I no longer have a headache, and my body doesn't feel like it's made of lead. I feel great. Completely at ease and enjoying myself because of… him.

Or the insanely powerful tonic I let burn through my system.

He says, "You know, instead of going into a convent, you can come live with me. I'll put you to work making silver blades and all kinds of other things whenever the fancy strikes."

"So we can spend a lifetime bickering with each other?"

"It almost sounds like a marriage to me," he says with a shrug, his tone teasing but slightly heavy. "Hear me out–"

"No," I grumble, wincing as I close the largest and most finicky section of the roof. My fingers ache to the bone.

"What if," he says anyway, bracing himself on the ladder, "instead of joining the cloth, you and I get *married*."

"Will you shut up? I'm trying to work."

"Just imagine it, Posey. You can have a little workshop in one of the spires at my castle and make your little trinkets until your fingers hurt, and then we can fight over dinner and what to watch on TV."

"Do I look like I watch TV in my downtime?"

"Well, you'd have to start, because I do. Sports. Scary movies. Movies about war. Shows about war. Podcasts–"

"*Oh, my Goddess,*" I whisper to myself, smoothing my palm over the ceiling to bridge the gaps of the smaller holes likely unseen by the naked eye.

"We'd have good looking kids."

My heart falls into the pit of my stomach. "Aris, please."

"I'm just saying… two birds, one stone."

"And what birds are those, huh?"

"You feeling like you need to run away and me needing to prove I can settle down and be the Shadowsynger Veiled Valley has needed since my grandfather was my age. The stone is *us*. Platonically, of course."

"And the act of making a kid is platonic?"

I know he's joking. He wouldn't ever consider someone like me for that role, but the teasing note to the conversation is making me feel light as air.

But then I meet his eyes. The way he's looking at me is... undoing the fabric of my world as I speak, and I don't even notice the way the ladder creaks, then cracks, and suddenly the slate beneath me, holding up my weight, gives way.

Aris shouts as I plummet.

I land in his arms, and he lands on the bed with me... straddling him, my hands braced on his chest.

He huffs a breath, laughs, and looks up at the mended ceiling. "Not bad, Pose. Are you sure you want to do this?"

"Do what? Marry you? Is that what we're still talking about?"

"Give all this up?" He sits up and grabs my aching fingers like he can feel the way they throb, how hot they are, how much power lives just there, in the tips. Those silver wells of endless power meet mine and hold. "Are you sure the temple is what you really want?"

"It doesn't matter what I want," I whisper, pulling my fingers out of his grasp.

CHECK

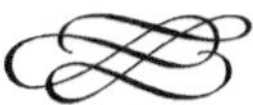

Nights falls on the cabin, but neither of us noticed the sunset until Aris mentioned something about the time, which I hadn't been keeping track of. It's still raining, and he's shifting again as it stands, probably to hunt for whatever he's going to eat raw for dinner seeing as our only other option for cooking is the wood stove, and while I'm capable of cooking like a dream, but not using that. That's a bit out of my wheelhouse.

Still, I twirl the second vial of contraceptive tonic between my fingers, watching the flakes of herbs dance in the milky liquid. I'd been too sick to my stomach to differentiate each herb, spice, and flower used to make it when I took the first draft, but this time I might be able to. If this heat isn't a one-time thing, I'll need this again, won't I? I should know what ingredients I'd need to make it for myself because I highly doubt the priestesses I'll be sharing the remainder of my life with will have them on hand.

A crash echoes from outside, and I go still. The tonic falls from my fingers and shatters on the floor at my feet. Unease ripples through me, making every fine, downy hair on the back of my neck stand on end as I move through the dimly lit main room to the door. There's only a few windows to the outside world, and none on this wall, and whatever's out there, lumbering through the rainy darkness, is *large*.

"Aris?" I say through the door, teeth chattering with fear. I swallow it back and slowly turn the doorknob, reminding myself this is a *private island* in the middle of a *secluded lake* in the Gem Lake districts, which is about as rural as Eastonia can get, other than, well, the far reaches of Tarsian where only sand survives. I yank open the door to two bright, silver eyes.

Aris is still in his wolf form, and it's… jarring. Speechless, I step back into the cover of the house while he lumbers up the porch steps, sopping wet, his deep, golden fur slack with water. He's huge for a wolf. His shoulder could brush the top of my head if he were to try to squeeze through the door, but instead, he stays in the rain, and drops a rabbit at my feet.

"Oh," I croak, feeling like my heart is going to leap out of my chest, whether in relief or something else, something deeper, I don't know. "Oh, that's so nice of you, but I'm not hungry."

His fluffy tail wags regardless. He nudges the rabbit with his snout—all wolf. Maybe even his mind, as it stands. He's been in this form for hours now.

I gingerly bend to pick up the rabbit, giving him a wobbly smile. He seems pleased, and turns, leaping off the porch into the darkness again. I promptly drop the rabbit beside the door and step inside, shaken to my core.

It feels strange. He hunted for me. Provided for me. It's a warm feeling, something that cuts through the slight ache in my temples and the fevered chills beginning to creep into existence as the moon rises far beyond the rain clouds.

I stand by the door, unsure what to do now.

So I wait.

He repeats the process three times.

By the fourth rabbit, I've had enough.

"We can't eat all of these, Aris, and I'm not hungry at all! I have no appetite. Isn't that part of the heat? That I won't be hungry?"

He just stares at me with those big wolfish eyes. He seems displeased. His tail doesn't wag this time, but he's refused to shift back into his human form or even come back into the house since earlier this afternoon. Maybe he's just as out of his mind as I am. Maybe my heat is messing with him, too.

I reach for him, smoothing my fingers over the short, glossy hair covering his snout. He huffs when my hand brushes the delicate, translucent whispers. It must tickle because his ears twitch, but he relaxes when I scratch behind his ears and hangs his head to give me better access.

"You're a glorious creature," I tell him, marveling at his build. I see wolves all the time. I shouldn't be this in awe. But I am. He's a powerful beast. All male energy and the promise of a swift death and as many rabbits as I could eat if there was nothing more tantalizing available.

I'm lost in the cozy, soft feeling of his fur when his massive teeth catch the fabric of my flannel–his flannel, that I pilfered and claimed as my own–and he pulls me out onto the porch. I hiss out a breath in surprise. When I don't take whatever hint he's trying to convey, he tugs on my shirt again until I'm forced to walk down the steps with him, his teeth precariously close to my skin.

"What do you want?" I ask, squinting against the gentle raindrops still pattering overhead. The air is sharp with his scent and ozone as the clouds hang low over the lake. "How about you come inside and warm up?"

He snorts–a very wolfish sound, obviously disagreeing with the offer, and turns and crouches low to the ground.

"You want me to climb on your back?"

He turns to look over his shoulder, those big silver eyes alight from within, and nods at me.

I clutch his fur. It's thick and surprisingly dry underneath the layer of damp overcoat. He's fluffy, just like his unruly hair in his human form. When I don't immediately do what he wants, he growls low in his throat.

I roll my eyes and scurry up his side, which is rather hard to do. It takes me several attempts to swing my leg over, and even then, I slide off to the side again, but the second I do manage to balance along his spine, my thighs gripping the taut muscle over his wide ribcage, he runs.

I can't even scream. The world rushes past while I sink my fingers into his fur, holding on for dear life, and that choked scream dies in my throat and is replaced by a wild laugh–a sound I don't think I've ever made before… like I'm suddenly alive.

He takes me all around the island in a matter of minutes, steady on his feet even on the uneven, slippery, rocky beach that lines the property. Then, he turns into the woods, racing uphill, where cypress trees grow thick, and vines hang from the canopy, blocking the clouds.

"Where are we going?!" I shout, laughing, but he keeps running, his body firm and powerful beneath mine, and this time when he drops down again, the cabin comes into view, lit from within, the windows radiating warm, golden light.

A flicker of disappointment blooms deep in my belly. I grip him a little harder as he slows to a trot, taking us around the back of the developed property. I want to dig in my heels and demand more when he stops at the porch and dutifully waits for me to slide off his back.

I do. I don't want to. His warmth and pure power were everything I needed, and the feeling replacing it makes me want to scream. I feel that same pounding ache in my temples when I back away from him, damp, my hair sticking to my cheeks, and he turns to look at me.

I wonder if he sees it. *Feels it*. The ache that's been growing since before the heat started. The thing that makes me question everything. The pinprick of knowledge that will forever keep me up at night with questions.

About him.

About me.

About his lips against mine and the heat between *us*.

Willow made it sound like this should be easy. Aris told me not every kiss has to mean something.

Maybe the first one didn't. But the second? The third?

The *fourth*?

Aris shifts back to his human form, and suddenly my entire field of vision is blocked by his body. His face. His hands caressing my cheeks before he pulls me toward him and collapses into me, his mouth on mine. It's the same rushed, aggressive kiss as before, when he was trying to shut me up, but deeper. Like every slow dive of his tongue against mine is searching for something he tasted before and has been thinking about ever since. He lifts me up. I wrap my legs around his waist. My hands travel down his naked back as he carries me inside, stepping over the rabbits he hunted for me.

Warm air rushes toward us, warming the chilled, damp fabric of my clothes. He shivers but kisses me deeply again, groaning into it like it's giving him life and I am...

He pulls away like he's coming back to reality, like he's just realized he's holding me, and he's not wearing any clothes, and we're here, at the cabin.

"Don't stop," I whisper against his lips, my voice small and pleading. "Aris–"

He turns, pressing me against the wall to ease some of the burden, and kisses me again and again.

I moan into his hair when he lowers his lips, his tongue gliding up the side of my neck. He inhales deeply with each breath, his muscles tight, his body so rigid I wonder if he'll snap, and I'll let him. Goddess, this is everything I never knew could be real. This feeling of being so utterly, desperately wanted? It's overwhelming the way he grips my thighs, spreading them open, pressing his hips into mine.

His cock is right there, pressed between us. The knowledge explodes through me like someone set a bomb off inside my brain, and I go completely fluid, willing and ready to do anything he could ever ask of me.

I would crawl. I would beg. Just to know what he feels like. What he could make me feel like.

He pulls us away from the wall and turns with me in his arms, walking into the center of the room, to the couch, to where I'd been standing when–

"Stop!"

Aris goes perfectly still, his mouth parting with mine with a sound that echoes through the cabin and allows real life to rush in, cold and empty. His eyes are wild and… horrified. He starts to put me down, but I grip his shoulders, shaking my head.

"I dropped–dropped the tonic. It shattered. Right there." I point to the ground a mere step from where he's standing.

He lets out his breath slowly. "Fuck, Posey–"

"I want to keep kissing you. The glass. That's all I meant."

"We cannot do this," he whispers, nose to nose. He curses under his breath when I hold him tighter, refusing to be put down.

I wet my lips, deranged, that fever spiraling back into existence, but I've never felt more clearheaded than I am now. "I want to know what this feels like before I go."

He shakes his head. "Posey."

"I want to have sex." It comes out as more of a whine. "*With you.*"

He takes another deep breath. "You're just in heat. That's why."

"I want to have sex with you. I trust you. *I want it to be you.*"

He drops his face into the crook of my neck, groaning. "Don't talk like that."

"Please?" I could cry. I want to cry, actually. My eyes sting. Desperation clouds my judgment. "Oh, Goddess, please–"

"You're not thinking straight. I can't–I won't do this to you while you're in heat."

"It's not about that. I've–since the first time you kissed me. I've known since then. I want to do this."

It strikes me then that he doesn't want to. Not with me. Dread cuts through the fever, clouding my nerves with overwhelming rejection. I push away from his shoulder, squirming until he carefully sets me down, and I flee, turning away from him before seeing him in all of his naked glory.

"Posey, wait!" I'm already halfway up the stairs. I slip, my shins slamming against the steps. Aris curses something, fabric snags, and then he's behind me, wearing pants now, at least, and grabbing me around the waist just as I reach the top step. He tosses me like a rag doll onto the bed and pins me down before I can protest.

There's fire in his eyes. He presses his body to mine, refusing to let up until I stop trying to squirm away.

"Do you think it's because I don't want you?"

I refuse to look him in the eyes, to see the cold, hard truth there. I'll swim back to the mainland if I have to, just to save myself the embarrassment of thinking he–the prince of Veiled Valley–would ever want someone, *something*, like me.

"Look at me," he rasps. "Posey, I want you to *look at me.*"

I close my eyes, turning my head to the side. He growls and leans down to nip the side of my neck. I gasp, but it quickly turns to a guttural, whimpering moan I can't stop fast enough.

He licks the spot where he just bit me and smiles against my skin. "If you think I haven't spent two weeks imaging all the ways I want to fuck you," he says slowly, darkly, "you'd be *so* wrong." He grabs the inside of my right thigh, forcing me to spread my legs and bend my knee, and he sinks between my legs until our hips are flush. "It's all I want. It's all I think about. But you're in heat, and you're out of your fucking mind if you think I'd take advantage of you–"

"I need you. Please, I want it to be you. I want to know–"

"Don't tempt me," he growls in warning, and I turn to look at him, at the darkness in his eyes, like it's taking all of his strength not to tear the clothes from my body and bend me to his will right here, right now.

I lace my fingers in his hair and lift my head just enough to bite him on the jaw.

And the prince of Veiled Valley, my older brother's best friend, decides to check another thing off my list.

JUST ONCE

"You've always been a whiny, demanding, pain in my ass," he pants, pinning my wrists above my head. His mouth is hot against the column of my throat as he traces a long, wet line with the flat of his tongue.

He likes it when I writhe beneath him. The smiles against my skin paint my body with heat almost as much as the rough, nibbling kisses I know will leave little marks that won't wash off for a few days—a brief reminder of tonight.

"Keep your hands above your head. Grip the pillow."

I obey, my fingers curled in the plush fabric. My heart races when he rises above me just enough to deftly unbutton the flannel I stole, revealing the white, damp tank top underneath. He takes a shaky breath and then chuckles darkly, greedily, and his eyes meet mine in the dim light.

"You're perfect."

"What?" I breathe, losing myself to the way his knee draws up between my legs and puts a breathtaking amount of pressure where I need it the most.

"Your breasts are a *masterpiece*." He kisses the rounded arch of my left breast and then the right, breathing heavy like he's desperate to hold himself back. "That's all Tate and Miles wanted to talk about. I considered beating the shit out of them for even looking in your direction."

Before I can gasp about the fact Miles and Tate were gawking at me, he pulls down the neckline of the tank top, ripping the fabric open, and buries his face between my breasts. Now, I'm gasping for an entirely different reason. My hands fly to his hair, tangling in the strands, and he licks my nipple, growling, "I told you to keep your hands on the pillow."

Every touch is absolutely glowingly unreal. Not too hard. Not too soft. Perfect. It's everything I've been looking for, I realize as Aris's ministrations travel lower, nipping down my belly, a swipe of his tongue against my fevered skin.

Whatever stupid nest I could have built wouldn't have ever come close to this.

"We need to set something straight," he says, pressing a kiss just above my navel.

"Yeah?" A breathy sigh sweeps the word away when he presses another rough kiss in the center of my belly, his hands braced against my hips.

He exhales deeply, his teeth grazing.

I shiver, clutching the pillow. "What–what do we need to set straight?"

"I'm trying really hard to be gentle with you," he replies with great effort, his voice low and tense. "I really don't want to be."

"Then don't be."

"That's what I need to set straight." He kisses up my stomach, lingering on my breasts with damning, passionate kisses and nibbles that leave me absolutely breathless. When he finally comes up for air, he continues, "I'm out of my fucking mind already, Posey. I thought shifting would help, but it only made it worse. If anything that happens next is out of your comfort zone, you need to tell me to stop. That's all you have to say. Just tell me to *stop*."

I nod, but he clutches my throat, forcing me to look him in the eyes. "What do you say when you don't like it or want it to end?"

"Stop."

He nods, giving me a cocky, somewhat wry smile. "Good girl."

His praise laces through me. He kisses me gently, drawing it out while slipping my shorts down my legs, taking my underwear with them. When his fingers trace up my slick inner thighs, I jump, surprised by the heat of his fingers. "I've never…. No one has ever–"

"It's okay." He presses the words against my neck and sighs, splitting my folds with a single finger. He curses something inaudible against my skin, but I'm lost, arching my hips into his touch, whimpering when he thumbs my clit. "Gods, you smell amazing." He buries his face in the crook of my neck and rocks his hips against my thigh. I can feel him there–hard. Massive. I'm not sure what I was expecting.

"Will it hurt?"

"I won't hurt you," he assures me. "You'll like it. I'll make sure you like it." He travels down my body again until his mouth is flush with my lower belly.

I scrunch the pillow, letting out a whiny gasp when he dips lower and kisses me somewhere new. I almost ask what he's doing. Willow never mentioned *this*. My lips part, the words sitting on the edge of my tongue, but the sound that comes out is a resounding *yes*.

He parts my folds with his tongue. My toes curl. My knees draw up on instinct, and he smiles against my pussy, chuckling under his breath, "I knew you'd be greedy. You better keep your hands on that pillow. I'm only giving you one more warning."

"And then what?" I pant, but he wrenches my legs further apart and dives deep. I turn my head to the side, choking on a scream of pleasure so deep I feel it in my bones.

The way he pleasures me is entirely wolfish. Using his tongue, his teeth, little bites to my inner thigh, the scratch of his stubble on my most sensitive skin. His groans and sighs only add to the madness enveloping me, threatening to send me catapulting over the deep end.

My lungs won't fully fill with air. My fingers ache from gripping the pillow. I want to touch him. I want to feel the muscles of his back slick with sweat. I want to trace his smile with my thumb.

I arch off the mattress when he slowly presses one large finger inside of me. I feel full but also incredibly empty–an utterly confusing combination. My fevered skin feels tight. The places where he kissed me before ache to be touched again. I want to crawl into his skin and stay there.

"Slowly," he whispers against my inner thigh.

"I need–Goddess, I–" I wince as my body tightens on the cusp of something so great I'll cry if I don't achieve it. That warm, throbbing feeling fades as he pulls his finger out and presses it back in past the first knuckle, stretching me further. The ache is bright and new.

"You are," he breathes, his voice trembling with effort, "very tight."

I'm beyond words. Maybe minutes pass. Maybe hours. Maybe this is all a dream. Aris works me with his mouth and fingers, taking his sweet, sweet time, refusing to let the pleasure build too much, refusing to let me come until I'm a compliant, whimpering puddle in his demanding hands.

But I realize, during the fourth time the pleasure peaks and sizzles into obscurity before I can fall over the edge, that he's purposefully holding me back.

"Why can't I?" I whine, frustrated, grinding against his mouth.

"We're not rushing this–"

"I want–*I want*–"

"I know what you want." His reply is hoarse as he nips my inner thigh and licks the imprint. Nothing hard enough to break the skin. "But I can't just fuck you, Posey. I could hurt you."

He looks up at me, his eyes so dark they're nearly black, and smiles wickedly as he spreads me with two fingers, then three.

I arch off the bed.

Aris is just as delirious as I am. He sighs against my clit and continues ravishing me with his tongue, his teeth, and his fingers until I'm dripping, begging him with words I've never once heard leave my mouth to just… take me. *Lay claim to what's his.*

Goddess, this heat is going to kill me if he doesn't do something about it. It's like he is the medicine I need. The cure. And he's just within reach but *so far away.*

"Please!" I nearly scream the word, finally letting go of the pillow to grip his shoulders. He sucks in a breath and rises over me. We fumble for a moment. I squirm out of the flannel with his help. He tosses both the flannel and torn tank top clean over the railing of the loft, where it falls silently in a heap a floor below. His pants are next.

It's only then, when we're down to nothing but our skin, that reality brushes against me. It's not a sweeping sensation of knowing, of the idea that we're doing something wrong, it's just…

"Are we crazy for this?" I whisper as he lays me back against the sheets. He's warm. His heat is delicious. I press my swollen lips to his shoulder and inhale deeply before kissing him there, my teeth grazing his skin, and he shudders.

"Yes," he answers simply, but then his mouth meets mine. "I suppose we are. Do you want to stop?"

"No."

"You can't take this back. We can't take this back."

"I want to know what it's like," I admit, meeting his eyes as he settles between my legs, smoothing a hand down the swell of my hip and the soft curve of my thigh.

"I can show you if you promise me something."

"Anything."

He nips my jaw and then slowly gathers my wrists above my head. "You'll rethink this whole convent thing."

"You know I can't–" I gasp, trembling, as the head of his cock parts my folds and rests at my entrance.

"Consider it," he whispers against my lips before his mouth parts in a grunt of pleasure. "Fuck, *Posey*…" He braces himself with his hands flat on the mattress on either side of my head, slowly pressing inside, just enough that I feel the stretch of him.

I bite my lip so hard it might bleed. "I don't think–Aris should it hurt–"

"Just for a moment." He kisses my nerves away. "I told you I wouldn't hurt you. You're more than ready. I saw to it. Clutch the pillow." I do. He thrusts in a little deeper this time, another inch giving way. I draw my knees in on instinct. "Good girl. You're so good. *You feel so good.*"

When I wince, he stops and waits, waits for me to say the word that would put an end to this forever. When I relax, taking a much needed breath, he slides in deeper, his eyes on mine–steady and unwavering–like he's watching me collapse and loving every second of me finally letting go.

"Do you know what I did after I kissed you for the first time?" he says against the shell of my ear, his cock pressing in slow, savoring the way I clutch him tightly.

I turn to him, our cheeks flush, perspiration dappling my temples. "What did you do?"

"I didn't sleep." He draws in a breath as he thrusts deeper, stretching me so wide I let out a breathy gasp. "I imagined this. The little noises you'd make with me inside of you. What you'd feel like with me buried between your thighs." Deeper. *Deeper.* He pulls out slowly, to the tip, with a groan. "I wondered what would have happened if I stayed."

He thrusts, pushing past that barrier, and makes me his.

For life.

It strikes me suddenly that there will never be anyone else after this.

His mouth is on mine as he slowly, carefully, spreads me open with each thrust of his cock. Pleasure winds through the base of my spine, turning my body molten.

It's everything I've ever wanted. It's everything my fevered brain is so desperate for. I was right. He is the cure to my heat.

My muscles begin to contract, rippling with tension. He whispers praise against my cheek, his hands clenched into fists on the mattress while he slowly savors every moment, keeping his pace aligned exactly where and how it feels the best for me.

"Don't hold back on my account," I want to say, but it comes out as a moan.

He smiles against my skin, thrusting hard as if in warning. "Hush. Let me give you this."

"I want you to feel good, too."

"Oh, Posey," he breathes, chuckling darkly, "you have no idea." His voice sounds like a rake is being dragged over his vocal cords—strained and deep.

I bring my arms down to splay my fingers over his back, but he stops me so swiftly I gasp, then whine, jostling my hips in a way that makes him grunt and still.

"No."

"Why can't I touch you?"

"Because if you do, I'll knot you, and you won't like it." His eyes are like quicksilver.

"What's knotting?"

"Oh, gods." He groans, dropping his face into the crook of my neck. "You're too innocent."

"Not anymore."

He lifts his head, a cocky, amused smirk touching his lips, and shakes his head. But as if in punishment for my behavior, he thrusts so deep I lose my grip on reality, and finally, finally, reach that peak again. He notices, lifts onto his knees, and drags me onto his cock with force, spreading my legs wide while pressing his hand flat over my stomach to pin me to the mattress.

"Good girl," he says, nodding, encouraging me. "Look at how perfect you are. How sweet. How *fucking* delicious. I want to fuck you every day for the rest of my life."

I arch off the mattress in a silent scream as pleasure pulsates through me. Aris rolls his neck and groans, the loft filling with the sound of our pleasure—our gasps, moans, and other sounds that only heighten each sensation.

With a sharp, frustrated grunt, he abruptly pulls out. The mattress sags when he angles to the edge, giving me his back as he pulls on his pants and rises, running his fingers through his hair.

I sit up, my fingers still prickling with the urge to touch him and the ghost of pleasure still washing through my body, carrying the heat fever away on a tide. "Aris?"

"It's all right. I need to shift, okay? Go to sleep." He turns to me looking so…. He quickly changes his expression and bends, bracing his hands on the mattress, and kisses me. "Go to sleep. I'm going to get more rabbits."

"We don't need more rabbits!"

"Have you seen how big I am in wolf form? I need to eat. Four rabbits aren't enough."

Another kiss effectively seals my fate, and I realize, as he walks down the stairs, that I'm utterly fucked. No pun intended.

I want to tell him everything. Even the thing I can't say out loud. The thing that would change *everything*.

THINK ABOUT IT

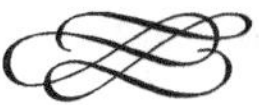

Posey

The fever returns in the morning when the sun rises. It's thick and syrupy with no end in sight. I sit up, surrounded by sheets and pillows I don't remember carrying up here from the couch. I'm wearing nothing but one of Aris's cut-off T-shirts, which I don't remember putting on. I rub my face on the worn fabric, inhaling deeply, trying to clasp onto whatever shred of reality I can find. All that takes up my mind is... here. Being here, in this cabin, with this man I've known my entire life. A man so far out of my league it's laughable.

The same man who made love to me last night like it was something fated. An act we've done a million times. Slow, tender, aching, the kind of touch I imagine comes from decades of knowing a lover's body.

I'm delusional when I walk downstairs, my brain split into sections. Sex. Lust. Greed. Possibly, hopefully, a single shred of who I am outside of this heat, but that section is the weakest of all. Sunlight pours through the open front door, casting the bare-bones furniture in hazy light I haven't seen in several days. It burns, honestly, after so long spent in the rain and fog. I shield my eyes but halt in front of the couch, gingerly stepping back, but the place where I dropped the tonic has been cleaned and swept thoroughly.

Aris... I don't think he came to bed last night at all.

Of course he wouldn't have. How stupid can I possibly be? Thinking Aris–the man, the myth, the fucking legend of Veiled Valley–would ever stoop to my level and snuggle with me until we both fell asleep. He can have anyone he wants. He *has* anyone he wants.

Last night, it was me. I'll guard that for the rest of my life. One single, deliciously deranged memory.

It has to be enough for me.

But this fever is just... relentless. My bones ache with every step I take into the strip of sunlight painting the rustic cabin bright gold. Only when my eyes adjust do I see Aris sitting on the front porch, shirtless, his back to me as he stares out over the lake, which is finally visible.

It strikes me then how far north we came. Instead of dense, humid forest, the horizon is dappled by shallow, evergreen mountains. Tucked deep in those mountains too far to see, and past a rolling river, Veiled Valley rests high above the river, and beyond that... home. I'm sure, if I stayed here long enough, I'd be able to pinpoint which of the towering ridges belongs to my father's territory.

A floorboard creaks below my foot as I step into the light. Aris turns slightly, notices me standing there, and rises methodically. He's sweaty, wearing nothing but a pair of briefs, and smells like the forest. He just got back from shifting. I can sense the wolf on him when he turns to face me. His pupils are still wide and dark, like he's not totally back in his human form yet.

A sharp ache clicks between us, and my fever spikes like it never has before. I swallow a whimper, my lower lip trembling. What's happening to me? *To us?*

He mouths my name, nostrils flaring, and suddenly, I'm in his arms, and he's carrying me across the house. He deposits me on the kitchen table and spreads my legs wide. I'm not wearing underwear. All he has to do is pull his briefs down just enough to free himself, and within seconds, and a sharp gasp, he's buried inside of me again.

There's nothing gentle about this. It's so *fierce*. So *passionate*. So… *overwhelmingly good*. I grip his shoulders, and he rolls his hips into mine, each thrust hitting deep points that set my blood on fire. I tangle my fingers in his hair at the base of his skull and encourage him, moaning and mewling without restraint. It's animalistic. The cabin fills with the sounds of our passion. He nips my neck as he picks up the pace, groaning against my skin when my inner muscles tighten abruptly and spasm in rhythmic, satisfied waves, the fever rolling away with each passing second.

He is the antidote. I wonder if he knows. He has to know.

"Look at what you've done to me," he rasps, groaning into my ear. "You're fucking perfect. You're so perfect, Posey. I'm a mess." He inhales sharply, thrusting as deep as he can go, his body shuddering. "I want to come inside you."

"I want you to," I whimper, my nails leaving claw marks on his back and shoulders.

He groans again, but he's frustrated, taking out that frustration with little bites to my neck and collarbone. His movements slow, but he's rigid.

"I want you to," I repeat, brushing the words over his chest. "I want you to come in my pussy."

"Fuck," he grunts, growling, and pulls out, his cock pressed between us. He holds me close, one hand splayed flat across my lower back to keep my upright and the other braced on the table.

"Why?" I ask as heartbreaking clarity fills the void left by the fever. "You did this last night, too. You didn't come."

"I can't."

"I can help you."

He chuckles darkly against my forehead. "Just looking at you does the trick. Trust me."

"Then why?"

He grabs my hand and brings it between us, folding my fingers around his thick shaft. He's *amazing*. A work of art. But he's the only man I've ever been with, and it's still all foreign. But then, when my hand reaches the base, he grows... hot and swollen. Much, much bigger than before.

I look up at him. He has his eyes closed, his mouth parted in what I can only describe as ecstasy when I tighten my grip. I start to move my hand, traveling up and down his length again, but he stops me at the base of his cock.

"What is it?"

"A knot," he replies hoarsely, licking his lips. He looks down at me through slits, his eyes hooded and heavy with heat that ripples through me, igniting another fire. "It happened last night, too."

"What does it mean?"

"It means my wolf wants to fuck you as much as I do. It would have fused us together. It would have hurt you."

"I want it–"

"No," he breathes, shaking his head. But his mouth quirks in a sly smile. "It's not possible."

I want to ask why not, but he presses me back down against the table and kneels, my legs draped over his shoulders, and silences me by licking me from base to clit, sucking and nibbling until I'm beyond words or sounds, and the cabin fades to nothing but bright, white light, and the fever dies for good.

Passing time with Aris is the equivalent to watching butter melt on freshly baked bread. It's perfect. Like nothing will ever be the same again between us but in the best way. I don't think many people get to see this side of him. The serious side. The side sitting on the ground with an old book, explaining his conspiracies and opinions about the past wars with animated detail. The side that laughs into the sun as we look for freshwater clam shells on the shore. The side that listens intently when I talk about my garden back home and the little trinkets I've made using alchemy. The quiet, contemplative side.

His warm body. The rhythmic beat of his heart as we look up at the stars, sprawled out on a blanket in nothing but our skin.

He checks everything off my list and then some, until the morning of our third day at the cabin dawns, and my heat slips through my fingers.

Reality doesn't seep in until the sailboat meets the dock at his manor in Ruby. We're still laughing, smiling and telling silly jokes when he helps me off the boat, and we turn toward the house.

My body instinctually begs to turn back, to climb aboard the little craft and sail back to that cabin where we can be just Aris and Posey again. Not the prince of Veiled Valley and the monster whose secrets are a death sentence.

I wanted to tell him the real reason I have to leave, but I can't. I can't bring myself to admit it. Even when he jokingly talked about marriage again, the children we'd have–with hair like mine and eyes like his–I couldn't tell him the truth. That there would never be a child because I cannot bring something else like me into the world. That it would break me to see the look on his face when he realized what I was, and who I am, and the secrets I guard like a dragon atop its hoard.

I might survive watching him slip through my fingers. I'll never survive his hatred and disgust.

"Are you okay?" he asks, but his voice is tight, and his gaze lingers on the house for several seconds before he meets my eyes. He looks as torn as I feel.

"It's been a..." I turn to him, aching to reach out and touch him. "Thank you, Aris. For everything. I know this isn't supposed to mean anything, but I'm really glad it was you."

He stares at me, those silver eyes gleaming in the sunlight. He hasn't shaved since we left. I yearn to reach up and run my fingers over the stubble–several shades darker than his golden hair. He looks looser and more relaxed this way, like he doesn't have a care in the world.

I wait for his boyish reply, that smirk. That roll of his eyes followed by a shrug that would scream, *"It wasn't a big deal. It meant nothing at all. If you want to fuck again with no strings attached, you have my number."*

But he bites his lip, his gaze locked on mine to the point I feel like he can see right through me and into the deepest, most closed off places in my soul. I'm in his spotlight, and I've never been warmer or more at ease.

In another world, in another life, I feel like this could have been the beginning of something.

"I asked you to consider something. Do you remember what it was?"

Now, I'm biting my lip. "Aris, we talked about this."

"You don't have to go into a convent."

"I don't have another choice."

"What if… the things we talked about. What if you knew I wasn't just joking around?"

Marriage. An entire semi-platonic life together. *Two birds, one stone.*

He steps closer, closing the distance between us.

"I could give you everything if you let me," he says. "I trust you, and I think you trust me. That's enough for me."

"You shouldn't," I whisper, and he presses two fingers to the underside of my chin and forces me to look up at him.

He searches my gaze. "What's going on with you, Posey? Did we not just establish that this is beyond friendship?"

My stomach hollows out.

I did not expect this from him. Not from Aris, the man whose sexual proclivity is well known throughout Eastonia and possibly Crescent Falls, as well. He could have anyone. I've been telling myself that for days, telling myself I should feel blessed. *Fucking lucky.* But the way he's looking at me now?

It's tearing me apart at the seams.

I watch the column of his throat bob as he swallows, leaning closer like he's about to kiss me. "What's stopping us, Posey?"

The sound of the glass door on the back patio sliding open steals both of our attention. Aris doesn't step away as a shadow moves into view.

My blood runs cold, and Aris's touch on the underside of my chin burns as Roman raises a hand to shield his eyes from the sun to look down at us across the yard.

I step away before his vision clears, and it feels wrong. Like I'm making a mistake. Like I'll regret this for the rest of my life.

And that's the worst part of it, that… I don't think I'm okay with that anymore. Pretending everything is okay. Being so completely, utterly alone.

I turn to Aris to just *say it*. To tell him everything before it's too late.

But Roman calls out our names, and Aris growls low under his breath, "What is he doing back so soon?"

ONE BIG MISTAKE

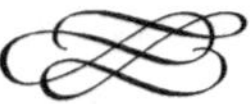

Aris

Roman steps into the light of the kitchen, scanning Posey from head to toe before turning his sights on me. "I've been calling like mad for a day straight. Where've you been?"

Posey shuffles her feet before stepping past me, but I stop her, setting one foot after the other, and let my shoulders hang, turning my skeptical expression to that charming smirk I'm known for. I have it down to a fucking science, after all, even if it feels strange wearing it now after so many days of just being… me. With her. Just us.

Roman's presence feels like an enemy has entered my territory and is currently threatening the woman trying to shrink into the shadow of the stainless steel refrigerator. I have no choice but to bite those feelings back.

"We went exploring on the boat and got caught up in that storm a few days ago. I took her to the hunting cabin up north to ride it out."

Roman nods, the tension in his shoulders easing. "Yeah, I got swept up in that, too."

"Why are you here?" Posey says with a squeak, and Roman looks at her like he's already forgotten his own sister is standing mere feet away. "You said you were coming back in ten days–"

"Well, that was the plan, but when I finally got back to Veiled Valley, planning on spending a day or two in the city before returning home, I heard rumors." He looks at me. "A fox? Have you heard anything about that?"

Posey goes perfectly still. I notice the way the color drains from her face. It's such a sharp contrast to the rosy blush she normally wears.

"You came all the way back because you heard a rumor there was a fox in the Gem Lake districts?" I lean over the kitchen island with my elbows braced on the surface, arching a brow. "Seriously?"

"I had Posey to think about, so of course I came back at the first mention of it. I didn't even bother confirming it. Hadn't even set foot off the ferry when we reached Veiled Valley, actually. I overheard two deckhands going on about it and made the decision to come back. I came straight here." He runs his fingers through his hair and snaps his fingers at Posey. "Go get your things. We're going home."

"Wh–" Posey looks at me. "What?"

"You're not staying here with a fox around."

"Nothing has been confirmed," I urge, but Roman rolls his eyes.

"It doesn't matter. When I finally got here after two days stuck in a storm, having to weather it out in some run-down, half abandoned village north of here, it's all anyone was talking about. Shops are shuttered. Hunting parties are gathering at night. I'm not putting the burden of her safety on you. You're not family. She's not your responsibility."

I can feel Posey staring at me. I can see her out of the corner of my eye, wondering how I'll react, what I'll say. No doubt she believes I'm about to spill our secret. I hate that. I hate it almost as much as what Roman says next.

"I don't care if there hasn't been a confirmed sighting of a fox shifter in over a century. I'm not risking it. The thought of one of those devils–those disgusting beasts–anywhere near–"

"Roman," I say with as much calm as I can manage, "fox shifters have been extinct for a very long time. It was likely just a wild fox."

"Posey," Roman says, snapping his fingers again and the noise… gods, I have to brace myself for impact, force the clawing sensation blooming deep within me to settle. "Go get your things. We're catching the noon ferry."

"It's unnecessary–" I try to say, but Roman turns to his sister, smiling and dripping with sudden brotherly affection I can see right through, his love, or lack thereof, as transparent as glass.

"Do you need help packing?" he says with a bit of a bite in his voice.

"No, I–"

"I'll help," I murmur, brushing past Roman and taking Posey by the arm. He doesn't even notice how I'm gripping her, leading her away from him… because he trusts me with her life.

I fucked his sister, and he has no idea.

I claimed her as mine, and I doubt she knows that, either.

When we get to her room, I shut the door behind us, ignoring the nest that now feels foreign without her fresh scent on the pillows. Snapping out of her heat haze had felt like a hangover, like all I wanted was another drink, just one more bite of her. She looks exhausted when she turns to face me, shaking her head, her lips parting, but I hold out a hand.

"I don't want you to go with him."

She stills, blinking up at me. "Aris, I have to!"

"You don't. That's what I've been trying to tell you for three days. Stay with me. Forget about the convent. Come to Veiled Valley with *me*. Your family will allow it–you know they will. Even Roman wouldn't be able to argue about his sister marrying the prince of Veiled Valley, and you know that. Our friendship be damned."

"I can't."

"Why not? I know you don't want to be a priestess–"

"Of course I do!"

"You didn't say a word about it the entire time we were gone. For someone as passionate and dedicated to the Goddess," I nearly snarl and realize too late where I'm going wrong, "you didn't act like it."

She gasps. "Aris!"

"Stay with me," I tell her again. "I'm not going to get on my knees and beg you, but you already know you're throwing your life away. I'm offering you a way out."

"So you can be unhappy with me for the rest of your life?" she says with a cruel laugh.

Shellshocked, I quickly reply, "What about the last three days makes you believe I was the least bit unhappy?"

"It doesn't matter. You'll get bored of me within weeks, Aris. It meant nothing, remember? It was just sex. You do that all that time. People do it all the time." Her bitter words are a sharp contrast to the suddenly terrified look on her face. I watch her unravel, spewing venom while her eyes fill with tears of... dread?

It doesn't make any sense.

"Was it just sex to you?"

"I was in heat! I barely knew what I was... wanting until it was... until you–" Tears glisten along her lower lashes. "I'm so sorry. I should have never led you believe that I could–that I wanted–"

"Don't lie to me."

"I'm not lying!" She is lying. I can taste the lie. Feel it in my bones.

"Then why are you doing this?"

"Why do you care?" Her voice breaks. "Aris, we can't do this. What happened between us–what you did for me... I..." She closes her eyes, tears dribbling down her cheeks. I resist the urge to reach out and swipe them away, but I'm worried that if I so much as touch her, I won't be able to let go.

"I'm going to tell you something, and I'm only going to say this once," I begin, curling my fingers into fists. "I've never felt this strongly about something. What you're doing is wrong. It feels *wrong* to me. It has felt wrong since the day I found out you were planning to sign your life away. If I had any notion that you were serious about this, that you actually wanted to pledge your life to the Goddess, Posey, I'd support it. But I look at you and see..."

"See what?" she says bitterly.

"I see someone lonely enough to believe that's all they're allowed to feel."

She scrunches her face, her lips pursed tight before she explodes, "You wouldn't know a Goddess-damned thing about that, Aris. You have a loving, supportive family. You can do whatever you want. Be whoever you want."

"And that's where you're wrong," I grind out. "I'm a Shadowsynger. The most powerful since my grandfather, and I have a sacred duty to Veiled Valley as a whole to remain there for the rest of my days, to keep the lights on and the shields up, no matter what, even if it means I stay in those towers overlooking the city every day for the rest of my miserable, lonely life."

She blinks up at me through tears.

I lick my lips, continuing, "I watched both of my sisters get their hearts torn out. I watched my cousin spiral into darkness and another get kidnapped and thrown into hell. I watch my parents and my aunts and uncles try to juggle the world they inherited while threats come from all angles, and I am not allowed to do anything about it. It's never my name that's called to come to the front. I was a forgotten middle child. My parents love me. Sure, they do. Wholeheartedly. But I was the one they didn't need to think about. My path was carved in iron, Posey. If you think you're lonely, you know nothing about it." My throat nearly closes around the admission. "And... and another thing, something I... when you were in heat... I'm not just–" Not just a wolf, I almost blurt. There's a part of me that tried to crawl to the surface when she was in my arms. The part I keep locked away for good reason, especially now, when the entire Ruby district is up in arms about the idea of something else like me being around.

"Posey!" Roman shouts from downstairs, and both of us jump.

She wipes her hand over her face. "I have to go. I know you don't understand, but this is best for everyone."

"It's not what's best for you."

"*Please*," she whispers. "You don't have to act like you actually care anymore, okay?"

"Do you really think I'm that dense? Of course I care!"

"You're acting like I belong to you know!"

"Maybe you do," I say and effectively silence her. She looks at me, and all I see is my reputation flashing behind her eyes. Maybe that's what this is about. I find it hard to believe, however, knowing Posey. She's never seen me like that.

She looks suddenly out of place against a backdrop of creams, baby blues, and taupe. Her features are too bright here. Too soft. I want her like she was at the cabin, her skin alight with silver and my shadows dancing over her curves.

Roman calls out her name again, and she turns, hastily dragging her larger suitcase from under the bed. "I have to go, Aris. Please don't make this any harder than it already is."

I watch her toss her belongings into the suitcase. She throws her textbooks like they mean nothing, which is the confirmation I need to know I'm right.

"Stay with me. Marry me. Let me fix everything."

"No," she says, shaking her head. "I can't!"

"Our future children will be set for life. They won't want for anything, and they will be so loved. They won't grow up like you had to!"

"I can't give you children," she hisses, her eyes so cloudy with tears I nearly fall to my knees at the sight of it. Her voice breaks, that earlier ice shattering. "*I can't.* Why do you think I'm throwing myself into a convent? You've offered me the entire world, and I can't give you what you really need in return, okay? *This is over.*"

"Posey–"

"Stop," she says tearfully, the one word I told her to say when she wanted it to end. She knows it, too, because she holds my gaze, waiting for me to step past my own boundaries, and I can't.

Half an hour later, Roman carries her suitcase out to his car and doesn't even help her into the front seat. This is where I should put an end to this idiocy. I should grab Roman by the neck and shake him. I should refuse to allow Posey to leave.

But instead, I stare at the tire marks in the white gravel until the sun sets. She's long gone, and I'm left feeling so removed from myself that I can't even rise from the front porch, even when the nearly full moon rises, riling up both my wolf and the fox within.

My fox is especially upset by her absence.

It's well after dark when I finish closing my summer house down and snap my fingers, Gem Lake swirling into the aether, replaced by familiar onyx stone and stained glass lit by moonlight.

I drop my bag on the smooth stone tiles, and the sound carries to the rafters, echoing down each corridor that branches off the grand foyer. I don't expect a welcoming committee. Those days–the warm days when the castle was full–ended a few years ago. Mom and Dad split their time between here, Moonrise, and the Deadlands. Grandpa Ryatt is constantly being called away to far-off lands, and more often than not, Grandma Ella goes with him.

The man who greets me tonight is unseen but familiar. His excitement riles the massive smokey quartz chandelier hanging precariously over my head. It's a gnawing, impeccably masculine presence. He's always been that way, whoever he is. The jokester. The mischievous poltergeist who thinks rattling Soren's nerves to the point he won't return to this castle unless Maeve twists his arm is the greatest of achievements.

But his presence is quickly swept out of the foyer by another force. Calm. Warm. The same feeling as being gently picked up off a couch as a child and tucked into bed by a beloved parent. *She* realizes something is wrong before her ghostly companion does, and while *he* drags my bag away into the darkness, she remains while I slump to my knees and hang my head, her unseen hand clasping my shoulder.

"It's nothing," I lie, and the chandelier rustles in answer.

MOVING ON

Aris

Four Months Later...

It never snows in Veiled Valley, even in the winter. At least, it shouldn't be snowing. Rain, yes. It rains often. So often, honestly, that I can tell what time it is just based on how the storm clouds begin to roll over the mountains with the promise of our nightly thunderstorms.

But snow?

I stare out the window at the silver landscape, narrowing my eyes at the guards posted at the gate. They're just as confused as I am, but at least they're enjoying it.

"I think it's a ridiculous name, but Soren has his heart set on it," Maeve says from somewhere behind me with a deep sigh. "Can you imagine naming a child after a fruit?"

"Is he particular to clementines?" Brie asks with a small laugh.

"No, he doesn't even like oranges. I have no idea what's gotten into him lately, but when we found out we were having another girl, he pitched the name, and I immediately laughed at him and told him over my dead body, but he's been calling her that, and now Fallon is calling her Clementine, too."

I look at my sisters over my shoulder. Brie is packing her things, and Maeve is waiting patiently for the herbs Brie has to take to travel to kick in. They've been here for the past week, and their only agenda, it seems, was to harass and pester me. In Brie's defense, she was worried Grandpa Ryatt was keeping me locked in one of the towers against my will, honing my Shadowsynger skills. Maeve, on the other hand, was disappointed that that wasn't the case.

"I think Clementine is a perfectly nice name." Brie neatly folds one of Kieran's sweaters and tucks it in her suitcase.

Maeve groans. "And what's next, then? A daughter named Watermelon?"

"Well, what would you name her otherwise?"

"Something tough, like *Elektra*."

"That sounds like a new electronic device for home security," I quip, and Maeve scowls, the pregnancy in question barely even beginning to show beneath her thick wool sweater and matching skirt.

"Well, no one gets an opinion on the matter because fate decided Fallon's name. Her long-dead Firestone ancestors will be the deciding voices in the end." She rests her hands on the swell of her belly and fixes us both with a look.

"Just be grateful you get to name another girl. Boy names are ridiculously hard to settle on. Lexa and Kaleb couldn't decide for nearly two months."

"Oh please," Maeve scoffs, rolling her eyes. "They named him *Ian*, for Goddess's sake. I was expecting something more exciting, like *Darragh* or *Ronan*. I know Kaleb was trying to convince her to name him Magnus for a while."

Brie wrinkles her nose.

Maeve smirks, flipping her thick mane of dark brown hair over her shoulder. "All better options than Clementine."

Brie shakes her head, amused but slowly starting to get annoyed. I recognize this little dance. Normally, by this point, they'd be at each other's throats, but some distance and different living situations has apparently turned them into calm, thoughtful beasts.

"Logan and I had a whole list of girl names," Brie sighs wistfully. "I was, of course, thrilled Griffon was a boy, but still, girl names are cute. We really liked Lilly or Lilac."

"Lilac?" Maeve arches a brow. "What is she, shampoo?"

The corner of Brie's mouth twitches. "Posey was Logan's favorite, but I explained we already have a friend with that name."

I haven't heard the name spoken aloud in months. It's like a knife twisting in my gut. I look down, half expecting my entrails to be scattered across the pristine emerald carpet.

"That's... one of the Sapphire Ridge kids, right? Alpha Farrow's daughter?"

I can feel both sisters looking at me, but I turn to the window to hide the pained expression spreading across my face.

"Roman's sister, yeah." Brie zips her suitcase with a nod. "Goddess, how much of the tonic did you give me this time?"

"Enough to knock you out cold." I can still feel Maeve's eyes boring holes between my shoulder blades. "What's up with you, weirdo?"

"Tired," I lie. My sisters exchange glances before Brie bows her head to aimlessly fluff a pillow on the couch, and Maeve moves in to pry, but Logan's presence in the second floor den immediately halts her progress.

He's holding both Griffon and Kieran, the former bright-eyed and bushy-tailed, excited to his see mother, and the former slumped over Logan's back like a sack of potatoes, fast asleep after a day spent terrorizing the castle to the point even the spirit of the house made himself scarce. "Are we ready?"

Brie sleepily nods, but I can still feel Maeve watching me like a hawk. While Logan passes Griffon to Brie, Maeve takes a few more determined steps in my direction, tilting her head as she rounds me to inspect my expression.

"Is Grandpa Ryatt torturing you?"

"No," I say with a soft smile, meeting her eyes. They're so unlike mine. She looks like Ella, our grandmother, with her startling sea-green gaze. Her powers swirl within, visible in the right lighting, which this is not. The castle in Veiled Valley is dark, cast in silver, even on the brightest days. Tonight is no exception. It's a new moon, barely a lick of light in the sky, especially with snow still spiraling down from the thick clouds hanging over the city like a wool blanket. "I've honestly enjoyed training with him."

"He thinks you're ready to be Alpha. He spoke to Mom about it."

Caught only slightly off guard, I ask, "How do you know?"

"Because she told me."

"Well, she never told me."

"I expect there to be some kind of announcement about Mom stepping down as Alpha of Veiled Valley during the Solstice gathering in Maatua." She turns to look out the window with me. "You know this is a long time coming for her. She's been a part-time Alpha at best, not the Alpha King Veiled Valley really needs."

I brace my hands on the windowsill, nodding. "I know."

"She just wants to be a midwife, and with the Ghosts mostly stationed in Moonrise these days, it makes sense for Mom and Dad to move there full time."

"I'm aware."

"Which means… this is all yours."

"I understand how it works, Maeve."

She chews her lower lip for a moment before adding, "You'll still report to me, technically."

"Hardly. Veiled Valley was never part of the Firestone domain, and that hasn't changed. The only reason you've had access to the inner dealings of this territory is because your mother is the leader."

"Well, I hope we'll at least stay on good terms." She squeezes my arm in a loving manner, which is unlike her, but then she takes a strained breath and looks over her shoulder at where Logan and Brie are preparing the boys to jump back to the Deadlands. "I heard a very strange rumor."

"Oh?"

She turns to me, taking a single step to close the distance between us so she's not overheard. "Are you... have you invited Princess Morgan of Celestoria to stay here?"

"For a week, yes."

"Why?"

My ribs ache. I absently rub my hand over my chest and refuse to meet her curious gaze. "She's single, a bit older than me but not by much, and her family has ties to ours. I met her a few weeks ago."

Maeve's brows rise with a disbelieving chuckle. "Ties? Her great-grandfather was the Alpha King who allowed Great-Aunt Maddy to fall into the hands of those breeder auctioneers. She's the niece of the current Alpha King!"

"And our cousins wouldn't exist had he not," I remark, twisting to face her. Maeve is exceedingly tall, just like Lexa, able to look me right in the eyes. She steps closer, her lips parting in disbelief.

"What business do you have with the Alpha King of Celestoria and his family?"

"None as it stands, but again, I met Morgan at a ball and we... talked about getting to know each other better."

"Her father is already boasting about a possible engagement."

"Nothing has been said in that regard."

"Maybe not on your end, but there's been rumbles, Aris."

"Rumbles about what, exactly?"

She shrugs, crossing her arms over her chest. "Well, for one, her father was in serious debt and had to be saved by the Alpha King, his own brother. It's caused some discord in the packs in Celestoria."

"That's none of my business."

"When you become Alpha King of Veiled Valley, it will be. They're part of the Allied Kingdoms just like you."

"Which is probably why her father reached out, trying to create a bridge between us."

Maeve narrows her eyes. "What are you up to, Aris? You're not considering marrying that self-righteous bitch, are you?"

"So you've met?" I smirk, and Maeve's glare turns cat-like and cutting.

"No, but I've heard rumors."

"Sounds like you hear a lot of rumors." My tone has more ice than I anticipated. Maeve turns away, huffing a breath.

"Whatever you're up to, I don't like it."

"You don't have to like it."

She looks at me again. Really looks at me. Sizes me up for several seconds before she angles her body toward Brie and Logan and walks off.

After brief, hushed goodbyes, the group disappears into thin air, and the castle groans all around me in silent triumph.

But when I reach the highest of the floors, just before the rooms above split off into the towers and spires, I realize I'm not alone.

Grandpa Ryatt moves from one side of his office to the other. It's a mid-sized room, a place he's laid claim to since he returned from Moonrise when Maeve came into power. The dark emerald walls and rich wood floors make the room look smaller than it is at first glance, and the dim lamplight casts long, inky shadows across the floorboards as I close the door behind me and sink my weight against it. He doesn't even look up from the papers in his hands. "Did they leave?"

"Yeah, just now. You didn't want to come down and say goodbye?"

"I spoke to the girls earlier today, when I arrived." He sits behind his desk and looks up at me, his dark hair and sharp, chiseled features looking decades younger than he is in the shadows. He was a startling handsome man once. There are a few photographs of them—him and Ella, as well as Isaac and Maddy, in their youth scattered around this castle. But he looks like something out of Grandma Ella's paintings now as he scans my face and bends his neck to scan the papers again before folding them neatly and tucking them in a drawer.

"I'll be in Maatua for the next two months, at least until after Solstice," he begins, motioning to one of the regal armchairs in front of his desk. He reaches for a bottle of the fine whiskey Isaac sends him and fills two glasses while I take a seat, sinking into the plush fabric cushions. "Are you planning on joining the family for Solstice?"

"Of course."

"Good."

I sip lightly, catching his gaze, waiting for him to confirm what Maeve brought up earlier.

"And what will you be doing with your time otherwise?"

"What needs to be done for Veiled Valley, I suppose."

He leans back in his chair to inspect me, his silver eyes, identical to mine, firm and inquisitive. "Blake has extended an invitation for the men to gather at his house before everyone leaves for Maatua."

"Blake is throwing a gentlemen's evening? That doesn't sound like him."

"It's likely something he and Soren cooked up. Those two have been attached at the hip lately."

I immediately think of Roman and banish his image from my mind. It's been a few weeks since we've spoken. It's all very formal when we do. His father is in the process of stepping down. Roman is engaged, getting married on Solstice to a woman from his pack. Tate and Miles are off in Tarsian with the Ghosts. Willow is on the air with that million-dollar smile in Crescent Falls, and the few times I've tuned in and seen her face, I wasn't able to tell whether or not Roman has grown a set of balls and rejected her.

But every time I think of Roman, I think of Posey, and I'd rather forget her entirely if I'm able to.

"Aris?" Grandpa Ryatt says to drag me out of my mind, and it works.

"Yeah?"

"You're aware of your mother's plans, I assume?"

I nod, but it's tight. "It's never been a secret that she longs to leave Veiled Valley and return to Moonrise to run the clinic."

"It's been her dream since she was a little girl," he says under his breath, a flash of grief lighting behind his eyes. "Being Alpha of Veiled Valley shouldn't have fallen on her, but we–" He halts, takes a slow breath, and continues, "we couldn't have more children, and she was enough, always has been."

I know for a fact Ryatt did everything he could to make sure Ella never went through another pregnancy. Not because it wasn't what they wanted, but because of what he had to witness the day my mother came into the world several months early, not breathing, dying beside her mother, his mate.

I used to not understand. My parents had the three of us. The house was always loud and busy. Mom loves babies, and I think she would have had more had Maeve not been breathing fire and getting herself lost in the aether before age one, but I digress. The look in my grandfather's eyes while he thinks about that time of his life, when he nearly lost his mate, I get it, for some odd, unreachable reason. Like I've felt that way before but can't place when or where.

"She's going to make the announcement during Solstice," he says, holding my gaze. "You'll ascend to Alpha of Veiled Valley and its territories. We'll hold the ceremony after the new year, so you have another two or three months to prepare and hone your skills."

"Sounds good to me."

One of his thick, dark brows twitches. "Does it?"

"I'm ready. I've been ready." I lean back in my chair. My phone buzzes in the pocket of my black slacks. I'm in the habit of ignoring it, finding every notification comes with a heavy dose of anxiety, of impending heartache.

"And what of the girl from Celestoria?"

"Who told you?"

"Your sisters." He arches a brow. "Is there anything you want to tell me, or is this going to be another damning surprise for the whole family?"

"I'm the last person you need to worry about, remember?"

GRAY LIKE ME

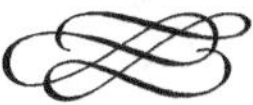

POSEY

SNOW COATS THE ANCIENT COBBLESTONE IN WET STREAKS OF SILVER. Flakes stick to my gray wool cloak, the hood pulled over my hair, which is braided down my back. I blend with the landscape in shades of steel and ash, but my black boots catch the gleam of lantern light swirling a familiar magic that settles in my bones and turns my heart to dust.

Roman walks beside me in silence, his phone screen illuminating the space between us in artificial blue-hued light. I try to swallow, but the knot of nerves pressing against my vocal cords makes it impossible.

"He knows I'm coming, right?" I ask in a croak that sounds like a toad. Roman nods, shrugging a shoulder like this isn't the end of the world as I know it. Like I haven't spent three months in a purgatory of my own making because of the man who lives in the castle now casting us in its snowy shadow. The castle itself is something out of a gothic fever dream. At least a half-dozen spires stretch into the thick clouds, and four towers stretch just as far. Stained glass windows cast dim light across a wide, circular driveway beyond the reach of the front gates, where a quartet of guards let us through, the steel grinding closed behind us.

I've been here before. Not in years, but I do have memories from this place. Warm, happy childhood moments that feel fuzzy and grainy when I try to think back on them. But now, in this uncommonly snowy weather, it feels like something out of my darkest nightmares, even after spending the last three months in an ancient temple continuing my studies as a priestess in training.

"When do you start at the local temple?" Roman asks, but his tone tells me he doesn't really care.

"Tomorrow. Immediately," I reply tightly, falling back a few steps. He approaches the absolutely massive front doors. This entire face of the castle is dark stone and stained glass, but it's dark enough that I wonder if anyone is home. I suppose it won't just be me and Aris here for the next month and a half or so, however long I'm stationed at the Temple of the Lunar Eclipse, the main temple of Veiled Valley. If all goes well, I'll say my vows just after the new year and can be stationed somewhere far, far away... perhaps Celestoria or even the furthest reaches of Tarsian. Hell, I've heard priestesses are being sent to the fae lands now. I could go there. Put hundreds upon thousands of miles between me and—

The doors open wide on a phantom wind. The breeze is warm, and it embraces me, thawing my chilled skin. But I feel like I'm pulled into the castle against my will. I take in my surroundings, trying to connect my blurry memories to the present, but a shadow moves into view and the doors close behind us. I hold my breath as Aris appears in... all of his glory.

Unfamiliar and dark.

His hair is much shorter than it was this summer. It's gelled back, which accentuates his sharp, chiseled features. He looks older and more refined, like he's been sculpted from smooth alabaster. His silver eyes are sharp and honed on Roman while he steps toward us, dressed in all black–a form fitting shirt and black trousers. His black cloak makes him look like the king he'll be one day soon.

His Shadowsynger bracelets of iron and gem catch the light of the dark crystal chandelier barely lighting the foyer.

I imagine him suddenly–a memory from this summer. Him leaning over the kitchen counter giving me a hard time about... something I can't remember while I cooked breakfast. It's a memory from before everything changed, before I ripped my own heart to shreds, and based on the cold look he gives me when he turns his gaze on mine, his heart, as well.

"How was the journey?" he asks Roman with no emotion in his voice whatsoever. It's deeper. Harder. Bitter.

"Snowy. You were right about that." Roman drops my trunk with a thud that echoes all around us. "I'm not staying long. I need to get back to Sapphire Ridge before the storm gets worse."

Aris nods. He's looking at Roman. His eyes won't even flicker in my direction. It's probably for the best because I can't take it. I hate that Roman is forcing my hand here. I hate that he still has authority over me even after three months away from home. *I hate that Aris agreed.*

"Have a drink with me before you go. We have business to discuss," Aris says, and his voice is so *foreign*. That iciness doesn't feel at all familiar. He turns on his heel, begins to walk away with Roman at his side, but stops, turning his head just enough that I can see the shadow of his profile. "Your room is on the fifth floor in the third tower. The house will show you there." He hesitates for a single second before walking away, leaving me in the foyer with my trunk.

I swallow back a sudden sob that makes the bones in my chest rattle.

A warm rush of air spirals around me before darting away, and suddenly my trunk is airborne and darting into the shadows of the corridor opposite of where Roman and Aris disappeared.

I'm sure most people would be thrown off in a situation like this– watching a trunk weighing more than a hundred pounds zipping through narrow, darkened corridors and up several flights of stairs, but I follow, unperturbed. I'm aware of the strange spirits here–a man and a woman, I believe, although I don't remember anyone speaking about them as separate entities. But I can feel the woman's presence now, beside me, while her partner dutifully carries the trunk to the highest reaches of my prison for the next six weeks... unless the Goddess really is on my side and strikes me dead, possibly with a fall down these insanely steep, narrow, uneven steps....

I glance behind me and feel pressure on my lower back, a soft *tsk* against the outer rim of my left ear, and a firm *no* whispered into my mind. I don't like the idea that these spirits can guess my every move, but I've studied entities like them for the past three months, so I know a lot of this is just my mind trying to rationalize what isn't in the least bit *rational*.

Before long, I'm tucked in a room that smells like clean linen and cashmere. A candle lights on its own accord along a wide, shallow dresser, scenting the room with hints of rosemary and vanilla. The dresser drawers open, and my clothing flies out of the trunk and into the drawers, perfectly folded. I whisper my thanks several times while I take in the room. The faded, dark floral wallpaper. The mural of the night sky on the ceiling. The arched windows of stained glass give a blurry view of the snowy landscape beyond. There's a bathroom attached to the room. It's not overly ornate but still decadent. Everything in this castle is dark wood, dark tile, and dark stone. It's glorious. It feels warm and cozy despite the frigid temperature outside. It's moody and overwhelming in the best way.

It's how I'd design a house, for sure. I curl my fingers into a fist on the bathroom counter and slowly look up at my reflection.

I barely recognize myself. I've lost weight unintentionally, and it shows in my face. My cheekbones are more pronounced, my lips slightly too full, and my eyes wan and lined with shadows. My hair definitely lost its luster after months spent inside in the depths of the royal library in Moonrise. Even more so in the ancient temple in Old Moonrise, since Prince Blake destroyed the other one, and it's currently being rebuilt using his own wealth, apparently. I wasn't much for the rumors and gossip among the priestesses and those in training, like me. Most of my time was spent studying what I hoped would be my specialty–the occult. Things beyond the veil of magic that spices our lands. Ghosts, paranormal activity, theories and lore that span thousands of years.

Surprisingly, at least to me, most of the trainees in my class want to be actual priestesses—the ones who hold the ceremonies and read the scriptures to the crowds. The ones that preside over marriage ceremonies and bless new babies.

I want to be forgotten, and what better way to do that than to chain myself to the deepest depths of academia and write papers about the unexplainable all day for the rest of my life?

I suppose I may be called to perform an exorcism eventually, but based on the fact there's only ever been three in our recorded history, probably not.

I'll wither like the books I've been reading.

"There are other rooms if this one is too dark for you."

I whirl toward Aris's voice. He's standing in the doorway looking like a god of death in all black. He takes a single step into the little light to be had, and the spirits hush. I sense them leaving the room. The silence left behind is so intense I can hear my heart beating.

"I like it. But I don't plan to stay." I twist toward the dresser and begin pulling my clothes out. "This was Roman's idea, not mine. The temple has an apartment I can use. All I need to do is say—"

"In the old rectory? With the collapsing roof?"

I clutch a dark brown, fluffy knit sweater between my hands. "I don't need to be here. I already feel like I'm invading your space. It wasn't my idea."

"You won't be in my way. It's just me here. Me and… a guest, who's arriving tomorrow. Roman explained that you're spending your days between the old temple and the archives in town. I agree with him that it's best if you stay here. You're closer to the archives that way. It's a five-minute walk."

"I really don't need—"

"Don't make this difficult for me," he says dryly, and I slowly look toward him over my shoulder. His eyes meet mine, completely, utterly void of emotion.

There's so much I want to say. So much I should have said this summer when I left. I ran out of time, and I realized it the second Roman snapped at me to go pack my things.

"I'm sorry," I whisper without meaning to. Maybe I do mean it. Maybe it's what I've wanted to say for months.

He just stares at me like he's looking right through me at the far wall, like I'm not even here.

"The house will do whatever you ask. Nothing is off limits to you. I have a small library but nothing like the archives. Dinner is served every night like clockwork at eight, but if you're not there, the house will bring food up to you."

"And breakfast and lunch?" I ask, my voice trembling. It's a stupid question. I shouldn't have spoken. I bite my lower lip, and his eyes dart to my mouth. My heart quickens at the memory of his lips–his mouth on my body... He looks away, pale, biting his lip and turning toward the door.

"I don't take formal meals right now. I'm very busy. I doubt you'll see me much, which I believe is best."

"Aris, can we–"

"Can we fuck again? No."

It's like I've been stabbed through the chest. I take a wobbly step back in surprise. His eyes are like cold fire as he holds my gaze, unbothered, not regretting the bite in his voice in the slightest.

"That's *not* what I was going to say."

"There's nothing to say. You made that very clear this summer. Goodnight, Posey."

He leaves and shuts the door with an aggressive snap. I yank at my dress–gray, like the rest of me. All the color seeped out long ago. I can't breathe. Maybe this is what I deserve. It's best that he hates me. If he hates me, he won't feel so conflicted in the end, will he?

When he finds out what I really am? I can't avoid spending a full moon here. My death at his hands would likely be swift.

SHE LIVES HERE NOW

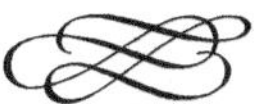

Aris

POSEY'S CLOAKED IN GRAY AS SHE APPROACHES THE CASTLE. I WATCH her through the window in my study, the way she's swallowed by the faint moonlight. The last remnants of sunset have been washed from the sky, driven back by the stars, but it does nothing to light her path after a day spent doing whatever the hell she does at the temple archives. I haven't asked in the few days she's been here. I haven't spoken to her at all since she arrived. She takes her meals in her room, just like me.

Seeing her again was startling. Seeing her here, lit by silver shadows? She looks like she is meant for this place, which is only making this worse.

The newspaper on my desk rustles as the house refills my glass of whiskey. I glance at the paper, at the headline on the front page, and stuff my fist in my pocket as I look away.

"Prince Aris of Veiled Valley engaged to Princess Morgan Ravenswood of Celestoria."

I was not the one to announce it. Neither was my family. Which

179

begs me to believe her idiot father was champing at the bit and spilled the beans before anything was confirmed. I had a single conversation with her at a ball I attended out of moral obligation to my aunts and uncles on that side of the family in Crescent Falls. Morgan had been there; we met, spoke briefly, and she'll do, I suppose. I don't feel strongly about it at all.

Maybe this is for the best. It's a weight off my shoulders. Finding my mate one day? It's damn near impossible, given what I am. It doesn't matter. I slide the paper in the trash can and sit behind my desk with a sigh.

Morgan is supposed to arrive tonight for a week-long stay which was, in the beginning, before an engagement was announced, supposed to be a time to get to know each other and for her to decide if she really wants to live in this dusty old castle. Based on the bright pink gown she wore to the ball, I highly doubt she'll like this place, but it doesn't really matter now, does it? She wants an entire horde of children, and I'll need a few heirs. She is tired of her social circles in Crescent Falls, and I'm never leaving Veiled Valley again if I can help it. She's single. I'm single. It makes sense to just say fuck it and sign on the dotted line.

I tuck back the drink in one swallow and move downstairs, my powers lighting the sconces before the house can get to them, much to their annoyance. I do need the practice.

I turn a corner and nearly run Posey over. She gasps in surprise, tripping over her feet on the stairs, but I grab her shoulders, move her to the side, and walk past her.

I don't look back, but my fingers flex and then curl into fists as her touch spirals through me and tangles into furious knots.

Her rejection aches. I'm not sure how to describe what the past several months have felt like, but I nearly told Roman no when he asked if Posey could stay here for the remainder of her training. Two months ago, if he'd asked the same question, I would have said that word without hesitation. *No,* she cannot stay here with me while she finishes her studies. *No,* I cannot and will not subject myself to her presence in my house, in my life.

I thought I was over it when he made that phone call and asked if Posey could stay here, that he'd feel better about her safety and care in my hands over the rectory. I agreed. I thought seeing Posey again would feel empty, a void of what was once there, and I could finally tell myself that there was nothing there to begin with.

How wrong I've been.

I walk straight outside into the gloom. The stars are bright overhead, but the ground is slick with ice. I make my way to the guard station. One of them turns to me, bowing slightly, and I nod, waving the formality off with a flick of my wrist. "Any word on Princess Morgan's arrival?"

"No, sir," the guard says with another bob of his head.

I should feel disappointed, shouldn't I? Instead, relief sweeps through me. I turn on my heel and walk back into the castle, kicking ice from my boots before gliding up the main staircase and into my wing of the house.

I shut the door and shed my cloak, tossing it over an armchair. The house groans around me, trembling slightly, and just as I'm unbuttoning my shirt, believing there's no way the princess–my future bride, by all means–is going to arrive tonight, my bedroom door snaps back open on a gust of fire-warmed wind and slams against the opposite wall.

"What?" I ask, looking up at the ceiling.

The door closes slightly and opens again with a crack. I hiss out a breath and stalk to the door, closing it tight and turning the deadbolt. The second I turn back around, the deadbolt slides free, and the door begins to open, but I slam my hand against it.

"What do you want?" I ask the house, trying to gauge which spirit is currently fucking with me. The woman carries that fire-warmed breeze. Cozy. Soft. Like sitting in front of a hearth on the chilliest day. She's also the most demanding. The male spirit is more likely to chuck a book across the room directly at my head to get my attention than repeatedly open and shut my bedroom door. Most inhabitants never even seem to notice there are two distinct entities here.

The door trembles slightly beneath my hand. Sighing, I release it, and it opens again.

She lights a single sconce in the hallway, letting it flicker several times. I scrub my hand over my face before ruffling my gelled hair, my shirt half unbuttoned, and slide back into my boots before following her into the hallway. The clouds are rolling in again, blocking out what little moon and starlight there is. The castle is nearly pitch black until she lights the sconces one by one, and I allow it. Normally, my powers keep the lights on, or Grandpa Ryatt's. Sometimes, my mom dabbles in her Shadowsynger gifts, but not so often anymore. And right now, it's just me here.

I end up in the formal dining room on the first floor, where I haven't dined in what feels like ages. The table is laid in a formal setting and piled with more food than one person could possibly eat.

"I'll take dinner in my room." I twist toward the door, which promptly slams shut and locks in my face.

That's when I hear a fork scrape against a porcelain plate.

Slowly, I turn back to the table. Posey sits several seats away from where the second and only other plate has been laid out. Her hair is tightly braided down her back, every strand in place, and her eyes are downcast as she stabs a piece of chicken with her fork but doesn't bring it to her mouth. She sets it down and begins to rise but winces when the spirit tucks her chair tightly against the table.

"You are not allowed to hold her against her will," I say to the room, glancing up at the chandelier, which rustles. In answer, the thick, ancient deadbolts on the door slide into place. I close my eyes and curl my fingers into my palms, trying to quiet the shadows threatening to burst to the surface and destroy the dining room altogether if it means getting out.

It takes a tremendous amount of effort to will my legs to work. I cross the room, sit at the table, and stare at my empty plate, my appetite completely forgotten.

"It's a man and a woman, isn't it?"

I lift my gaze to Posey. She's not looking at me, but that blush that haunts my dreams stains her cheeks, deepening every second that passes.

"The spirits that run the house? There're two." She tears a small bite of a dinner roll with her fingers but doesn't eat it.

I want her to look at me. I want to just see her eyes, see if they've changed as much as she has in the past several months. "You're correct."

Her smile is tight and faint–barely a quiver.

"How'd you figure it out?" I ask as I scan the spread, deciding on a glass of wine instead of actual food. "Not many people realize it."

"They've very distinct personalities. The female... she's the guardian, isn't she?" Posey finally meets my gaze. Her eyes are spectacular in this light–the deepest, most brilliant green I've ever witnessed.

I nod, my chest suddenly tight. "I believe she's the one that keeps everything running."

"And her mate is the trickster?"

"Her mate?" I hold her gaze.

She arches a brow, slightly confused. "You didn't know? They're definitely mates. I think... whoever they are, and whatever happened to them... it happened together. Here, in the house."

"Isn't that how hauntings work?" I sip my wine, letting the alcohol bloom through my veins to match my already disheveled appearance.

"They're not haunting the castle. They're... it's hard to explain. They're bound to it somehow." Silence falls over the table, highlighting the distance between us, which spans only a few platters of food neither of us are touching but feels like an ocean.

I run the base of my hands down my thighs and begin to apologize for how I spoke to her earlier even though... I know I meant every word, meant the hurt in my voice, but she didn't deserve that. It was just sex. I've never wanted it to mean more until it came to her, and I've been trying to reckon with that for months. It wasn't fair to her. I owe her–

"Congratulations," she says under her breath.

"For what?" My voice is hollow and void as I bring the wine to my lips.

"Your engagement. I just read the news."

I lower the glass, the wine suddenly foul and acidic. "Posey–"

She rises, and the deadbolts slide open. I notice a small copper band on her ring finger then, and the healed burn on her skin just beneath it. I rise, walking rapidly to catch her at the end of the table. She startles when I grab her by the wrist and pull her to a rough stop.

"What is that?"

She tries to twist out of my grasp, but I hold firm, sliding the ring back with my thumb until the deep, twisting scar is fully visible.

"Aris, stop!"

"What have you done to yourself?"

The doors fly open, and five figures waltz out of the shadows. I don't break Posey's gaze until a lifted female voice says, "Well, this place is absolutely… monstrous."

I drop Posey's hand and turn to the group. The woman at the center arches a brow as she looks around, chuckling. Her companion, a young man I've never met, follows suit, smirking and rolling his eyes at the gothic state of my ancestral home like they don't even see me standing here.

A trio of maids brings up the rear, carrying several heavy suitcases and trunks.

Far more than my fiancé needs for a week.

Princess Morgan's dark brown hair is perfectly curled and tied back. She steps into the room, the dim light casting her in shadows that make her look severe. She's tall and thin, her body shrouded in a bright pink pantsuit and matching wool coat that dusts her ankles. Her dark-eyed gaze falls on me, and she curtseys.

I lick my lips, taking a restorative breath, and say, "Princess Morgan. You're quite late."

"Let's drop the formalities, shall we? I fear we're past that already." She giggles, glancing at the man. I wait for her to introduce him, but she turns her attention to Posey, her smile fading. "And who is this?"

Everything. "Posey Sapphire. She's the sister of my friend and ally, the prince of Sapphire Ridge. She's a priestess in training." The words feel thick and wrong. I say them anyway. "She won't be in our way."

"Well, thank goodness for that. We have much to discuss, don't we, my dear?" Another lifted laugh, and then she snaps her fingers at the maids. "Where can they bring my things?"

"I'll show you to your room—"

Posey disappears in a flash of gray, skirting around the group without a glance back in my direction, and that ache in my chest blooms into real, bright pain when I take Morgan by the elbow to give her a tour of her... new home.

HE'S BEEN REJECTED

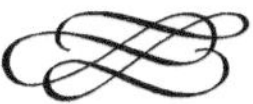

POSEY

WILLOW'S VOICE IS SOFT. I PRESS MY PHONE TO MY EAR WITH MY shoulder, the recesses of the archives spanning out before me in dusty shelves and varying shades of black. I'm at least four levels underground, and the air is thin and murky as I zigzag, trying to find the table I claimed for myself earlier this morning.

"So, wait, you're staying with Aris?"

"Yeah," I murmur, trying to keep my voice low even though I might be the first person to take an interest in this section of the archives in like a thousand years. I balance the heavy books, standing on my toes to peer over the shorter shelves toward the lamplight that seems like it's leagues away. "It wasn't my decision."

"Tell me again about this Morgan chick. She sounds awful."

"She's… gorgeous. Tall and lean, you know, like the models in your fashion magazines."

Willow snorts. "Come on, Posey. Their engagement is all over the news, but the royals haven't uttered a word about it. Is he for real?"

"I think so. I haven't spoken to him since she arrived."

Willow doesn't know about this summer. I have to remind myself that when I set the books down and sit with a huff. Shadows dance all around me. I adjust the lamp and set my phone down, pressing "speaker." Most of the time, I play music to fill the darkness, but tonight, Willow's voice is my welcome companion.

"Girl, you need to get me some insider info." She hisses and then laughs, the buzz of her fancy office building in Crescent Falls filling the void around me. "The public is clawing for information! Even Celestoria is quiet about this, but I mean, their news cycle is nothing like mine, as medieval as they are."

"I'd hardly consider Celestoria medieval." I laugh, cracking open a fresh text. Withered, yellow pages spread before me, smelling of parchment and faded ink from an era long lost to time.

"Oh, please. Have you ever been? Anyway, what do you know about her?"

"Less than you, probably."

"You're probably right." She lets out another rich laugh. I smile. I can't help it. Hearing Willow happy again? It feeds my soul in a way it hasn't been nourished in months. "Listen, I'm not saying you should sneak around and be my informant, but... I could... maybe... pay you to get a scoop for me?"

"I'm training to be a priestess, remember? What good is money to me?"

"*Boo,*" she sighs, and I imagine her rolling her eyes. "You know I hate being reminded of that."

"Look, she's... beautiful. Like a model. But she's mean, okay? When she saw me in the dining room last night, she looked like she wanted to scratch my eyes out just for being in Aris's presence, and I didn't like it."

"Well, he stuck up for you, right? I mean, Aris totally had the hots for you this summer..." She waits for me to argue, and I can't. Goddess, if she only knew. If I could just tell her... It would be such a weight off my chest. He didn't stick up for me. I'm not sure what I expected him to say.

"He... yeah. It's fine. I doubt I'll see either of them much. I'm busy."

"Reading dusty books about ghosts? Have you ever heard of lead poisoning? It's a real problem for historians because of all that ink."

"I'm not going to get lead poisoning," I grumble, but the ink is flaking off the pages when I turn them. "And I don't study ghosts."

"What else would you call it?"

"Uh, the spirit realm?"

"Boring," she giggles, and my eyes water. I miss her. I wish this summer had been different for *me* and *her*.

"Willow," I whisper, knowing only spirits and the Goddess Herself can overhear the conversation, "can I ask you something?"

"Only if it's not about Roman."

I take a deep, dusty breath. "Please?"

She's quiet for several seconds before grunting, which I take as submission.

"Did he reject you?"

"Do you really want to know?"

"Of course I do!"

"Don't hate me for what I'm about to say, okay?"

"I wouldn't–"

"And don't tell anyone I told you this."

"Who would I tell? You're my only friend."

"You better keep it that way. I don't like to share."

I smile. It's wet and wobbly. "Pinky promise."

"Good." She lowers her voice to a whisper like she has her lips pressed to the phone. "Posey, *I* rejected *him*. He came to Crescent Falls, came to my work, and demanded an audience with me. He..." She tapers off, and it sends my mind into a tailspin. I feel a sudden sense of dread drop over my shoulders like someone is pressing their hands into my flesh, baring down. "Posey... he offered to step—"

The call drops unexpectedly. "Willow?" I grab the phone as it beeps, staring at the single bar of service before it flickers and disappears. "Shit. Willow?" I try to call her back, but it's no use. I run my fingers through my hair, loosening the braid. It's late. Nearly midnight at this point, which I didn't realize until I see the time on my phone. Of course, Willow answered the phone. She works nights. Where has my brain been?

I try to call her back a second time, but just as the call drops, a crash sounds out in the distance behind me, echoing toward me and bouncing off every ancient shelf. I jump to my feet, my entire body tingling with adrenaline, and gather the books. "Nope," I whisper, sniffling as I fist the lamp–battery operated and the best purchase I've made so far for my new career–and whirl toward the sound. Blood rushes in my ears. I scan my murky surroundings and decide in an instant that I'm probably done for the day–at least here.

I've been avoiding the castle all day. I snuck out before the sun rose, sat in the temple for several hours, and scurried into the archives the second it opened for the day. Arthur, the little… *guy* that runs this place, whatever he is, knows I'm down here, because I'm, apparently, the only one brave enough to travel this deeply into his horde of knowledge since he was a child… which I believe might have been centuries ago. I'm too afraid to brooch the subject.

The brisk night air is a welcome relief to my lungs. I drink it in, my breath coming in misty white puffs. I move through the darkness carrying my books, which, technically, I shouldn't be allowed to just take from the archives, but Arthur watched me stalk by and simply glanced at me over the rims of his ridiculously thick half-moon spectacles.

The castle guards roll back the front gate without so much as a glance in my direction, having grown used to my comings and goings, and I'm thankful for it. I'm even more thankful when I reach my room without running into another soul.

I feel jittery and off center when I dump my books on my bedspread and change out of my gray cloak and my basic gray temple trainee robe. Technically, I don't need to wear them daily, especially here, where I'm nothing more than a researcher, studying to go into what the head priestesses in Moonrise deemed my "calling"… living in the dark, alone.

So be it.

The castle rustles around me–the spirits well aware of my presence—as I change into thick pajamas to combat the chill in the air tonight. But when I finish getting ready for bed and rifle through the books to find the text I'd been working on when I called Willow... I realize I left it in the archives.

"*No*," I whisper, rubbing my eyes. I'm too jittery to even think of falling asleep. My conversation with Willow plagues me as I debate my options. The text I needed was just a somewhat basic guide to ancient astronomy. I could likely find something similar here, in the castle's library.

With a sigh, I slip my feet into slippers and creep through the castle again, one of the spirits—the man, I think—lighting the way with each sconce that flares to life.

I remember the library from my childhood. It's wide at the base and funnels with each level, each subsequent floor spiraling into one of the spires of the castle and growing darker and darker with the climb. Small, arched windows let in moonlight when I move into the center of the main floor, but the lights are already on and dimmed, probably because the spirits realized I was coming this way and took care of that for me.

It's hard not to get distracted. This place is just... beautiful. Dark wood, black stone, silver finishes.... Yeah. I'd like to just disappear here. I'd have everything I'd ever need. Solitude. Books. The ever-watchful eye of the spirits who can drop food out of thin air. My fingertips graze spines of leather and fabric as I walk up the spiral staircase lined with shelves. Millions of books live here, I bet. I'd spend an entire lifetime counting. My fingers graze a leather-bound spine, and I stop, freeing a thick, incredibly old text about astronomy from its resting place.

"Nice," I murmur with a rough sigh and an ever quieter prayer.

I find a little nook on the third floor where an alcove rests in the embrace of three windows. A large, comfortable looking armchair swims in moonlight. I sit and crack open the book, my surroundings fading into obscurity.

A touch on my elbow has my arm, and the book, flying, my body whirling with force. I scream with effort as the book meets something hard.

Aris steps back with a pained grunt, covering his face with his arm.

"Oh, my Goddess! You scared me to death!" I rush out, flying out of my chair, my fingers thrumming with adrenaline. I gasp for breath as he lowers his arm, glowering.

He prods his cheekbone, which is reddened from the impact. "What the hell is the matter with you?"

"Me? You sn-snuck up on me!"

"This is my house. My library."

"It's past midnight! Why are you even awake?"

"I could ask you the same question." His gaze cuts me like a knife, and my heart relaxes enough for my mind to catch up with the fact I'm looking at *Aris*. I'm sharing space with *him. I just hit him in the face with an impossibly heavy book.*

"Oh–oh, I'm so sorry! I didn't–You scared me. It was an accident!"

He looks me up and down and rubs his cheek. "Obviously."

"I didn't know you were here."

"You didn't notice me sitting on the second floor, mere feet from the staircase?"

I shake my head and then notice the bottle in his hands when it catches the light. Whiskey. It's half empty, and I can smell it on his breath. He's wearing a casual sweatshirt and jeans, and for a moment, I feel like I'm back in his summer manor, at the side-table between us is the kitchen island, and he's smiling at me instead of cutting me to pieces with his glare.

He bends to pick the book up off the ground, scanning the cover. "What does astronomy have to do with our church?"

"A lot, actually."

He shrugs, handing the book back, but I hesitate to take it. I hate this. I hate this so much I could scream.

The words burble out of me before I can stop them.

"I'm sorry, Aris. I am. I really, really am."

"I've been hit harder. Trust me."

"No, for—for this summer." I can feel his gaze raking over my face, but I keep my eyes on the book in my hands. "I feel like—I hurt you in some way. That I ruined our friendship. I was in heat. I didn't know it was going to happen. I shouldn't have pressured you into—into sleeping with me—"

He takes a single step in my direction, his body suddenly rigid as steel. "You think you pressured me into sleeping with you?"

I wince. "I thought—I didn't stop us."

"I agreed to it."

I finally meet his eyes. For a moment, he's Aris again. Those silver eyes soften, boyish, gleaming in the moonlight. The same eyes that begged me to *stay with him*. I've spent months trying to rationalize his reasoning for offering that lifeline. He felt sorry for me, I'm sure. Felt some kind of ownership of me, like he owed me protection after everything. I've convinced myself it wasn't because he actually wanted me. *He couldn't have actually wanted me.*

My throat closes into a knot.

He scans my face, seeing the doubt, the shields I put back up, and his eyes turn icy again. He chuckles darkly, shaking his head. "You haven't changed a bit."

"What's that supposed to mean?" I bite out, every emotion I've felt the past months rushing to the surface. I hold them back, breathing deep, counting to ten in my head as he closes the distance between us.

Aris cages me in against the wall of the alcove.

DON'T GO SO DEEP

Posey

"You're lying to me about something," Aris says. My back hits the wall of the alcove. He braces a hand against the wall beside my head, tsking, his hooded eyes meeting mine under the cover of his lashes. "I've been trying to figure it out, you know? You felt like you didn't have any options when it came to the trajectory of your life, and I offered you an out." The words brush over my temple.

"You offered to marry me, Aris."

"And?"

"You don't love me. Doesn't that matter to you?"

He arches a brow. He smells like whiskey and smoke. Like he's been resting in front of a fire staring into the flames for hours. "I'm fucking *engaged* to someone I've met once. You tell me."

"You're drunk," I accuse him, and he smiles wryly, his brows arched.

"How'd you figure that one out?"

I lick my lips as his scent curls around my senses. Memories flash before me–a moment just like this, his body inches from mine, but his eyes had been dark with something other than hatred then. This is the side of Aris I don't know, even when we were kids and he bullied and teased me. This is who he can be. Cold. Dominant. Hateful. This is the side he shows others, the side that makes him an Alpha.

It hurts so much.

"Why do you hate me?" I ask, my voice trembling.

The question seems to catch him off guard. He lowers his hand from the wall and takes a step back, but his eyes catch on the ring on my finger. He rolls his lower lip between his teeth and meets my gaze again. "I don't *hate* you."

"Then what is your problem with me? Give me a straight answer because I can't take this."

"You want an answer, Posey? An answer to what, exactly? Why I can't stand to be in your presence? Why it feels like I need to rip out of my own fucking heart whenever I look at you?" The vitriol in his tone slices through me like the silver blades he joked about me making for him. Looking back, he wasn't joking, was he? He doesn't need the blades after all. His quicksilver eyes are doing just fine. "You did something to me this summer. Something about you–" He bares his teeth, struggling to put his mangled, drunken thoughts in order. He points at me, chuckling. "You know what, no. I'm not having this conversation with you."

"Then leave me alone."

"I live here!"

"Then, I will leave!" I go to step past him, but he blocks my exit, his hand braced on the railing overlooking the drop to the bottom floor of the library. "Move."

"What are you hiding?"

My heart stops. Panic blurs my senses. "I don't know what you mean."

"I offered you everything. You still said no. Still threw yourself into a life of solitude."

"I like being alone!"

"Do you think I don't know how you're spending your time here? Arthur is a long-time family friend. I've been in those same archives dozens of times, Posey. But you go deep underground where the books go to rot. Why?"

"Because I need—I need them for my research—"

"My cousin Blake," he seethes, "is a mystic. *The King of Mystics.* Anything you need to know about the spirit realm, you can ask him. I could call him here *now.*"

"Leave me alone," I warn as prickles of unease whisper over my skin, but he grabs my hand and yanks the copper ring off my finger so swiftly I don't realize it's happened until the unmarred skin burns anew, and I shriek, pulling my hand back against my chest.

He catches me before I collapse to my knees, my bubbling, blistering skin reddened and throbbing. He kneels with me pressed to his chest, and I don't fight it, not when it's taking all of my energy to remain me. Fight or flight is clawing for dominance, and one wrong move, one wrong breath, and I'll die, right here, in this beautiful library, and Aris will be the one to do it.

"It's to stop you from using your alchemy gifts, isn't it? I wondered when I saw it last night. You can't bend metals when your body is constantly trying to heal itself."

Tears sting my eyes. I'm transported back to those two nights at the hunting cabin, safe and warm in his arms. I try to stay there in those moments a little longer, but he continues, "If I catch you wearing it again..."

"What will you do, Aris? Kill me?"

"Worse. I'll lock you up here. I'll never let you leave."

Something heavy settles in my chest. His words and actions... Goddess, it's ridiculous. *It's mean.* I shouldn't be leaning so heavily into him right now, but there's only ever been one person who has come close to seeing through my bullshit, and it's him.

Which is why he's so dangerous right now.

His free hand ghosts up my back to clasp the nape of my neck, his fingers drumming against my pulse. He's counting my heartbeats, quietly holding me until my heart begins to calm, and my mind clears enough to...

"How would your fiancée feel about this?" I whisper and regret it immediately.

He doesn't move, but I can feel his wicked smile against the top of my head. "This means nothing, Posey. You made that perfectly clear this summer."

He abruptly lets go and rises like my touch is enough to burn his skin. The bottle of whiskey catches the light as he snatches it off the side table, glancing at what's left of the amber liquid and tucking it under his arm. He looks down at me where I'm still kneeling on the ground as if praying to his altar, unwilling to move, and smirks, dropping my ring in his pocket.

He looks at his palm with a slightly surprised expression that fades as quickly as it came and angles his hand to show me the circular burn on his skin. "Apparently, copper doesn't like me much, either."

My chest quivers with confusion, but he turns and stalks into the shadows out of sight.

The next morning when I fail to rise to my usual 5:00 A.M. alarm, I find a thick bandage on my finger and a jar of healing salve beside my bed. It wasn't the spirits. Aris's scent is faint when I slide my legs out of bed and look around. The astronomy book I left in the library rests on the little table beneath the windows, where wintery, silver sunlight bleeds through the curtains, and a note is lodged between the aging pages.

"Do not go into the depths of the archives again without me." Aris. I crumple the note and toss it in a little wastebasket in the bathroom and try to put last night behind me.

There's obviously something incredibly unsteady between us that wasn't there before. It yanks and pulls whenever he's near, and it hurts. I don't know how else to explain it.

I get ready for another day in the archives, disregarding Aris's note completely, and while walking through the castle, try to call Willow again, but she doesn't pick up. She's asleep, most likely.

The female spirit is with me when I head toward the foyer. She bustles around me like a little bird I can't see, but I have to say her presence is surprisingly calming. Like I'm alone but not totally. I don't mind it.

"Do you want to come with me? To the archives?" I ask in a whisper, and she flutters, making my hair lift off my shoulders. But her presence is suddenly swept away when I reach the final narrow hallway leading to the foyer, and I look around for any physical evidence that she's still here.

All I see is a door opened just a crack.

Muffled voices drift into the hallway. I crane my neck and hear Morgan speaking in low tones to her male companion, Talon, I believe is his name. He laughs under his breath and says, "Imagine what can be done here."

"Here? It's terrible. I feel like I'm catching a cold just from being here with all this dust."

My nose crinkles. It's not dusty in the slightest. The spirits keep this place so tidy.

"I feel like I haven't seen the sun in days, Talon. It's awful."

"A few more weeks, and we can return home, and all will be well."

"That's so easy for you to say," she coos. "You don't have to seduce the man."

He chuckles under his breath, followed by the sound of furniture shifting, like he's moving closer to her on a couch or bed. "Once the marriage is finalized, you'll be a wealthy woman, and you can do whatever you want. He can't keep you here."

I feel that same glimmer of unease from last night creeping back into existence. I take a single step down the hallway and stop, clutching the books I need to return to the archives. The back of my neck prickles. I slowly turn around.

"Are you spying on me, little church mouse?" Morgan steps out of the room in a glorious velvet robe that makes her look like she's floating over the black tiles. She closes the door with a soft click.

I say nothing. I just look at her, taking her in, watching the way her dark, cat-like eyes scan my face. She clicks her tongue and folds her arms under her chest.

I turn from her and hurry down the hallway, wincing at her

chuckle, but that uneasy feeling remains even after morning prayers at the temple and several hours spent in the archives, this time in the upper levels helping a priestess catalog books borrowed by the temple and putting them back in their places. Her name is Maria, and she's several decades older than me. Old enough to be my grandmother, at least, and just as kind.

"I find it hard to believe you're willingly going into the studies of the occult," she says as we sort through several volumes related to old church doctrines.

"Someone has to do it. Mother Anabella made it sound like no one has chosen this course of study in a long time."

"Well, she's correct." I can feel Maria's diamond blue gaze scanning my profile. "I know I haven't known you long, my dear, but I have a very hard time believing you're choosing this for yourself."

"I find study of the occult and spiritual realm fascinating. There're so many unanswered questions about our world and why we are the way we are."

"I'm talking about you, dear. You were a teacher before this. I did read your file when you were transferred from Moonrise."

I flinch. "I was."

"Did you not like it?"

"I loved it. I've always been good with children." *Every time I looked at my students, I saw a future I couldn't have. It was crushing. It was a constant reminder of what I am.* I blink, pulling myself back to the present.

"I've spoken to the head priestess of the temple in Lunaria. They're interested in you. I believe, once you take your vows, you may be called to join the North Star Temple. Would that interest you?"

Thousands of miles north? In a land where the sun barely rises? So far away from Aris that the memory of his warmth against my skin might fade?

My chest convulses, but I nod, turning back to our task.

I'm sent away when the sun sets by Arthur himself, who chides me about being in the lower levels alone, warning me in vivid detail that he's not sure whatever was imprisoned down there centuries ago has died yet, whatever that means, which is effective enough. Still, when I arrive at the castle and close myself in my room, the female spirit is already there. A gown of deep, glossy emerald flies out of the armoire I haven't so much as opened and hangs itself on the canopy of my bed.

I stare at the dress, at the way the silk ripples.

"Why?" I ask, and only a flutter of air answers.

BLOOD IN THE FOREST

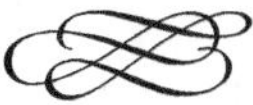

Aris

C RISP, CLEAR MOONLIGHT SNAKES BETWEEN THE GNARLED, FROST covered trees. My paws pound shallow snow, but I don't feel the cold bite. I needed this. Desperately. I needed to be out in my wolf form while leaving the rest of the world behind, even if just for a moment.

The castle fades into the distance. I race over hills and into shallow valleys, following the curve of a mountain creek, still burbling. Ice glimmers on the water's surface and starts to solidify the higher I climb, but the silver surface begins to darken, which catches my attention after an hour spent running, barely thinking, unable to form a single rational thought.

The human side of me spots blood before my wolf senses catch up to what I'm seeing.

I skid to a stop next to the creek, taking in the rich, iron scent. I follow the trail—bloody droplets at first, then a puddle, then a path where something large was dragged several yards into a clearing.

It's a deer.

I halt at the edge of the clearing, hackles raised, sniffing the air for any other signs of life nearby, but I'm alone, and this deer... it's obvious whoever preyed on it was doing it for the thrill of the kill and nothing more.

I shift back into my human form, my Shadowsynger bracelets and ghost-issued gloves cover my body in thick, winter armor. The deer's neck is in pieces, and she died with her eyes wide and glassy with fear, which strikes me in the chest. I get it, I suppose, the urge to hunt, to kill, to eat. But this deer wasn't killed for food, which I find incredibly wasteful, and based on the half dozen wolf prints littering the clearing, her torment was a group effort.

Veiled Valley has strict laws when it comes to hunting and access to what we consider our sacred mountains. My family, for eons practically, have been the guardians of this place and all who live here, which includes the mangled deer.

A hunt like this would have had to have been cleared by an Alpha and the meat salvaged for the pack, which begs me to believe this was a sporting match for the wolves responsible, and they left her here to rot, which boils my blood.

I crouch, examining her, running my gloved hands through her smooth fur. "What a waste," I hiss, furious, and then a twig snaps on the other side of the clearing, and my shadows ignite without warning.

The clearing fills with tendrils of depthless black, but they pull back when they reach the tree line. Whatever I felt that made me sense a threat fades and is quickly replaced by heartbreak.

A newborn fawn trembles in the shadow of the tree where it sought refuge, too terrified to make a noise. It's another female, I believe, her hide covered in frost. I slowly rise from my knees, clicking my tongue and making low, soft sounds so I don't startle her. Fawns should have been born months ago, in the spring, but she's fresh, likely only a few days old, young enough that her mother's demise is a death sentence.

"You're all right," I say like the animal can understand a Goddess-damned thing. She's too cold to move, to run away, which means it's only a matter of hours before she dies from the elements or something large makes her death swift, but for whatever reason, the moment I pick her up with every intent to make her death calm and quiet, I can't do it.

She's a soft, shivering bundle of weight in my arms. She's the victim here. Her mother is dead. There's no one to teach her how to survive on her own. She's in the arms of the enemy and too weak to do anything about it. She curls her head, tucking her nose against my chest—and submits.

TALON IS MORGAN'S GUARD. HE'S A TALL, PINCHED-FACED MAN WITH A ravenous appetite and has a total disregard for decorum as far as I've been able to tell, especially as he fills his third plate of food, chomping and slurping while Morgan watches me, a coy, tilted smile on her painted lips.

"I have some ideas for the wedding," she says causally, cutting a dainty slice of flesh from her steak.

"I think we're far from discussing a wedding at this point in time. We've known each other for the equivalent of thirty-six hours."

"People have been married in less time," she argues, rolling her eyes. "Don't they marry this quickly in the Deadlands, in those tribes?"

"No," I say.

Talon chuckles. "They just steal their brides, I believe."

"They have the tradition of paying bride prices, actually." I take a bite of steak, eyeing Talon from down the table. He only has eyes for his food.

"Anyway, I thought it would be best to have a wedding in Moon-risc, at the palace."

I laugh under my breath. "Uh, why?"

"Well, it would be a royal wedding. You're the queen's brother."

"Exactly. I have my own kingdom. We'll hold the wedding here."

She frowns and glances at Talon, who shrugs and goes back to his trough.

Morgan chews her lower lip in distaste and stares at me. I want to ask why she rushed the news of the engagement before an engagement was even discussed between us, but footsteps echo in the corridor beyond the dining room and a shadow appears before its owner does.

When Posey steps into the room, I suddenly find myself standing and walking in her direction before my dog brain catches up to my body. Curves. All of them. All of them on display in a deep, gorgeous, emerald silk dress that makes her rosy, alabaster skin gleam like moonlight on rose petals.

Her expression, however, when I pull out a seat near the head of the long table, is tight and uncomfortable. She wordlessly sinks into the chair and doesn't meet my gaze, but Morgan stares at us with venom swirling behind her eyes, and her gaze follows me to my seat and doesn't break until I'm seated and back to eating my dinner.

She rests her chin on her fist and smiles at Posey, but it's cruel, lifted in more of a grimace than anything sincere. "So, our resident church mouse takes dinner in our formal dining room," she muses, her eyes flicking to mine.

"Our?" I say before Posey's cheeks can color. "I wasn't aware we were married yet, but perhaps I'm wrong, seeing as I was also unaware of an engagement?"

Morgan frowns, but when I discreetly look in Posey's direction, I notice the deep breath she takes and the way her muscles relax.

"Anyway," Morgan damn near growls, her eyes rolling to mine. "If we're holding the wedding here, everything is going to need to be redone. This castle is just… too dark. I can barely see a foot in front of me."

She goes on and on, which is exactly what the past two days of her week-long stay have been like. Morgan talking about how ugly the castle is. Morgan talking about dresses and shoes. Morgan frowning at the idea of introducing herself to the leading ladies of Veiled Valley society. Morgan wanting to see the family vault and jewels.

I zone out and wonder if she knows I've stopped listening, and before long, Morgan and Talon leave the dining room altogether, and the air seems to return to the space, warming, like the house was purposefully keeping it so chilled my fiancée and her guard would be forced to leave eventually.

"You look nice," I say before my brain can catch up with my tongue.

Posey is several seats away on the opposite side of the table and once again not even touching her food. Her collarbone is on display, and I hate it. I want to cover it with my hands and bury my face in the side of her neck, just once, just to feel that warmth and comfort again.

She flexes her jaw before replying, "The spirit chose it. She wouldn't let me leave the room until I put it on. She's rather persuasive."

"Did she dangle her precious books over the bathtub?"

Her eyes flick in my direction before landing on her plate again. "No. Out the window."

I sigh, feeling some of the tension leave my chest, making room for the ever growing gaping void spreading there since this summer.

I rise, bracing my hands on the table for several seconds in thought, then ask, "Can I show you something?"

Her mouth twitches, but she hesitates before asking, "Are you giving me my ring back?"

"Never."

Her nostrils flare. She inhales, her eyes locking on mine—sharp and serious. "What do you want to show me?"

"Come." I tilt my head toward a side door, an idea striking me. She rises and follows but stays several steps behind as we move into the older part of the castle, where maids and servants used to live. Now, these rooms are mostly used for storage, but there is one room my grandparents renovated even though the spirits, somehow, keep us fed without it.

The kitchen is grand and opulent in shades of deep blue, gray, and black stone. A center island of black granite separates the kitchen into two parts, and I watch Posey walk around it, examining shelves and appliances, before she rounds the island and stops in her tracks.

The oven is on, blasting heat, and she stares at the ground, just out of my line of sight for several long, silent seconds before her eyes meet mine again, wide and unsure.

She kneels and disappears from sight behind the island.

I take several restorative breaths before walking around it from the other side.

"Where did you find it?"

"In the woods about ten miles north of here." I kneel on the other side of the cushion where the fawn is still asleep, thawing out. "I came across its mother first. She was dead. The fawn was born way late in the year, obviously, and couldn't survive without her mother."

Posey smooths her hand over the fawn's soft, short hide. Her stunning green eyes meet mine.

"I couldn't kill her. I thought about it. It would have probably been the merciful thing to do–"

"She's just a baby. I don't blame you." Her gaze holds firm for several seconds more before the fawn grunts, and she pets her some more. "What are you going to do with her now?"

I shrug, stretching my legs out in front of me. "I don't know. I haven't thought far ahead, but I couldn't leave her in the cold, and whatever group hunted her mother for blood sport might return, or something else would have taken her. I just… I know how it feels to be alone."

Posey purses her lips and tucks the fawn in tight.

"She's just a deer. Just a baby. It isn't fair, what happened to her."

"It's kind of you to care."

"She can't help what she is."

Posey looks right at me, her cheeks dusted pink as she toys with a loose thread on the blanket the fawn lies on.

I grind my jaw, trying to loosen the tension there. "Anyway, I notice you haven't been eating. You're thin. If you want to cook, this place is yours. No one will bother you here, and whatever ingredients you need, the spirits can bring you. Just ask, and it's yours."

"I–I don't need to do that. It would just be me eating."

"I would…" I taper off, take another breath, and continue, "I miss it. Having you cook for me like you did this summer."

Her smile is wistful. "Really?"

"Of course."

I don't think I've been able to bring myself to look at her this closely since she arrived. It hurts. It hurts in a way I didn't expect but probably should have anticipated after I kissed her for the first time and felt like my life was never going to be the same.

I walk her out of the kitchen after ten minutes spent convincing her that the fawn will be all right down here and that the female spirit has it covered, but when we walk through the old servants' quarters, she asks about the closed doors and winding, narrow staircases splitting off in multiple directions.

"This place is an actual maze, and most of the rooms in this area of the house are rotting. Stay out of them, please. I don't want you falling through the floor. That's the last thing I need."

She smiles again. It's faint, but gods, it kills me. I've been such a fucking dick, and I should say something about that, try to explain why but…

She asks, "Why are you doing it?"

"Doing what?"

"Marrying Morgan?"

I grit my teeth. "This was just supposed to be a visit. I was unprepared for the engagement announcement."

"But you're going through with it?"

"I guess so."

"Why?"

"Why not? Obviously I'm not attached to the idea of marrying for love."

"But you… hate her." Posey sounds so incredulous it almost makes me laugh. "And she hates the castle. I wanted to stab her with my fork when she started talking about replacing the stained glass in the foyer!"

"I need a wife." I catch her gaze on the staircase leading back to the dining room. *It could have been you. Probably should have been you, if I'm being honest.*

"You could have anyone, Aris, and you're choosing someone so vastly outside of what you actually need."

"I can't have anyone I want," I tell her, my voice low and gravelly.

"Of course you can–"

"Posey," I breathe, my hand gripping the doorknob. "Did you hear a single word I said to you this summer? I wanted *you*, and you didn't want me. Not like this." I open the door but can't bring myself to step into the light just yet. She looks radiant in my shadows, like she was meant for this, for moonlight and dark stone. For stained glass and magic in the air.

"I can't give you what you need," she says, her voice breaking. "And I hate that you hate me for it."

"I don't hate you. I could never hate–"

"There you are. I was looking all over for you!" Morgan's voice is thick with frustration as she rushes into the dining room.

Posey steps back into the shadows, turning to walk down to the kitchen, and I want nothing more than to go with her.

But I close the door.

THIS ISN'T WONDERLAND

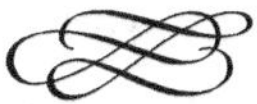

Posey

I LEAN ON THE DOOR AND TAKE SEVERAL ACHING BREATHS AS ARIS'S muffled voice replies to Morgan's incessant questions.

"I wanted you, and you didn't want me."

I close my eyes against the memory of his omission, but the words bounce through my skull, funneling deep into my gray matter, where hurt blooms into regret.

To make matters worse, knowing what I know now... I hear Aris say, "What can I do to please you, Morgan?" and it wrecks me more than anything I've ever felt or ever known. He sounds so defeated. So tired and broken, and it's my fault.

But I can't tell him the truth. It would hurt us both even further, and I don't think I'm strong enough for that.

I slink away from the door, carefully gliding down the stone steps in the thin, slipper-like shoes that match my dress. The air feels unnervingly cold until I reach the kitchen again and round the island, telling myself I'm here to check on the fawn and not to burst into tears without anyone seeing me. I crouch to run my fingers through the deer's short hair, remembering the baby girl needs a name. I flinch at a loud thud somewhere in the kitchen, followed by several clangs and echoes that reverberate throughout the space. The fawn twitches, but she doesn't wake up. I rise and scan the items now resting on the island that weren't there seconds ago. A huge bag of flour. A jar of yeast. A pitcher of warm water. I rest my hand on a massive wooden mixing bowl to stop it from rattling. That fire-warmed sensation blossoms around the room before settling like someone is standing at my side. I turn to her, the spirit, trying to imagine what she might have looked like and how old she was when she became trapped here, but she's nothing but air.

"Bread?" I ask like she'll suddenly speak and give me an answer. My fingers already ache from lack of use, lack of the copper ring that kept my alchemy at bay. It might be nice to mold and knead something even if it's not the iron and silver I long for, and maybe she knows that.

I dab my wet cheeks with the back of my hands, glancing around the room, taking in the sleek kitchen–impeccably clean. Only a small bottle rests in the sink where I wash my hands. I suppose it's for the fawn, who's sleeping so soundly she doesn't stir as the water runs.

Wordlessly, I get to work. After twenty minutes of measuring, letting the yeast bloom in warm water and honey, and mixing, I begin the arduous but blissful task of kneading the bread. I love the ache in my shoulders and triceps. The slight pinch in my wrists. The feeling of doing something for me instead of wringing my sore fingers and flipping pages to keep my hands busy.

The female spirit comes and goes mostly to check on the fawn, and I realize she's taken over the baby's care. I watch a wet rag slide over the countertop nearby, collecting bits of flour, and smile to myself. "What do you think he's going to do with the fawn? I doubt he can keep her. She won't stay this little forever."

"He's lonely."

I jump as the words skitter through my brain and down my spine. It's not at all like the mind-link. It's like she whispered directly against my ear, her voice soft and girlish, making me wonder if she was young when this, whatever it was, happened to her.

I continue kneading the dough long past the point I feel it's ready to proof. I watch the spirit move things around. She tucks the fawn in over and over, adjusting the blankets and the oven, which is still on and blasting heat. It's rather nice being here alone but not totally. I could get used to something like this.

The longer I spend here, the easier it is to determine when she's nearby. She's a warm presence–soft and cozy. She lifts my hair and brushes against my back when she passes, like she wants me to know she's here so she doesn't scare me, and I like that.

The male spirit, on the other hand, is more difficult to decipher.

I drop the dough in a bowl to rise and rinse my hands again, careful of the sleeping fawn, and feel the female presence rush out of the room, leaving a chill in her wake. I stand still for a moment, wondering where she went and why, then step into the hallway outside of the kitchen. It's unlit, swamped in shadows, and that bitter chill makes the darkness feel a thousand times larger than the hallway itself. The stairs leading up to the dining room gleam in fractals of light spilling from beneath the doorway where Aris looked at me like I'd absolutely shredded his heart this summer, and my body rejects the idea of going anywhere near that door, so I don't. I do exactly what he told me not to do and use my moment of total freedom from watchful eyes to peek into every single room on this floor of the castle. This level rests just below the main floor and seems to be carved into the cliffside. A few rooms on one side of the hallway have small angular windows letting in dusty moonlight, and Aris was right about these old rooms being used for storage now. The other, spider-like staircase is calling my name, however, and instead of traveling up, I walk down into the gloom, letting my hand drift along the wall, which grows damp and cold as the steps wind into the shadows.

Water drips on my head when I step into another hallway. I blink and narrow my eyes to squint into the darkness and several doors come into view. My exploration is brief–the first three rooms I find are old bedrooms, likely for servants. Beds made of wood lie in heaps, cracked and disintegrating with age.

I'm about to turn back to the staircase to check on the progress of my dough when my fingers begin to ache so violently I hiss out a breath and wring them out, and when I look up, I find the single door I've yet to open.

I probably shouldn't.

I desperately want to.

The second my fingers curl around the doorknob, I feel it. Iron. That slippery, moldable feeling that settles in my bones and sends my senses into a frenzy. I turn the knob, careful not to use my powers to mold the metal inadvertently, and push the door open with effort, choking on thick, stale air and dust the second I take a breath.

Moonlight illuminates wooden crates stacked to the ceiling. A worktable coated in centuries of dust rests in the center of a circular room, tools scattered like whoever used this space last left and never returned.

Metal spices the air. I step inside without thinking, the door snapping shut on a phantom wind behind me, sealing me inside what I can only describe as the workstation of my dreams.

A small forge rests along the exterior wall—long dormant and cold to the touch—but just a brush of my fingertips gives me a glimpse of the metals once melted here. I greedily pick through the layers of dust, grabbing handfuls of iron ore. Another crate is full of non-ferrous metals, but I'm more careful with those. My fingertips burn when they brush against clumps of raw copper. Bricks of gold line the bottom of one crate, while another holds a wealth of silver, which I find especially interesting.

I'm in heaven. I lose track of time completely, moving from one crate to the other, then to the wall where a wealth of alchemy tools hang in perfectly organized suspension on little hooks and—

"Wow," I whisper, carefully taking a heavy wooden box down from a shelf and resting it on the worktable. My fingers tingle as I pull a vial from its velvet-lined grave, holding the glass to the moonlight. A syrupy liquid slithers within, likely far, far past its prime, but I pop the cork anyway, which instantly crumbles in my hand.

Alchemy tonics. This one is… wild cherry pits, and… charcoal, and…. I take a step back to try to angle myself deeper in the moonlight to catch the color of the liquid, but the ground creaks painfully beneath me, then cracks.

My scream of alarm is swallowed by the sound of the floor giving way. The tonic drops from my hand, followed by the sound of glass shattering, and I have approximately one single second to reach for what remains of the floorboards before my body careens into thick shadows that will swallow me whole. My flailing hand grasps splintered wood for a second but then fails—and I fall for what seems like an eternity and then land with a thud that knocks the wind from my lungs.

"Oh…my…fucking…Goddess…." I gasp, trying to force my lungs to work, but the impact with what feels like stone has my body vibrating with pain. I gulp for air. Above me, a sliver of moonlight is the only view of the floor I just fell through, which is far above my head, and the floor is still crumbling. I manage to shield my face from the worst of the debris, but shards of wood pepper my legs and stomach for the several minutes it takes me to come back to my senses.

The sound of running water in the distance is the only noise other than my rapid heartbeat. I don't move until I can feel the pain in my body, thankfully only a dull ache. I wiggle my toes, gently bend my knees to ensure I haven't broken anything, then slowly sit up.

The air is sulfuric and heavy. I blink to clear my vision and look around. Darkness as black as pitch begins to form shapes and jagged angles while I debate what I quickly realize are limited options. I need to be able to see fully to get out of here. Aris is already going to kill me for disobeying him and exploring because what happened just now is exactly what he warned me about, so…

A sharp ache wanders up my spine. I take a greedy, dusty breath and open my eyes wide. A tingling sensation curls through my body, and my eyes glow.

My surroundings are... insane. This has to be an old part of the castle. Based on the carved stone, the outline of what I think might have been a grand hallway at one point, and shadows of doorways long crumbled to heaps of debris.

But as I start to move, my gown and slippers shredded, the landscape changes. Whatever building stood here before shifts to tunnels of stone and crystal. This is a cave.

I grip the wall to steady my shaking legs and keep moving, following the main path, trying to remember the layout of the castle above me. Shadows stretch for what feels like miles, and there's nothing here, but... destruction. Something terrible happened here. That's the only feeling lodged in my chest when the sound of dripping water fades, and is replaced by...

"Hello?" I croak, pausing at the entrance of an area so dark even my powers can't cut through it. Cold winter air makes me shiver, but it's fresh. Clean.

Whispers through the darkness reach me. A soft giggle. A guttural moan. Sounds of pleasure and pain, laughter and sorrow, mingled together in a rush. A breeze lifts my hair from my shoulders, and my fingers begin to ache anew.

I'm in the caves. Those ancient, sacred caves that run beneath Veiled Valley. The caves that call Shadowsyngers to what we've long called the ascension or the calling.

My throat bobs, but it's impossible to swallow. The darkness begins to flicker. I gasp as I take a single, determined step, and the walls of the cave shine with gems.

And objects.

Weapons and the remains of a bloody, terrible battle. Bones jut out from the rocky walls. Skulls lie shattered at my feet.

"*Come,*" whispers a voice against my ear, firm but uncertain. It's him, the male spirit. I feel his touch on my fingers and turn to him, his masculine, unshakable presence my only guide out of the darkness, and he knows exactly where he's leading me because we walk through a slice of shadow into an ancient, narrow, cave that bleeds into what remains of a corridor, and then a door appears. It's small and insignificant, and it groans against the act of a deadbolt sliding free after centuries of lack of use, and when it opens, I feel like I'm stepping back into the present, into the richness of the castle above.

The door closes behind me, and the spirit titters, checking me for injuries. My glowing eyes fade, and before me, nestled in the golden haze of sconces on either wall, a massive metal vault door stretches in every direction. Judging by the thundering footsteps on the spiral staircase just to my left…I shouldn't be here, and I'm about to die… or want to.

A creeping, icy sensation sweeps through me. I hear a scream. An anguished, terrified howl that cuts me to the core.

It's coming from the vault.

"What the fuck are you doing down here?"

BEHIND THE DOOR

Aris

Morgan's long fingers trace over the top of my hand, her red painted nails shining in the firelight as she smiles at me, cat-like, her dark eyes giving away nothing. When I don't react to her touch, she leans away to refill her glass of sparkling wine, clicking her tongue. She rises and turns around the room, that smile angling into a frown.

I bring my glass of scotch to my lips. I've been drinking more than I'd like. I feel sluggish, and the booze is doing nothing to fill the creeping void spreading in my chest with every hour that ticks by.

"My maids have been saying this place is haunted," she says with a small disbelieving laugh. "Idiots. It's just an old castle. I keep telling them that."

Her guard is asleep in an armchair by the fire, sprawled out and snoring. She passes him without a glance but comes to a stop near one of the windows. Icy silver lights fan over her skin, washing her out. What am I thinking?

"Was there a reason you chose to announce an engagement that hadn't happened yet?"

She looks at me over her slender shoulder. Her velvet robe falls over the shoulder in question–bare, her skin oiled and gleaming. "I thought, based on our correspondence over the past few weeks, that things were already set in motion. My father is proud."

"Your father jumped ahead in line without so much as speaking to me."

"You have to understand," she says in a low, seductive purr, "my father is merely the brother of an Alpha King. He doesn't even have his own pack anymore. No sons. No standing outside of his name and his familial relations. I have always been his greatest asset."

"Something to marry off?" I take a giant gulp of my drink, wincing and baring my teeth as the scotch burns down my throat.

"Precisely." She flips her hair over her shoulder and moves in my direction like a wolf stalking its prey. Silent, but sure. She sits beside me again, her hand resting on my upper thigh. Her touch has none of the warmth I need or want. It does nothing for me, but she's trying. Maybe I should try, too. "Look, Aris. You and I both need something out of this. I need status, and you need an heir. They're no details to work out."

"You hate this castle."

"I'm sure everyone does." She wrinkles her nose and looks around but then leans closer, nearly draping herself over my lap. "But we can change some things."

"No."

She recoils. I bring my drink to my lips again, staring into the fire. "Aris. Don't be like this. I want good things for us." Her hand moves higher. "You're a lonely man, aren't you? You seem like it. Imagine me here, warming this castle, bringing color back to your life."

I grip her fingers before she reaches my groin and move her hand away.

"I need to set something straight. First of all, this visit was meant to be just that–a visit. You'll return to Celestoria in four days' time."

She yanks her hand away and scowls.

"Then, I will make my decision."

"We're already engaged!"

"I do not see a ring on your finger." My voice is as bitter cold as ice. This isn't me. This seething, steely tone belongs to a man I've never met but apparently lives inside me. "Anything that has been announced is just rumor. It doesn't mean a thing unless it comes from the royal family directly. From me directly."

She rolls her neck, her perfume of roses and lilac heavy in the air between us. "Don't do this. This is what you wanted. You *agreed.*"

"I agreed to a visit so you could see where you'd be living and meet the people you'd be ruling over as Luna, and so far, all you've done is complain about the castle." I rise as a breeze ruffles the curtains. An uneasy feeling drifts through the room. I told the house spirits to leave Morgan alone, and so far, they have. Now, however, the female spirit's presence is thick and alarmed as she rattles the chandelier to get my attention, but outside, the wind is howling, carrying thick snow. Morgan probably believes the constant rattle is just the wind against the spires.

"It's an adjustment, to be sure." She places her hand on my chest, toying with the buttons. "But… remember when we met, Aris? At that ball? How much fun we had together? It can be like that again."

The glass is suddenly ripped from my hand by the spirit. It bounces off the rug, spilling ice.

Morgan frowns but doesn't move away while I scan the room, watching as the breeze skitters through the curtains in warning.

"This is about the church mouse, isn't it?"

"What?" I look down at her.

"Posey, that little ghost that haunts your castle. Why is she even here? The way you look at her makes me wonder if she's your paramour or something. I doubt the temple would like that." There's a warning in her voice, a silent challenge that immediately enrages me.

"Do not," I growl, "say her name again."

Morgan scoffs, but the chandelier rattles violently, and her grunt of displeasure shifts to a gasp of alarm.

"Excuse me," I say under my breath and whirl toward the door. Behind me, Morgan murmurs some curse under her breath, but the door closes with a snap, and then every sconce in the hallway flickers to life like a heartbeat.

My chest is in knots. I watch my powers flare in each bulb. My shadows beg to stretch, to seek.

A jolt of awareness has me moving before my mind can catch up, and then I'm in the dining room, the table still laid, wine glasses half empty and food uneaten.

"Where is she?" I shout at the room, and the door to the kitchen and old servants' quarters rips open. Now, I'm running.

I skid to a stop in the entrance of the kitchen. The fawn is still asleep, but a bowl of bread dough overflows, expanding over the kitchen counter. With a hiss, I search every room, ignoring the house trying to pull me in the direction of those ancient stairwells because… she better not have taken them down into the deepest levels of the castle. I told her to stay out of there.

Fucking Posey. This woman will be the death of me.

My anger reaches a peak when I find an open door in the lowest level of the castle. I've never been in this room before, but I can see why she ended up here. Her fingerprints are everywhere. She went through every crate, touched anything that could be touched, totally ignoring the danger she was in with every step she took in those fucking satin slippers. A smear of blood on the edge of the hole in the floor makes my stomach tumble to my toes. Dread renders my senses useless. I nearly jump, but the male spirit catches me by the shirt, holding fast.

"Where the fuck is she?!" I bellow.

When I find her…. Fuck. Any anger I feel vanishes.

I use my common sense and follow the male spirit to a safer path. I step off the last step leading to the family vault, which rises above us in a wall of pure iron. She's standing in the glare of two sconces, her gown in shambles, her body damp and covered in grime and small scrapes and bruises. Her hair is flattened against her head—wet, and full of shards of wood. She looks pitiful but uncharacteristically furious as she meets my gaze through her golden lashes, her cheeks crimson with a blush that's undoing me at the seams in real time.

I lean on the railing, giving myself a few seconds to collect myself, but it's no use. I explode.

"What the fuck are you doing down here? What the hell were you thinking? Posey? You fell through the fucking floor–"

"I'm aware," she grinds out, choked, her voice small but furious.

"You could have died. I warned you about this, didn't I? Or did you not listen to a word I said about–"

She cuts me off by pointing to the vault, her body shockingly still. Her shoulders are squared, her breathing coming in deep, even pulls, like she suddenly fell into a trance.

I step off the stairs, glancing at the vault door before approaching her. "What?"

She says nothing, just points, her fingers steady and unyielding.

I cock my head, closing the distance between us, and then I see it, the way her eyes are glowing faintly enough for me to notice. Her fingertips are hot when I grip her hand and try to drag her toward the staircase, but she fights it, her slippered feet sliding over the tiles. "What is the matter with you? Are you concussed?" I look down at her bloody, swollen fingers. She has dozens of splinters, likely from clawing and then hanging from the floorboards before she fell into the... into the fucking caves.

I let go of her hand and tuck mine in my pockets to stop myself from picking her up and throwing her over my shoulder. I have it in mind to chain her to my bed to keep her in one spot... in a totally innocent way, of course. Not that I wouldn't like to see her tied up in not much less than she's wearing now.

Her gown is barely holding together as she steps to the side and puts her hand on the vault.

"Don't you fucking dare," I warn, but the inner mechanisms click widely as she uses her alchemy to undo the intricate, magically warded room. "Stop it. Right now."

The door groans as the locks slide free–dozens. Some larger than others. I bite the inside of my cheek, torn between watching her use her insanely impressive magic and putting an end to this madness. In the end, I let her do it out of sheer awe.

"Posey."

She licks her lips, her eyes still glowing, and draws her hand away as the seam pops. The vault opens just enough for a sliver of light to fan over my body. I grab her before she can slip into the room. "I don't think so."

She clutches one of my bracelets in warning, arching a brow. It's so uncharacteristic of her, but I don't think she's totally in control right now. I guess I'm used to seeing this kind of behavior in people like Maeve and Blake–people with real, tangible magic that sometimes becomes too much. Magic that takes over and overwhelms everything else, and right now, Posey is thrumming with energy I can feel in my shadows, which shockingly, unnervingly, get excited at the prospect.

"What are you doing?" I ask slowly, reaching up to tuck a lock of her filthy hair behind her ear. "Snap out of it and talk to me."

"Your mask is broken, isn't it? It's why you don't wear it."

"It weighs more than you, for one. Two, it's ugly as fuck. Three, there's no point–"

"It's part of you. It calls out to you like it's been calling out to me since I came here." She doesn't sound like herself, and it's making the spirits dancing around us worried. The female titters nervously while the male shifts from one end of the room to the other like he doesn't know where exactly to hover. "I need to see it."

"No."

"Yes." She bares her teeth. I narrow my eyes, feeling suddenly uneasy.

"Posey, do you know where you are?"

She doesn't answer. Her hand is still wrapped around my wrist, and the metal is starting to warm, but her grip is insane.

"Posey?"

"I need it. I need to fix it. I need–to–I need to fix it." Her eyes suddenly roll back into her head. I catch her before she slumps backward. She goes totally, completely limp in my arms.

A great sigh of relief skitters around the room. The female spirit rushes around us.

"I don't need this," I tell myself. I carry her up the stairs, then more stairs, *and more stairs*, until I reach her bedroom. "This is the last thing I need right now."

"The mystic," the male spirit whispers against my ear, and I close my eyes, shaking my head.

"What is he going to do, huh? He's not the same, you know. He gave all that up."

"Impossible," he replies in that ghostly, low tone that skitters up my spine.

"She needs an outlet for this power," his female companion says on my other side, but she's further away. *"She'll fade. She locks so much of herself up."*

"You know it freaks me out when we speak like this," I remind them, and they go quiet. As I sit at her bedside, picking splinters from her heated fingers into the later hours of the night, I begin to wonder what exactly Posey has been hiding because–this power she has?

It's going to be an enormous problem for both of us.

YOU'RE DONE

Aris

"Do not make an enemy out of her."

Blake's violet eyes hold my gaze for several seconds before flicking to the corner of the room, where Skye is busy playing with Maeve's old dollhouse with the help of the female spirit, who seems incredibly fond of the girl. It's no wonder. Skye is like warm sunshine on the coldest day, even if she's strange and unreadable like her freak of a father.

Who... came when I called. Almost immediately.

"She hates me on a personal level already. I doubt that'll change much in the negative."

Blake tucks his hands in the pockets of his jacket, sucking his cheeks in thought. It's strange seeing him like this—casual. Laid back. Like whatever darkness that lived within has been stripped from his soul... or, my theory, he finally accepted it and stopped it from ruling his life.

The God of Death inspects the carpet with the toe of his boot before sinking into an armchair and leveling me with a firm look. "I'm serious. If she wants something to meld, give it to her."

"She fell through the floor and passed out in my arms last night. I'm not keen on giving her anything but a stern talking to."

"If you must." He leans back, crossing an ankle over his knee. "Alchemists are, by far, the most closely guarded secret in our family."

"This is Posey. She's not like that."

"You told me she doesn't use her gifts. I find it hard to believe she's been able to keep them contained thus far, as powerful as she is."

"I doubt she understands what she can do. She keeps them a secret from her own family." I tap my fingers on my thigh in thought. "I want you to look into her head–"

"No."

"Blake."

"It's not even that it would be crossing a boundary, but I can't."

"What do you mean, you can't?"

"She's different. Alchemists are... made different. I don't know how else to explain it. They can naturally capture power and turn it into something else. If she hasn't been properly trained in her powers, she could do so much harm to someone like me, or Skye, or you."

I roll my eyes, but Blake arches a brow.

"You don't believe me."

"I don't think it's that deep. She's hiding something, and I need to know what it is for her own safety."

"You're one to talk, seeing as you have a princess of Celestoria in this castle right now."

Now I'm leaning back in my chair and leveling him with the same icy scowl he used to be known for. Fatherhood has softened him. Hanging out with Soren constantly has roughed him up around the edges. He used to be a man of blunt honesty and smooth, immoveable lines.

Now, he's just Blake. My weird cousin with mind-bending powers and an aura that still makes me squirm. But still.... "Morgan is only here for a visit. The engagement is a rumor."

"We all figured as much."

"So the family is talking about it?"

"The grandparents, yeah. I took Marianna and the kids to visit Maddy and Isaac recently in Maatua–"

I wave a hand to shut him up. "I don't care about that right now. Morgan doesn't matter. What do I do about Posey?"

"Give her what she wants." He shrugs.

"Access to the family vault?" I snort a laugh, shaking my head. "No."

"Her powers took over last night, completely wiping her brain clean. That's a bad thing, *idiot*. What do you think happens when my powers, or Maeve's powers, or, hell, Lexa's beast form takes over completely?"

"A temple gets blown up?"

Blake glares. I count it as a win. "Give her the mask. Let her do what she needs to with it. Give her an outlet."

I don't mention that the spirits of the house said the Goddess-damned same thing, but the words settle like an anvil, and I kind of have to give it to her now, don't I?

Blake rises and stares at his daughter, the smallest of smiles on his face, but then he looks down at me, and that smile fades in an instant. He becomes serious. "I expect your presence at Solstice. Soren and I–"

"Your gentlemen's evening?" I smirk, and his glare deepens.

"It's an important gathering of the ruling men in our generation, yes."

Something sharp twists in my stomach. "Succession already?"

He nods. It's short and sharp, and he looks at Skye again with a sigh he tries hard to stifle. "You've been holed up here, so you haven't heard the news, but Adrien found his mate a few weeks ago."

I think of Misty and Cole's son–their oldest. The son she was pregnant with during the war against the Arcane Umbra. I don't like Blake's tone as he continues, "He traveled to Tarsian to visit the Alpha King of Oasia with Cole. Cole's friend Declan is still a prince, you know, his father–"

"I'm aware of the connection." And history, for Goddess' sake, especially the fact that Cole gave up the title of Alpha King to Declan's father after the war.

"Declan and Georgia's daughter, Eva, is Adrien's mate. Any child of theirs in the future will have a claim to Tarsian, and Maeve is already scheming to use that to her advantage."

"It would create an official monopoly of power for our family."

"Yes." Blake checks his watch. "And with Soren's ascension as the Alpha King of the Roguelands, and our family to the south in the Deadlands… we have a lot to discuss about who gets what when these kids come of age. Your kingdom, of course, is its own. Whatever children you have with Morgan–"

"I'm undecided on that front."

I can feel Blake staring, but I refuse to meet his gaze. He's silent for several seconds, the quiet broken by Skye's squeals of delight when the spirit makes the dollhouse's lights flicker.

Finally, he asks, "Do you want me to speak to Posey about what we discussed?"

"No. I'll handle it."

"If she fights it, say it's by royal decree. We need her. She's invaluable to our family."

I exhale deeply. He has no idea how fucking stubborn that woman can be. I doubt a decree will make a Goddess-damned difference. Again, I imagine having to chain her to the bed to keep her here, and that's looking more likely with each passing second.

POSEY

BANDAGES WEAVE LIGHTLY AROUND MY FINGERTIPS. I EXAMINE THEM IN the silvery winter sunlight fanning through the thick curtains. I stopped trying to escape my room two hours ago, when it became evident that I'd been given some type of tonic to calm my nerves, which also successfully blocked most of my resonance, which meant bending the iron door jamb wasn't an option.

Still, when the door finally opens midmorning, I fly out of bed only to stop short when Aris darkens the doorway.

I grip the fourposter for support. He steps into the light, kicking the door shut behind him, his face set in neutrality as he carries a heavy wooden box toward me.

"We need to talk," he says, and I expected this. *Of course I did.* I fell through the floor and then, essentially, blacked out. I have vague memories of last night, but they're jumbled, broken by that sharp pain in my fingers that grows worse when he sets the box on the foot of my bed and lets his shadows creep from his fingertips, unlocking it with his powers.

I chew my lip. I should move, step out of his way and angle my body for a full view of the box's contents, but the cold look on his face is killing me.

"Is the fawn okay?" I ask, and his expression softens for several seconds before hardening to ice again.

"She's fine. Your dough, on the other hand, had to be tossed out."

He reaches into the box and pulls out... *Goddess.*

"I need you to listen to me very carefully. Do not speak. Do not give me an answer until you hear me out."

He turns the... *Holy shit. The Shadowsynger mask.* He angles it into the sunlight, and it's....

I find it hard to swallow. My powers rile. I choke them down, wishing I had that copper ring again. So badly.

The mask is hard to explain. It's very old and meant to completely cover his face. Three prongs of iron protect the cheeks, the nose, and chin. Gems of unnatural origin are dotted throughout, but several are missing, and one of the prongs is mangled, like whoever wore it last took a catastrophic blow to the side of the face, which is likely what happened judging by the state of the artifact. It's so old. It looks like it'll shatter in his hands with one wrong move.

It can't hold his powers in this state. Not like his bracelets or his grandfather's sword of shadow can.

"You're useful to me," he says under his breath like it's painful, like he doesn't want to be saying it, "and therefore… *priceless* to my kingdom. To my family. You shouldn't have been able to open the vault. No one can do it unless they're like me, my mother, or my grandfather. It was built that way."

"My father–"

"Can't. I confirmed it. It can only be opened by a Shadowsynger or…"

I don't understand. "Aris–"

"You're an incredibly powerful alchemist, Posey, and I cannot allow that to be wasted. My family cannot allow it, and that means you are no longer *allowed* to become a priestess."

He finally meets my eyes.

I hadn't expected them to be shining with what I can only describe as guilt. I should argue. In any other circumstance, I would, but the look he's giving me is almost enough to bring me to my knees.

"What?"

"You were pulled from the training program this morning. Your robes were returned. Your name will be scrubbed from the list of trainees. You're no longer a priestess in training. You're mine. My alchemist. And you're going to fix this for me."

He shoves the mask into my hands. I almost drop it. It's heavy. Much heavier than I expected it to be.

"I–I can't. Aris, I can't stay here–"

"Neither of us have a choice now, Posey." He turns toward the door and takes several determined steps in its direction, then stops, saying over his shoulder, "I'll show you your new workspace when it's ready."

"Aris, I can't stay here!" I shout, clutching the mask for dear life.

"Why? Are you ready to tell me the truth?"

Dread knocks me sideways. Somehow, someway, I remain standing, gripping the mask like it's my only lifeline. I think about the moon cycle, about my heat this summer, how I haven't had one since. I count the days until the next full moon. Barely a week.

When I don't reply and instead clamp my mouth shut, he turns ever so slightly, brows raised. "Are you in love with someone else?"

"What? No."

"Were you really dead set on being a priestess, then? Was it really what you wanted? Tell me the truth."

"You won't believe me. You never have."

"I'll believe you now. Tell me you want to be a priestess, and I'll make it happen, my sister and cousin be damned. What do you want? Do you want this?" He points at the mask. I wonder if he can see the excitement in my eyes, if he can see the dread dripping off me like sweat, if he notices how I'm falling to pieces right in front of him. "Or do you want to go? Because I cannot stand here in your presence any longer. It's killing me. You being here is killing me, Posey. I'm supposed to be bonding with my fiancé. If you leave–if you want to be a priestess, I'll make it happen even if I don't think you should."

"I'm sorry I'm getting in your way of that–"

He raises a hand and looks at the floor like he can't stand to hold my gaze for another second. *I did this to us. This is my fault...*

"Do you want freedom to use your alchemy with my family's protection or to be a priestess? If it's the latter, I'll have you stationed elsewhere."

"Can I ask a few questions?"

He rolls his eyes to the ceiling and laughs, but it's bitter. "Alchemy it is."

"Wait!"

"If you're going to ask if your family will find out, don't bother. They won't."

"But how?"

"It's not your problem."

"It is because if they know I can do alchemy, they'll think I can shift!"

"Can you?" His tone slices the air between us into pieces. He hates me. *Hates me so much, and it's killing me, but it's what I deserve.*

Another lie slips free. "No. I can't."

Silence fills the room like poisonous gas–suffocating and caustic. I watch Aris's chest rise and fall, watch the way his fingers clench into fists at his sides, and wait.

"Do not leave this room until I come back."

"Am I your prisoner?" I spit, letting my tangled thoughts turn to fury.

The door clicking shut and locking in his wake is my answer.

WE HAVE TO GO TOGETHER

POSEY

THE SUN SETS OVER THE MOUNTAINS WHEN ARIS RETURNS. HIS shadows pierce the bright pink light of the alpine glow, his boots moving across the floor, disrupting the stillness that's been enveloping me for hours.

I've been sitting in the same position since he left, dressed in the same thin nightgown, holding the mask in my hands. I've been in a trance, letting my powers dance in a way they never have while inspecting and investigating every groove and divot, every master's brush of hot iron and alloys to strengthen the mask.

Whatever I do, I can't think about my current situation. I'll fall apart. Falling apart means losing my grip on reality, and if I lose that...

"Posey."

I look up. My eyes feel dry and scratchy. I'm not sure I've blinked since he left... hours ago.

The door is wide open. His shadows dance around the room—

which is much emptier than I remember it being, like everything has been cleared out since this morning right from underneath my nose.

We wordlessly weave through the castle. He lets me hold the mask. He doesn't even move to take it from my hands, which are surprisingly steady. I let my mind wander, let fractured thoughts and memories creep in before banishing them. I wonder what Morgan is up to, what kind of schemes she has planned. I wonder about Roman. I wonder about Willow, and I stop in my tracks. "My phone–"

"Is on a charger in your new quarters," Aris replies without skipping a beat.

"Aris?"

He slips into the shadows when we round a curve, and when the sconces light, I watch his body move through the dim haze and through the slit of two heavy black velvet curtains.

My stomach dips to my toes, but I follow. I have no choice. It's not like I've ever had a choice.

Becoming a priestess was the only thing I ever decided for myself.

I swallow back my gasp. It rumbles through my lungs and comes out as a strangled whimper.

We're in one of the spires, at its base, where the rooms are almost circular and covered in narrow, angular windows letting in strips of violet light. Stars are just beginning to flicker to life beyond the glass.

But it's the room that's taking up every thought and feeling. Aris comes to a stop in the center of the space, watching me, his arms crossed over his chest and his face cast in shadow of his own making. His power thrums off him. I can feel it in the air between us like an electric current driven by his emotions… primarily anger. Righteous, perfectly placed rage. I don't blame him. I can't. I did this to us.

"I had everything moved here, where the floor is stable." He motions to the floor, which is sturdy, a mix of wood and iron beams running throughout. "I don't have the ability to make you a forge here, but Blake has it in mind to have you moved to Moonrise."

"I don't need a forge," I whisper, my eyes on the work tables, the shelves, and the tools. It's mostly bare but won't be for long. Not if I–

"Aris?"

"Yes, Posey?"

I love you. I love you. *I love you.* "Are you sure?"

"Are you?"

"It kind of sounds like I don't have a choice in the matter."

"If you can get into our family vault, you can fix the mask... and other things. You can create necklaces and bracelets to keep our powers safely contained. You can create weapons."

"I know what I can do."

I set the mask down on the nearest worktable and turn my back to Aris to scan the crates I've already picked through. Everything from that old room is here. I run my fingers over the old tools, however, and recoil when my fingertips trace hints of copper alloy. "I can't use these."

"I'll have new tools ordered. Whatever you need."

"I can make my own." I slowly turn back to him, but my eyes are on the ceiling where a spider's web of rafters funnels upward into the dark heights of the spire. This was my dream once, when I thought I still had a future. Days and nights spent practicing alchemy. Being useful. Being wanted for something.

Now, it feels like a blade in my heart.

I have only days here. That's it. Unless I somehow throw myself headfirst into alchemy, let it consume me. Eat and breathe metal until there's nothing left of me but my skill set.

"I need–"

"Herbs for tinctures and tonics, I know. The house has it covered. The kitchen is yours."

My eyes fall to Aris's face. Exhaustion lines his eyes, making him look older and harder, all traces of those innocent moments at the hunting cabin lost in the hell I made for us personally. "You'll have full access to the castle still as it stands, but you're forbidden from going to the temple and archives until Blake smooths this over and scrubs your history from them."

"Why would he need to do that?"

"So that no one knows who you are and what you can do. For your own safety."

I stare at him, trying to read behind the neutral, unaffected expression painting his face in cold shadow.

He steps toward me, tucking his hands behind his back, and begins to pace. "Anything you need is yours. Supplies, tonics, research materials. Ask, and you'll have it. You'll be paid for your work, of course. You'll live here for the time being until Blake and Maeve decide–"

"Why would they get a say? Shadowsyngers and alchemists are, historically, one unit."

He stops pacing and looks at me over his shoulder, and I swear I see a hint of a smile. "I know. They're trying to argue their point, that you're useful to all of us and not just me."

"The Firestones had their own forges once. They were notoriously wary of alchemists."

"I'm aware of the history," he replies, but his voice is lighter, and his silver eyes hold mine as I walk across the room, feeling the resonance of the iron beneath my feet hum against my powers.

"I do not work for the Firestones nor mystics. It's never been that way. I work for… you. I have to work for you."

I turn back to him, the distance between us like a great, violent ocean. Shadows shift over his body, and he angles to face me, his hands in his pockets, and asks, "Then you'll stay?"

"My other option is becoming a priestess."

"Your only other option is letting your unused powers consume you, like they almost did last night. You'd die eventually from it, you know. It would eat away at you until it grew too much for your body to handle."

"So this is all I can do," I whisper, more to myself than to him.

"I don't know how to fix this for you, Posey." *You won't let me fix it. You are killing me with every passing second I have to spend in your presence. What did I do wrong?*

I blink, looking down at my feet in confusion at what I'm sure were his inner thoughts drifting through my mind in a whisper. I'm imagining things, obviously. I'm going insane.

When I don't speak for several moments, he says, "I know you've felt trapped your entire life. You've never had a choice in anything until you choose to become a priestess. If you don't want to do this, to be this, at any point, I will release you from your duty to me and Veiled Valley, but as long as you're here, working for me, I will guard you and protect you. In the spring, when the snow clears, I'll have one of the guest houses cleared out and renovated for you. I'll build a new workshop so we're not..." *Sharing space. So I don't have to see you while spending my days with Morgan, or whoever comes next, because I can't take it. What is wrong with me? What's wrong with us?*

I squeeze my eyes shut and rub my temples.

"Are you all right?"

"Just a headache," I lie while my body thrums with a sudden knowing. "Did you–did you give me something last night?"

"A healing tonic–"

"No, did you use your powers on me in any way?"

He shakes his head. "No. Is something wrong? Are you hurt?"

I glance at him and then at where I left the mask resting on the worktable. "I think it's the mask. It's broken, and my powers are... I'd like to fix it soon so it leaves me alone."

He takes a single step in my direction, but it's guarded, like he isn't sure if he should continue. "What do you need?"

I take a deep breath to settle myself, to let my mind function properly again. "I think I have everything I need already, supply wise. I do need some new tonics for myself, though, because the mask has alloys I don't recognize, and confirming how it was made and what alloys were used is going to take a tremendous amount of power and strength, and I'm... untrained."

"You are very powerful, Posey." His voice is low and level. I steal a glance, my heart skipping a beat when I notice his gaze on my neck, his eyes wan and hooded by shadows. Sad, aching shadows.

I chew my lower lip before replying, "I need a few books from the archives."

"No."

"I need to research. It's not that big of a deal. I need to make the tonics myself because alchemy tonics are very hard to acquire. Roman can attest to that. I made tonics for him and my dad all the time, but what I need is different. I also need some studying material on alloys and nonferrous metals because my resonance is profoundly iron leaning and things like copper–"

"Burn."

"Yes," I breathe, feeling more confident. "Exactly. I'll hurt us both if I'm not totally sure I have everything I need, and I like to research instead of just going for it." He looks at the mask for several seconds, scanning the same bent and gnarled metal. I step toward him this time, and that ocean between us narrows to a river. "I need to know how this happened, how this kind of damage was done. So much was lost during the Great War. Do you know what happened to the man who wore this mask?"

"No," Aris admits, his voice low and gravelly. He hangs his head for a moment in thought before adding, "You're correct. My great-grandfather Westfall was enslaved by King Kane and was a child when Veiled Valley lost its Alpha King, his grandfather. He doesn't know what happened to his parents. They were young when he was separated from them. He raised my grandpa in Moonrise as a warrior trainee to try to keep him safe, to try to continue to keep Veiled Valley safe, and brought Grandpa Ryatt to the caves for the ascension cere-mony. That was the first time the caves called to anyone and the last time they called to anyone until me. Everything before that is a mess. We don't know what happened."

"But the spirits of the house do," I offer, taking another step. He notices, stiffens, then relaxes when I step past him to run my finger-tips over the mask. "And Arthur might have something in those archives."

"You're not going back down there."

"You said I couldn't go without you."

He grinds his teeth, and I notice the flicker of unease. I arch a brow. "Are you scared of the archives?"

"The depths you've gone to? Yes."

"It's not that bad if you have a lantern."

"I can have Arthur fetch anything you need."

"He won't go down there either, which is why I went down there myself."

"Posey–"

We're close enough now that the river between us is a creek.

"You have to wear the mask while I'm doing the more complicated repairs," I explain, my voice suddenly tight. "I could hurt you, Aris. I want to make sure I'm doing it right, that I have everything I need so I don't hurt you."

"You've already–" He cuts himself off abruptly and then turns, giving me his back. His golden hair shines in the moonlight. He runs his fingers through it with a sigh. "We'll go to the archives tomorrow morning. Whatever you need." He takes a steadying breath before facing me. "I have to leave in four days for a meeting with my cousins in Moonrise. You'll have the castle to yourself."

"What about Morgan?"

He rolls his lower lip between his teeth, and his gaze locks on mine. I shiver under the weight of it, of the movement of his teeth and tongue. "What about her?"

"Are you…. Is she…" I look down at my hands, wringing them. The bandages are still tight, but my skin is warm, reminding me of the heat from the fever I had months ago.

"I'll do what I have to do for my pack and kingdom," he says, his voice low and every ounce the Alpha that he'll be one day. But he reaches out to tuck a lock of hair behind my ear, and when I meet his eyes again, they're soft. He pulls away, tucking his hand back in his pocket like touching me burned him.

"Tomorrow morning, then." With that, he leaves in the shadows, and I turn back to the mask, wondering why the Goddess is punishing me like this. I suppose I already know.

PLEASURE AND PAIN

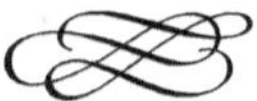

POSEY

I DON'T DESERVE THIS FOR WHAT I'VE DONE. THIS ROOM. THIS DREAM of mine coming to fruition. I run my fingers over every surface, count the steps from one side of the room to the other, and stare out of the trio of windows along the curve of the wall for a long time.

The stars hang heavy when I finally ask the spirits of the house for help. The female is eager, pleased with the state of the room and the list I give her, which is quickly whisked away and disappears into the shadows of the highest rafters, where my footsteps echo as the male spirit moves things around and reorients the space for me. I only leave to change out of my pajamas in the adjoining bedroom, which is small but cozy and well furnished, when I realize there is no way I'm sleeping tonight, not with my thoughts so tangled and my heart wracked by guilt.

I try to call Willow in the earliest hours of the morning, when the nearly full moon is high, and the sky turns a milky violet, but the call goes to voicemail, and I can't bring myself to even say, "Hey, I really need someone to talk to. There's so much I need to say to just…

anyone." Then, I just walked around, weaving through quiet hallways, trying to still my thoughts.

The castle is dark and coated in shadows when I make my way back to my new rooms. My booted footsteps sound on the staircase leading up to my spire, where the door is still slightly ajar. I rub my eyes to make sure the scene in front of me is real. A basket of dried herbs rests on the worktable, which is now positioned under the windows, drenched in moonlight, and along the far wall, a table-top burner stove is seated on one of the counters running the length of the room, and pots and pans are stacked on the shelves above. Glass vials that glimmer in the starlight–empty and ready for the tonics I need to make–are also situated there. A rocking chair gently creaks near the roaring fireplace.

It's cozy. It smells like metal and herbs. Outside, the moonlight flickers through clouds, and it's dark again. Snow begins to fall while I spend the rest of the night, and the first light of morning, running my fingers over the mask, trying to figure out why it feels incomplete. It doesn't make any sense. A mask like this was incredibly hard to make, I believe. It would have taken an alchemist of tremendous skill to meld the pieces and inlay gems as thick as this. They would have used a forge, I think. They would have had to. Unless... whoever made this is as powerful as I am, apparently.

I run my thumb over one of the thick prongs. The iron heats, glowing under my touch, and the jagged, bent edges of the broken piece smooth... almost too easily.

I set the mask down and step back, massaging my aching fingers and shaking my head.

I have no formal alchemy training, but I developed my gifts early, before Roman was even experimenting in our father's alchemy room. My skill set wasn't the priority–Roman's was. No one asked; no one would have cared if I brought up the fact I was bending iron ore and knew nickel and silver were my alloys of choice by the time I was thirteen, so I never mentioned it.

Females of an alchemist line are never this powerful. At least, that's what I was told. Our purpose was solely ensuring alchemy was passed down through the generations, and for a while, until I knew I was different, I figured my impressive skills would make my parents proud when it came time for me to marry and... breed.

I look at my hands. At my narrow fingers. My soft palms. I turn them over, inspecting them like they're new to me, wondering what Aris sees in me that I haven't seen in myself. What his family sees in me. What I've done that's so impressive compared to my father and brother, who've worked with his family for years.

I finally snap out of it and leave the spire but take my time weaving through the castle. I don't wear a watch, but I'm sure Aris means to fetch me soon to go to the archives, and that's the priority right now, at least for me.

I must have taken a wrong turn because I end up in the western wing of the castle by accident, which I'm not familiar with. It's a maze of small hallways until I reach the second floor, which is more open and modern compared to the rooms I occupy upstairs. An unlit corridor of red carpet and creamy white walls stretches into the darkest shadows—silent, and just as I begin to turn back the way I came, to descend the stairs again and backtrack to the eastern wing... a sconce lights at the very end of the hallway.

My heart jumps into my throat when it flickers. I've learned to tell the difference between the milky golden haze the spirit of the house produces and Aris's silver light... and this isn't Aris.

It flickers again, beckoning, and I follow on silent feet, creeping with one hand against the wall. Unease nearly chokes me as the stillness grows so thick I can hear my blood rushing in my veins, but then a murmured voice reaches from the shadows, then a girlish, pitched laugh, then a... moan.

My cheeks blaze as the moaning continues—shallow and rushed—like whoever it is currently in the final throws of ecstasy I know so well because I... I've felt that. With *him*.

"No," I whisper, squeezing my eyes shut. Morgan's resounding *"Yes!"* splits the hallway into pieces, my heart cracking so violently I shudder. "I don't want to see this!" I whirl and sprint down the hallway, tripping, falling to my knees so hard the thud vibrates down the hallway, but I get up, tears blurring my vision as an awful, clawing jealousy and misplaced betrayal tears through my chest.

Aris isn't mine. He's never been mine. He can't be mine, and I made that so completely *crystal clear*. My tears feel like acid on my skin. He has every right to fuck Morgan. She's going to be his wife, for fuck's sake. The mother of his future children. Maybe they're getting a head start...

I stifle a sob and brace myself on a cold, dark stone column over-looking the foyer. My body shatters under the weight of my heart-break. I've been doing so good so far, haven't I? I've only cried myself to sleep... six nights out of the week on average so far. I've been eating again... just a little bit. Food still tastes like sand, like forcing Aris through my fingers took everything good and sweet out of my life.

He offered me the world. I gave it up. I shattered his heart and mine and this widening void in my chest is what I deserve–

"Why are you crying?"

I shriek, covering my ears, startled by the noise that just tore from my mouth, and slowly turn to Aris, who's standing with his arms crossed in the center of the foyer below, squinting up at me through the haze of chandelier light.

"Posey?"

"What–I–" I slowly lower my hands and grip the balcony, finding it impossible to fill my lungs. Adrenaline courses like a rapidly spreading wildfire through my body, and I know without a doubt my skin is prickling, turning from peach to a fiery pink. "How'd you get down here so fast?"

"What?" He steps out of the center of the foyer, his boots sending an echo up to the highest rafters. "I've been down here waiting for you for twenty minutes. I was about to go wake you up. I want to get to the archives before Arthur rises for the day. Otherwise, he's going to pester us–"

"You weren't–you weren't with–" I pinch my mouth shut before I say something I know I'll regret. It's none of my business. His arrangement with Morgan is *none of my business.*

He scans my face. His eyes narrow for a moment before he sighs and motions for me to come downstairs. "Get down here."

"I–" I should tell him, shouldn't I? That his fiancé is sleeping with someone else in his own house? Unless he… finished… and I blacked out again and have been wandering around for twenty minutes or so….

"Posey, for the love of the Goddess, get over here. If you're wondering if I know that my fiancé is fucking her bodyguard, yes. I'm fully aware. She's not very good at hiding it."

My lungs quiver. I almost laugh but choke instead. The corner of his mouth twists into a wry kind of smile.

"Can we go? Or do you need me to explain this to you in detail?"

"You're okay with this?" I start down the grand, curved staircase but step at the center, looking down at him. "With the woman you're going to marry sleeping with someone else?"

"Of course I'm not, but I'd rather not go into detail here. Her maids are shameless spies, which is how I found out about Morgan and Talon in the first place, on their first night here. Their first two hours in the castle, actually. I've been enjoying dangling this engagement in front of her, knowing I'm sending her home in a few days' time and will never see her again."

"Aris," I whisper, shocked by his level, dry tone. He seems totally unaffected.

He shrugs as I reach his side. My cloak, which I forgot to bring with me, drops from thin air into his hand. He shakes it out and drapes it over my shoulders. "She's after my money, Posey."

"Isn't anyone you marry going to be interested in that? Given your terrible reputation?"

His touch lingers on my shoulders, searing through my wool cloak and my equally thick gray sweater to warm my skin. "Morgan's reputation might be worse, which is why I thought we'd be perfect together. As it turns out, she hates my house, which makes me hate her."

I feel all toasty and off kilter when the doors open wide for us, revealing at least a foot of fresh snow and a landscape swept in silver.

It's gorgeous. The most beautiful morning I've ever seen in my life. "Was finding someone who wants to live here your only requirement?"

"I felt like I'd know for sure when I saw her here, against the stone and stained glass. I'd know she was supposed to be here with me, and so far only one person has walked into this ancient place and… glowed." He catches my elbow, tucking me behind him as he carefully stomps through the snow, clearing a path for me to walk.

His words, however, linger in the air between us, booming through the vacuum of snowy silence as fresh flakes fall from the cloudy skin.

"Well, I'm sorry you're not getting married."

"No, you're not."

"I am. I really am. You deserve to be happy."

He places his hand on my arm again when we pass through the gate where the guards are actively digging out the security booth. He doesn't say another word for what feels like an eternity. Five minutes, in fact. When we finally reach the wide doors to the archives, the building built into a cliff face overlooking the valley and city of bridges below, he hesitates at the door, his fingers curled around the brass knob.

I can feel him looking at me, his gaze boring into my profile. I know the second I look him in the eyes it's going to break my heart all over again.

I was happy. For two days I was happier than I've ever been and will ever be again.

I roll my neck, wincing at the ghost of his voice invading my thoughts. I'm imagining it again. I have to be. I'm making things up to soften my own suffering.

"Don't run off while we're in the lower levels, okay? I don't know what's down there. I don't really want to know." He yanks open the door, and we're sprayed with warm air.

The frost on my eyelashes melts. I blink the moisture away. Warm, golden light of the main levels of the archives expands all around us, but then my heart skips a beat, and I resist the urge to fold into myself at the sight of a trio of priestesses and their proteges, women I know from the training program.

Mother Maria looks up from a book and stares at me for several seconds. To my great surprise, she gives me a relieved smile and a sharply knowing nod.

I suck in my lower lip and smile in greeting before Aris whirls us toward the doors leading into the depths of the archives.

I immediately step into the shadows, but he's reluctant to follow.

"What?" I ask, blinking up at him.

He glares into the darkness for several seconds before sighing heavily and running his fingers through his hair.

"You're scared, aren't you?"

"I'm not scared."

I turn to face him. "You are!"

"I hate the fact you came down here several times without someone escorting you."

"I've been fine. I like the dark, actually. It's quiet down there. No one bothers me, hovers over me, which is exactly what you mean to do, so please, let me find the books I need without breathing down my neck the entire time, okay?" I step into the shadows, biting back a smile as he curses above me, and then there he is, directly behind me, his hand gripping my waist as we navigate the stairwell into the depths of the mountain.

GET OUT, NOW!

It's a silent hunt for any books related to alchemy, metal, and forges. I find a few texts about old methods of ironsmithing I'm sure will be useful. Most of the alchemy books are tarnished, faded, and damn near useless at this point. Back when the skill was openly taught to anyone who brandished the powers, a different language was used. I don't know it. Aris is just as puzzled, but he gathers old books in his arms nonetheless, his original hesitation shifting to curiosity as we walk the stacks together. He lights the old lanterns with his shimmering powers, and his shadows stretch all around us, dancing in the grainy light. I'm sure, when he's like this, drenched in his own magic, most people would find him intimidating. *I think he's glorious.*

"What are you going to do with the fawn?" I ask when the silence becomes too much. I slide another heavy book into his hands, this one about apothecary remedies, hopefully old enough to have something for the use of alchemists within its yellowed pages.

"I don't know," he says with a heavy, slightly defeated sigh. "She's so small. I can't bottle feed her like this and then thrust her back into the wild."

"You've been feeding her? I thought it was the spirits."

He bites back a small smile. "I kind of enjoy it–taking care of her. She's cute. Little. She likes me, I think. At least one thing in the house does."

I like you. "Have you named her?"

"No, not yet. She's a deer. She doesn't understand us."

"You've never had a pet, have you?"

"I'm a wolf. I'm my own pet."

Somewhere in the recesses of the shadows, a thud echoes toward us. I shiver, stepping closer to Aris, who's squinting into darkness of his own making. His shadows funnel toward the sound.

"I caught a bat when I was little. I kept it in my room."

"Why?"

"Why not? I was alone most of the time if I wasn't with Roman, or you, when we used to visit. She liked it there. I'd leave my window open for her so she could come and go at night."

I notice the way he places his hand on my waist and carefully pulls me toward him, positioning himself between me and the shadows.

"There's a group of wolves hunting in our sacred forest. They're the ones that got her mother, and until I know who they are, the fawn is staying with us. Come spring, I'll build her a little enclosure in the garden. Something small, likely next to the greenhouse I'm planning for you and your herbs, or whatever." He's still looking into the shadows with narrowed eyes, rambling, likely unaware of the promise of the future we don't have lacing through the stale air between us.

"What is it?"

He makes a very male noise–a grunt–before replying, "I have no idea. A spirit, probably. Or the shelves are starting to collapse under the weight of all these books. Arthur should do something about it."

"The ghost or the ancient wooden shelves?"

A crash rattles the nearby shelves, and Aris tugs me against his chest. I gasp, whirling as if in slow motion, tucked in the folds of his cloak. The books in his arms fall to the ground. I feel his muscles jerk and flex as he raises his hands, his bracelets shining, and the space around us suddenly glows with silver. He vibrates with power I can feel in my bones. I wrap my arms around his waist and steal a glance over my shoulder, biting back a gasp as books lift off the ground and his shadows dance in the shape of... wolves.

"Aris?"

A roar rips from the darkness. I can't choke back the scream of alarm that escapes my throat, especially when Aris whirls around, shoves me into the shadows, and disappears in a gust of silver smoke. He's completely invisible. A shadow.

And then... the battle ensues.

❀

"You need to explain why," Aris snarls, his hands braced on Arthur's cluttered desk, "why the *fuck* you had a hellhound hidden in the archives!"

Arthur stares at him over the rims of his half-moon spectacles, so thick his eyes are at least ten times their actual size, totally unperturbed. "I don't remember putting it there."

"Well, it was there. It nearly took my hand off. Does my grandfather know about this?"

"I doubt it. He won't go down there. She's the only person who's been brave enough to venture down that far." He points at me, seemingly impressed. I blush. I can't help it.

Aris, meanwhile, is scowling at both me and Arthur. He has smears of blood on his cheeks and his eyes are still wild and wolflike. He shakes his head, hissing a curse, and points at Arthur. "Enough. Close it off to everyone. Is there anything else down there I should know about?"

"Hopefully not, but in my defense, I haven't been down there in a century or two."

My brows arch against my will. Aris slowly straightens, fuming.

253

He grips my upper arm, nostrils flaring, glaring at Arthur before turning on his heel and marching us out.

"Are you okay?" I meekly ask. He's not. I'm having a hard time myself after what I witnessed less than twenty minutes ago. Aris, shifting between his wolf form and a shadow of the darkest black fighting against a creature I've only ever read about. He tore it apart, limb by limb, until the creature croaked and literally disintegrated into ash.

I don't think my heart beat a single time during the entire three minute ordeal.

His jaw clenches, and he makes a small noise in his throat, nodding tightly, his eyes on the snowy landscape ahead of us while he tromps through thick snow. It's still snowing, and even for midmorning, it's dark, the mountains cloaked in clouds and sheets upon sheets of pure white. Snowflakes stick to my cheeks and eyelashes, and his too, softening the furious expression etching shadows across the plains of his face.

"Aris?"

"You were down there by yourself with that thing."

I stop walking. He stops, too, but doesn't face me. His hands are clenched into fists.

"Aris, it didn't–it never bothered me. We were at least three floors below where I normally set up my study station."

"You have no way to protect yourself. I told you this summer–" He runs his fingers through his hair. "Don't *ever* go back there. Not without me!"

"*I'm fine.* I was fine!"

"Do you realize how close you came to dying today? If I hadn't been there–"

"You don't need to worry about me–"

"*I love you.*"

I startle. The world around us fades until it's just me and him and the pearly white snow all around us. Aris is looking at me so intensely I feel him in my soul, rewiring my brain chemistry.

"I love you, Posey, for fuck's sake, I'm *in love* with *you,* and the idea of you being hurt–being killed by a fucking hellhound in my fucking territory…" He looks down at his boots, closing his eyes.

"Aris, I–" I reach for him. I just need to touch him. I'm on the verge of tears when he holds up a hand to stop me.

"Go home."

"Please–"

"*Go home*. I have shit to handle." He disappears, his silver-flaked power riling the snow. It falls in heaps at my feet, his body replaced by mist, then… nothing.

My cheeks are wet with tears when I press my chilled fingers to my skin, sniffling. An icy pain radiates through my chest. I look up and see a slightly familiar woman standing in the snow, staring at me.

She ducks her head and hurries into the storm, her body disappearing against the heavy snow.

I don't go back to the castle right away. I wander, letting my mind go blank. A group of kids in heavy snowsuits pass me on a makeshift sled made of cardboard, their father, or perhaps an older brother of shifting age, in his wolf form pulling the sled as fast as he can to the delight of the little boys screaming in glee. Every shop is lit up with Solstice lights that glimmer like gems against the wintery backdrop. I can't remember the last time it snowed like this in Veiled Valley. It's normally so warm, eternally tropical. This is a treat for everyone.

In another life, I imagine Aris and me shopping for gifts for his enormous family. I'd find something silly and girly for Willow, who loves the aetherial fashion of Veiled Valley, and we'd sit on a bench, happy, our fingers entwined.

It's a stupid, useless dream that carries me back to the castle.

I close my eyes the second the heavy doors close behind me, blocking the view of the foyer. My breath comes in a shallow rasp while my numb fingers stumble over my cloak clasp. Ice clings to my lashes. I open my eyes, wondering why my vision is so hazy and pink, but then I'm knocked sideways by a force so strong I barely have time to feel the floor biting into my shoulder when I land hard.

"You conniving little bitch!" Morgan roars.

My cheek prickles with a searing heat, throbbing and puffy. I reach up with a gasp and touch my skin where a swollen imprint of her fist is now engraved in my face. My fingers are wet and crimson when I draw them back.

"You!" she screams, her dark hair falling like a curtain over her face, hiding her wild, furious eyes from view. She grabs a handful of my hair and pulls until I screech in pain. "You little slut! Aris is *my* fiancé! I'm going to be Luna of Veiled Valley, and you're not getting in my way!" She yanks my hair so hard I feel a chunk leave my scalp. "I didn't come to this disgusting castle for nothing!"

"He knows about you and your guard," I grit out, grabbing her wrist, her jingling bracelets slipping under my palm. Gold. Plated gold with something underneath. I just need to find its resonance–I scream in pain when she kicks my thigh with her pointed-toe heel, but then she's crying out, letting me go, and stumbling backward holding her wrist.

Burnt skin spices the air.

"What did you do!" she shouts, sniffling. "What did you fucking do!"

A whoosh rips through the foyer. The lights flicker out, and a groan sounds, gusting through every now pitch black hallway.

"What the fuck was that?" Morgan bellows, panting. She looks up at the chandelier, which rattles violently, and her glossy brown eyes meet mine in horror. "STOP! What are you doing! Witch!" She sprints toward me, her pink satin robe flaring out around her like wings, but then she's knocked on her ass and dragged by her hair by an unseen force, and her screams of terror and rage fade after a few seconds, followed by the sound of a door slamming shut somewhere in the recesses of the castle.

"Thank you," I croak, wincing. I bring my shaking fingers to my face. The female spirit's presence envelopes me in a warm, worried embrace, and after a few moments of encouragement, I rise and hobble into the dining room, then through the door leading downstairs, to the kitchen.

I drop like a dead weight in front of the stove. The fawn bounces toward me, jumping on and off my thighs, her little hooves pinching my skin but I barely feel it. Blood rushes to my face and fingers while I stare aimlessly at the cabinets. My brain refuses to function from the shock of my homecoming, and honestly, I'm thankful for it.

Heavy boot tread echoes, then stops. I don't look in Aris's direction when he rounds the kitchen island and crouches next to me.

"Am I bald?" I ask weakly, closing my eyes when I feel his touch on my chin, his thumb grazing what I think are three deep claw marks across my cheek.

He doesn't say a word and leaves as quickly as he came.

The next morning, I watch Morgan, her guard and likely future baby daddy, and her trio of covert spies—also known as maids—hustle out into the snowstorm dragging her luggage behind her. She doesn't look back at the castle. Not once.

I'LL KNOW IF YOU DO

Aris

Posey's fingers are unnaturally warm as she carefully fits the mask to my face. She tilts my head back, then to the side, smoothing her thumbs over my cheek where the third prong should be. I can't stop looking at her when she's like this–hyper-focused, her green eyes sharp and unyielding. It's the same side of her I got to witness this summer every time I barged into her room to harass her and waste her time while she tried to study into the later hours of the night.

I feel like we've both lived an entire lifetime since then.

"How does it feel?"

"A little small."

Her brow furrows. She angles the mask upwards so the middle prong rests directly over my nose, which feels wrong, and judging by the frustration behind her eyes, she knows it, too. "It's missing something. You're sure this is all you found?"

"Well, the third prong is missing."

She tsks and sets the mask down on her worktable, which is now covered by a slab of pure white granite. Yesterday morning, when I'd come here to coax her into taking a healing draft for the scratches Morgan left on her face, which she'd refused, she'd explained that granite doesn't absorb resonance, which makes it perfect for practicing alchemy. That is also why all the temples in Eastonia are made of granite, and then I zoned out, watching her hands smooth raw iron ore into thin, sharp picks and curved blades–tools, I realized. She made them all without even blinking, all while talking, giving me a complete history of her kind.

And I'd been just as transfixed as I am now.

"There's a piece missing," she huffs, frustrated, her hands outstretched in surrender as she looks down at the mask. "It's not the third prong, either. There's something else. A piece here. A head-piece–no–a helmet. That's it." She reaches into her soot covered apron and tosses a small, already half-full notebook on the table and brushes her black fingertips off on the apron's cream colored fabric. Her pencil is already worn down as she scribbles, and I just sit here, watching her, watching her chew her lower lip in thought. "It was a helmet, not just a mask. Where is the rest of it?"

"Huh?"

She's looking at me now, a strand of hair falling loose from the messy bun I watched her wind and tie back half an hour ago, imagining the curve of her spine and the indent between her shoulders, the same places I kissed–

"Aris?"

"What?"

"Are you listening? This mask is supposed to be connected to a head guard–it's a helmet. That's why it won't fit over your face and why it's so heavy."

"Well, shit."

"*Well, shit,*" she parrots, her hands pressed to her hips. "The caves, then?"

"No." I rise, clearing my throat to try to stop from laughing. Her gaze is incredulous. "Don't look at me like that."

"I–"

"You are not permitted to access those caves under *any* circumstances." I already know she's not going to heed any warning or listen to a Goddess-damned word I say.

"Why not?"

"Are you fucking serious?" I step toward her. She doesn't shy away. In fact, she tilts her chin to continue looking me directly in the eyes while I tower over her. I'm tempted to close her against the worktable, but I refrain because I've had months of practice doing just that at this point. I'm a bundle of nerves and pure, undying heat on my better days. Today isn't one of them. Yesterday nearly undid me on a molecular level.

It was the most beautiful day I'd ever seen in my entire life. Endless crystal blue skies. A white-washed landscape buried in more snow than Veiled Valley had ever experienced. The city was alive, everyone in the streets, kids screaming with joy and Solstice music blaring.

I spent the majority of the day dealing with pack business, which was only reports of kids throwing snowballs at businesses and elderly neighbors. I also got in touch with Maeve about the Morgan situation, giving her the go-ahead to spread an official statement from her office instead of mine about the fabricated report of my engagement.

By midmorning, however, reality sank in. Posey was up in her spire, hard at work or avoiding me and the world entirely, I wasn't sure. I wandered the castle, replaying the fact *I told her I loved her, and she didn't say a word* over and over until I felt like it would be more comfortable to peel my flesh from my bones than remain in that memory another second.

But when it comes to her, I'm a weak man.

"What does this do?"

"Don't touch that."

"If I eat this, what will happen?"

"Aris, put that down."

"AH! What the fuck–"

"That was literally just on fire! Why are you in here? Don't you have other things to do?"

Mostly, for the rest of the afternoon, I sat in that rocking chair under the window, watching her. Watching her move. Watching her reach for those shiny glass vials. Watching her grind herbs and dunk her new tools in vats of cool water.

I'm not used to being alone in the quiet. She thrives in it. My presence, as long as I'm not in her way, touching her things, doesn't seem to bother her.

I kept enough of a distance I didn't feel like my skin would combust if I didn't touch her, and on occasion, I did feel her gaze… brief, but curious. Brief but heartsick.

I can't figure her out. She's a maze. Her mind is built like the vault door below the castle–impenetrable–and she's the only one who holds the key. I'd give this up, let myself succumb to the fact that she isn't interested if her eyes didn't glisten and her body lean toward mine during every conversation. I'd let this festering, heartbreaking rejection fade if she gave me a real reason she hates me, but she hasn't. She won't. She doesn't.

Now, she's fitting a new prong onto the mask knowing full well it won't fix it, and I'm refusing to give her what she's pouting about.

"Do you understand why I won't let you go into the caves?"

"No, I don't." Metal sizzles under her touch, turning molten. She quickly grabs a tool I'm not even going to try to name to score the mask before carefully putting the new prong in place. Her fingers stain black with soot but otherwise remain perfectly intact. It's amazing.

"It's dangerous."

Her forest green eyes meet mine for several seconds in a searing glare before they drop back to her task, and she sighs heavily, shaking her head. "It's your loss. You need the entire helmet."

"Just make me a new one."

"It doesn't work like that."

"How does it work, then?"

"I don't know! You're the Shadowsynger. You tell me!"

"Well, you're an alchemist, the same kind of fire breathing creature who made this shit in the first place." I motion to the mask.

She scoffs. I mimic the sound. She points to the door and doesn't blink until I take several determined steps out of her way. "I'm leaving tonight. I'll be back in two days, give or take."

"I heard you the first time."

"Don't go into the caves."

She doesn't reply and instead yanks a stool beneath her and sits with a huff, propping her chin on her fist. I linger in the doorway for several seconds, gripping the top of the frame. *Antagonize her some more, that little voice in my head demands. Ruffle her notebook pages. Make her see you.*

"Aris?"

"Yeah?"

I don't turn to the sound of her voice, but she's closer, light on her feet like always.

"Are we going to be able to do this? Work together?"

"My only other option is sending you back to Sapphire Ridge."

Silence. It's heavy and suffocating.

"We should... talk about Morgan."

I turn, bracing myself on the doorframe. "Why?"

She's standing only a few feet away, her stained fingers fiddling with her apron. She reaches up to pull the clip out of her hair. It falls over her shoulders like strawberry silk, somehow more vibrant in the faint silver glow beginning to drift through the frosted glass of the windows behind her.

I asked her if she'd ever been in the sun before. Now, I hope the weather will always be gray because she's stunning in this light. So beautiful it hurts.

I'd crawl through fire for her. I'd give her anything she wants other than access to the fucking caves. That's where I have to draw the line. A wide, immovable one.

"You sent her away because she..."

"Hurt you?"

"I handled it."

"By lying down and taking it."

"I wasn't going to strike the future Luna–"

"I was never going to marry her."

"You only decided that after I came back into your life and that isn't fair to you."

Why can't you just say it back? Do you not feel it, this terrible, all-consuming yearning? This feeling like we'll die if we don't just... touch? I'm dying here, Posey. I'd rather you took a knife to my throat and just ended it. Gods, I'd die happy for just a touch.

I lick my lips, biting back a bitter laugh. "I have options. I can use a breeder. I can find one of those anywhere."

Her cheeks flush. I can't take it. It's so much easier to be around her when she's annoyed with me, or mad, or doing anything but being soft and kind.

"You said... you loved me."

Fuck. "I know."

"You shouldn't."

My eyes close against the pained look on her face. "Posey."

"I... can never give you what you need. You need an heir. I can't give that to you."

We could adopt. We could hope and pray Maeve has a son, or even a daughter who isn't fully Firestone and has a single drop of Shadowsynger blood passed down from our grandfather and our mother. I'd give it all up. I'd fucking walk. If I knew I had the option of being with you, I would do it in a heartbeat.

"I talked to Willow about Roman. The call dropped, but... I was sure she was going to say that Roman wanted to... step down."

I open my eyes to slits just to see the troubled look on her face, and it's damning. The fear in her eyes is palpable.

"He loves her, doesn't he? That night at the manor? She was the one who ended things, not him. He didn't hurt her. It was her. Did you know he went to Crescent Falls to talk to her? That he told her he'd step down so she could stay there, keep her dream job? That he was willing to step down and not be Alpha of Sapphire Ridge?" she asks.

"I didn't."

"Aris," she whispers, tears in her eyes. I feel like my chest is being bent apart, my heart and lungs on display. "Don't."

Don't step down for her.

That's the worst part about this. *I can't.* I'm the only male of my line, the only one of my siblings with these powers. I'm the strongest Shadowsynger since my grandfather. The caves called out to me, and... I need kids. A family. Promises that my powers will be passed down and Veiled Valley and its endless secrets and sacred mountains will remain protected.

Posey cannot have children.

We were doomed from the beginning.

"I care about you," she says, her voice pinched. "I hate this. If I'd known how hard it'd be, I wouldn't have–this summer–"

"Do you regret it? What we did?"

"No," she whispers. "Never. Not for a second. I wish things were different."

I can't take it. I'll shatter like glass right here, right now, if she so much as touches me. When she steps toward me, reaching for me like she always does without realizing what it does to me, I step into the shadows, putting that gaping ocean of distance between us once more.

"The spirits will report to me if you've been in the caves. Don't do it. That's all I ask."

I don't even bother packing a bag. Fuck it. Fuck the broken look in her eyes and the way her fingers clench into tight fists. I want to hate her for this so much. I want to bend her to my will, force her to break and tell me the truth. There has to be more to this than her inability to give me an heir. It's not Roman. It's not her family. It's something else. Something she can't say. The thing driving every self-deprecating decision.

"Do not go in the caves, Posey." I tear myself into pieces, letting it hurt, pushing myself to the limit on purpose, and when my powers sing and writhe, begging for mercy, Blake's ugly, impossibly open and massive modern living room comes into view.

I run my hand over my face, knowing full well that impossible, untrainable, aggravating, utterly *perfect* woman is going to the caves *right now*.

"You look like you could use a drink," Soren says, his voice bouncing off the Tarsian-plastered walls.

"A whole bottle might do, for now."

SECRETS OF THE CAVES

LUCKILY FOR ARIS, I'M TOO BUSY TRYING DESPERATELY TO KEEP MY mind and heart away from the thought of him in general to disobey his direct orders. Unluckily for him, after a night of tossing and turning, with very little sleep, I wake up the next morning alone in the castle for the first time, staring at the mask, at my scattered, useless tools, and my mind wanders again.

Trying to ignore my wanderlust, I get back to work, popping out the old jewels and busying myself by placing new ones, ones I made myself out of silver and melded until they shone like diamonds. The fawn bounces around my feet while I do my work. Silver is great for this–creating gems. Most alchemists can't touch silver without a variety of specialized tools and a heavy duty forge, none of which I have, but it doesn't affect me. Silver feels beautiful under my touch– like silky cream. Like pure, cold water. It makes me shiver as I press shards of silver into stainless steel molds, heating them until the silver within is reduced to shards of what looks like hot glass. It takes a while–all of my morning–to replace each and every tiny gem that once peppered the mask, but I complete it by midafternoon, and still…

"It's worthless in this condition," I say to the room, my mind made up.

The foyer is ice cold for some reason. Maybe it's my nerves, the gnawing sense of knowing that I'm about to do exactly what Aris forbid me to do, but I can't just sit here, alone, alone with my own stupid, incessant thoughts, and wait for him to find the rest of the mask's components. In fact, I already know he doesn't care. Repairing the mask is meant to keep me busy, to keep me here, and in a way, it's working. I'm of one mind. One single, idiotic brain cell. One focus. One task to complete. Everything else–the time, the day, the fact I haven't eaten since last night and that I've barely slept, fades away as I secure my apron tight around my waist and drape my cloak over my shoulders. Yesterday, I found a large basket in a cupboard in the kitchen and filled it with some rags, bandages, and a few healing drafts I made myself just in case, so I'll bring that along.

But I have no idea how to access the vault and the tiny door in its shadow.

"I have two options," I say to the foyer at large. "I can either jump through the hole in the floor, or you can show me how to get to the vault."

The chandelier above my head rustles. The dust hanging in the strips of golden winter sunlight panics, zooming as something–someone unseen–walks through it to stand at my side. It's the male spirit. He takes up more space, more oxygen, and his presence carries a strange, almost icy, feel to it. It's impossible to explain. He feels like he was a warrior at some point in his life–that he was important and hasn't forgotten.

Still, his counterpart is now causing a ruckus. The castle groans in protest, a popping, grinding sound funneling toward me, and I turn my head and capture the moment a door that wasn't there before appears directly in the stones under the staircase. The stones themselves have pulled away, revealing a shadowed entrance.

"Creepy," I muse but smile, and the male spirit brushes my loose hair behind my shoulders before ghostly footsteps edge toward the opening, beckoning me to follow. "He'll be angry."

"*He needs you.*"

"*Don't,*" the female voice whispers. Their unearthly voices send shivers up and down my spine. It's like they're whispering directly against my ear, more a hum than noise. It's the only time I've ever felt afraid of them, like I have to be reminded of what they are. Ghosts. Apparitions. Maybe even demons trapped in a cage.

"*Careful,*" she whispers to me when she realizes I can't just… turn around, not now, not when her companion is willing to show me the way.

I hold my breath and descend a twisted, decaying wooden staircase into the gloom, the deepest depths of this ancient, beautiful place. At its base, the vault comes into focus, and that's it. Only one way in and out, I suppose, but when that little side door creaks open, and the cave system's gaping maw expands in my field of vision, I shiver again, and this time with fear—palpable fear.

I clutch my basket tightly and say a small prayer I know will go unanswered, and take one step forward and then another.

Soon after I begin my explorations, I realize there are at least four different entrances to this cave system, and only one leads directly to and from the castle. Which, I deduce, means the original castle was built directly on top of the tunnels and channels made by an underground creek, which I sometimes have to carefully cross during my hours of exploration.

My battery-powered lantern shudders several times, holding on for dear life. I came prepared for most possibilities, but I did not bring batteries since Aris and his family members can use their magic for that, and they don't have a single battery in the castle. I looked. For a while.

I'm ready for everything else though, I hope.

I'm not sure what I'm even looking for. Back at the cabin this summer, I laid in Aris's arms while we listened to the rain. He told me about his descent into the caves. He'd been fifteen, which seems incredibly young. Fifteen and full of hormones and spite, he'd said, which drove him forward when the cave walls and darkness closed in on him. When I asked how he found his bracelets, he said it wasn't like he just stumbled upon them and grabbed the first thing he saw. He was led to them. He told me he'd heard voices in the darkness, unintelligible, but they grew louder and more frantic, and finally he found what the cave had called him for.

"I found the mask on my way out, though. It was just sitting there, like I'd stepped over it on my way in without seeing it the first time, so I grabbed it, too, but it never lit for me or responded to my powers like these." I had the bracelets in my hand at the time. He'd taken them off to show me. I fell asleep with my fingers curled around them, my hand against his chest.

The memory is so warm, I stop and ponder taking off my cloak, but a whisper echoes toward me, bouncing off every glimmering wall of crystal.

I freeze, holding my breath to still my thundering heart so I can hear past the blood rushing in my ears—and wait.

It's a laugh—bright and girlish, followed by more whispers and giggles, the sound of someone falling in love.

My heart skips a beat. I turn toward the sound, my brain shutting off entirely and my senses taking over. It's a rush, like whatever energy is reaching out to me with long, spidery fingers has its own electric current. It pulls me, guiding me into the darkness until I come back to my senses and realize I've gone further into this underground maze than I ever meant to.

The air here is so cold and wet it sticks to the back of my throat when I take a deep, sulfuric breath. Water glistens in what little light there is to be had in the haze of my lantern, which illuminates stalactites and other impressive, otherworldly crystal formations that have grown over what appears to be columns of onyx. I blink, that tunnel vision evaporating in a single heartbeat, and look down at the floor. Marble tiles—cracked, of course, with veins of crystal growing through the breaks.

I feel a whoosh behind me. Warm air creeps through my cloak. I swear a firm but small hand wraps around mine, the one holding up the lantern to spray light across my surroundings, which I believe might have been a temple.

An altar rests in several pieces ahead of me. The underground creek runs directly through the center of the room now, pooling just a few yards away, creating a glassy, crystal pool.

The female spirit clutches me tight. It's a strange feeling, like being compressed by air itself.

"You didn't need to follow me."

She says nothing but allows me to take a few steps, where I lift the lantern high and…

A gleam catches my attention. It's duller than the crystals all around us. Metal. The sheen of… iron.

I stomp through the crystal pool, the icy water biting my skin at knee level, and come to a halt just before the altar.

A small, thin band of iron meant to be worn as a diadem, I think, rests on the ground. Crystals grow through the small, intricate detailing of the crown piece, where several settings for gems have been long empty. One moonstone remains, but it's cracked—shattered, actually. I kneel, my wet cloak spreading out behind me, and tentatively reach for it when I notice what's lying beside it… and behind it.

The helmet is only a few feet away. Bones of pure white lie scattered between the diadem and helmet. More than one person rests here eternally. Finger bones reach for each other, the digits in exactly the same position they were when the owners of the skulls died here, their hands intertwined.

My heart caves in, sinking like a dead weight against my ribs, refusing to beat.

I think of the mask, of how I figured the broken prong was that way because of a devastating, absolutely catastrophic blow to the face. It would have been deadly.

Instead of reaching for the helmet, my fingers ache, stretching through the diadem. The second my fingertips brush against the ice cold metal, my eyes fill with visions and voices like I'm flipping through the pages of a book.

Raven black hair flutters as she runs down a hallway, laughing, that same girlish laugh I'd heard just moments ago. Silver eyes blink like stars as she turns to grin at him–the owner of the helmet. The helmet she made for him after they married.

"*He's lonely,*" she tells her mother in the tower of a castle far north of here. I recognize the mountains, the valleys, but the village beyond is ancient, older than anything I've ever seen. Miles away, against the setting sun, I see the ridge my pack is named after. "*He's my mate, Mother. What am I to do?*"

It's a violent time. I watch through her eyes as soldiers march down dirt roads. People dressed in strange, outdated homespun beg and kneel in front of a young man with soft brown hair and eyes like iron, begging for news about family and friends from Moonrise and beyond. Some are asking for news from *Rifthold.*

"*The Great War cost our kind so much blood,*" a deeper female voice says as the image plays out before me like a movie. "*Isolde, you must be careful. You're the last of our pack. It's just you now.*"

"*He'll take care of me. He promised. Mama, I love him. He loves me.*" An image of a young hand pressing a withered one to her belly expands before me behind a grainy, distorted veil.

"*Stop.*" I snap out of it the second the female spirit's presence presses down against my shoulder. I almost drop the diadem. "*I remember now.*"

I look up, expecting to see nothing but the glare of my lantern against the crystals, I see her clearly–like she's made of mist. Long, dark hair. Eyes of polished silver. She looks like King Ryatt. Like–Aris but darker–with the same eyes.

"Oh, my Goddess."

She shushes me, her sad, tired eyes meeting mine. "*I remember now. Oh, but he doesn't remember. Neither of us remembered.*"

I think I might be dreaming all of this. Her, the cave, the images still branded in the back of my mind. I can't really be picking up the helmet next. I can't really be oh so carefully tucking both artifacts into my basket. I can't be contemplating taking the skulls with me, can I?

My gaze holds on the bones, on the interlocked fingers, before sliding back to the female spirit, who's still kneeling, her eyes fixed on the same bones.

"Isolde?"

She slowly looks up at me, her shattered expression cracking my heart into pieces. "*He promised me we'd go together. He swore if there came a moment when all was lost that we'd... we'd go. He wouldn't let them take me. He'd kill all three of us both before–*" She looks up from her ghostly, translucent hands and stares at the broken altar.

I crouch at her side. "You've been in the castle this whole time? Why?"

"*We promised each other. It was our home. We couldn't let King Kane take it from us. Over our dead bodies, we said. All else be damned. Our son–*" She looks up at me, shaking her head in despair. "*I don't remember now. Why don't I remember what happened?*"

A creeping sensation skitters up my spine. The cave groans. Crystal shards hurtle to the ground before the air goes still again. I make the executive decision to take their skulls with me, neatly wrapping them both in rags. I begin to walk out of the cave but stop, turning back to the altar and Isolde, but she's no longer there.

My clothes are damp, and my brain is reduced to mush when I finally reach my workspace in the spire, my legs aching and begging for me to sit down and never even look at a staircase again. I have big plans. Things to fix. Questions to unravel and find the answers to. The sun sets as I repair the helmet.

The golden light of day fades to twilight when I secure the mask to the headpiece. It warms under my touch–ready. Fixed.

"Isolde!" I call out to the empty room, excited, wondering if she'll bring the male spirit with her so we can–

Silver moonlight drifts over my boots, stretching across the room as the full moon rises–glorious. Huge.

"Oh no," I rush out as tingles of awareness rip up my spine, and that clawing, deprived monster whines inside of me. "No, no..."

How could I forget?

DREAD

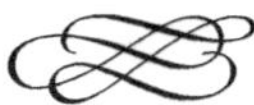

Aris

Soren leans against the thick charcoal gray cushions of the L-shaped couch in Blake's atrocious modern living room. It's... sunken. I nearly cracked my head open within seconds of appearing in his house twelve hours earlier than I told him I'd be here, but apparently Blake, Soren, and to my surprise, Logan have been expecting me. Or they were getting the party started early. We've wasted most of the day. I slept until the late afternoon. Logan cooked dinner, which was surprisingly good, and now?

Blake got the good whiskey out for the occasion, whatever that occasion is, because nothing about succession has been spoken about yet.

Logan, propped on the armrest on the far side of the couch, crosses his arms over his chest and looks down at where I'm sitting on the floor. My back is against the curved base of the wall-to-wall fireplace. Everything in this house–save for Skye's scattered pink and purple toys–is smooth, curved or leaning at impossible angles–all dark glass, gray plaster, and pale wood.

Everyone else in the family thinks the house is a masterpiece, a true marvel of modern engineering. I often wonder if Blake based the blueprints on one of Kieran's absolutely insane drawings because, to me, none of it makes sense.

The bottle of scotch resting between my knees catches the light of a hand-blown chandelier. I tip it to my lips while Logan and Soren continue commiserating over their beloved wives–my sisters. Who they adore. Who they won't stop talking about. They're men who look like they could beat the shit out of anyone at any time. Yet, they go soft and fluffy at the mention of their mates' names.

"I miss the girl. I'm not gonna lie," Soren says, stretching his arms over his head with a soft groan. "Fallon's newest vocal stim is 'fuck.' She's been saying it repeatedly, and it drives Maeve mad, but... she's definitely the one who taught her that."

"Yeah, Kieran went through that, too. It gets better as they get older. I can just tell him no now, and he moves on to the next cuss word on his list."

"What's his current favorite?"

"He heard Ryan call someone from a neighboring pack a bastard, so of course, it's that."

Soren chuckles, and the conversation drifts away without me, but I haven't been following most of it. This is supposed to be a guys weekend, according to Soren, who planned the whole thing mostly to get acquainted with the impressively large flat-screen TV upstairs in Blake's den, but when Blake returns to the living room with more drinks, I notice the shadows under his eyes and the way he catches Logan's eyes.

I can't ignore the elephant in the room anymore. "Where the fuck is Kaleb?"

Soren sighs, grumbling under his breath as he stretches out on the couch, legs splayed. "I can't blame the guy for not coming. He doesn't know us well."

"He barely speaks the language yet as it stands," Logan adds with a nod. "Plus, they've got Ian."

"He didn't like the idea of leaving Lexa behind. An evening away from his mate and child carries a very different connotation to him after everything they've gone through recently. I doubt they'll leave each other's sides again." Blake sets a fresh bottle of scotch beside me, eyeing me with interest before he sits down a few feet away on the ottoman.

"Should we talk about succession, then? That's the reason we're all here." I drain the rest of the first bottle, the booze going down far easier than it should, but slowly lower it when I notice all eyes on me. "What?"

"Why is it snowing in Veiled Valley?" Blake asks pointedly, his dark brows arched and voice smooth and cold as ice.

"Fuck if I know," I murmur, reaching for the second bottle, which he snatches quicker than I can react.

"Your emotions and powers are directly tied to the stability in that territory. You've turned a tropical rainforest into a winter hellscape."

"I don't know where you're getting your information, but I am not Alpha King of Veiled Valley. Not yet, at least. Last I checked, my mom's still the Alpha and Grandpa Ryatt–"

"What's going on with you?" It's Soren this time, and I shoot daggers at my brother-in-law from across the room. He's more amused than anything.

"Fuck off. I came here to talk about succession, and if we're not doing that, I'm going home." I rise, but all three men remain seated, staring. Waiting for me to break. Normally, I wouldn't give them the satisfaction... ever. Especially Logan, that old fuck. He used to beat the absolute shit out of me and my friends during our years in warrior training when he was our unit trainer, and he enjoyed it. Now, he's married and mated to my sister, and he's looked smug as hell about it for years.

"Fine." I snatch my cloak off the back of the couch while striding out of the room and immediately stumble over the step leading up from the sunken area. I curse, then whirl to face the men. The closest things to brothers I've ever had. "You know what?"

"What?" Blake sighs, popping the cork off the fresh bottle of scotch like he... already knows what I'm about to say.

I've bottled these feelings up for months. The rejection. The heartache. The confusion, and honestly, the fear. Fear I had a taste of something I'll never have again. Fear I'll roll over in the morning to pull my wife closer, and she's not soft and warm and doesn't smell like fucking cherries.

"You fucking bastard. You know. You looked into my head!"

Logan and Soren rise methodically, poised to intervene, but I ignore them, taking several determined steps toward Blake, but he doesn't stand. He takes a pull from the bottle and then shakes his head. "I didn't have to."

"What is that supposed to mean?"

Soren tucks his hands in his pockets and bites back a knowing smile.

"Fuck. Skye?" I gape, and Blake shrugs.

"She's exceptional."

"You haven't taught her it's bad form to look into someone's head?"

"You wear your feelings on your sleeve. You always have, which is why I was shocked to find out you had them for others in the first place." Blake rises and rests the bottle on the mantel and then folds his arms over his chest. "What happened with Morgan? Did she reject you?"

Apparently, Skye isn't as exceptional as her freak of a father thinks she is. "No. I kicked her out after she put her hands on my–"

The room falls silent, which isn't that hard to do. Even the crackling fire is sucked into the vacuum of stillness created by what I know are impeccably sound-proofed walls.

"Posey Sapphire." Blake rolls her name over his tongue, violet eyes holding mine. Just the sound of her name is enough to undo me. The scotch washes over me in a wave, dragging me to the floor, where I slump on the step, resting my face against my palm.

I was, proudly, the family slut. The one with a heart of steel that couldn't be broken or invaded. I could party, riot, and rage without a second thought. I've been rumored to have slept my way through Eastonia, and... it's an honor, truly, but still....

I'm fucked up. My best friend's little sister fucked me up. She could have run me over with a car, backed up, and done it again, and it would have hurt less than this.

"I told her I loved her," I admit, my voice steadier than I assumed it would be. "I told her I'm *in love* with her, and she won't…. She feels the same way, which is why this entire fucked up situation I'm in is just impossible. She won't say it. She won't just accept it. She won't budge."

"She's an alchemist, Aris. This is in their nature." Blake paces to the far side of the room to look out the window.

"And what nature is that? To be stubborn and immovable?"

"She's bound to duty to not only her pack but her powers–"

"She was going to join a convent," I snarl.

"Have you…" Soren tapers off, glancing at Logan before arching a brow. "Slept with her?"

I laugh. It's bitter. Wanting. Like just thinking back on this summer is like a knife to my vocal cords. I run my tongue along the edge of my bottom teeth. "Yeah." I glance at Blake. He's looking at me again, but I can't feel his tendrils of power anywhere near me, thank the Goddess. "Do you guys want a play-by-play, or something?" I scan each man's face. "Any takers? Anyone care to know that I practically begged her not to go into that asinine priestess training program and to stay with me instead, to marry me, so she could live in peace away from her family?"

"What does her family have to do with this?" Logan's voice is low, calm, like he's talking to a live bomb. Maybe I am. My shadows rile, curling between my fingers.

"She can't shift. She doesn't have a wolf. Blake, who knows fucking everything, can attest to the fact that it's a bad thing for her family's reputation and her brother's ability to ascend to Alpha soon. All the Sapphire Ridge pack cares about is their ability to use alchemy, which is supposed to be directly tied to the ability to shift. It determines everything–marriages, children. And–" I laugh because I'll throw the empty bottle across the room to shatter against the window if I don't, "She can't have kids, apparently, and a few hours ago she looked me dead in the eyes and told me not to step down for her."

"You offered that?" It's Logan again. He sits back on the couch, stretching out his legs. He almost looks impressed.

"I couldn't even if I wanted to." I look right at Blake, who apparently is Ryatt's heir as ringleader of this generation of the family, which feels a little unfair. We should, I don't know, hold a vote about who's really in charge. I'd vote for myself, of course.

"Is she your mate?"

The clouds shift, and moonlight stretches across the living room. It's full and brighter than I've seen it in months. The second the moonlight sweeps over my feet, I feel both forms vibrate in wait, but my fox form…

I stiffen, slowly clutching my shirt. My heart pounds before racing, and I feel…

"Are Maeve's shields up?" I ask Soren, who narrows his eyes.

"Of course, why?"

Logan shifts his weight uncomfortably, glancing out the window in the direction of the palace, where my sisters, Marianna, and the kids are having their own girls weekend… plus the twins and Brie's boys.

Another pang rips through my heart in warning. Something's off. I either drank enough to officially give myself alcohol poisoning, and I'm about to pass out, or…

She did it. She went into the caves. I knew she would. Fuck.

"I have to go." It's all I can manage before my shadows erupt and wrap around me against the shouts of alarm from all three men. I close my eyes, and the world goes black. I open them to the blurry outline of Posey's alchemy room. My vision clears, revealing startlingly bright moonlight filling every inch of the room. She's not here.

The fawn is asleep on a pillow under the window. She doesn't stir when I take a step, then another, scanning the room like someone or something is about to jump out and attack, but then I see *it* and confirm the worst.

The mask... and the helmet. The helmet I've never seen–that didn't call to me in the caves. The helmet that's humming with so much energy now I can taste it. It's mended completely. New gems glisten in the quicksilver glow of the moon.

But beside it, in a basket, rest two human skulls and a diadem.

"What the–"

Howls drift from the forest beyond the castle. That's not uncommon for a full moon, but the ache in my chest as the howls drift away and the racing of my heart nearly brings me to my knees.

"Where is she?" I ask the house. "Did she go back into the caves?"

Only the male spirit makes himself known.

"*Where. Did. She. Go?*" I snarl. The air shifts nearby, and then the helmet slides across the granite tabletop, rattling as it comes to a rest. The wolves howl again; they're on the hunt.

I look out the window as dread like I've never known fills my body and renders my human senses useless.

I turn to the door I hadn't used to enter the room, and a pile of shredded clothing glimmers in the moonlight.

She lied to me about being able to shift... but why?

FADE INTO SHADOWS

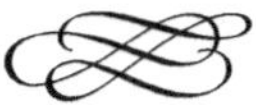

Posey

The snow is far too deep, but the air is crisp, and icy fog hangs low. I bounce and weave between trees, my body and mind feeling freer than it has in a long time. I would stay like this forever if I could, but... I'm untrained. Also, if I'm caught, I'll be killed and made into a pair of expensive mittens, which I'd rather avoid.

It's been months since I let the moon take over. When I was training in Moonrise, I spent three full months in the temple, sweating and in debilitating pain while chugging vial after vial of healing tonic to try to keep the shift from happening. I prayed for mercy. I often prayed for death. I mostly thought about Aris and let my mind stay in those golden memories from this summer, even though at any other point in time, I did my best not to remember.

But tonight wasn't an option. I should have seen the signs this morning–my one-track mind and my inability to keep still. I couldn't sleep, for one. I was ravenously hungry, thirsty, and bouncing off the walls with bursts of unusual energy that I funneled into my alchemy.

And, most pointedly, when I was in the caves, my senses were sharp as a knife, and my fear was at an all-time low.

The last night I shifted was this summer, the night I arrived at Aris's summer house. I hadn't been able to schedule my arrival for the next day because Willow was driving and in control of the timeline, but they gave me an out when they went to that bar, leaving me behind to "study." I shifted, made it quick, and tried to be as discreet about my scent as possible, running with the wind to carry my scent away from the house. I showered and had just settled my thundering heart when Aris came home in a panic over an unfamiliar scent outside. He'd come so close to catching me.

I often wonder what would have happened if he had, if everything that happened this summer ended there, on my first night in Gem Lake.

A rabbit bounds out of the brush. I chase it for the thrill. It's nearly as big as me, all things considered, and the same flawless winter white. Being this pale had shocked me at first, especially when I got my first look at my snow-white paws. During the summer, my fur was an orangey pink, matching the season. I'm small but powerful. Sleek and quick. My senses bloom as my blood soars through my veins, leaving little room for rational thought. I chase the rabbit for a while. I'll never catch it, but that's really the point. Just moving like this, bounding through snow so deep I have to pounce through it, feels incredible. I get distracted when I disrupt a family of voles. They're far more fun to chase, and the rabbit disappears into the swirling, glittering fog to be someone else's snack later.

The voles race between my legs in a tizzy. I let out a foxy, barking laugh, delighted. Absolutely light as air. What if I just... stayed this way? Raced into the distant mountains? Found a little hollow to sleep in? How bad would that be, to leave everything behind? To live for this—survival instead of heartbreak and the damning reality of what I am?

I'd miss him. That's the hang-up. I've already been researching potions, and admittedly, dark magic, which I know it's illegal, but if there's a way to get rid of this affliction, I'll do it, even if… this is the best I've ever felt.

I wish I could just be this. Be accepted. Not be seen as a monster. I've always found it odd that people told stories about my kind like we snuck through open windows and stole babies in the night right out of their cribs and licked the tears of weeping mothers.

Me? This form? I'm barely a foot off the ground. My teeth are minuscule in comparison to a wolf. My cat-like claws are barely enough to puncture a vole, let alone a person.

The voles scurry into the hollow of a tree too small for me to follow, so I spend some time digging for them before growing bored and catching a new scent.

Copper. Iron. *Metal.*

Blood.

I follow the scent. The forest thickens, and the deep snow becomes more manageable. I'm not sure how far I've gone from the castle, but it can't be that far, surely. Again, my brain bounces between rational and animalistic. The scent deepens–fresh and hot. I can't help but follow it, even when prickles of unease begin to skitter down my spine.

I enter a clearing lit by moonlight filtering through the fog. It's so cold that the trees are covered in frost, every branch coated in white and silver ice crystals. It could be daytime based on the way the moon reflects on the ice, highlighting the gentle shadows of the forest floor–and the puddle of blood just a few feet away.

The rabbit I chased is shredded, its white fur scattered in puffs across the snow now dappled red. What's left of its body is still.

I lift a paw, then another, finding it suddenly, inexplicably cold.

A soft click of teeth hits my ears. A crunch of snow. A twig snapping.

All of my fur stands on end. My ears twitch toward the sound.

My heart pounds just once, and then I'm running for my life.

A snarl breaks the snowy silence. A howl pierces the air, then more, until what sounds like six wolves make their proximity known.

One is on my tail, far enough away it's only chasing my scent, but now their thick, bloody, smell is all around me.

I sprint through the forest, zig-zagging to try to lead them astray, but there are so many. Their howls make my blood race. My human brain and senses fight for dominance as reality settles in. I'm so much smaller. I'm not as fast. I need to *hide*.

Another clearing expands before me. I race toward a tree where a hollow rests just out of view in the snow, but the snow is deeper here, and it slows me down to a near crawl as I fight through it.

A snarl rips through the air above me, and I screech when teeth latch onto my back left thigh, and then I'm airborne.

The second I hit the ground, I disappear into three feet of powdery snow that slips and deepens when I try to roll onto my belly, to find my footing, but it's no use. A second wolf enters the clearing and begins the chase, the torture. I'm tossed back and forth like a rag doll, scratching and snarling, biting when I can, but they could crush my head in their jaws, and my narrow neck could snap with just one bite.

But I fight. Puncture wounds pepper my legs. I scratch, bite, and scream in pain but... everything grows blurry. My body feels slow and sluggish. My vision darkens, and the clearing is suddenly wet and warm. My blood is... everywhere.

One of the wolves bites down on my hip and tosses me again. My back hits a tree, and I slide to its base, where I lie limp, and my powers of shifting begin to fizzle. They must think I'm a wild fox. Some exceedingly rare toy to toss around like a rag doll. They're not hunting me to eat me. No, the way they slowly approach, all six of them now, makes me believe this is just for fun. My gruesome, tortuous death will be for sport.

The snow around my body vibrates, pulling toward the center of the clearing. The wolves stop, hackles raised as they glance around, their gaping maws wet with my blood.

I see the shadow of a new wolf before they do. It rises out of the fog, twice their size, a deep, endless, unnatural black.

Then, it just goes... hazy. All these wolfen bodies. All the blood.

New blood. Their blood. It washes over the clearing in a crimson wave that coats every frostbitten tree. I feel myself slip out of my fox form against my will, too injured to fight the change. My body curls into my human form, naked, and blood-soaked. My hair falls over my shoulders to cover my breasts, but otherwise, I'm totally exposed to the deepening, frozen chill.

With the last of my strength, I pull my knees to my chest and hug them, barely able to make out the shadows of the battle taking place ahead of me.

Three dead wolves lie in pieces only a few yards away. The fog lifts to reveal two more. The clearing goes dark as a moonless night when thick, heavy clouds roll in, and it begins to snow in earnest—thick flakes that stick to my hair and shoulders. I'm being buried, gently, in a snow-white casket.

This is gentler than I thought it'd be. Going into death... I always pictured it being violent, and it was at first, but now... I just feel warm and light. Dying terrifies me, honestly. I'm not a wolf. I won't go to the Goddess's kingdom. I'm not sure where I'll end up. Somewhere dark, I think. Somewhere where demons like me are punished for eternity for things our ancestors, the ones who passed this curse through my bloodline, go.

Somewhere in my dwindling subconscious, I feel another presence. Someone warm and solid reaching out to me, tugging on the threads that bind us. I've been wondering about that. Those little strings in my chest that pluck like piano strings, filling me with either hurt or a deep, secure kind of warmth. Love. Security. Togetherness. Or dread. Pain and rejection.

It used to be just a fleeting, faraway feeling, like a whisper across a void. Now, as my blood drains, and my battered legs go numb, I feel these emotions like fingers curling around my heart, keeping it beating, like this is my final punishment, and this new wolf is here to finish me off in the violent way I deserve.

"Tell him I loved him," I whisper, my lips nearly frozen from the cold. "I loved him so much it could have killed me. I wanted him. A life with him. I have so many regrets."

The battle with the final wolf continues in slow motion, the black wolf tearing into its back and dragging it across the clearing under the disorienting snowfall. Snow is already starting to coat the other bodies, their hot blood sending mist into the air.

"I love him." I choke, tears spilling and freezing against my cheeks. "I love *Aris*. I wanted to tell him. I should have told him, but I knew how much I was hurting him already." My final confession is barely a whisper, no more than a puff of icy mist. "I did it all for him. So he could have a future with someone like him. Someone who isn't a fox, who isn't a monster. I'm sorry. I'm so sorry."

An unearthly roar rocks ice crystals from the tallest trees, and then a tearing, popping sound cuts me to pieces. I choke on dread, on fear, as the black wolf rips the spine from his opponent, and the clearing falls silent.

Then, he turns to me, his body and face distorted by the heavy snowfall.

But I feel it in my bones. The familiarity. The shadows that pour from him... I know them. They're the same shadows that dance around my room at night to keep me company when I can't sleep. The same shadows that curl between Aris's fingers when he's upset, or even... immensely happy. The same shadows I let him paint over my naked skin in throes of passion.

"No," I whisper, tears blurring my vision. "Goddess, *no*."

JUST LIKE YOU

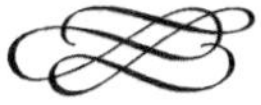

POSEY

THE SHADOW SHIFTS FORM, THE MASSIVE WOLF FINALLY COMING INTO full view just seconds before his body rolls into its human form, cloaked in tendrils of night. Silver eyes. A mask that gleams in the moonlight–all those gems. All that iron. Minerals I've touched. Mended to fit. Armor of black coating his body. His usual cloak. I'm not imagining it.

He's wearing the newly mended helmet, and it glows with his powers.

Blood seeps down my legs as I curl them against my chest, trying to wiggle back as far as I can against the tree.

His determined steps align with my rapidly beating heart. Dread worse than being thrown and bitten by those wolves rips through my senses. Tears blur my vision. I extend a trembling hand like I can push him away. "Please–" I croak, choking on a sob. "P-please don't, Aris. Don't h–hurt me! I–I don't want to–to die like this–I just–" Sobs cut through the words. I can barely get them out. "Please don't hurt me!

Please don't! I can't help it! I never–I never–I never asked for this–*I can hide it*–oh, Goddess–please don't–"

Strong arms scoop me off the ground. I try to scream, but it comes out as a mangled sob. His hand comes up to rest against the back of my head. My body stiffens. I try to muffle my cries, waiting for him to snap my neck, but his fingers curl in my hair, and his touch is so warm, so soft. My mouth opens against his armor in a silent cry I can't hold back, and he wraps his cloak around both of us, shielding my naked, shredded body from the cold. I might be dying anyway. The world fades, and warmth rushes in, numbing my body to the point I can't feel a thing. Stars streak overhead before disappearing, and a strange, twisting sensation pulls me apart until I just give in, slumping, my mind ceasing to function.

I don't remember closing my eyes, but when I open them again, I'm in an unfamiliar room. Another starry mural covers the ceiling, and the deep, dark blue velvet canopy covering the four-poster bed is half drawn, shielding one half of a room that smells like Aris from view.

His room.

His bed.

Oh Goddess. Oh... no. No, no, no...

I fly out of bed. I'm in one of his shirts. A black button down that's soft to the touch. The wounds on my legs are completely healed, nothing but silver streaks against the cool alabaster of my skin. The second my bare feet touch the shallow, soft as cashmere carpet, I see him, sitting in a winged-back armchair next to a roaring fireplace. He doesn't say a word. He doesn't move. He just stares at me, his face painted in shadow, those silver eyes searing mine from the inside out.

I back up until my thighs hit the bed. "Aris." My heart thuds before breaking into a sprint.

"You're a fox." His voice is deep and dangerous, quicksilver eyes unreadable and honed on my face, like he's looking right through me, inside of me, peeling me apart piece by piece.

My lungs ache as I draw in a shuddering breath.

He uncrosses his legs and splays them in a very male way–unbothered, damn near relaxed as he inspects me. He looks livid. Ready to kill.

"I–I can explain–"

"This *entire time,*" he says, but his voice breaks with a scolding laugh, and for a moment he struggles to continue, "this *whole* time, Posey, *this* was the reason you rejected me? The whole fucking reason you kept me at arm's length?"

"I'm a monster." That's all I can manage. The sniffling that comes after is against my will, but I've never felt fear like this. I knew that one day I would be found out. I prayed it wouldn't happen, that burying myself in a temple and forsaking love and company would spare my own miserable life but…. He rises and takes two steps in my direction before stopping.

"No one can know," I beg, holding out my hands in surrender. "Please! My family doesn't know! They can't. It would ruin them. They'd be killed if–if anyone thought maybe they were like me–"

"No one is going to touch them. You have my word."

"They're not like me, *I swear.* They're wolves. I promise they are! No one else knows. Just you. I faked those tests. I led my family astray for their own safety. I was going into the cloth and taking my vows so that no one would ever know. So I couldn't get married. *I won't have children,* I swear. I won't pass this on!" I nod several times as tears spill down my cheeks. I begin to fall to my knees, but my legs won't bend. I'm not sure what I'm begging for anymore. The words spill without my consent. "Just–make it quick. *Please.* I don't want to hurt. I don't want anyone to get hurt because of me. That's why I've done every-thing I had to do. All the lies. I tried to be discreet at the manor in Gem Lake, but when the moon is full, I can't–*I can't help it.*"

"I understand." I look up at him. He's closer than before. Close enough I can see the way his eyes gloss over. I wince when he raises a hand and reaches for me.

"Just make it quick," I croak, drawing back my breath with a tangled sob. "Just break my neck. I won't fight it. I swear I won't. I'm sorry. I'm so sorry, Aris. Oh, Goddess, I am so sorry–"

His hand wraps around my neck. I close my eyes, praying my last prayer. Not for Her forgiveness. But for *his*. How I wanted to tell him that I was in love with him. That I dream of him. That those two nights in his arms at the cabin were the best moments of my stupid, insignificant life.

That I'm grateful he's the one to end it all for me.

But the twist doesn't come.

He steps into me, closing the distance between us, and kisses me.

I shove him away, gasping for breath, but he pulls me back with a deep growl. "Stop."

"Don't touch me. I'm disgusting. I'm a monster. I'm a fox, Aris, you saw it!" I shove him again, hard, and he backs up, raising his hands in surrender, but it's the look on his face that rattles me so greatly my fear vanishes in a heartbeat, replaced by confusion.

He's smiling. It's almost deranged. And when he barks a laugh, I startle. "Are you fucking joking, Posey? This whole fucking time? All of this–" He waves a hand around the room and laughs again, much louder this time. "You going into the temple and throwing your life away was because you're a *fox*?" Another laugh, this one so hard he groans in pain and clutches his chest.

My cheeks flare with heat, turning crimson. "What is so funny? You fucking bastard! Is this some form of torture? Some sick game before you let me loose, hunt me down, and kill me?"

"I'm not going to fucking kill you, Posey."

"Then what–"

"What I'd really like to do," he says, each word clipped and severe as he closes the distance between us again, "is fuck you until you're screaming my name. I want to do everything I've been dreaming about since this summer. Everything I think about when I see you haunting my castle, in the very places I've imagined bending you over and punishing you for *what you did to us*."

"What?" I rasp. My brain shuts down for several seconds before rebooting.

He simply shrugs and closes me against the bed, forcing me to sit, his hands braced on either side of the mattress by my hips.

"I feel like an idiot," he admits, sucking his lower lip and then letting it go. "I should have caught on, you know? Gods, when you were in heat? I thought I was losing my fucking mind over you."

"What is this?" I rush out, my body tingling under the weight of his attention as his gaze rakes over me like hot coals.

"And this whole time, I was right."

"Right about what?"

"*You*. Why I felt like you'd ripped my heart out of my chest when you left Gem Lake. *You fucking did*. You cunning little *fox*. I should have known then and confirmed it the second you stepped back into my life. I was totally foxed up."

"What are you saying?"

The next kiss is so overwhelming, I can't fight it. I don't want to. He growls against my mouth until I part my lips for him, and then he's ravishing me with his tongue. He doesn't stop until we're both trembling for air. "Aris–"

"I love you," he says against my mouth. There's nothing tender about it. It's all consuming. Meant to lay claim. "I love you. I'm not going to kill you, but I kind of want to for what you put us through the past couple of months. You should have told me in the beginning."

"You would have hurt me."

"I would have *protected* you." He pulls back so I can see his eyes, and there is he, the Aris I fell in love with this summer. "Like I'm going to protect you *now*."

I shake my head. "We can't. You cannot be with a fox. You can't do it. If we had children, Aris, there's a risk they could be like–"

"Like us?"

I stare at him, sure my brain just short-circuited, but he smiles down at me and presses his hand against my heart.

"What are you talking about?"

"What do you feel right here?" He taps my skin. "What do you feel when you look at me? What did it feel like when Morgan was in my presence or when you found out about her and Talon and thought he was *me*?"

I can't look away from him. My heart rate skyrockets. The sky could be falling, and I wouldn't know.

He leans forward, his hand traveling down over the slope of my breast to my stomach, then lower, his fingers brushing my inner thighs. I let out an involuntary huff of air trying to hold back a moan.

"Did you know that knots are impossible unless a man is with his mate, Posey?" he says against my forehead, his lips parting in an involuntary grunt when he feels the wetness pooling under his touch. "That's one thing I couldn't stop thinking about. I thought it was a fluke, that I was just desperate for any kind of real connection, and my body responded in that way, but look at us now."

"We can't be mates. I'm a fox and you're a wolf."

"Look at me," he commands sternly, and I do, but my eyes are full of tears. "Any children we have, because we *will* have kids, Posey. And we *will* get married. And you *will* allow me to protect you for the rest of our lives… our kids will be like us because *I'm* like *you*."

"You're not–"

"My grandmother Amanda? She's a full fox, just like you. I thought she was, up until an hour again when I saw you getting torn to fucking shreds–" He cuts himself off with a growl, trembling, but his fingers move upward, and I sigh into the touch, mouthing his name. "She was the only one. My dad and I have both forms. But now there's you. *My mate.* I knew it this summer but couldn't confirm it and didn't understand why I felt that way. I couldn't put my finger on what you'd done to me, but then I saw you in your fox form, defenseless, untrained. *My mate.*" He presses two fingers through my folds, and my head rolls back, giving him access to my neck, which he greedily accepts, groaning into my skin before biting down. He releases me, breathless, and says, "I felt it like a knife through the heart. You're *mine*. You've been mine this whole time, and I'm not letting you go. I can't. Stay with me, Posey. *Stay here with me.*"

I'm beyond breath. I can barely form the words I want to say as he slides his fingers deeper, his body shuddering and my inner walls spasming. A single touch is all it took to bring me to the edge. He licks down my neck to that spot he loves.

"Stay with me. Say you will. Tell me who you belong to now."

"I'm yours," I say weakly, too overcome to say what I really want to tell him. Everything blends together into a sensation that sweeps me off my feet. "I've been yours. I'll always be yours. I love–love you. I'm so sorry for what I did to us. I love you."

He tangles his hand in my hair and tilts my head to the side, licking me again, wetting my skin and sucking until I'm crying out.

"Say it again."

"I'm yours. I'm yours. I'm–"

Aris's teeth sink into my neck, breaking the skin.

Golden threads flood between us, and I cry out his name.

DO YOU WANT THIS?

POSEY

ARIS PANTS AGAINST MY NECK. PLEASURE LIKE I'VE NEVER KNOWN washes through me. Toe-curling, mind-numbing bliss that I drown in for several seconds until the room comes back into focus, and I remember myself.

His eyes are dark and hooded in the firelight. The curtains are drawn to the storm beyond, and it's still nighttime, I think. Aris is leaning over me, one hand resting between my thighs, and his other hand is still splayed against my back to keep me upright. His gaze holds mine in disbelief before he dips his head to lick the wound he just left clean, the puncture marks fading into scars under his tongue. His mark on my skin feels like I've been branded by liquid silver. It feels heavy and amazing.

"You should hate me," I whisper, closing my eyes and leaning my cheek against his. I'm so tired. I've never felt exhaustion like this before. My fingers ache to the bone. All I did today was build the helmet, repair every gem, turning silver into diamonds and moonstones to hold his power, without him there to test each jewel. It worked regardless. Now I know why.

Mates. I did this to my mate. I broke his heart and let it fester like that for months.

"I wanted to," he admits, then leans back and straightens to look down at me, at my tangled hair that he brushes off my shoulders. "Now I understand."

"I thought I was protecting you."

"You were." His voice is so soft and reassuring. It's maddening, actually. He should still hate me. I took advantage of him this summer. Used him for my heat. And now, here? Knowing he was pining, *yearning*, that he was breaking apart in my presence, and I didn't run away like I should have? I didn't want to. *I wanted him.* It's the most selfish thing I've ever done.

"Shhh," he whispers, pressing an open-mouthed kiss to my forehead while I unravel. I press my hands to his chest, bunching the fabric of his shirt while tears roll down my cheeks. We stay like that for a long time. Me, resting on the edge of the bed, my cheek pressed to his chest, reckoning with what I've done to us. Him, leaning down, whispering soft reassurances into my hair. His mark settles on my neck, a lick of heat reminding me how close he is, how close his body is to mine again.

He only pulls away to run a bath. His hands are firm but all business as he helps me out of the shirt. I shy away even though his ensuite is dim and beyond the frosty windows it's as dark as my soot stained fingers after a day spent doing alchemy, and I instantly regret my involuntary flinch when he touches my arm to turn me toward the water.

He leaves the room, which smells like him—his soap. His shampoo. His aftershave and toothpaste. I want to drown in this moment to keep it safe. I'm afraid to leave the bath even after it grows tepid, and I've untangled my hair. I don't know what I'll find behind that door because my entire future lies beyond it.

I'm his mate. He loves me. He wants me and my body. *He wants us.*

But there's so much we need to talk about.

Wrapped in a towel, I slowly open the door into the bedroom, which is warm and dim. He's sitting in that winged-back chair facing the bed, his head tipped back and eyes open to slits like he was sleeping until he sensed my presence.

I stand here, unsure of what to do or what to say.

He scans my face before saying in a rough, almost choked whisper, "Come here."

The floor is warm and soft beneath my bare feet. His hands are steady and firm on my waist when he pulls me into his lap so I'm straddling him, only some thin fabric separating us.

His fingertips have their own electric current. Just the act of brushing my hair away from my neck makes my chest tighten.

"Did it hurt?" he asks, his voice low and gravelly. His thumb traces the half-moon scar, and his eyes lift to mine. I nod weakly, and he leans forward, pressing a kiss to my mark, which ignites. I shiver as warmth rushes down my spine to flood into pure, molten heat at its base, tingling and impossible to ignore.

"We need to talk," I whisper into his hair.

His wry smile against the mark makes me quiver. "About the skulls? Or the helmet? Or the fact you went into the caves when I explicitly told you not to?"

The column of my throat bobs when I force myself to swallow. My body feels electric, like one innocent touch from him is enough, but his tongue against the side of my neck is *indecent*.

"We have time," he breathes, then gently bites down over the mark again like he can't help himself. "You need to eat something and sleep."

I grip his shoulders, sighing into the sensation of his mouth against my skin. That same hunger from this summer pulsates through my muscles, the heat settling in my bone marrow. I don't want to eat. I really don't want to sleep. A whiny, pitiful sound leaves my trembling lips when he kisses down my neck to my chest and stops, breathing hard, his grip on my waist tightening.

He's so restrained. Tension pours from his body with every kiss and nip of his teeth.

"I never thought I'd touch you again," he says against my skin, and it's my undoing.

A choked sob escapes my throat, and his mouth is on mine in an instant, shushing me, pulling me closer until we're flush, and his heat envelopes me.

I hesitate for a moment before kissing him back. Everything else vanishes. It's just me and him. His hands ghosting up my sides. His tongue gliding over mine in deep, exploratory strokes. I wrap my arms around his neck, my fingers curling in his hair. Touching him again is like coming home. It makes me want to weep, to pray, to fucking smile for the first time in months.

But he sighs against my parted lips and breaks the kiss. His eyes are dark silver in the fading light of the dying fire. "You need to sleep."

I nod, but the last place I want to be is anywhere other than his lap. I can feel him straining between us, his cock rigid and full, pressed against my stomach.

He angles his mouth over mine but doesn't kiss me, like he's doing everything to talk himself out of it, of this in general. "I need to sleep, too."

"Then come to bed."

He smiles, shaking his head. "You're killing me, Posey."

His hands drop to my thighs, drifting upward under the towel.

"You're too thin," he murmurs, dropping his mouth to my collarbone. "I'm going to get you something to eat."

"The spirits–"

"Have made themselves scarce after I felt something was off and came back here and found out you were being attacked by wolves in the forest, ten miles north of here. They're hiding from my wrath, I think."

He nips at my skin, grunting at the effort of keeping his hands still at the juncture of my thighs and hips.

"Do you know how to cook?" My head falls back when he kisses just above my breasts.

"No." It's breathy, and his fingers twitch before gripping me harder, like he's on his last nerve. The towel slips a few inches, revealing the slope of my breasts, and a resounding growl vibrates through him. He meets my eyes briefly. Hunger deepens the silver until it's as dark as raw iron. My arms slowly unravel from his neck.

He tilts his head while I reach for the towel.

"Posey..."

Fire warmed air makes my skin prickle, but the look on Aris's face has me shivering despite the heat.

He leans his head back against the chair, lost in a trance. His eyes track the movement of the towel as it unravels, leaving me in just my skin.

"*Fuck.*" His mouth barely moves. He hisses out a breath and adjusts his hips, grinding against me, the motion making my chest bounce ever so slightly.

I take his hand and guide it to my breast. My heart leaps, blood thrumming through my veins at the sensation of his heat against my skin.

"Can I touch you?" The words are barely audible, but the desperation in my voice is loud and clear. This summer, when he'd held my wrists above my head, it had been in an effort to keep himself under control.

I angle my hips to meet his, and he grunts, hissing through his teeth. I do it again and again, chasing the friction of his cock through the rough fabric of his pants, making a mess of both of us. He grips my hips, his eyes narrowed to slits and focused on my breasts. His breath comes in sharp, shallow rasps as I lose control of myself, my rational brain slipping into oblivion. And the noises that leave my lips?

"Please?" I whine, and he exhales deeply, his eyes shut and his body so tense I can feel every hard, bulging muscle beneath his shirt.

"I'm not going to last," he replies with a short, rough chuckle, like he's in pain. "If you so much as touch me, I'm going to come."

"I want you to. You haven't. Not once when we're together." He pulls me closer to press an open-mouthed kiss to my cheek, slopping and frantic just like I feel while I writhe on his lap.

"Do you know how often we do this in my dreams? Every night,

Posey. I imagine you here, in my room, in my bed, every single Goddess-damned night, and now I have the real thing, and I can't...." He hisses the last words while I pull down his zipper. He nips my earlobe. "Greedy."

His hand roams to my ass, and he adjusts my weight on his lap with a soft sigh. Then, his mouth is on mine again, hungry and hot.

He doesn't let me take what I want, though. He pulls my hands away from his zipper and holds my wrists behind my back, kissing me slowly, thoroughly, until I'm warmed to the bone. The raging fire, his heat, his mouth... It's like being lulled into a trance. I'm sleepy. My body feels amazing and soft, and I just want him to let me give him something he's been going without.

He licks the mark again, shivering, pulling me as close as possible until my breasts are flush with his chest. "I dream about this. Every. Single. Night."

He cups the back of my head and tilts my face to the side to gain more access to my neck.

"I'm obsessed with this spot, right here," he whispers into my skin before biting over the mark again, grunting, groaning, his body vibrating. "I love when you wear your hair up so I can see your neck."

I feel like I'm floating in a warm pool. His body relaxes with mine. This has nothing to do with sex, and I quickly realize it, some of that overwhelming desperation flickering away to make room for something great, and it nearly brings me to tears.

"I regret not telling you before," I say into his hair. His hands drift up my sides. "I feel like I wasted so much time we could have spent together."

"Do you want this?" His tone drops, darkening.

"Of course—"

"Not sex, Posey. That's not what I'm asking. I'll fuck you. I'll lay you down and ravage you, but I want more than that." He leans forward slightly, his hands steadying me as we drift, and he rises, carrying me to the bed. His sheets are warm and soft, and they smell like him. He lays me down, his arm braced beneath me, his eyes like quicksilver.

I smooth my hand against his cheek. His stubble scratches my palm. He closes his eyes and leans into the touch.

"I want this, too. I want to stay here with you. I think I can be the kind of Luna you need."

He opens his eyes, leans in for a kiss, but my hand drops to the mattress, and within the space of a heartbeat, I drift into a deep sleep. It's endless. I don't dream. I don't hear voices, and my sore fingers don't wake me up in the middle of the night incessantly.

I wake up to warm sunshine for the first time in weeks. The frost on the windows has begun to melt, and streaks of gold wash over the bed, where Aris is tucked beside me, his body curled against mine, our fingers intertwined.

I close my eyes again. I'm not in a rush.

For the first time in my life… I get to *live*.

ON THE WORKTABLE

Aris

I LIFT THE SMALLER SKULL AND BALANCE IT IN MY HAND WHILE POSEY moves in the background. The midmorning air is scented with the herbs she uses for her potions and hand creams. Little bells and chimes ping through the air as her timer goes off. I glance at her, the sunlight casting a halo around her face. She's pouring a cooled tincture of whistlethorne and dried cherry into a large vial.

It's not even noon, and her fingers are already stained black.

I set the skull down and look at the tools arranged on the granite, some still cooling, sending puffs of steam into the air. "You have a whole collection now," I muse, and her smile is soft, no teeth, just a twitch of her lips.

"I have a ways to go to replace everything from the old alchemy room downstairs."

"I could… order some, take the burden off your shoulders."

She throws me an incredulous look that makes my heart squeeze.

"Or not." I ease onto the stool I brought upstairs so I could sit here and watch her from a closer distance than my chair far across the room. After last night, we've breached that invisible boundary.

I'm not sure why I didn't pick up on the fact that she is a fox. I can see it now in the way she moves. Her small, delicate, but skilled hands. Even the curve of her eyes and chin are foxlike, and her hair?

"You're almost completely red in the summer, aren't you?"

She glances up from a book about herbal remedies and catches my gaze, again with that soft but not quite full smile. "Just about–with tinges of pink, I think. I'm still strawberry-blonde, even in my fox form. But… I haven't had much of a chance to look at myself in a mirror in that form or even a pond."

"Can you shift at will?"

"Yeah. I can." She turns to the other counter along the wall. I watch the movement, the way she takes a deep breath.

"You've never been able to talk to anyone about this before."

"No," she replies quickly and then clears her throat. She looks at me over her shoulder and smiles. "Just you."

My heart lurches. It's not the first time it's done that this morning, either. Waking up with her in my arms, soft and warm… gods, it had been everything I prayed for. Everything I incessantly dreamed about come to life, and I really don't want to fuck it up by moving too fast.

Or by trapping her, which is why I didn't take her last night, even after marking her. Marking her while my fox form held dominance over my senses.

I shift my weight on the stool, interlocking my fingers over the granite slab. "Posey… if this isn't what you want… if you want to…" How do I even begin?

"Aris." She turns, her hands on her hips, and for the first time in months, I see her again, Posey from this summer, grumpy and busy, but this time, she's mine, and it shows as her smile widens. "I've been in love with you for a long time." She licks her lips, just as speechless as I feel. "I thought I could handle it. This summer, when we slept together? Even if we weren't mates, I think I would have felt the same way I have all fall and winter, like my heart went through a meat grinder, and I didn't know how to put it back together. And I hate being here with you because I knew how much it was hurting you, and I couldn't just say I didn't want you because that would have been a lie, and I'd been lying for so long already."

I rise, but she backs up into the juncture of the counter, wringing her fingers like they ache, and I know they do. I can feel that now. Those little whispers of discomfort that rile my senses through our bond.

"I'm very good at lying, but I can't lie about how I feel, not with you," she whispers.

"I know. I couldn't either." I take a few steps in her direction, but she doesn't notice.

"When I found out about Morgan, I was devastated," she admits, breathless, her cheeks turning a rosy pink that floods down her neck and chest. Her breasts rise, and she takes a deep breath, and my vision hones on her soft curves. "And I felt so terrible about that. How much I wished it could have been me. How much I wanted to go with you instead of Roman. I would have–if I'd known, if I hadn't been so scared."

"Did you think I was going to hurt you?" If what she was muttering when I found her is any indication, I already know the answer. I reach for her, dragging my knuckles over the sharp curve of her waist, imagining her like she was last night, her skin warm from the fire and naked for me to see. All of her. All of her softness. I wanted to bite her all over.

"Yes." The word trembles with guilt. "I did. I thought you'd kill me. Everyone hates foxes. They're scared of them, even wild ones. And I messed up this summer, didn't I? Other people caught my scent, and it sent the Ruby pack into a frenzy."

I was a very good boy last night, in my opinion. I wasn't going to bend her over the bed and fuck her after she was nearly torn limb-from-limb by that rogue pack of wolves. Oh, but I wanted to. So badly it killed me to lay her in my bed and watch her drift to sleep. More so, this morning, when I sat across from her and watched her eat for what I think was the first time in days. I wanted to sweep every plate off the table and drag her to me, seating her on my lap, ripping the fabric of her shirt open until those glorious breasts were mine for the taking.

"Aris?"

I look into her eyes. "People are always going to be afraid of what they don't understand." I kiss her hard, unable to stop myself as every damning, delicious, utterly indecent thought I've had about this woman before me rips my other senses to shreds.

She gasps against my mouth, but it's over. I can't stop, not when she grips my shoulders and moans against my mouth. The world goes dark, and everything else fades.

We're alone. There's no one else here. She can scream to the rafters, and no one would hear her. The spirits... I'll deal with them later. They're being weird. The female won't respond to us, and her companion has a freezing, bitter presence when he's near that I recognize as a mate doing everything in his power to make his mate's world a little smaller and more secure for her comfort.

I don't realize I've picked Posey up and splayed her out on her worktable until her metal tools ping off the floorboards, and empty glass vials shatter. She rips at my shirt, tearing it open, pressing her hands flat against my chest.

Her touch is enough to send me spiraling.

"Fuck," I grunt, tearing her shirt down the center. She's not wearing a bra which makes me weak in the knees, and before I can finish shredding her clothes from her skin, I bury my face between her breasts, and she squeals in delight. Those little giggles...

I nip at the top of her right breast to give myself a moment to calm down. "I should have marked you here." I move to the other side, catching her gaze. "Or here." I bite down a little harder than I mean to, but she takes it. She's *so good* to me.

Her whimpering makes me feel completely feral. She's fumbling with my belt loop while I press kisses all over her chest and down her belly until I'm forced to rise and undress myself, my hand pressed down on her stomach to keep her pinned on the table exactly where I want her. I pull her apron off. Her skirt is next. I hook my thumbs in her panties and pull them down over her knees, tossing them to the other side of the room. My pants are a heap at my feet that I kick to the side, but I'm out of breath, thrumming with desire so strong I think I'll come before I'm even inside of her.

My hands travel up her smooth, soft thighs.

"I'm going to knot in you. I'm not going to be able to help it," I warn, breathless, my voice ragged. It's the only warning she gets.

My cock splits her folds. The resistance is insane. Her beautiful, wet pussy hugs me so tight I can't breathe until I'm buried to the hilt, and her muscles quiver around my length. Her breathy, shaky inhale of breath makes me see stars.

"Is this okay?" I whisper, bracing a hand on the table and leaning over her to press my lips to hers. Her mouth parts in a moan. Her legs are already shaking, and she's so tight. Fuck, I'm not a fucking marathon runner by any means.

The knot is already happening. I thrust in deep, grinding to find the perfect spot, the perfect depth. Posey trembles, her body flushed and tight. She grips my arms, and I slowly move inside of her, her clit throbbing like a drumbeat.

"Does it hurt?" she whispers.

I choke on a rough laugh. "This?" I move ever so slightly. She's full of me. There's no more space. She fits me like a glove, and I could die right here, right now, a happy man. She gasps when I pull out and press back in until our hips are flush. Her legs tighten around my waist, ankles interlocked. "I've never felt anything like you, Posey. You're a fucking dream."

Another hard thrust. I grab the edge of the table, my chest only inches from hers, and press in again. She arches her hips to meet each thrust while I suck and nibble on her breasts, leaving a sensation she'll feel for days, and then I'll give her new ones.

I wrap an arm under her back and hoist her upright. The new position is like liquid heaven–molten–and I'm so deep she's crying out my name.

Her gasp of shock rocks me back to myself. The room around us is still blurry, and my heart thunders as the knot expands. Pleasure like

I've never known soars through me, and then I'm coming, and she's crying my name, her muscles spasming.

"Good girl," I pant against her temple, the pleasure almost edging on pain as I fill her to her breaking point. "Take it. You're doing so well."

"It's so big," she moans, shivering, her arms wrapped around my neck and fingers tangled in my hair. She shimmies her hips, and the movement rockets down my spine and explodes into another orgasm that has me crying out her name this time. I grip her like my life depends on it. Maybe it does. Losing this woman… I can't even think about it without wanting to scorch the world to ash and embers. If anyone even looks at her funny, it will be the last thing they do. I want to keep her here, where she's safe. Where she's safe with me.

"I love you," she whispers against my cheek.

"Prove it," I dare, my voice strangely stern. "Give me your mark."

She whimpers with heat, burying her face against my shoulder. I move in slow, rhythmic jerks, unable to thrust into her again with the knot keeping us together, but every slow movement has her grip tightening, and body her tenses when she comes again, I'm right there with her.

"Fuck! Posey!" I growl, grunting. Her pussy clamps around my knot in rhythmic spasms, so tight I could shout.

But then she bites down on the ridge of my shoulder so hard it breaks the skin, and she holds on, riding out our bliss while leaving her mark on me. Her mate. Her man. I'm going to marry this woman. Tonight. I'm taking her to the temple right after this, everything else be damned.

A distant chiming sound barely registers in my brain. It fades but then comes again.

"What is that?" Posey asks breathlessly, resting her cheek against mine.

I'm out of breath as I look over my shoulder at my discarded pants and the flicker of blue-hued light lighting up one pocket.

A few minutes later, after cleaning us up and making sure I haven't maimed my own mate beyond repair, I pull on my pants and whip out my phone, slightly annoyed that anyone would dare to call me and interrupt.

A single line of text from my mom lights up the screen. I can sense how frantic she was when she wrote it, and every sense tightens when I slowly turn back to Posey.

She notices, her eyes widening as she scans my face while simultaneously tying her apron strings. "Aris? What happened?"

STUCK IN A SHIFT

Aris

"Are you okay? Dizzy?" Posey's cheeks are warm and flushed between my gloved hands. She nods, but it's short and sharp, and I can tell she's lying about feeling anything but insanely nauseous and out-of-body.

I've jumped with her before, when I brought her mangled, bleeding body back to the castle and dosed her with so many healing drafts I wondered if I'd inadvertently killed her with them instead of healing her injuries, but unlike Brie and some of the other normal people in our family, she has powers, and she recovers within seconds of being torn between realms and stitched back together again.

It's early evening in the Deadlands. Silverhide glows in the pale golden haze of the first light of sunset. The snow-covered landscape shines pink as the sun dips below the ridges, turning the sky a stunning violet, but we're not here on a sightseeing tour.

"Come here," I murmur, tugging her closer to fix her cloak, which tangled during the journey. She stands stunned, looking to the side at the village nearby. "Never been?"

"To the Deadlands? No. Of course not." She blinks and meets my eyes. "Why are we here?"

"I have no idea, but my mom said it was urgent." I didn't give her much of a choice about coming with me. Her mark on my neck isn't even an hour old, and no part of me was about to separate myself from my mate this soon.

I turn her toward a steep wooden staircase leading to the wide deck of the Alpha's King's house, the railing lined with frost covered garland and blinking Solstice lights. I've always loved Silverhide and Ryan's simple, cozy home here, but tonight, the very second I open the door, it feels like the air has been removed from every room despite the Solstice decorations and the scent of cranberry and evergreen.

Dad turns at the same moment Uncle Ryan kicks off the wall in a fighting stance. I tuck Posey behind me on instinct as tension I can taste suffocates the room, and we're only in the doorway as it stands.

But Ryan relaxes, running his fingers through his hair and cursing into the palm of his hand. Dad glances at him before moving in my direction and taking me by the shoulder to lead me back outside, and then he spots Posey.

"Oh," Evander, my father and the head of the Ghost army, says in shock. "Posey?" He meets my eyes. "What–"

"Later. Where's mom? She sent me a text and said it was urgent."

Dad stares at Posey for several seconds. His deep green eyes are a kaleidoscope of colors against the Solstice lights.

"Dad?"

"She's inside."

"Aris."

I take a breath and turn to the voice coming up the stairs behind me. Grandpa Ryatt is dressed in his usual black, the shadowsword strapped in a halter along his spine. Humming voices drift between us. My bracelets react to the sword's proximity. It calls out to me. It has for a very long time.

It's mine.

I blink back the involuntary thought, tucking Posey against my side. Her fingers are like ice. "Is anyone going to explain what's going on?" I look between my father and grandfather, but Grandpa Ryatt turns to Dad, tilting his head toward the door.

"Ryan needs to leave for a while. He's upset, and his pack mates are catching on. This needs to be kept quiet until we know how to fix this."

Posey's fingers snake between mine and squeeze. I look uneasily through the door. Aunt Aviva comes into view looking like she's been recently dragged through hell. She stops at Ryan's side, her head bowed while talking in low tones, and he nods, eyes closed, before cursing under his breath and turning with her into one of the bedrooms on the main floor.

What the hell is going on?

"We haven't formally met," Ryatt says, and I snap back to the scene on the frosty exterior deck. He steps forward and extends a hand to Posey, who looks up at him slightly dumbfounded. "Posey Sapphire, correct? I know your father well."

She lets go of my hand. Dad's eyes slowly meet mine, one dark blond brow arched in a silent question, but I ignore him, fuming.

I want to be back home for once in my life. I want to lock myself away with Posey in my bedroom. I want to move all of her stuff there and never leave. Not for a while, at least. There's only a week and a half left before Solstice, and once that's over, my parents and grandparents will descend on the castle again, and nothing will be as quiet or as private as it is right now.

Before I realize what's happening, Grandpa Ryatt unsheathes the shadowsword in one swift, practiced motion. The glint of metal against the Solstice lights is momentarily blinding, and before I can think, I'm standing between him and Posey.

"What are you doing?" I seethe, shoving Posey behind me, but she fights it, huffing under her breath before stepping to the side and accepting the sword's hilt.

She smiles at Grandpa Ryatt.

I feel like I want to break something. I want to rip someone, possibly him, to shreds for even looking in her direction.

"Son?" Dad grips my shoulder firmly and drags me into the house. I jerk, trying to rip my arm out of his iron grip, but he shoves me against the wall in the kitchen, hard enough to rattle picture frames and pots hanging from the walls, his forearm pressed over my chest. He points out the window beside us. "She's right there, see? She's within sight."

I shake my head, trying to rid myself of this weird, overwhelming fight or flight feeling.

Dad leans in, keeping his weight steady on my chest. "Mates?"

"How did you guess?"

"You were about to kill your own grandfather for speaking to her."

I close my eyes for several seconds and take a breath. He lets up on the pressure against my lungs but doesn't let me go. "He's just showing her the sword. That's all. Her family made it long ago."

Posey's soft laugh drifts from outside, and that urge to shred something fills me up again. Dad presses me to the wall with a sigh. "How long ago did you mark her?"

"Last night."

"Fuck." Dad grinds his teeth with a short nod. "All right." He looks toward the hallway where muffled voices drift from the shadows. "We didn't know. Otherwise, I would have told your mother not to reach out to you for a few days, at least."

"Why," I grind out, "am I here?"

Mom appears around the corner looking just as unnerved as Aviva had moments ago. She gasps, rushing toward me with her arms outstretched, but halts when she sees Grandpa Ryatt and Posey through the window.

Then, she notices Dad has me firmly pinned to the wall. She blinks, looks at each of us deeply for several seconds, and then smiles.

"You found your mate?" She looks from me to him, her worn expression brightening several shades.

Dad sighs and nods.

"Oh, my Goddess! It's a Solstice miracle!"

"Why did you text me saying I needed to come to Silverhide immediately?" I snarl, losing my patience, but then Posey walks in, her cheeks burning pink when she notices me plastered against the wall and being held back by my father. Her lips pop open. I'm a single second away from head-butting my dad, shifting, and snatching my mate away when Misty steps around the corner with a long, defeated sigh.

The look on her face effectively evaporates the tension.

"There's nothing I can do."

Mom whirls to face her. "You're sure?"

"It's not a curse, Kenna. You're right. Honestly, I have no idea. I've never seen anything like this before other than... Maeve."

Dad straightens, letting me go. I step to the side, discreetly taking Posey by the arm, but her eyes are on Misty as well.

"Maeve was one when her powers began to show, right?" Misty asks, scratching her head.

"This is different, Misty," Mom replies under her breath, befuddled.

"What's the matter?" I step into the light of the kitchen, looking down at Mom and Misty.

Mom purses her lips and opens her mouth to explain, but Grandpa Ryatt, standing silently in the doorway, says, "Show him, Kenna. Let his shadows do their job."

"Blake has already come and gone. You did the same. There's nothing left to try," Misty cuts in with a huff, but I'm already stepping past them. Posey's fingers slip from mine. It takes only a matter of six determined steps to reach the small but cozy wood-lined bedroom on the first floor, which is packed as it stands.

Aviva spots me and smiles gravely. Ryan is too busy talking in low, serious tones to Kaleb in that strange, otherworldly language I haven't bothered to learn. Cole is kneeling, his medical kit open on the ground beside him.

And Lexa sits on the bed with a bundle in her arms that... doesn't look right.

Her exhausted dark blue eyes meet mine with a silent plea I can't decipher.

"I came as soon as I could!" Maeve's voice is like a shrill scream in my ear as she bustles into the room behind me, panting. "What's the matter?" Her mouth falls open when Cole pulls back the blanket covering the baby in Lexa's lap. Ian. He's a cute little thing with curly dark hair, sharply pointed ears and large, hazel-blue eyes.

At least, he was.

"Goddess above," I murmur, suddenly dizzy with shock.

Maeve gasps and doesn't bother to hide her recoil, her long pointed nails gripping my upper arm for support.

Lexa forces herself to swallow and hugs the... *wolf pup* closer while Cole listens to his chest with his stethoscope.

"Lexa?" Maeve steps forward, her sea-glass eyes shining brighter than they ever have against the sudden paleness of her skin.

Kaleb looks like he's on the verge of shouting at everyone to leave his mate and child alone. I take a step back, then another, until my back hits the closet door. Lexa shakes her head at Maeve while Cole continues a thorough examination of the tiny wolf pup. On *Ian*.

"It happened this morning, and then he shifted back," Lexa tearfully explains. "He's a quarter fae." She looks at Kaleb, who immediately comes to her side and braces his hand on her shoulders. She speaks rapidly in his language for several sentences while he stands stoically at her side but I can feel it, that ice. That need to protect, to close Lexa off from everything bad and uncomfortable. His grip on her shoulder is like iron.

I get it now. Having a mate isn't easy. It's not supposed to be easy.

She turns her attention back to Maeve to continue, "During the last Trial in the arena, when Blake–" She takes a choked breath. "When everything started to fracture, I was struck right in the abdomen by the king's powers. It sliced through me, but I was unharmed on the outside. I thought he'd hurt the baby, that he knew about him, but Ian was fine throughout the pregnancy, and the birth was easy. He's been fine. All of a sudden, when he overslept during his nap and I went to check on him, I found him like this. He was asleep. I couldn't wake him up right away. And when he did wake up, he panicked and shifted back. Then, a few hours ago, when we came here for help." She looks toward the doorway where Misty and Aviva are standing side by side in quiet solidarity. "It happened when he was in my mom's arms. He hasn't been able to shift back. He's barely six months old. He doesn't know how, and there's no way to teach him like this."

"He's stable, Lexa." Cole tries to reassure her, but she screws her face into a pinched, furious frown.

"He's cursed. The king did this. He had to have done this." She drops back into the old tongue of the Deadlands. Kaleb whispers to her, easing onto his knees. Ryan, standing nearby, grits his teeth and mouths another gruff, silent curse, motioning for everyone to leave.

"I can help him."

I turn toward Posey's voice. Maeve whips around, and Posey blushes deeply under the gaze of several notable members of my family. The column of her throat bobs as she looks at Lexa, offering her a small, unsure smile.

She points halfheartedly at Maeve and says, "Just like Maeve's old necklace. I can make something like that for him. To absorb these powers, for now. I can do it. I'm sure I can do it."

HELP ME PROTECT HER

Aris

POSEY DISAPPEARS IN A FLURRY OF GRAY WOOL THE SECOND MY POWERS fade like tendrils of smoke across the dark mosaic tiles of the grand foyer. Her footsteps echo down a darkened corridor, the only sound for what feels like an eternity–an eternity spent willing myself to stand still and not chase after her.

We just returned from Silverhide moments ago. Me, my mate, and my parents and grandfather. Posey's role is clear as I tuck my hands in my pockets. She's going to help Ian using her alchemy. My parents, on the other hand, came here because...

I don't feel like myself and they sense that and are concerned... among other things, like the fact I have a mate and she's... powerful. So powerful. There's a monster inside of me with a one-track mind, and it's only thought is her, my mate. My mate and her comfort, her protection. My mate and her body under mine. My mate locked away somewhere only I can find her for the foreseeable future.

It's a grating, unnerving sense of possessiveness that has burrowed so deep in my bone marrow that I feel like every nerve ending and insignificant cell in my body has been rewired and fine-tuned to her wellbeing. I want to scratch my eyes out. I want to scratch my family member's eyes out for even looking at her. I want to rage and bite something. *I want to bite her again.*

"Aris?"

I close my eyes for a moment, take several deep breaths, and slowly turn to the trio waiting in the shadows for me to come back to my senses.

Mom steps forward, Dad and Grandpa Ryatt falling into her shadow. Her smile is sweet and genuine, and her silver eyes glimmer in the faint amber light of the chandelier glimmering several stories above her head. Her hair falls loosely around her shoulders. She begins to approach me, and for whatever reason, I bristle, the idea of her touch like someone pressing a molten rod to my bare skin.

"Kenna," Dad says in warning, and she halts, that smile fading so quickly I wonder if she even smiled at all.

Grandpa Ryatt's footsteps are the loudest as the men approach. Dad takes Mom by the elbow and walks her back into the smooth curve of the foyer, putting what would usually be an unnecessary distance between us, like I'm a live bomb of power ready to explode if she so much as breathes too close to me.

I know, somewhere deep in the still functioning recesses of my mind, what's happening to me. I know what this is. I don't like it–the violence brewing. The knowledge that other people are aware, and my family is walking on eggshells around me. I've heard the stories of the effect a fresh mate bond can have on a man, Ryan's being the one that stands out the most, seeing as he felt so out of control that he wasn't able to rein in his beast form, but thankfully Aviva took that in stride.

My shadows feel like lead. I'm holding on for dear life against the pull to drift into those shadows, to disappear and guard my mate like a dragon curls around its hoard of gold and gems. The worst part of this is that Posey and I have a lot to discuss about the future. I want to be sure this is actually what she wants because she's never been given the opportunity to make a decision for herself. That knowledge curls around the desire to pin her down and never let go.

"We're not going to stay long," Ryatt says, eyeing me with overt sympathy. "I'll return after the Solstice celebrations are done."

I nod, my jaw clenched and flexed to the point of pain. I've been here alone for weeks now while my parents tended to my sisters and their growing families and my grandparents semi-retired in Maatua. I was… lonely. Clawing at the silence of the normally loud, busy castle, and now, all I want is everyone to just… *get the fuck out my house.*

Grandpa Ryatt takes a tentative step forward and stops, his cloak swaying around his feet. "Does she have everything she needs?"

I angle my body away from the trio and run my fingers through my hair. Outside, another storm rages, this one wetter and warmer than before but guaranteed to coat Veiled Valley in ice, nonetheless.

Silverhide has real seasons. Winter there is just as glorious as the rest of the year–calm, stable, steady. Ryan and Aviva's had been warm and cozy, smelling like cedar and evergreen, a perfect nook to rest in the gleam of the Solstice season, and yet, all I could see was the way Posey's cloak flared as she knelt in front of Lexa and placed her skilled hands on Ian's wolfish body, reading his resonance, she calls it, and that's all she needed to do to know how to fix this when several other powerful, incredibly skilled members of my family came up short.

She hid this for so long.

She is so precious, so priceless.

I am, forever more, tasked with guarding her life with my own. Gladly.

"She does. If she doesn't, she'll know how to source and make what she needs." I eye Grandpa as the words slip from my mouth, booming through the foyer. He reads between the lines just like I knew he would.

He knows. Everyone has to know by now that Posey is powerful. Maybe more than Blake, Maeve, or me in her own way.

But she's *mine.*

Mom makes a small noise in her throat and pries Dad's fingers from her arm. I'd feel awful about the way he's keeping her away from me, her own son, if I didn't have a grasp on the situation and how dangerous I could be to her right now. It kills me the way he assesses me like I'm a threat, but he's right, I am.

"I'd like to talk to her, if that's okay. I won't touch her, Aris. But she seems very tired, and she's a lot thinner than the last time I saw her. Granted, it's been a year or more since I visited Sapphire Ridge," Mom says softly.

"I would appreciate that." I force the words out even if my body screams against the idea of anyone in Posey's space. "She's in the eastern spire, the one overlooking the forest. I've had a hard time getting her to eat or sleep."

Mom nods, glancing at Dad, and he grits his teeth and gives her a knowing look. Mom slips into the shadows at a hurried pace while I clench my fists to stop from chasing her down and stopping her.

Dad makes a move, crossing the distance between us to stand beside Grandpa Ryatt, angling his body to block the corridor where his mate's footfalls are fading.

I close my eyes to my dad's voice telling me to take my time and breathe. Ryatt agrees, adding that they've been through this, it's normal, but I'm having an especially hard time.

And then it all comes out.

"She's a fox," I grind out, opening my eyes to fierce slits. "She is a fox shifter, fully, no wolf at all. And she's been hiding from her family for years. She's been secretly practicing alchemy for years, right under their noises. And she's brilliant, and I don't know what to do or how to keep her safe."

Dad moves in, but I step away, shaking my head in warning. "Don't. Don't touch me right now."

"She's a fox," Dad says slowly, rolling the word "fox" over his tongue. "You're completely sure?"

"I saw her. I thought–there was something about her I couldn't figure out, something that nagged at me for months, since this summer." I nearly bring up her heat, which now makes glaring sense. It was *my* fault. I kissed her. I kissed my mate for the first time under the pretext of crossing something off a mental wish list, and it dragged us both through the coals within days. I put my mate into heat before either of us understood what was happening between us, that there was a bond there, trapped behind our primary powers, waiting for a spark.

That spark had ignited when I saw her getting tossed like a rag doll in her fox form. I hate that. I wasted so much time.

Grandpa Ryatt is looking down at his boots in thought. Dad runs his fingers through his hair exactly the same way I do. "This is serious."

"Do you think I don't know that?" My voice trembles, threatening to break. "I have an obligation to her family to tell them I plan to marry her. In fact, I will be marrying her as soon as fucking possible, with or without their consent. She cannot be without protection. Mine–and yours." I eye each man, my voice deadly serious.

"Her father is a smart man. I find it hard to believe he isn't aware of the level of skill she possesses," Dad argues, but Grandpa's looking right at me, those quicksilver eyes shining like pure steel.

"Her father was willing to marry her off to whomever had even a slice of the power she kept secret to keep their precious bloodline strong!" I spit out.

"You cannot make enemies of the Sapphire Ridge pack. They're the only Alchemists left. Her family in particular." Grandpa Ryatt finally steps forward, his sword catching the light of the chandelier.

"They put her in an impossible situation," I protest. "I owe them… very little, as it stands."

"And what about Roman?" Dad's voice drops several decibels. It's nearly a whisper between us.

"What about him?" It's bitter. Like acid on my tongue as I continue, "He was only worried about Posey's lack of wolf abilities affecting his marriage prospects and his rise to his father's throne. She has always been secondary to everyone but me." I look at Grandpa Ryatt, then my father, silently… begging. Fuck, I'd fall to my knees. "How do I keep her safe?" The words come in a strangled whisper. It's agony, this torture. Maybe they can see it, sense it flooding off my skin because Dad takes one more tentative step forward and grips my shoulder.

"This feeling is going to pass."

I shrug him off, turning for the shadows. "Don't!"

Grandpa Ryatt sighs heavily and moves into the faint light trickling through the windows, which makes the silver shine reflect like water on the tiles. "Posey is, and will continue to be, powerful. Her powers are only going to grow the more she practices her alchemy. Alchemists are rumored to have been the ones who built the Firestone forges, their magic the ones that filled those basins and allowed the Firestones to build their fortresses and weapons, but that's only rumor. A myth. A fairytale. We know so little about that war, even with people like Aviva and the Fae in Pantharas able to fill in some gaps, but it's never going to be enough. One thing is true, Aris, and that's that you, out of all your siblings and your cousins in this generation, have the heaviest burden on your shoulders."

I blink at him, narrowing my eyes like that'll help me decipher his words more clearly.

Dad grits his teeth. "Ryatt, not now. Not when he's like this."

"It's better this way. Let him hear it, Evander, while he feels like he would tear the world in two for his mate."

Grandpa Ryatt unsheathes the shadowsword in a fluid, silent motion. The tip clangs against the tile, with light, rapidly moving silver and deep blue shadows skirting all around us and up to the rafters. The castle trembles and groans, and my bracelets awaken, riling my powers as they shine.

"Take it," he commands sternly.

I look at Dad, whose eyes are lined with dark circles, his face washed out by the shadows he's known about his entire life. His mate used that sword when she went through the Shadowsynger ceremony to pass the kingdom from one hand to the other. Grandpa Ryatt has warred and killed with the same blade. Kingdoms have fallen against its edges and risen in its wake.

And it calls to me like never before.

"Take it, Aris. It's yours. It's made its decision known." He looks toward the corridor, to the shadows dancing under his control. "It's calling out to her, as well."

"What?" Dad and I echo, glancing at each other before looking at Grandpa Ryatt again.

"Has she… been to the caves?"

I lunge, my teeth bared, and I lose whatever sense of control I had over my wolfish urges and overwhelming emotions.

Everything goes black.

I'M A FREAK

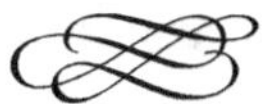

POSEY

I PRESS ANOTHER COOL, WET RAG AGAINST ARIS'S BATTERED FACE, sighing deeply at the gouge across his forehead, expertly stitched by his mother. A welt the size of Tarsian slashes from temple to jaw on the left side of his face, and he has a black eye, but I'm sure he's looked worse at some point in his life. This is just the worst I've ever seen him, and my stomach curls into tight knots when he frowns and hisses in pain against the cold press of the rag.

"Don't be a baby about it," I scold, dunking the rag in ice water again and wringing it out to continue torturing him. "It was, wholeheartedly, your fault."

He grunts in reply, unable to fully open his left eye, but the right one is fixed on my face, narrowed into a foxlike slit.

I reach for the small vial of healing draft on the bedside table, but he catches my wrist. "No. I did deserve this, after all. Might as well suffer for a few more hours."

"You look like you've been through a meat-grinder." I smile down at him. He presses my hand to his chest and closes his eyes with a deep, pained sigh.

"I attacked my grandfather, the most powerful and feared bastard in all of Eastonia. I knew better."

"Why would you do that?"

Aris settles with another sigh. I press the rag to his mangled face with my free hand, easing up on the pressure this time. "He mentioned you going into the caves, asked if you'd been, and I just snapped."

"What's wrong with you exactly? You seem off."

"Attacking my own grandfather makes you think I seem off? How so?" The sarcasm is impossible to miss.

"Aris." I toss the rag in the bowl and lean over him, brushing a rogue wave behind his ear. "What is the matter?"

"You. You're killing me."

"I've been killing you for months, it seems."

"That's true. I suppose now you've moved onto slow torture." He squints and rubs his thumb over the mark he left on my neck. His smile is beautiful. Just a flicker on the outer corners of his mouth, like just the feeling of the scar under his fingertip is enough to lighten his mood. "I'm a man, Posey. Me being absolutely out of my mind right now is a curse from the Goddess Herself."

I cock my head to the side. "And why are you out of your mind?"

"Because of you. And this." He smooths his thumb over the mark again, slowly, tenderly, his good eye fixed on the silver scar forever branded on my skin. "I want to hurt anyone who even thinks about you. Which, apparently, includes everyone in my family."

"It sounds like you need to sleep."

"I'd like to fuck you first," he deadpans, but his voice shifts, like it's his wolf talking and not necessarily him. It does fill me with liquid heat, but I have to resist for now.

"You have twelve stitches in your forehead and can only see out of one eye."

"Turn the lights off, and you won't notice how ugly I am."

"You need to go to *bed*."

"So it's only okay if you tell me what to do?" He grins, and it's foxlike, which confirms my suspicions. The Aris I know and love is barely here, hanging on by a thread, while his animalistic counterparts are feuding for control.

I lean forward and press a gentle kiss to his forehead where the skin is not broken. He winces, and maybe decides that I'm right, that his grandfather taking him to the floor in one punch probably means he does, in fact, need to just close his eyes and sleep it off, but he still wraps an arm around my back and holds me close, inhaling deeply against my neck and into my hair, and we stay like that until his grip loosens, and he drifts off. I spike his glass of water with the healing draft he's so far refused, tidy up, and pull my arms through my apron before heading back upstairs to the spire.

I'm not alone in the room, however, when I follow my shadow over the threshold. I expected Kenna to be here. I spent a few minutes alone with her going over my health, her welcoming me joyously to the family, and a brief explanation as to what I plan to make for baby Ian.

But it's not her.

The shadow staring at my already full shelves and tools hanging neatly from hooks along the wall belongs to the man who just put a gash on the side of my mate's face.

The King of Shadows turns around to face me, his arms crossed, towering over me. My stomach dips to my toes, and I bow my head, my heart thudding to a stop before skittering back to life at the speed of light, just like it did when he offered to show me his shadowsword while we were in Silverhide.

Being alone with him, however?

It feels like standing amongst Aris's shadows, but heavier, like Ryatt has only grown more powerful with age.

Except that's not true.

I felt it when I held his sword—the lackluster weight. The dimness in the gems. The age. Gods, the sword is thousands of years old. It has to be. Now, it's lying on the granite surface of my worktable, right next to where I left the thin, lightweight chain necklace I'm making for Ian. He glances at the jewelry when he notices my gaze on the table and his prized possession.

"I hit my grandson in the face and knocked him on his ass because he lunged for me, and I knew he would do everything in his power to peel the flesh from my bones while I still breathed had I not stopped him—for his own safety, of course."

"Of course." My voice rattles as I approach. I tuck my hands in my apron. "It's a mate thing. That's what Kenna said."

"She's correct. Your kind—women—have it easier. It's barely noticeable, from what I've been told. We male beasts, on the other hand, get a little... unhinged. You'll meet Ella, my mate, during Solstice when we're all in Maatua, and she'll confirm that I was a raging lunatic once we finally accepted our mate bond, and I marked her." He smiles softly at some memory before meeting my gaze. "Unless, of course, you're planning on spending Solstice with your family?"

I haven't thought that far ahead. "No, I don't suppose I am."

This is what he's here for. Me. My connections in Sapphire Ridge. During Ryatt's reign over Veiled Valley, things were different. My family wasn't trusting of him when he returned to claim what was his. Kenna and Evander, however, needed us. Isaac, once the King of Crescent Falls, had created several prototypes for special armor that could shift with its owner from human to wolf form and back. Evander took over Ryatt's special unit of warriors, the Ghost Army, and brought those prototypes to my pack to inquire if anything could be done to make them on a larger scale, and he was right to do so.

Every Ghost warrior wears specially crafted gloves that mold and meld into armor, finely woven, pillow-soft threads of metal—mostly iron and steel, with nickel alloy—that can change form and take an impressive beating.

Alchemists are to thank for those advances. My father is to thank.

But then there's me.

"You did go into the caves alone, didn't you?" His voice is soft and curious, almost amused. It's unnerving, honestly, because his tone doesn't match his stern face and heavily tattooed hands and neck.

I lick my lips and sink onto my usual stool, pulling Ian's unfinished necklace toward me. "They called to me."

"I thought so."

I dip my fingers into a bowl of flaked silver shards, which turn to balls of liquid in the palm of my hand, which I'll form into beads shortly, once it cools enough to take shape. Ryatt watches with interest, stepping closer to the table. "I'm plating the silver in iron with nickel alloy, like the Ghost gloves. Ian won't feel the silver. It won't hurt him at all, but the silver will prevent him from shifting into his wolf form. It should… snap him right out of it when they put it on him for the first time. And he won't be able to take it off and choke on it, I swear."

Ryatt's mouth ticks into a wry smile. Charming. Handsome. For a moment, I see the resemblance between him and Aris, and then it fades, reminding me that Aris generally prefers his father's side of the family looks-wise.

"Blake's daughter, Skye… you'll meet her at Solstice. She might be in the market for something like this, as well. She's very girly, so something pretty. A necklace or a bracelet–"

"A charm bracelet?"

"Perhaps. I'm sure she'll tell you exactly what she likes." He leans on the counter to continue watching me work. "And Fallon… she's Maeve's daughter. She's only one and hasn't burned any houses down yet, but that'll come in time."

I lick my lips again, finding them dry. "My dad made Maeve's necklace." I toy with the nearly finished necklace and attach another piece, then another. "I can make Fallon something as well. I just need to… touch her. Her and Skye, and whoever else might be in need."

"And that's the difference between you and any other alchemist alive, Posey. It took your father months to figure out the best metals and gems to use for Maeve, and meanwhile, she burned down two rooms in the palace in Moonrise and spirited all over the Allied Kingdoms before her second birthday."

I attach the final element to the necklace. It took me three hours to make from start to finish. That's it. Problem solved.

I feel pale and flushed under his gaze when I rise and hand him the necklace. "It'll work. Immediately. I can add more links as he grows, and when he's older and able to control this a little better, he can stop wearing it all the time." I drop the necklace into Ryatt's palm.

I'm a freak. Some kind of witch or demon. My powers are so different–so precise and focused compared to my family members… and even if they knew, it wouldn't have changed anything. I wouldn't be Alpha. I wouldn't have had my own alchemy room or access to my father's tools. I would have been someone else's quiet wife. A dutiful, submissive, silent breeder.

Ryatt barely looks at the necklace before tucking it into his jacket pocket. His eyes catch on the shelf housing the diadem… and the skulls. I still have questions about them and also think they're cool. Whatever. He can think I'm weird.

But he says, "We don't know for sure what happened to the original owner of this sword. My father believed he was an ancestor of ours, possibly the son of the last true Alpha King of Veiled Valley." He takes a deep breath and meets my eyes. "What I've always wondered, however, is who made this for that man." His hand hovers over the sword like it embodies a specific spirit. "Who made him this, and the helmet, and the wealth of what I believe is a full suit of armor?" His eyes land on the diadem I haven't repaired. Not yet. I'm waiting for Isolde to return from what I believe is a voluntary confinement, letting the male spirit handle the day-to-day tasks of running the castle, and he's not nearly as good at it.

Ryatt doesn't have to say it. He's thinking what I am, what I've been wondering since I had those strange visions in the cave of the woman with raven black hair and silver eyes.

She was an alchemist like me.

And like me, she loved a Shadowsynger.

She made the shadowsword and the helmet for him, and he placed that iron diadem on her head and vowed *forever*.

And they've had forever, here, in this castle, guarding their ancient, sacred bloodline–for centuries.

"This belongs to Aris now. I believe you might be more convincing on that front given what happened," he says under his breath, sliding the sword in my direction. His fingertips slip over the jagged, worn blade, but his eyes catch on the diadem again. "And I believe that means it also belongs to you." He bows his head, and my gut instinct, surprisingly, is to tilt my chin in a proud, regal manner and accept this... ascension that was written in the stars for us.

Luna of Veiled Valley.

Willow is going to *freak* when I tell her.

THE TABLES HAVE TURNED

POSEY

BRIGHT WARM MORNING SUNLIGHT DANCES THROUGH THE CURTAINS. The frost of the windows melts in real time as I sit up, my back stiff and aching. I fell asleep in the chair by the fireplace by accident, a book on modern apothecary sprawled across my lap, still open to the page Kenna said would have some more up-to-date applications for relieving the aches and pains associated with using my fingers like tools.

Aris is fast asleep in a ray of sunshine, his glass of healing draft spiked water empty and his face, thankfully, looking normal, if not still a little bruised. I rise, my thin nightgown falling down my thighs when my toes touch the floorboards.

Aris's eyes pop open. He sits up, running his hand over his face, and looks right at me.

"Good morning." I set the book on the chair. This moment feels slightly odd, like a recreation of the night I stumbled out of this same bed to find him sprawled in the chair, watching me like a hawk while I unraveled in fear and heartbreak in the moonlight.

This morning, it's sunny. His eyes shine like polished silver as he extends a hand, silently beckoning me to the bed. The second our fingers brush, he grabs mine, yanking me into the sheets. We both laugh and roll until I'm on my back, and he's on top of me, his knee drawing up between my thighs while he pins me to the mattress.

"Sneaky fox. I was planning on looking like I lost a bar fight at least until after Solstice so my grandpa had to remember his fist meeting the side of his grandson's face every time he looked at me."

I grin against his mouth. "We've already been over this. You deserved it. I only snuck a healing draft into your water because I didn't want to scream and wake up the entire castle when I saw your mangled face again this morning." The words turn to a playful screech and giggles when he nibbles my neck, nipping at my mark, his body rolling against mine.

Heat blossoms deep in my belly, intensified by the press of his hard cock against my thigh. He's only wearing boxers, and he's so warm and smells like his evergreen body wash, and my brain turns to mush the second his eyes meet mine, and he gives me a cocky, wry grin.

This feels like this summer at the cabin. I feel like I did this summer, and it's nearly enough to bring me to tears.

"Hey," I mouth, my fingertips drifting over his cheekbone. He shaved yesterday before we went to Silverhide, and it's been so long that I've seen him this smooth that I've forgotten about the little silver scars peppering his jaw.

"Hey," he whispers, brushing the word over my lips.

Those tiny golden threads between us vibrate with pleasure I've never known could be real. It's easy and wonderful and makes me tingle from the tips of my toes to my chin.

"My parents are still here," he says with a soft groan that ends in a kiss to the corner of my jaw. "They're wondering if I'm stable enough to join them for breakfast this morning, with you, of course." Another kiss, with tongue, makes my eyelids flutter closed. His hands drift up to grip my ribs. "I said no."

"Aren't you hungry? You didn't eat dinner yesterday."

"Did you?" He drags the flat of his tongue up my neck. I shiver.

"Yes, I did. With your parents and your grandpa. I like them a lot. Your dad is a bit concerned you've lost your mind entirely when I showed them the fawn, though."

"How is our little darling?"

I try to chuckle, but it comes out as a breathy sigh. He bunches up my nightgown until my belly is exposed, the fabric hanging just below my breasts.

"She's–" He presses a hot, wet, open mouth kiss to my sternum over the fabric of my nightgown, his hands slowly roving to my hips. "She's using the kitchen as a jungle gym. She needs a–a real place to live. A barn, or some–something–oooh–" I arch my hips against his mouth. His tongue laps over the thin, already drenched cotton of my panties, and he growls with satisfaction.

"I'll fix it," he murmurs, his voice dripping with heat. He slowly pulls my panties down, but they're barely around my thighs when he sucks my clit and groans so deeply the vibration nearly sends me into a tailspin already. "I love this. I think of this all the time. You're unreal."

I fist the pillow and press my hips against his mouth, desperate, whiny moans filling the silence all around us.

I've never really taken in the small details of his room. It's so dark, so masculine, so overwhelming in a delicious way. The velvet canopy is still half drawn, like he prefers to sleep within it, in a little cocoon of darkness, and I love that. I love the way his tongue slowly parts my folds, and he grunts with pleasure, like the taste of me is the Goddess's nectar, and he's praying at Her altar while he nips and sucks, sliding his fingers through me until I'm full.

Only when I'm silently gasping, riding the edge of oblivion, does he draw his boxers down and enter me in one swift, overwhelming thrust, giving me something big and hard to clench around when I come utterly, completely unglued.

The orgasm sweeps through me, through us, like a tidal wave, and after several moments, we both drift down to reality, and it's... beautiful.

He's still hard, on the verge of knotting me, but it's clear he's in no rush, and I'm thankful for it. His warm body covers mine, pressing me into his sheets, making me feel like something small and delicate, something he covets and buries away for only himself. We laugh and kiss and let our hands wander while he presses into me in slow, exploratory thrusts, and that goes on for some time until we're both glistening with sweat, and the pleasure builds to a crescendo, and I'm looking up at him, mouthing his name. He stills, lips parted in awe and… love. Real love. The kind of love I thought was reserved for fairytales and the occasional romance novel I'll never admit to buying and hiding under my bed.

I clench around his cock in rhythmic spasms that make him groan and close his eyes, his forehead resting on mine, our lips barely touching.

"I'm going to knot you again," he warns, drawing out a deep grunt as it begins. I wiggle beneath him, taking him deeper, and he blows out his breath, opening his eyes to slits. "Greedy like always."

I angle my hips, and he slips in so deep he hisses and grips my hip to keep me still, one brow arched.

"Posey. We're going to have *a lot* of kids if you keep that up." His knot expands, stretching me so wide it starts to sting, but my body melts into the sensation, and when he presses deeper, thrusting in shallow strokes to find the perfect fit, I come again, and it's long and slow and delicious. He fills me completely.

He groans into my neck, nipping my mark, his tongue lapping at the scar he left.

Tears sting my eyes, but I blink them back, smiling up at the sunlit canopy, my fingers stroking through my mate's hair.

"WE'RE GOING TO STAY ON THE GROUNDS FOR NOW," ARIS SAYS, untying his boots in the glare of the warm sun against the rapidly melting snow. The trees are still coated in snow, and the air is chilled but far warmer than it's been lately, and when I shed my cloak and hang it over an old stone wall, my skin doesn't feel like it'll freeze immediately, but I still shiver in nothing but the nightgown I wore to bed last night that I haven't changed out of, mostly because it smells like Aris, and I want to bury my face in it.

He looks up at me from the steps, squinting against the sun, and tilts his head toward the patchwork of overgrown hedges.

"How far do the grounds go?"

"Well, it depends on who you ask. There's a lot of outbuildings and old cottages scattered just there, in that small valley. That belongs to us. Then, over there, there's a small lake and–"

"An underwater entrance to the caves?" Wrong thing to say.

He frowns, but the furrow between his brows isn't nearly as deep as it could be. "Perhaps." He licks his lips, making a show of slowly unbuttoning his shirt. "Maybe I should toss you in the lake and see if you can find it?"

I scoff, but the sound turns to a gargled hum when he slips his shirt off and drapes it over the railing, standing there in the glistening sun, all muscle, scars, and overtly masculine energy.

I glance at the castle. We're on the far side where the windows are scarce, but still, the idea of taking off my nightgown and being naked… shifting in front of someone for the first time?

My skin's been prickling from nerves since we stepped outside.

"It's not nerves. You're under my shadow right now. No one can see you but me. And it doesn't matter anyway; we're alone now. My parents left with Ryatt for Silverhide again an hour ago. We should have news about your success with the necklace when we get back." He steps toward me, but I frown.

Did he just read my mind? "I'm… what?"

"My shadow. You're in it. Invisible."

I look around, shivering, hugging my bare arms. "Really?"

He nods like this is no big deal. "You don't feel it?"

I shake my head, and the motion has the thin straps of my gown falling off my shoulders. His gaze flicks to the slope of my left shoulder, darkening. "Interesting. Normally, it feels like being covered in snakes."

"Wh-what?"

Another lazy shrug, but he's taking steps in my direction, his eyes following the curve of my shoulder, my upper arm. "The shadows must like you as much as I do." His words are almost slurred by lust. He kisses my shoulder, then my neck, lingering on the mark for a moment like he just can't help himself, and I'm a puddle in his arms. "There's something I want to show you."

"Will there be extra clothes there?" I shiver, but not from the cold. His hand roams up my spine, gathering the fabric.

"I have a small stash. You'll be fine." He steps back and pulls the nightgown over my head, leaving me in nothing but my panties. He bites his lower lip and nods to himself.

"Did you just mouth *nice?*" I hiss, but he smirks, motioning to my underwear.

"Those, too."

I hesitate for several seconds. This is suddenly very real. I'm about to shift in front of him. I'm about to be in my *fox form* with *him*.

I slip my panties down my thighs and step out of them, kicking them under my discarded gown. Aris silently inspects me like I'm an ancient statue in the royal museum in Moonrise. My skin glows a rosy pink under his thorough gaze.

"Don't be nervous."

"I can't help it."

"Have you ever shifted when you wanted to before?"

I shake my head. "I… I can, though. It's voluntary. Will you be shifting into a fox, too?"

"Yes. It's been a while though, so cut me some slack." It happens in a split second. Aris is standing in front of me, but then he's just… gone.

What remains is a sleek golden fox, an unnatural color that matches his hair. His eyes, however, are so sharply silver that they resemble polished steel.

I slip into my fox form without meaning to do so. Unlike when the moon is full, it doesn't hurt, there's no blood involved, and instead of practically tearing out of my skin, it feels lazy and unhurried, almost… nice.

I see my foxy reflection in his eyes.

I never thought I'd have this.

Someone to share this with.

"*Try to keep up,*" he says into my mind.

A SHIFT IN DISPOSITION

POSEY

THE SNOW IS WET AND THICK BENEATH MY PAWS, UNLIKE A FEW DAYS ago when everything was a frozen wasteland. I can prance easily, staying mostly on top of the snow instead of sinking into it, and the air feels cold but in a good way instead of that teeth-rattling chill.

I have no idea where we're going, and I don't think Aris does either. He's quick and sure-footed, but so am I, and while we race and weave between trees and leap off rocks jutting out of the snow, our movements begin to sync until I'm beside him instead of behind him.

The forest thins to reveal the shallow valley he was talking about earlier. The ground beneath us tilts into the valley, slippery and uneven.

When I slow and carefully pick my way down, Aris has other plans. He pounces on me, sending us both careening through the snow, and the play fight that ensues has birds soaring from the trees in alarm. He pins me twice, rolling me onto my back, dragging me over the snow and delighting in my little squeals, but I've *never* had this much fun.

He even chases voles with me.

During our jaunt through the old village, abandoned village in the valley, while we explore the outbuildings and rotting homes, he occasionally stops to nip my neck and nuzzle against where my mark is in my human form. It feels insanely good. Everything about this is what I've missed out on as a fox before.

When the sun begins to set and paints the sky a vivid crimson, instead of turning back to the castle, he takes us deeper into the valley, back through the tree line where a small lake rests, covered in ice.

I hang back while he trots ahead of me, his ears pinned like he's prepared to strike, but his body is relaxed while he carefully picks a path for us across the ice.

Then I see it. The reason we're here. What he wanted to show me.

I nearly burst out of my fox form in shock.

At the edge of the lake, cloaked in icy fog and tucked in a thick overgrowth of gnarled trees, a structure of obsidian rises out of the fog, overgrown with frozen, frosted vines.

The entrance is nothing but a gaping void of light, the shadows within stretching for what looks like miles.

Aris glances over his shoulder, his eyes meeting mine, before he slips into the entrance and disappears.

I trust him. I really do. But I really don't want to go in there. I want to stay in the sunshine for once in my life, with him, rolling in the snow, but I follow, shivering, my paws slipping over ice that continues through the entrance, and... I was right about the lake having an entrance to the caves.

A few minutes later, dressed in thick slacks and a loose-fitting shirt that reminds me of something out of a romance novel about pirates or knights from a time of old, Aris kneels in his human form. My gaze is on our murky, glittering surroundings. He secures a length of rope through the belt loops of the men's pants he asked me to put on, tightening the rope around my waist to keep them up. My cloak is twice as long as it needs to be for my height, but with the men's sweater underneath, rolled up my wrists, I'm toasty warm.

"The boots aren't going to fit at all, but they'll have to do," he murmurs. I absently slip my feet into them, still gazing at the stone archways high above our heads and the crystal formations hanging from them. Water drips in the distance. Behind us, the lake is glassy, reflective ice, stopping at the beginnings of what I believe might have been a massive cathedral now buried in the mountainside.

"Tell me about this place." I whisper, but my words carry, echoing into obscurity.

"It was the original temple of Veiled Valley. The castle was actually built against it, above it, following the slope of the valley."

"So our castle is… the top of the structure, essentially?"

He smiles softly when I say *our*. "Yep. The top six floors or so."

"Wow! The original castle would have been absolutely massive!"

"It is." He nods as he rises to adjust the fit of my cloak and smooth back my hair. "What we call the caves is just the old castle, really. Some areas have fallen into caverns, sure, but this place? It's one of my favorites." He looks over the top of my head at the entrance, chewing his lower lip for a moment in thought. "But this is the first time I've been able to access it this way, with the lake frozen."

A rush of cold air groans over us. Crystal fragments fall from the archways, crashing to the ground, but Aris doesn't seem bothered.

"I thought you didn't want me to come here."

He smooths his thumb over my mark, his eyes going distant for a moment, like he's trapped in some thought, then he replies, "I already know you're not going to listen. And if you're drawn to this place, maybe there's something here calling out to you that didn't call out to me during my ascension. I'd like to know what that is." The shadows groan again, and his bracelets illuminate, casting a gentle silver glow around us.

It's enough light to see… Goddess!

"What happened here?"

"Something bad."

Armor rusts in shambles beneath our feet. Bones disintegrate into dust under Aris's boots. I follow him, waiting for those whispers to begin, but it's silent, save for the occasional rumbling groan of phantom wind coming from doorways where the wooden doors themselves have long rotted and fallen away.

We explore the main sanctuary for a while before I decide there's nothing here. Nothing with ties to the helmet and diadem, but then we cross through another part of the temple and the corridor grows narrow, and instead of grand archways, the ceiling drops, and the cave structures jut from the remains of stone walls.

Some rooms are totally closed off by crystals, but one thing is clear. "We're in the old castle now."

He nods, using his bracelets to light our way. Stone walls give way to raw earth and back again. I feel like we've been walking for miles, somehow moving upward into the valley again. The floor beneath us, rough stone littered with rust from ancient armor and the occasional piece of pottery or other artifact, tilts upward, and Aris guides us up a gently curving staircase etched from stone, his hand wrapped around my elbow.

Water trickles down the wall to our left. It's surprisingly loud, but other than our footsteps, it's the only tangible sound.

Something raw and painful expands through my chest. My heart lurches and squeezes tight. I stop short, accidentally yanking Aris back a step, and he whirls, eyes blazing silver in the darkness.

"It's okay," I murmur a bit breathlessly. "I just feel weird."

"Light headed? We're moving up, and the air will be less heavy soon." He leans down a bit to look me in my eyes, but I shake my head.

"No, just…" I scrub my chest beneath my cloak. "I found a room I thought was the temple, but now I think I was wrong. It's where I found the helmet, diadem, and the skulls. It's where the spirits of the house died, I think. Where is it?"

"I don't know. I've likely never seen it."

I feel disoriented in the dark. I can feel Aris's nerves tightening as I collect myself and urge him forward in our exploration, but the further we travel, the more my chest aches.

Aris starts to move us down a wide corridor where the ceiling tilts again, closing us into another ancient section of the castle, but my legs suddenly refuse to move, and I turn to the sound of whispers directly behind us. His bracelets shudder before glowing again. He stiffens behind me, his hand folding over my hip. "What do you feel, Posey?"

I flex my fingers, which tingle, growing increasingly warm.

"Posey?"

In the darkness, through a slit in the shadows, I feel a pull, like someone's reaching through my cloak and yanking me to the side.

There is, in fact, a small cleft in the wall of the corridor. I move through it. Aris barely fits, and his hiss of pain and grunt of effort behind me as he squeezes through the cleft barely registers in my head as sound because it's all whispers now. Whispers at first, and then full, startling, barely discernible conversations.

Our boots slash through stale water. Darkness sweeps in, and the air grows thin and empty.

"Oh, my Goddess," Aris breathes, lifting his arm and letting his powers dance. His shadows expand with flashes of throbbing blue light, illuminating a great, cavernous space.

A ballroom.

"Wait," he rushes out, grabbing my shoulder before I can take a step, and we look down at the littered floor.

"Oh, no." The whisper leaves my lips in a pained moan. This is a burial ground. Piles of bones and armor. Tables in shambles, turned to rot. The remains of plates and cutlery rusted and buried beneath decades—no, centuries—of stillness.

And at the very back of the room is a door.

I immediately know where it leads, and my heart sinks to my too-big boots.

The altar room sits beyond the ballroom, through another break in what used to be a wall and small servants' corridor. The hallway itself is in shambles, littered with artifacts and bones, like whatever battle took place spilled over into the closed off, private wings of the castle.

The whispers stop once I reach the watery grave of the spirits who've been so kind to me, to us, the guardians of the Shadowsyngers who came after them despite all odds.

Aris crouches to examine the bones of Isolde and her mate and sighs.

"I saw her," I explain, telling him in detail about my time here. "She's been so quiet since then. I can barely feel her anymore."

"And the male spirit is in protective mode," Aris agrees with a grunt, like he somehow gets it. "Do they talk to you? Can you hear them?"

I nod, and he seems pleased with the answer. He takes a deep breath and squints into the shadows.

I say the thing that's been weighing on my mind for several days now. "Do you think... once we've found all the missing pieces of the armor, that they'll... go away?"

"I don't think it's possible for us to find everything," he admits. "The ascension... Look, you found the helmet. You're connected to this. I think, being my mate, and being an alchemist, it called out to you for me. You were meant to mend it, and you have."

"But the diadem–"

He steps toward me, closing the distance between us. He's warm and solid–something real, something I can touch to keep me grounded as an ancient world long buried thrums all around us.

Aris smooths my hair back, his thumb ghosting across my lower lip, and then he kisses me. It's lovely and soft while equally possessive. "You're going to be the Luna Queen of Veiled Valley. My mate. My queen. My *wife*. If that diadem called to you, it's because you're meant to wear it."

"This whole thing kind of put a damper on shifting," I mumble, but I'm blushing so deeply I'm sure my cheeks are bringing the temperature of the caves up by ten or more degrees.

He cups the back of my head and angles my face upward to meet him, pressing a kiss to my forehead, whispering, "We have time. Solstice is next week, and then we have so much time to figure all of this out, and better yet, just to be us. Here, in this creepy, dusty old castle."

"I love it here." Our fingers intertwine, mirroring the eternal embrace of our ghostly companions' bones on the ground nearby. I can wholeheartedly understand why they didn't leave if it was voluntary.

"There's something I want to ask you," Aris says against my skin.

A PROPOSAL AND A PROMISE

THE FAWN IS ALL LEGS IN ARIS'S ARMS AS HE WALKS HER OUT OF MY alchemy room, where she's been bouncing across the floorboards for the last hour, jumping on any flat surface and threatening to lose her life repeatedly around everything hard and sharp.

Heat pours from my fingertips. I smooth a length of silver flat, the molten metal reflecting red against the granite, when Aris returns in a huff, sweaty, new bruises on his forearms when he rolls up his sleeves.

He tsks, giving me an incredulous look before easing into his resigned seat at my worktable–the only stool strong enough to hold his impressive stature and weight. "You may have been right."

"About what?" I tease, picking up the tools I need to begin etching the strip of silver.

"That our darling daughter is a wild animal and would be better suited to a life outside."

"Our daughter?" I laugh, and it's pitched. "Aris!"

"Do that again." He braces his hands on the granite and eases up, leaning forward.

"Do what?"

"Smile like that again."

The tools become leaden weights in my hands. His eyes are so bright and yearning that I do smile with utter and sincere happiness.

He traces the curve of my mouth. "You are the most beautiful thing I've ever witnessed."

I used to think butterflies in my stomach were only reserved for the great, fictional romances. Someone will write a book about me one day. About us.

Today has been nothing short of a fever dream. We left the caves only an hour or two ago, Aris whisking us back to the surface using his powers. I showered off the grime and cold and immediately felt called to work on the diadem. I'm hoping, if fate allows, that Isolde will return from whatever alcove she's been hiding in and tell us more about what happened to her and the male spirit. So, I've been etching and weaving lengths of pressed silver before coating it in flakes of raw iron, heating them until they meld into a loose, almost fragile alloy, then coating it again in an alloy of iron of chromium to strengthen the bond, trapping the silver inside. The braids of coated silver are scattered across my work table, ready to be fitted to the missing pieces of the diadem, but my hands suddenly don't want to work. They want to press against Aris's broad chest, undo the buttons on his shirt, and sink lower, and lower...

But he's been a little weird since we got back.

First, in the caves, he pressed a kiss to my forehead and whispered that he had something to ask me. It sounded like he hadn't meant to say it out loud, like his internal thoughts lurched out of him before he could stop them. He'd taken a moment to look around and then brought us back. He's been hovering, nervous energy flooding off him in torrents, vicious and hard to ignore.

"You're acting weird," I accuse him, and he grunts in agreement before pulling back and sitting down. He crosses his arms on the granite and leans down to watch me work at hand-level.

"I have a hunch," he murmurs, his eyes meeting mine briefly, "that you can't wear just any kind of ring, can you?"

My throat feels suddenly thick when I swallow. "You're correct. Metals are temperamental against my skin, yes." I smooth another length of silver and heat it until it shines crimson.

He tilts his head, enthralled by my fingers and wrists, like he can see and sense the strange, shapeshifting powers of heat pouring like invisible thread from my hands.

"I want you to make me something."

"What would you like?"

He makes me wait several aching, unnecessary seconds for an answer.

"A ring." His silver gaze leaves no room for misinterpretation. "And a matching one for yourself."

I set my tools down and lean toward him, the space between us narrowing into a slice of air. Nearly nose to nose, I ask cheekily, "Are you going to ask me something? Perhaps whatever was on your mind in the caves, Prince Aris?"

He narrows his eyes and rises, keeping his eyes on me as he rounds the worktable to stand in front of me. I angle to meet him, soot-stained fingers on my hips.

"You do enjoying watching me grovel for your affection?" He smiles.

"It's my favorite thing in the world."

He kisses me tenderly, possessively, groaning into my mouth in a way that makes me lean in, desperate for more, but then he pulls away slightly and kneels, taking my fingers in his hand.

"Marry me," he whispers for only us to hear.

"Say please."

"You are the biggest pain in my ass."

"And yet, you're still on your knees, Aris."

He squeezes my fingers. "Be my wife. I'll beg if you want me to. I'll crawl."

I know he will, and maybe that's why I'm on the verge of tears. Maybe that's why I'm already crying, imagining myself tucked in that bed at his summer house, books I couldn't care less about sprawled all around me. Me, wearing the glasses I haven't needed since I started letting my powers flare through my veins, melding with my blood to create something new and powerful, something that makes me whole and knits all the jagged pieces of my psyche together.

Me, watching him brace himself in the doorway, teasing me, his eyes having a very hard time staying fixed on my face.

I love him. I've loved him.

He's mine. All mine.

"Posey Sapphire," he whispers, "make me a ring so I can wear it every day for the rest of my life and feel you there when we're apart. I love you. I don't deserve you, but I'll try, Posey, for Goddess' sake, I'll do my best, even if it kills me. Even if you're the one to kill me."

"You're–" I suck in a sob, trying to keep the mood light. "You're barely selling this."

His eyes are wet and glassy when he smiles and takes a breath to try again. "I love you. I want to wake up beside you every morning. I want to fuck you into our mattress every night."

"Aris," I sniffle, laughing despite the glowing warmth in my chest.

"I want to hold our child in my arms and witness something we made together. I want to grow old and wrinkly with you by my side. I want it all. I want you, just as you are, quiet, shy, and easily entertained by silence and something to do with your hands. I want to sit there on that stool and watch you create masterpieces with just a touch. I want that. I'd do anything for that. I'd do anything for you."

"I know." My heart lurches. My throat aches with a sob I'm not sure I can hold back. "I want that, too."

"Then say you will."

"I'll marry you."

He rises, cheeks damp with tears, and leans down, his mouth angled over mine. "Say it again."

"Yes. I'll marry you, Aris. I'll make us rings. I'll make them right now."

I make his out of iron with gems made from nickel and platinum, turned into smoky diamonds under my touch. My ring is a thinner band, but the same. A beautiful, imperfect duet. He inspects them as they rest on the granite to cool, perfectly sized and glittering in the light of the setting sun, and I move on, my powers beautifully stable as I begin to piece the diadem back together, repairing lengths of iron that remind me vividly of the spires of the castle. In fact, it has exactly the same number of prongs as the spires themselves.

"I like the smoky diamonds," he says around a mouthful of food.

He leans over with his fork, forcing me to take the offered bite. I appease him and continue the finishing touches on the crown.

"I think I'll add a few… sapphires." The iron in my palm warms, separating into balls of liquid metal before taking form. Raw, glimmering sapphires appear when I unfurl my fingertips, sizzling and steaming against my skin, but I don't feel a thing. My hands are torched black by now, however.

"I can't let Maeve know you can do that so easily. She'll send you an entire list of things to make for her. She's got a penchant for things that shine, like a crab."

I choke on a laugh, and he feeds me another bite of food.

"I think," I say mostly to myself, "it's done. What do you think?"

"Try it on," he says, standing.

I hesitate. "Well, it's not mine. It's Isolde's."

"She was the wife of the Alpha King, or one of his heirs. If she wore that, it means you have every right to do so, as well. I want to see it on you."

The diadem feels light as air despite it being made of mostly iron. It looks so Gothic. Haunted, honestly. The alchemized gems glisten in the glow of the nearby hearth. It is, honestly, the most beautiful thing I've ever made.

But while I consider it, Aris moves toward me. The sword Ryatt left behind rests on a shelf above my head. I thought maybe he meant for me to repair it, but after a thorough examination, it's not something that needs to be done. I could smooth the blade and replace the gems, sure, but it's not just a hunk of metal. Every skill, every conquer, adds to its magic. That's not something even my powers should manipulate.

With a deep breath, I raise the diadem and place it on my head. Aris has just grabbed the hilt of the sword at that very moment, his powers roaming through it, illuminating every gem in shades of blue and silver.

His bracelets ignite.

The gems on the diadem flare with light when our eyes meet and lock. "Aris, what–"

A shudder runs through the castle. It starts as a small, insignificant vibration, like wind howling against the spires, but erupts into a bone-rattling combustion, and then the room is alight. Neither of us moves, though. Light and sound storm around us. Figures of shadow dance in a slow, haunting waltz. Murmurs of conversation in a language lost to time and the whine of string instruments is broken by sudden chaos. I can see it all clearly, as if I've fallen back through time.

There's a battle raging in the temple that spills into the castle despite an army of guards at the ready. Dark, vicious magic spreads like poisoning gas, stopping wolves and armed guards before they can even turn to unseen enemies.

The ballroom is next. The stench of death is too much.

"Aris?" My voice is weak. I can't breathe. But his eyes are open and full of shadow as he holds my gaze, mouthing, "Wait."

A man who towers above the rest fights with the same sword Aris holds. The same corridors we traveled earlier in the day come into view as he's shoved back further and further until he's guarding the doorway of the altar room, the place he carved out for his wife.

Not an altar of granite.. Not a place of worship.

That room was Isolde's alchemy room.

Her scream of terror splits my eardrums as she's attacked. He tries to save her, taking a fatal blow in the process, his helmet breaking, his Shadowsynger powers running dry.

They made promises to each other. They wouldn't leave. They'd guard this place, their home, where they fell so madly in love they could watch the world burn and it wouldn't matter as long as they were together.

But their world did burn.

The image suddenly extinguishes. I rear back, my hips biting against the worktable. I reach to snatch the diadem from my head, but Aris clutches my wrist to stop me and turns me to the strip of moonlight filtering through the windows.

Isolde stands, ghost-like, nearly transparent. Her wobbly smile fades, however, when she says, "He doesn't remember yet."

WHY WAIT?

Aris

I've seen things in my life I can't explain.

This is, by far, the most intense.

I was perfectly fine staying ignorant of the fact that the spirits who keep the castle running like a well-oiled machine were once people, and that Soren was right about being unnerved by their ghostly presence.

But this is…. This is just…

Posey steps forward to stand between me and the young woman draped in silver moonlight, her gown like something out of the ancient books in Arthur's archives. It's strange seeing the haunting outline of the diadem on her head, her dark, tightly curled hair woven through the slits of metal in an intricate updo compared to Posey, soot-stained and gorgeous, still in her apron, the diadem resting on top of her thick, strawberry-blonde waves.

Two princesses separated by death and centuries stare at each other for a very long time.

I feel the male spirit's presence nearby, but he's invisible, just a touch of air on the side of my cheek.

Isolde, that's what Posey calls her. An old name.

"I remember," Isolde says, closing her eyes.

"Who did this to you?" Posey asks with heartbreaking quiet.

Isolde opens her eyes again and looks directly over my shoulder like the man who used to draw the very sword in my hands is standing right behind me.

"In the time of the old kings," she says in an ethereal voice, "after the Great War and the Goddess's veil we were safe here, in the valley. The Shadowsyngers never fought in the war against the fae gods. They wouldn't. They saw it as the losing battle it was and chose to protect our sacred people instead, including mine. Ours." She looks at Posey with overt sympathy. "It used to be the women who were the most powerful alchemists, Posey. Long ago, when there were hundreds of us. I was one of the last." Isolde looks down at her hands—misty silver streaks as she moves, turning to look out the window. "The Alpha King at the time, my father-in-law, paid my father a fortune to have me brought to this castle. I was tasked with making weapons. Terrible, powerful weapons for every Shadowsynger, man, woman, and child. That's how I met Levi." She turns again to look behind me, and her smile is so full of yearning, so heartbroken, I have to brace a hand on Posey's worktable to keep myself upright.

"We fell in love as a new king rose to power in Rifthold, this one worse than the last. King Kane. He was young and hungry for the dwindling powers of his fae ancestors, and he took everything from everyone—all those shifters. All those witches. He enslaved Eastonia in a matter of years, and with his power, he grew in influence."

She walks in a tight oval, wringing her hands. "Veiled Valley was supposed to be protected. We were hidden for so long even some of the last Firestone queens didn't know about us until it was too late for them to beg for our help. I was eighteen when Levi and I married in secret, against his father's wishes. Nineteen when I built him that armor to house his powers, and gods, he was so powerful." Her voice cracks painfully. "And he made me promise that if he died in that armor, his powers would remain, that he would remain with each piece so he could continue guarding the valley until those fit, those of our bloodline, could rise to power again, called back to the home we vowed we'd die for." Her eyes land on the sword. "And I agreed, but only as long as I got to stay with him, so when I built the sword... I took some of the gems and used them in the diadem I crafted for our wedding day, binding myself to his magic so that we'd stay together, and we have." She smiles. It's soft and wistful, just like her words.

"But we were betrayed. His father was slain. The elders encouraged a ball in our honor, to usher in my mate's reign as Alpha King, but it was a trap. I tried to tell him. I kissed our infant son goodbye and sent him away with the witches to be kept hidden in Moonrise, where the rebellion had taken hold. It was safe there. King Kane had infiltrated Veiled Valley, swayed our elders against us, promised eternal life and power, but he lied. His army killed everyone. Every last Shadowsynger. Our streets ran red for decades." She turns away from us, her hand pressed against the window.

"But our son survived. The witches taught him what little they knew about his kind. He had a son, and you are a direct descendent. It's where you get your family name." She looks right at me over her shoulder.

"Westfall?"

She nods. "And you must know his story, how your great-grandfather was caught and enslaved by Kane, how he escaped with young Ryatt. And Ryatt found the sword and the castle. We came to life again, able to watch what's left of our kind grow and thrive. I watched you grow up, Aris." Her voice edges on a sob. "I didn't get to see my son grow up. I wasn't there to witness his first steps, his first words, or his first love, but you gave us that." She looks over my shoulder again. "Both of us. Levi?"

The male presence is warm beside me, like it's his hand pressed on my shoulder, squeezing in agreement.

But Isolde looks at Posey, her eyes wan, glimmering with moonlight. "And you found my diadem. I wondered if anyone would ever find it. And it was you, an alchemist like me. He'll need you in the years to come. Everyone will. You are, wholeheartedly, the glue that will hold Veiled Valley together. It's what we're for as alchemists."

A tear trails down Posey's cheek.

Isolde looks at Levi, again, smiling softly. "Do you remember now?"

His answer isn't meant for me and Posey, but his warmth is like nothing I've ever felt.

Isolde fades, and the castle shudders, and then it's clear we're alone again. I give myself a moment to collect my nerves and tuck them away. Then, I set the sword on the shelf, feeling more than a little out of body.

Posey doesn't take off the diadem. She's looking at the spot where our resident ghost stood, her eyes searching the shadows in a longing way that both breaks my heart and makes me smile softly.

"They're not leaving, you know."

"How do you know that?" She wipes her tears, transferring soot from her hands to her cheeks.

"Because, according to Levi–Goddess, it's nice to have a name for him finally–he has unfinished business."

"What? What business does he have?" She blinks up at me, confused, and I smile again.

"He's been really enjoying tormenting Maeve's mate, Soren. You'll meet him during Solstice."

She furrows her brow. "They're staying because he wants to harass your sister's mate?"

I nod. "Yep." Maybe that's not the only reason, but it's certainly the funniest.

"Aris, that's asinine!"

"Take it up with him." Enough of this. I'm ready to go to bed. I'm ready to fall asleep on a couch in the library while Posey picks through another book about apothecary medicine or the romance novels she thinks I don't know about. Some of them make our trysts in the sheets look tame. "Where were we?"

I tug her close, folding my arms around her back. She melts into the touch with a sigh. "We were playing dress up while we waited for the rings to cool off."

"They look cooled off now."

She turns her head to look down at the worktable. "It's late. We should probably go to bed."

"I don't know. Do you know anyone at the temple who could marry us?"

"Tonight?"

"Why not?

Her lips part in a gasp. "But–"

"I know you don't want a wedding." I lean down, caging her in against the worktable. "I know the last thing you want is to have to walk down the aisle in a huge dress while everyone stares at you. I also know you'd rather throw yourself from one of the spires than have to gut through a reception afterward."

She can't argue. Her guilty sigh burrows through me. "But… what about what you want?"

"I'd like to marry you and come home, alone with you, and lie in bed until morning, alone with you, and wake up to just you in a quiet house, and then… fuck you in every room."

"Aris, be serious."

"I'm dead serious. I don't want to wait."

"What about your family?"

"What about yours?"

She frowns. I kiss it away. "My family will live, trust me. I'd rather be married with your ring on my finger when I go drag your father through the coals, anyway."

"What about Roman?"

Ah, fuck. That. My best friend… and his little sister, who I'm now propping up on the table, spreading her legs, preparing to bury myself deep between her thighs.

"I'll handle it."

THE TEMPLE IS SHROUDED IN SHADOW WHEN WE APPROACH THE ELDERLY priestess waiting for us at the altar. Posey's wearing the most beautiful cream satin gown I've ever seen–long sleeved and fitted around her waist. I'm not sure where it came from, but then again, neither is she. Isolde is my guess.

Posey bows her head to the priestess who smiles fondly down at her in a way a mother would, and I realize this woman is likely the mentor Posey told me about during quiet hours over the past week or so, when we were lying in just our skin, watching the mural in my bedroom shift from starry night to day.

I never considered myself a romantic until Posey bulldozed her way into my heart. I'd write sonnets if I had a lick of creative ability, something more than, *"You have massive, amazing breasts. I want to bury my face between them for the rest of my life,"* which, admittedly, I considered adding to our vows because, *hell*, that's all I'm thinking about when we're silently commanded to kneel, and the satin fabric pulls over her chest, her nipples peaked against the chilled air. I'd fall on my sword for this amazing woman, more than once if it doesn't kill me the first time. I'd do anything she asked.

Life without her feels suddenly foreign, like my entire life up to this moment in time meant very little.

It's a simple, quiet ceremony. There's no fanfare, no applause, no hoots and hollers. Petals don't rain down from the ceiling. My mom isn't in the wings bawling her eyes out from happiness.

I'll make it up to my parents one day.

I'll make her parents wish they'd treated her better.

I don't feel the bead of silver weighed against the length of silk as our hands are bound, a test of our bond. But when I slide the ring on her finger, it feels like a miracle. The Goddess is here, finally smiling on me, pleased with my behavior and ability to pull such a stunner. Fuck. I am the luckiest man alive tonight. I in no way deserve this. I'm acutely aware of how I didn't listen to a Goddess-damned thing the priestess said during the ceremony. I'm acutely aware of the feeling of taking Posey in my arms and kissing her like the priestess isn't watching, however, and Posey's smile against my lips, and how good it feels to pick her up and run out into the street, spinning her in a circle before spiriting her back to the castle, to our room, where we fall into the sheets, and the satin dress becomes strips of torn fabric in a matter of seconds because we're both too impatient to exercise restraint and use the zipper.

I watch her sleep until the first hints of the sunrise fan through the curtains. Outside, it's as warm as spring, the snow melting.

I count the freckles on the bridge of her nose and press a kiss to her forehead. "I'll be back," I promise, kissing her lips, and she burrows into the pillow with a yawn.

I really don't want to leave, but I might need to make her an orphan this morning if her father gives me any flack.

And also, I need to buy her a Solstice gift.

OUT OF THE SHADOWS

Aris

SAPPHIRE RIDGE ISN'T A BEAUTIFUL PLACE BY ANY MEANS. COMPARED TO the sub-tropical, evergreen landscape of the capital, the Ridge is, for the most part, buried in several feet of fog on even the sunniest of days. Today is no exception.

It's raining. Pouring, to be completely, brutally honest. The hood of my cloak is sopping wet by the time I reach the gate of the castle, which opens wide with the help of a quartet of guards who either sensed my presence or open the gate for anyone who comes near, the latter being more likely. Sapphire Ridge is secluded, rural, and not friendly to outsiders. Everyone here–all two-hundred pack members or so–are related loosely, I believe. Distance cousins–at best–are given the preference to marry and reproduce for alchemy power over love or even the mate bond.

The castle of Sapphire Ridge is a boxy fortress of moss-eaten gray stone that casts the rest of the village buildings in its shadow. Built into the side of the mountain, its grounds are little more than stretches of stone and more modern concrete additions and paved over gardens. But, as I round the front of the castle, set on entering through the back, more intimate entrance, I spot a building I've never seen before during my infrequent visits that span my entire memorable life as Roman's best friend.

I haven't been here for years. Nothing has changed–not the village. Not the villagers who spend the majority of time in their wolf forms. Not the gray hue to every person, place, and object as far as the eye can see.

Nothing but the patina green of rusted copper catching in the glare of the rain.

A greenhouse rests in the fog several years away, tucked in a thicket of overgrown trees. The glass is covered in condensation, but the garden around it is severely overgrown and frostbitten, like it hasn't been tended to in months.

Of course it hasn't. That greenhouse belongs to Posey. My mate. My wife. It was the one Goddess-damned thing her family was willing to give her for herself as long as she behaved and fell in line, and knowing Posey, she always did.

Until now.

A guard stops me at the back entrance to the castle but stiffens and bows his head when I lower my hood. "Price Aris," he murmurs, embarrassment biting through each syllable.

"I'm looking for Alpha Farrow." I could've spirited directly inside, but this is more dramatic.

"He's in his study, Your Highness." He gives me another bow, deeper than the last. I resist the urge to roll my eyes and slip through the door, opened by a second guard who decides keeping his mouth shut is better than putting his foot in it, and I appreciate the silence.

There's no doubt in my mind that the guards have alerted their Alpha to my presence by now. The castle is alive with activity, but no one goes out of their way to pay me any mind.

The undercurrent of frantic activity makes sense. I've barely heard from Roman in the past several weeks, if not months. He returned here from Gem Lake and almost immediately became engaged, and that wedding is supposed to take place within the next week. The wedding I was formally invited to but only heard about because of the formal invitation delivered by a Sapphire Ridge messenger, not Roman's mouth.

A wedding Posey hasn't mentioned. Not once.

I want to believe the marriage wasn't totally Roman's idea, but knowing him and his priorities of late…. Yeah, he's going through with it, whether he's ever met the woman or not, whether they're cousins in some way, shape, or form, or not.

I follow a familiar route to the upper floors of the castle, doing my best to keep my mind blank, trying not to think too hard on what I'm going to say when I face Posey's father, possibly her mother, and Roman. It seems pretty straightforward to me. She is mine. *Mine.* The most precious, deserving woman in all of Veiled Valley and the world beyond. She's a master of her craft, so talented she puts her entire born pack to shame. How dare they make her believe she was worthless? How dare they raise her to be someone's dutiful puppet? How dare they–

I stop short in the shadow of a side staircase, backtracking two steps to squint into the dimly lit corridor to my left.

Two shadowed figures whisper in low tones, the taller one gesturing between them as the shorter one runs her fingers through her hair before desperately agreeing with whatever the man said.

It takes all of two seconds for their faces to come into view.

Willow and Roman have no idea I'm standing at the base of the corridor watching them, not even bothering to step into the sanctuary of a nearby alcove to spy.

"You shouldn't have come," he tells her, but his voice is strained.

"You invited me."

He steps into her space, his deep sapphire eyes lighting with frustration. "I felt obligated to do so given our–our history."

"Because I'm your mate, and you're marrying someone else?" Her freshly manicured nails trill on her hipbones as she tilts her chin to look into his eyes. "Fucker!"

"Did you come here just to rub this in my face a little more? You rejected me. I told you I'd–I'd do it, Willow. I said–"

"First of all, I never rejected you. Secondly, you were the one who stormed off when I asked if we could talk about this another time. I was at work, Roman. My job. My very important job that you offered to leave your rightful role as Alpha to allow me to keep!" She shoves him back a step. "And then I get a fucking invitation to your wedding?"

"Willow," he grinds out, his voice hushed. "Do you think, for even a second, that I want to be doing this? I wanted you. I made that clear months ago. You didn't give me a choice in the matter. I respected your wishes. I left you alone, gave you space, or whatever."

"No, you didn't give me space–you straight up left. I got off work an hour after that, and you were gone, and I had no way to get in touch with you."

"Why are you here, Willow?"

"Are you going to deny it? That you ran?"

"Did you not run from me the morning after we realized we were mates?"

Willow's nostrils flare, but the statement knocks her down a few pegs, for sure. "That didn't stop you from seeking me out three times after that, Roman. We've been hooking up, and you failed to tell me you were fucking engaged to be married!"

"I want to be marrying you," he whisper-shouts. Goddess, I chose the right time to arrive. "I would give anything to have you take her place. So, if you're here to continue ripping my heart out of my chest, there's nothing more I can say. I won't reject you. It goes against everything I feel, but I sure as hell am not going to stand here and continue making a fool of myself–"

"You're going to be the Alpha of a pack in Eastonia, Roman. Not even just that, but the Alpha of a pack with special witchcraft! I'm a news anchor!"

"You're also my mate. That trumps everything!"

"I would fucking hope so."

He turns his head slightly, and then both of them startle. He grabs her and defensively tucks her behind his large frame, but the damage is done. The couple sees me, realizes I've been listening for quite some time, and they both pale to the point I think they're about to collapse.

"Aris, what are you doing here?" Roman looks utterly surprised. "Did you–"

"Hear everything? Yes, but it's not news to me. Hi, Willow. Were you going to tell Posey you were in town? She's been trying to get a hold of you for a while now."

The mention of Posey has Roman's hackles raised. Great.

Willow peaks out from behind him looking flushed and uncomfortable, but she gives me a small, subdued smile nonetheless. "Hi, Aris. I was–I was going to drop in. I heard she's staying with you."

"She is." I walk toward them, swishing my cloak behind me, my ring on full display, the little gems that are normally so dark they blend with the iron rippling silver with my powers.

Roman notices the ring and stiffens, rolling his lower lip between his teeth. "I heard the rumor you'd proposed to some princess from Celestoria but didn't realize you'd gone through with the marriage."

"I didn't. Princess Morgan is safely back in Celestoria for all I know."

"Then who?" Roman's brows furrow deeply, but Willow steps out from behind him, and the look in her eyes…. Women are a lot quicker than men, for sure.

"My wife is at home, resting. We're leaving for my family's Solstice celebrations in a few days."

Willow's eyes grow wide, but she doesn't utter a word. Roman, on the other hand, continues to look like a deer in headlights. "Then why are you here?"

"I need to speak to your father and also convey my deepest, most heartfelt apologies that I won't be attending your wedding, but it seems like there may not be a wedding after all." I wink at Willow, who flushes.

Roman relaxes, nodding like me being here, in Sapphire Ridge, on Alpha King business, is a totally reasonable thing for me to do. In theory, it is.

In reality, however…

"Is Posey okay?" Willow takes another step in my direction. "Is she… doing better? She's supposed to be taking her vows soon, right?"

"She is better, yes. As for her vows, no. She won't be taking them."

Roman flinches and looks right at me. "What?"

Neither of them notices the shadow looming further down the hallway. A tall, broad man who looks exactly like Roman but three decades his senior silently comes into view and stops short of making his presence known. I look past Roman and Willow, wondering if I'm doing the right thing by being a total asshole about this, but as much as I love Roman… as much as I respect him… as much as I understand the situation he's in, because I've been there myself, recently…

"Posey is no longer training with the priestesses."

"Why not?" Roman steps toward me, but Willow grabs his arm to stop his approach, and like a good mate, he obeys. Farrow, still lurking in the shadows, notices, and goes still as stone.

"Because she is mine. My wife."

The floor under Roman's feet could have collapsed, and it would have had the same effect. He gasps, chuckles, then stares at me like I slapped him. "Uh, come on, man. What's going on?"

I look down at my ring with a saccharine smile. "Alpha Farrow, I find it hard to believe you weren't aware of her skills. She bends iron like water. She made this ring. The little gems, too. They hold my power so expertly."

Roman slowly turns around to face his father. He doesn't shake Willow's hand off his wrist, and she is too stunned to speak as she stares at the ring. Her eyes, however, are wet with unshed tears.

Tears of relief. Joy. Pride, I think.

I step toward Roman, passing him, and angle myself in a way I can face both men, tucking my hands behind my back.

"Prince Aris," Farrow says sternly, trying to bite back the acid in his voice. "What is the meaning of this lie?"

"How dare you assume I'd lie, Alpha. Your daughter puts the rest of you alchemists to shame. She hid her powers to ensure Roman took his rightful seat on your throne. Did you know that? Or did you have a hand in how she was treated and forced to hide her gifts?"

Farrow looks murderous, but I continue, "I love her, if that's any consolation."

"What?" Roman rasps, and I know, without a shadow of a doubt, I may have just carved an impassable rift between the two of us.

But if I play my cards right and take the heat, he might have a real chance of happiness for himself.

Willow can sense it, I think, when I tell them everything, leaving Posey's bigger secret, her fox form, out of the conversation entirely.

All the while, her hand remains on his wrist, slowly creeping down until their fingers are intertwined.

HOW IT WENT DOWN

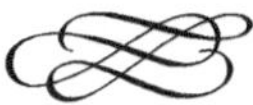

Posey

"I don't think I understand." I set the letter down and turn to Aris, who's leaning against the hearth in our bedroom. "My father wrote this?"

"It's his blessing." He crouches, inspecting the fire with a poker.

I resist the urge to crumple the letter but set it neatly on the bed instead. "In what world did you think I needed or wanted his blessing?"

"It was not my idea, trust me."

Aris returned minutes ago from Sapphire Ridge. When he mentioned he'd fix this, I hadn't realized he meant now, as soon as possible, slipping away in the quiet hours of the morning, leaving me wondering where the hell he was and why.

I spent the morning in the kitchen, mostly playing with the fawn that we've taken to calling "Darling," mostly because Aris calls her that. Then, I wandered the library. Then, I sat on a stool in my workshop twiddling my thumbs. Then, I came here to pace our bedroom, nursing an irrational fear that he'd suddenly developed cold feet and regretted our spur-of-the-moment nuptials and was scouring the Roguelands for a rogue witch who could cast a spell on me to make me forget any of this had ever happened.

Now, this. A letter in my father's neat, aggressive scrawl, a formally, law abiding contract for my care and well-being.

A passing of ownership of me from hand to hand.

I close my eyes, take a deep, furious breath, and snatch the letter off the bed and toss it into the flames Aris is actively coaxing back into existence.

He says nothing but watches me closely as I pick up my pacing again. Minutes go by. The canopy over the bed rustles as one of the spirits, Isolde, I believe, pops in to see what the issue is before she senses the tension and quickly leaves again to hang from the rafters in the foyer, or whatever she does with her free time.

My phone rings for the first time in what feels like weeks, vibrating in a lazy circle on the dresser. Willow's name flashes across the screen before it goes black once more.

"You should have answered that."

"She's been avoiding my calls for over a week now. I'll call her back later."

"She... had a perfectly acceptable reason to avoid your calls recently."

"What are you talking about?" I try to remind myself that this isn't about Aris. It's not his fault my father is a pompous jackass. Aris doesn't see me as cattle and doesn't think he has ownership over me. It's different. He's different. The look in his eyes right now–concerned–is evidence of that.

"You're putting tracks in the carpet. You'll burn right through it if you keep pacing."

I halt, wrapping my arm around the four-poster. "Aris, what the hell is going on?"

"This is what I know for sure." He rises, sets the fire-poker down, and edges toward me cautiously, like I'm at risk of exploding. "Your father seemed livid at first, but then he realized his daughter is marrying the future Alpha King of Veiled Valley and quickly bit his tongue. He gave us his blessing."

"That piece of paper was a contract giving me to you."

"I understand, and I hope you don't think I believe I have any type of claim to you. Not like that. You're my mate, Posey. My wife. I love you. Your father can go to hell for all I care."

I settle just a touch, but waves of righteous fury continue to wash over my body. "And Roman? What does he have to say?"

My phone rings again. It's Willow. I grip the bed for moral support.

Aris waits for the phone to stop ringing before replying, "Roman's got a lot going on right now."

"Like what?"

"Did you forget he's getting married in like… three days?"

"No, I haven't. I was just ignoring the fact. No one will notice if I'm not there."

"He will notice, trust me. And… so will Willow."

I laugh, then realize he just said Willow's name. "What? Why would Willow notice if I'm not there? She won't be there."

"On the contrary. She will be. She's playing a rather important role, actually." He scratches his head, looking suddenly boyish, trying so hard not to smile it's almost comical.

"Aris, I swear on the Goddess, if you don't tell me what's going on, I'll cry."

"You are not going to cry." He arches an eyebrow, rolling his eyes to the ceiling with a sigh. "Gods, I kind of wish you'd been there, but you looked so peaceful and cute, and I wasn't going to wake you up."

"Aris!"

"In three days' time, we're going to Sapphire Ridge to watch your brother and your best friend get married."

My stomach dips to my toes.

"I stumbled upon them at your father's fortress of a house, walked right into the middle of a lovers' spat."

"She rejected him."

"She lied to you. Not with malicious intent. She didn't want you to be worried about her, not after what happened this summer. She worried about your friendship going forward. Apparently, your friend sleeping with your older brother is totally fine, but staying mated to your brother and putting them both in absolute agony for almost six months is the line she wasn't willing to cross, so she hid it. From you. In reality, they've both been pining and in utter pieces for months, and she just so happened to arrive just before I did."

He takes another step in my direction, then another, smiling softly.

"And they're getting married now? But, her job–"

"I have a meeting with the editor of the local news here, in the capital, tomorrow morning. I might have sweetened the deal and made it easier for those two idiots to see that throwing their mate bond away wasn't the answer by removing the obstacles in their way, which means she has a job here now if she wants it, and I think she was sick of reporting about what brand of trousers my cousin Liam was wearing in his latest paparazzi pictures. Reporting on Maeve's summit meetings with the fae in Pantharas seems far more up her alley."

"She's moving to Veiled Valley?"

He nods with another smile. "Are you happy?"

"Oh, my Goddess, Aris!" I lunge for him, my body moving before my brain can keep up.

"Happy Solstice," he says into my hair. I bunch his shirt between my fingers.

"It's not Solstice yet."

"Do you even like Solstice?"

"I do. It feels…. We don't have a tree yet."

He chuckles, gathering me close. "We'll put up a tree. I'll go cut one down right now and drag it back to the castle with my teeth if I must."

I pull back to look him in the eyes. "Does my dad know that I'm a…"

"That you're a fox? Absolutely not. I left that out. He does know, as does Roman, that you're exceedingly talented in alchemy, and I have a feeling your father knew that the entire time."

My heart sinks a bit. I try not to let it show, but Aris leans down, his hands braced on my shoulders. "I will never ask you to make yourself smaller for me, Posey. You're my equal. You're better than me in so many ways, and I hope you always will be, because I was half the man I am today when I saw you again this summer. I love you. I love everything about you. This situation with your pack? It doesn't matter now."

He practically reads my mind when I look down at my toes and squeeze my eyes shut around a nagging thought I haven't been able to dispel.

He slips his fingers under my chin, tilting my face to meet his gaze.

"Our children will not grow up in the shadows like you had to do. I swear. It doesn't matter if they're foxes like us, or alchemists, or giant squids–"

"Giant squids?"

He nods like that's a totally rational thing to say, and I can't help myself. I burst out laughing, and he kisses me, sealing our fate again and again.

We spend most of the early afternoon in bed, locked together, my hands memorizing every inch of his body while he maps mine with his tongue. In the late afternoon, he finally rolls out of bed with a burst of energy that results in a massive evergreen tree being propped up in the foyer with the help of the male spirit, Levi, while Isolde raids every closet and storage room for Solstice decorations. I sit in the center of the foyer with a few of my alchemy tools, crafting orbs of translucent crystal out of iron that Isolde strings like beads along a length of twine, and by the time the stars are out and gleaming in the heavens, our slightly uneven, towering behemoth of a Solstice tree is up and lit from within with Aris's powers.

For whatever reason, we end up on the roof, a special place Aris used to sit and watch the stars when he was young. The weather has shifted aggressively back to the Veiled Valley's eternal summer, and the air is blissfully warm on my bare skin as I lean back into the crook of his shoulder, nothing but the stars above us and the breeze rustling my hair.

We make plans for the future–a warm, happy home here in our Gothic, spooky castle. We discuss throwing a party for Levi and Isolde even though, so far, we're the only people they talk to. We whisper about our future children that Aris says will have hair like mine and eyes like his, and how one day, when they're old enough to shift, we'll go romp as a family in our fox forms, teaching them how to chase voles and rabbits.

We talk about the fact that after Solstice he'll likely be the Alpha King, which means I'll be… Luna Queen of Veiled Valley.

Old Posey would be wondering if I was ready. If I'd studied enough, prepared myself thoroughly. If I deserved to be known, seen, and heard.

Now, I feel bad for the girl I once was. She had no idea what gift was coming her way.

Days pass in domestic bliss. I practice new alchemy techniques and gather a satchel of tools, metals, and alloys I might need on the go. Aris and I travel to Sapphire Ridge for Willow and Roman's wedding, which is a strange, strained, but otherwise happy affair… for the four of us, at least. Our fourth cousin twice removed isn't nearly as joyous during the nuptials, however, seeing as she now has to marry a less good-looking cousin instead of Roman, but I digress. Maybe Aris will force Sapphire Ridge out of the genetic Stone Age once he's king.

Three days before Solstice, we stand in the foyer, dressed for a journey that for anyone without Aris's powers would take a week, maybe longer. The satchel feels heavy on my shoulder as Aris looks at our Solstice tree with a soft, wistful smile. There're only three presents beneath it. One for Levi, one for Isolde, and one for our fawn, Darling. Levi's getting a framed, candid picture of Soren, which Aris thought was a hilarious idea. Darling, whose favorite thing is kicking my favorite oversized metal bowl in the kitchen, is getting one of her own, handcrafted by me.

Isolde was harder to shop for.

I wrote her a letter instead. Promises. Vows. I'm stepping into her shoes now. The first true Luna of Veiled Valley in over a century. I know the burden she's passing onto me, and I want nothing more than to make her proud.

"Do we have everything?" Aris asks somewhat nervously.

"I think so. Are you… worried?"

"Why would I be worried? It's not like I got married in secret without inviting anyone." He smirks, presses a kiss to my forehead, and weaves his fingers between mine.

For whatever reason, my last cognitive thought before he spirits us into the aether is the memory of standing on the shore of Gem Lake after I overheard him talking to Roman about me, about being a priestess, and he'd followed me when I took off to make sure I was okay.

I think I loved him then.

Now, I get to love him forever.

"Let's go." I smile and squeeze his hand.

A UNIVERSE IN HER EYES

Ryatt

"*Dance with me.*"

"*I don't dance with men who won't even tell me their last names.*"

I fidget on the edge of the dreamworld again, the same scene playing through my memories. Ella, so young, so beautiful, in that too-tight red gown against a sea of vibrant color in a ballroom that at the time was considered enemy territory.

Now, I've been to countless events and weddings there, watched the sun set and rise through the same ceiling height windows, the same creamy golden walls, a thousand times.

Some would say, after being together as long as we have, that the memory of that first meeting should feel like a lifetime ago.

In reality, it was. We're so old now. But I dream about it every night, the same memories of our youth, that tumultuous first year. Her in the gown at Isaac's twenty-first birthday. Her in the pouring rain at that dilapidated cottage in the middle of nowhere after I finally caught up to her in the Roguelands. Her in only moonlight, my face buried between her legs, my teeth breaking the skin of her inner thigh to mark her as mine.

Her rising out of the lake in Moonrise like a siren, eyes glowing crimson, when I fell to my knees in awe.

Now, I'm pulling her against me. She grumbles something under her breath, still asleep, but melts against my chest. The blinds are closed to another warm, sunny morning in Maatua, but I hear the waves beating against the beach beyond the sanctuary of Isaac and Maddy's house.

"GG?"

I close my eyes for a moment as the door creaks open, followed by the telltale, thundering, boulder heavy footsteps of our great-grandson, Kieran, who calls us both GG interchangeably. We're working on it. Brie has thumbed her nose at the prospect of *Great-Grandfather Ryatt Westfall* so far.

The mattress dips, and the sheets shift. Ella mumbles again, settling closer as Kieran climbs over my legs and plops directly on my chest, big, round, hazel eyes blinking down at me expectantly.

"Good morning, Kieran."

"The Solstice Wolf didn't come last night. I checked."

"It's not Solstice yet. The Solstice Wolf is coming in three days… if you're good. According to your mom and dad, you're firmly on the naughty list this year."

He frowns and rubs his eyes. His thick dark curls stick straight up at odd angles, and his jaw cracking yawn makes his cheeks puff out. Gods, he looks like his mother when she was his age.

"Where's your Mom?" I whisper.

He topples to the side and rolls off the bed, done with me already. "Sweeping."

"Sleeping or sweeping?"

"Sweeeeping," he says, still working hard on those Ls, it seems. "Daddy's awake."

"I'll come down soon."

He trips on his way out the door and leaves it wide open. I lean back, staring at the ceiling, listening to the early morning sounds of the house beginning to filter upstairs. A door opens and closes down the hallway followed by Cole's and Misty's voices lifted in a soft laugh. Logan calls out for Kieran, murmuring something about how quickly the boy wanders away as he comes up the stairs. Isaac's voice cuts through the murmur while explaining from the expansive living room below about how plastic Solstice trees are a menace to society and tradition, and Maddy laughs at him, of course, reminding him that last year he complained about the flurry of pine needles and the scent of evergreen for weeks on end.

I roll to the side again, closing my arm around Ella's waist, and close my eyes. "I know you're awake."

"You're warm. I'm just enjoying it."

I press my mouth to her shoulder, nuzzling her skin, relaxing into the softness of decades together.

Decades I was sure we didn't have when this all began.

She rises before I do, drifting out the door, smoothing her hands down a thin robe, her dark, thick hair piled messily on the top of her head. I remain glued to the mattress for several more minutes, and when I finally sit up and ease out of bed, I'm reminded, for a moment, of how long it's really been since I met her for the first time and made it possible for our side of the family to fill this house to the brim every year. My body aches in ways it didn't use to. Sometimes I have trouble remembering small details. My hair has gone a soft gray around my face. Every time I look in the mirror these days, I see my father, and now I get it. The feeling that's been weighing on me heavily for the past twenty years or so. Have I done enough? Do they have what they need?

Is it almost my time to go?

The kitchen is full and already loud when I make my grand appearance. Soren's making what sounds like the third pot of coffee already this morning. Skye is propped on the counter watching Isaac bitch and moan while dutifully making her a pancake shaped like a unicorn. Maddy and Ella are on the porch with Maeve, Brie, Misty, and Josie, drinking coffee in the quiet morning air, watching the tide roll out.

Who are we missing?

"Where's Blake?" I lean my thigh against the counter, scanning the room at large. Marianna has her arms folded around Ian, now back in his human form and fast asleep, the glint of his silver chain necklace catching the sun's glint. Lexa has Blake and Marianna's twins in her lap, feeding them pieces of pancake while deep in conversation with Marianna.

Soren presses a fresh mug of coffee into my hand and shrugs. Above him, resting precariously on his shoulders, Fallon blinks down at me with those huge sea-green eyes, her lips pulled back in a gummy smile. I smirk at her, and she giggles wildly, leaning forward over Soren's head and reaching for me, her favorite person by far, at least, in my opinion.

I set my coffee down and let her fall into my arms.

"Blake and Kaleb went on a run, I think." Soren presses his mug to his lower lip and glances at Maeve, and then smiles softly, turning back to accept Fallon when she leans toward him.

"If you see him before I do, tell him I need to talk to him."

I begin to move toward the back deck, but the front door opens and shuts, and a few gasps and excited greetings ring out from the living room, where the rest of the family is gathered. I hear Nora and her mate, Trent, talking to whoever just arrived, and then Ryan chimes in that they're late.

Skye bounds out of the kitchen with her plate, curious about the newcomers, and Isaac comes to stand by my side just as Aris and Posey come into view, both dressed in dark grays and blacks, looking like they just stepped out of another realm.

In a way, they have.

"Look at him," Isaac says beside me, smoothing his hands down his ridiculous apron printed with little radishes.

"I see him." I also see the wedding band on his finger–both of their fingers. Kenna's going to lose it. I better warn Evander.

"He looks like you did," Isaac says absently, like he didn't mean to say it out loud. "During those first few years of peace."

Aris smiles down at where Ryan and Aviva are resting in the

sunken living room with Nora and her mate, laughing at something Aviva said, and as the sun blots over his wrists, I see his Shadowsynger bracelets illuminate, every gem swirling with the full brunt of his gifts. Our gifts.

He seems so happy when he looks at Posey, his eyes darkening with the same heavy emotion I know so well from years of looking at Ella and Kenna, the stars I've orbited around since my late twenties.

He'd nearly broken me into pieces that day in the foyer when I followed him from Silverhide to Veiled Valley, watching him come undone at the seams over the idea of anything happening to her.

Shadowsyngers are brutally loyal dogs to not only our crown but our women. It's a burden he'll carry for the rest of his life.

But he's ready. He's stepping into the role our ancestors protected and kept hidden with their lives.

I wish my father were still here to see this.

"Well," Isaac says with a rough sigh, his mouth curving into a smile at the edges. "I guess that's it for you. All your grandkids are settled. Now you can die."

"You'd love that, ,wouldn't you? You fuckin' bastard."

He claps me on the shoulder. "I need you to stick around a while longer. I have a few left unmated, and Sydney is pulling his hair out over Briar and Noah. I don't want you getting any funny ideas about going first and haunting me."

"I'm sure I'll have better things to do in the afterlife."

He snorts, turning back to the stovetop. I lean on the frame of the archway separating the living area and the kitchen, watching. Watching Ryan, who went through hell and back last year, converse with Trent, the least problematic of the men in his direct line.

But then I notice Skye tentatively approaching Posey, her eyes shining a brighter violet than they normally do.

Posey watches her like she's being stalked by something threatening, and for a moment, I wonder if I should intervene, to rein the powerful little girl in by calling out her name and mentioning that her great-grandfather is willing to make her another complicated pancake, possibly in the shape of the elusive Solstice Wolf, which would undoubtedly chap Isaac's ass, but then Skye reaches out and runs her fingers over the leather satchel draped over Posey's shoulder.

"Do you want to see it?" Posey asks, her forest-green eyes taking in Skye's dark hair and high cheekbones. Skye nods excitedly, giggling as they crouch, ignoring the conversation taking place next to them.

Posey brought several alchemy tools and little boxes of raw metals and alloys.

"I love rocks," Skye states, and Posey laughs, murmuring something about the chunks of iron ore in the box now in Skye's hands.

But then they touch. It's a single brush of Posey's fingertips on the top of Skye's hand. Innocent. Accidental. Posey goes perfectly still, her fingers still resting on Skye's skin.

Aris notices the exchange and stiffens. Posey takes Skye's hand in hers, closing her fingers over Skye's palm, and I've never seen Skye surrender like this.

Posey searches her eyes, brow furrowed, and then looks right at me.

I don't need to question what Posey might be seeing because my guess would be the entire universe in that little girl's hand.

She blinks, smiling at Skye, and says, "Do you like pretty things?"

Skye nods.

"Do you want me to make you a bracelet like Aris has? See these?" She takes Aris's wrist and drags him a step closer. "I can make one that you can hang charms from."

"I want that!"

"Okay," Posey says breathlessly, but there's a slice of panic and confusion in her eyes. She squeezes Aris's hand before letting go to rummage through her bag, looking for something she's not going to find. Something strong enough to keep Skye's enormous powers of sight in check.

"What's your favorite kind of rock?" Posey asks, blinking up at Skye.

"Daddy found me a meteor. Do you know what that is? It's a rock from outer space! He said it came from farther than the tapestry!"

Isaac has moved closer, silently, now standing at my side to watch the exchange, spatula in hand.

"Amazing. Do you have it with you?"

Skye nods, beaming with excitement. There's nothing she loves more than showing off her treasures. She zooms away, and Posey slowly rises, whispering something to Aris that seems to calm him down and erase the tension in his shoulders, but her eyes meet mine again.

She gives me the faintest of nods.

"What do you suppose that was about?" Isaac mumbles.

Another weight settles directly over my heart when Skye returns with the meteor, no bigger than her thumb, and Posey sighs with relief, nodding, and says, "Yes. This is exactly what we need to make your bracelet."

"I have a feeling we're going to find out," I reply to my lifelong friend and companion, my old, grouchy brother-in-law, and turn from the scene to join my mate on the porch.

Thank you for reading! Book 18 will be out soon! Sign up for my newsletter so you never miss out! Download this free story on Bookfunnel, and you're in!

The Beta and the Maid

Bella Moondragon
THE BETA
AND THE
MAID
The Alpha King's Breeder
A Novella

The Culling

The Kingdom

The Conquered

Pregnant With Four Alphas' Babies

Chosen As the Breeder

Mated to Four Alphas

Threats Against the Breeder

At War for the Breeder

The Stolen Breeder

Four Alphas, Four Babies

Becoming the Luna Queen

Descendants of the Breeder

Desired by the Devil series

Whispers of the Devil

Banter of the Devil

Murmurs of the Devil

The Mafia Kings series

Indebted to the Mafia King

<u>Loved by the Mafia King</u>

Claimed by the Mafia King

Secrets of the Mafia King

Burned by the Mafia King

Kidnapped by the Mafia King

Dark Stalker Romance series

Tempted by Sin

Fated to Sin

Secret Billionaires series

Finding the Secret Billionaire by Olivia Bhelle Kildare

Falling for My Secret Billionaire by Bella Moondragon

Driven by the Secret Billionaire by ID Johnson

Wolf Shifter Alpha Kings series

Ravens and Ruins

Sundrops and Shadows

Snowflakes and Sabotage

Waves and Wickedness

Breezes and Bodies—coming soon!

The Vampire King's Feeder series

Claiming the Alpha's Daughter

Loving the Alpha's Daughter

Finding the Alpha's Daughter

Bewitching by the Alpha's Son

Writing as B. Moon

The Boy Who Died

Sign up for Bella's newsletter here.

Or get a free novella from The Alpha King's Breeder series when you sign up here:
The Beta and the Maid

Follow Bella on Facebook here.

Follow Bella on Bookbub here.